ANGELINA'S RESOLVE

Village *of* Women

Book One

CINDY ERVIN HUFF

SMITTEN
HISTORICAL ROMANCE
IMPRINT OF IRON STREAM MEDIA

Smitten Historical Romance is an imprint of LPCBooks
a division of Iron Stream Media
100 Missionary Ridge, Birmingham, AL 35242
ShopLPC.com

Cover design by Hannah Linder Designs

Iron Stream Media serves its authors as they express their views, which may not express the views of the publisher.

This is a work of fiction. Names, characters, and incidents are all products of the author's imagination or are used for fictional purposes. Any mentioned brand names, places, and trademarks remain the property of their respective owners, bear no association with the author or the publisher, and are used for fictional purposes only.

Library of Congress Control Number: 2021940075

All Scripture quotations, unless otherwise indicated, are taken from the Holy Bible, King James Version.

ISBN-13: 978-1-64526-336-4
Ebook ISBN: 978-1-64526-337-1

PRAISE FOR *ANGELINA'S RESOLVE*

Cindy Ervin Huff has done it again! *Angelina's Resolve* is a compelling tale of a female architect who is cut out of her family business, so she puts her knowledge and skills toward creating her own "village of women." With memorable characters, plenty of conflict, and several twists and turns, you won't want to miss this exciting story.

~Jennifer Uhlarik
Winner of the Will Rogers Medallion Award for *Sand Creek Serenade*

Cindy Ervin Huff's delightful book shows the fortitude of women literally building their own town in 1860s Kansas. Readers who like strong women characters who overcome adversaries will enjoy Angelina's journey toward proving her worth—and falling in love.

~Sarah Hamaker
Author of *Illusion of Love*

Historical romance fans are sure to enjoy this heart-warming tale from Cindy Huff that showcases the bravery, fortitude, and power of a community of women willing to forge a place for themselves. Journey to Resolve and see what happens as this eclectic group strives to build Angelina's dream of the best civilization has to offer in the middle of the prairie.

~Candee Fick
Author of the *Within the Castle Gates* Series

Author Cindy Huff has crafted another winning title in *Angelina's Resolve*. Take a female architect with a strong dose of independence and a strong will, then add in a carpenter with entrepreneurial aspirations following the Civil War, and you have certain drama in the works. Neither wants to back down, yet both have protective feelings for the other. Can—should—will they realize the depth of their emotions? No spoiler alert here, except to praise Huff for her well-written, tender story of love and healing. Loved the details of history that added to the characters and the story.

~Donna Schlachter
Author of *Double Jeopardy* and other historicals

DEDICATION

To my daughter-in-law,
Anabelle Lotao Huff, engineer and
the smartest woman I know

ACKNOWLEDGMENTS

I am so grateful for my husband, Charles Huff, who reads every word many times and encourages me along the journey. He listens to me talk about my characters as if they are real without thinking me crazy. Without my ACFW Scribes242 critique group and Word Weavers critique groups, this manuscript would still be an idea in my head. Special thanks to Denise Weimer for her awesome editing and Iron Stream Media for believing in my story enough to give me a contract. I give the highest praise to my Lord Jesus for giving me the gift of storytelling.

CHAPTER 1

Chicago, July 1868

The paneled walls pressed in on Angelina DuBois as she listened to the reading of her father's will. Her corset prevented her from taking the deep breath necessary to gain control. She patted her perfectly coiffured hair, searching for a stray tendril to occupy her fidgety fingers.

The lawyer's droning tone hammered into her soul with the words, "I, Robert Archibald DuBois, leave DuBois Architectural Interests to my nephew, Hiram Oswald DuBois, in accordance with my late brother John Henry DuBois' Last Will and Testament, bequeathing the firm to his son after my death."

Hiram straightened, and a smug smile formed on his face.

No!

Angelina pressed her lips tight to keep from screaming. Father had promised. He promised the company to her. She wrestled slumping shoulders into submission and straightened her spine. In the end, Father couldn't retract his promise to his dying brother, even if it meant Hiram's inept leadership would be disastrous for DuBois Architectural.

The balding lawyer with hairy jowls took her hand in his sweaty palm. "My condolences, Miss DuBois. Your father was a fine man."

"Yes. Thank you, Mr. Pruitt."

Hiram shook Mr. Pruitt's hand, then hurried to take her arm before she could put distance between them.

His tall, gangly frame hovered too close. She pulled her arm free and turned to face him on the street in front of the law firm. "I assume I'll be your assistant as I was Father's?" The irksome thought

1

produced bile in her throat. Father's failing sight had required her help in sketching his designs. She'd corrected many of Hiram's mistakes. Now he would get even more accolades from her work.

Hiram pointed to a nearby bench. A gentleman would have wiped off the seat with his handkerchief. Her cousin was no gentleman. She inspected the bench before sitting. He leaned over her, adjusting his top hat while his leering eyes traveled over her frame. *You don't intimidate me, you dolt.* She scowled at him, placed her reticule in her lap, and crossed her arms.

"Are we going to discuss my role in the firm? Am I to be your assistant, or do you have another position for me?"

A *you-poor-thing* pout appeared on his face. "No to both. A woman in that position would be very inappropriate. Uncle Robert may have indulged you, but I will not. Clean out your office tomorrow."

"You're firing me?" Her outburst drew curious glances from two children who scampered by, playing tag, as an emotional tug-of-war raced through her. *The horrid cockroach fires me after all I've done to ensure his designs were flawless.*

Hiram sat beside her and adjusted his cravat. "Dear Angelina, I believe your time would be better spent securing a husband." He touched her face. Angelina quavered and moved away. "Perhaps you might consider marriage to me."

And let you get your hands on the DuBois fortune? The notion of marriage to her adopted first cousin was repugnant.

Doves cooed in the trees. The urge to throw a rock at the innocent creatures flickered in her mind.

Angelina rose and straightened the front of her skirt. "I am long past the age of majority, and you have no hold over my life. Father left me a sizable inheritance and the skills to manage it. Financially, I'll be comfortable for the rest of my days. I'll not be seeking a husband anytime soon, if ever. I shall empty my office this afternoon. Good day."

She glared at him one last time, then strode toward home. Angelina's high-top shoes beat a pace of irritation. It might be unseemly for a woman to walk in public unescorted, but a lorry ride would cover the distance before her mind had calmed.

Men were such selfish brutes. Even though Father had indulged her wish to get an architectural degree, she'd never used it. Then his fading eyesight made her his assistant. All her designs bore his name. Not even Hiram knew Father's secret.

Never will another man have control over my life.

Angelina sat stoically in her sitting room, her chest constricted. Her personal maid and friend, Bridget O'Malley, poured tea while her best friend, Teresa Shilling, stirred her cup. Both eyed her with concern, the sentiment comforting yet annoying. Her mind and heart had not settled enough to enjoy Teresa's weekly visit. She took a deep breath, then sipped her tea.

Teresa leaned forward. "Why so glum?" She reached for a finger sandwich and nibbled as she focused on Angelina and waited.

"I'm not glum." Angelina gave a wooden smile, then focused on wiping imagined crumbs from her black satin gown.

"Look at me." Teresa, a widow several years her senior, had a tone that commanded attention. Her taffeta gown ruffled as she moved to capture Angelina's chin in her hand. "Angelina Elizabeth DuBois, you can't keep secrets from me."

Angelina moved her chin, sighed, and stirred her tea absentmindedly. "I don't wish to cast aspersions …"

"Talking about my troubles always makes me feel better." Teresa smiled and nodded encouragement.

"Tell her, ma'am." Bridget rarely spoke without being addressed in the presence of Angelina's guests, but now her face creased with concern. "You've had a grave injustice thrust upon ye. Don't let it press ye down."

"Hear, hear." Teresa clapped her approval.

Angelina sighed in surrender. She motioned for Bridget to sit by her. Surrounded by her two dearest friends, she cried bitter tears, then recounted the events of the previous day. "Hiram is a greedy scarecrow trying to wear the DuBois name like a king's crown."

"I'm relieved you did not agree to marry the braggart." Bridget patted Angelina's hand.

"The thought gives me shivers." Teresa shook away the imagined discomfort.

"I have no need for a man, particularly one of his ilk." Angelina wiped her eyes with her lace hankie. "What will I do? I love designing buildings. No one will hire me."

"What about the buildings all over town you designed?" Teresa straightened and lifted her teacup.

"My father or Hiram's names are on those designs. I've no portfolio to share with a potential client."

"Why not start your own firm? You could show 'em all." Bridget rose and retrieved the teapot. "Let me warm your tea a bit."

"I said I have no portfolio."

"Then buy some land and build something." Teresa cocked her head to the side and smiled.

Her enthusiasm spread to Angelina. "I've been reading in the paper the many editorials by Horace Greeley regarding utopian experiments."

Bridget offered them a plate of cookies. "You mean the communes?" She took her place again. "Don't look so surprised—I read the paper."

"I have no interest in a commune run by controlling, idealistic men." Angelina scoffed as she reached for a sandwich, her appetite returning with the free flow of ideas.

"Build one run by women. We both know how difficult it is for educated women to make their way. Greeley is a great example of male hypocrisy. He supported antislavery legislation before the war but does not support women's suffrage." Teresa huffed.

"We women need the right to vote, show them what's what." Bridget brought her hands together with a loud clap.

"That sounds interesting. But I don't want to build a commune."

The clock chimed three, and three male figurines slid to the clock face and sawed wood, then slid back inside when the chime completed. Angelina stared at the clock as an idea formed. "What about a town? I could design the layout of the streets and parks, the building designs."

Teresa began to pace. "A town where women own the businesses and govern the city. I've always wanted to run for mayor."

"'Twould be quite an undertaking, ma'am, but yer up to the task." Bridget cleared away the empty plate.

"How would we persuade people to move to this town?" Angelina's mind began to fill with creative designs. "I don't want to create a utopia, just a nice place for families and a legacy for DuBois Architecture that is still standing after Hiram destroys what Father built. The idea of women owning businesses and running things is appealing." Hiram's sour expression entered her musing. "Yes, I like it a lot."

"While you're planning this, ma'am, can me and my friends find opportunity in your town? I always wanted to open a bakery."

"You are a wonderful baker. I've the only personal maid who makes cookies for my guests." Angelina hugged Bridget. "Of course, in the spirit of women's suffrage, let's find a way to make it easy for even women with less education to succeed."

"Aye, ma'am, if we put our heads together, we shall." Bridget fisted her hand, cocked her elbow, and punched the air. A satisfied smile appeared on her face.

"There is so much to be done. I'll need help with the legal end. Teresa, don't you have a law degree?"

"Indeed, I do. I wrote all my late husband's legal and business contracts. I even litigated a suit defending my husband's manufacturing plant against a disgruntled employee. We won, of course." Teresa bowed, then slumped in her chair. "Although the only other time was defending my right to inherit my late husband's estate."

"Well, Attorney Shilling, now is your chance. We've a lot to do before we can advertise for residence."

CHAPTER 2

Chicago, October 1868

Edward Pritchard reached the door of his flat and wrenched off his tie. Three rejections on the same day. He knew how to build, but the snobbish businessmen preferred to hire established companies. His work in the Army Corps of Engineers didn't seem to matter to prospective clients either. Those six years of military service could never be reclaimed.

The smell of bean soup filled the apartment. His sister, Caroline, sat at the table, her blonde locks draped over her face as she perused the newspaper. Papers cluttered the kitchen table.

"It smells like you've managed to not burn dinner while you research ideas for articles."

Caroline rose and kissed his cheeks. "By your expression, there is no good news? And yes, I am trying my hand at writing an article for the *Chicago Times*."

Edward picked up her pages. "An exposé on the evils of drink." He winked at her. "Writing from experience?" He laughed, and she gave him a playful swat.

"I'm using the pen name C.A. Pritchard." Caroline stroked an imaginary mustache.

"Good luck, then." Maybe the *Times* would be more open to her talents than architecture firms had been to his.

"Brother, you'll find work. We still have funds from Father's estate to sustain us for the year. Surely, a job will come before then. Maybe C.A. Pritchard will get hired by the *Times*."

Edward appreciated her youthful optimism. If it were a tonic, he'd be drinking it by the gallon. Caroline set the table, and Edward poured water into the wash basin and cleaned the grime of the city from his face and hands.

"Can you be a dear and drop my article by the paper tomorrow?"

"Why not do it yourself?" Edward's plans for the next day took him in the opposite direction.

"We both know articles on important issues written by women are not taken seriously. I refuse to write about garden parties and the latest fashion. If you drop it by, they will assume C.A. Pritchard is a man."

Caroline's hopeful expression as she held her hands in a prayerful plea always turned his resolve to mush. "Fine." Edward sighed and began stacking all the papers in a pile to make room for soup bowls. "I might place an advertisement for my carpentry service while I am there. Perhaps some companies of note will see the ad. Those contracts could open doors to build for the wealthy and influential. And a few smaller jobs would put more money in our bank account for the present."

"Very wise." Caroline smiled and placed steaming bowls of bean soup and a plate of store-bought bread on the table. Edward poured milk into two crystal glasses. After grace, only the sound of the mantel clock accompanied their meal.

"Let me show you …" Caroline plucked the newspaper from the stack of papers. "I found a job you might be interested in." She folded the paper to reveal only the ad. "I'm thinking about applying."

He continued to eat as he read, then stared at Caroline. "Is this a joke?" He pulled the paper closer to examine the print in more detail. "A quarter-page ad of foolishness." He flung it down and resumed eating.

"Edward Alan Pritchard, I thought you were a more open-minded, modern-thinking man." When he ignored her, Caroline scooped up the paper and read aloud. "'Seeking women of many skills, education, and backgrounds to populate a new town in Kansas. I am looking for qualified women to run a variety of businesses such as a bank, mercantile, and newspaper. Prospects with skills in retail, medical, legal, and livery may present a résumé and three letters of recommendation. Purveyors of many other occupations are welcome to apply. My goal is to design a well-appointed town and give women a chance to succeed in their chosen careers. I am also seeking builders of good reputation who are not only skilled but of a nature to respect a female employer. Men will be evaluated on a case-by-case basis. We welcome families. Farmland is also available. This will be a dry town that supports women's suffrage. Those of a different persuasion need not apply."

Edward bookended her impassioned reading with a long slurp of milk.

Caroline sighed and held the paper to her chest. "Does that not sound perfect? I could run the newspaper, and you could build the town."

"You're serious."

"Look at the signature at the bottom of the advertisement."

Edward grabbed the paper. "Angelina DuBois." His mind churned to place the familiar name. "That's not—"

"Yes, the daughter of Robert DuBois of DuBois Architectural Interests. He passed and left DuBois Architectural Interests to his nephew, Hiram DuBois." Caroline leaned forward. "According to Mary Allen, who heard from her cousin who works in the DuBois mansion as a chambermaid, Miss DuBois is an architect in her own right. She assisted her father. And they say Hiram couldn't design a chicken coop."

Now that put things in a different light. "I wonder if she's got a female builder in mind." Edward pushed his chair back and started pacing. "If I could persuade her to hire me, I'd have a nice project under my belt with the DuBois name on it." His pacing ended, and he stared at his sister. "Or … every opportunity might be closed to me because I worked for a woman."

"Don't fret so, Eddie. I'm going to work on my résumé after dinner. Maybe I won't be an editor, but surely, she needs a reporter."

"Who will be your three references? You haven't actually gotten an article published."

"Miss Hyatt, my English instructor, already gave me a lovely letter of recommendation when I graduated. Miss Harriet, our neighbor, would surely write a character reference. And of course, you, dear brother, will write a wonderful letter about my diligence and determination."

Their laughter eased his discouraged heart. Edward already had several letters of recommendation. Would this woman even bother to read them? All his past interviews hadn't resulted in the seals even being broken on the envelopes. Still … he couldn't believe he was willing to give this fool scheme a whirl. "Well, let's clean up and clear away space on the table. We have work to do."

CHAPTER 3

Angelina, Teresa, and Bridget finished setting up chairs and placing a table in front of the library door.

Teresa brought the printed forms and set up the reception area. "Bridget, are you capable of keeping ne'er-do-wells from disturbing things?"

"Me brother Shamus is going to come and sit in the corner over there. If there's any trouble, he'll see to it. He used to be a pugilist. Truly, his size alone will keep things peaceable."

Angelina gauged the distance between the corner chair and the door. "It is kind of him to help." There might not even be any applicants to be concerned about.

"He's hoping you'll find him useful. A new start for his family and putting boxing behind him is what he be wanting."

Angelina's hand went to her chest as she considered the request. Did she want a fighter in her town? "What other skills does he have?"

Bridget smiled. "He's a gentle soul with a sweet wife and darling daughters. He'll do what needs doin' without complaint."

"I'll take it under consideration. We'll interview him last."

Bridget gave her an odd look. "I've mentioned to my kin that you'd consider laborers and those willing to learn new skills." She crossed her arms and added, "It's been my experience that those with knowledge aren't always willing to work hard."

Angelina laughed. "True. I hope to acquire both knowledge and a good work ethic in those who come. But I'd take those willing to work and learn a new skill over those who spout knowledge."

Bridget gave an approving nod and took her place at the table.

Teresa placed a sign on the door instructing prospects to enter and sign in. "We don't need to wear out the butler nor waste precious time with formalities." She gave the nail a final whack and handed the hammer to Bridget. "Keep it close at hand."

"You seriously expect a riot over this?" Angelina checked her appearance in the mirror as the clock chimed nine. Her sense of calm overshadowed any doubts. That calm had always directed her.

"Always be prepared." Teresa followed her into the library.

Angelina's heart raced as the library door opened. Would she be able to make good choices? Her legs wiggled, and her breathing became shallow. Teresa squeezed her hand. A couple entered. The tall, bearded man had broad shoulders and a bandage secured around his neck. The woman resembled him, but thinner.

Angelina indicated the chairs in front of the table. "Miss Jameson and Mr. Jameson, please come in. We received references for you, Mr. Jameson—wonderful references toward your character and your skill as a blacksmith. But we received none for you, Miss Jameson. It is not my intention to hire men and the women keep house."

"No ma'am. I'm the bookkeeper and talk to clients. My brother's neck received a saber wound during the war, and he can't speak now. He writes notes, and we've learned sign language to make it easier for us. He is a wonderful blacksmith, but people treat him as though he's deaf and ignorant. I'm good at keeping books and would be happy to help others."

Her brother made hand signals, and Miss Jameson explained. "Michael is willing to help build. He's a hard worker and wants to be part of making the town a success."

Angelina sized up the man. No caution settled in her heart. Still, she addressed the question that needed asking to Michael. "Are you a drinking man?"

He spoke in sign language again.

His sister answered. "My brother said he did after the war. But God got ahold of his heart, and I helped him find his way back. He's not touched another drop and is happy to know there will be no saloons in the new town."

Teresa nodded at Angelina and handed a packet to Miss Jameson. "Miss Jameson, may we call you by your Christian name? We are all family in this endeavor."

"Yes, of course. It's Emily."

"Emily, you and your brother are what we're looking for." Angelina shook their hands and returned their bright smiles. *Now if we can only have more applicants like these.* "Read your packet carefully and be ready to board the train on May first."

"We will." Emily held the folder against her as though it was a life vest.

Angelina added a word of caution. "Please understand you will be living in tents for most of the summer while we build shelters. Each business will be two-story, so the women or families can live above it. I'll have to change that design for a blacksmith shop."

Michael tapped Emily to get her attention, then his hands went into a flurry of gestures.

Emily turned to Angelina and translated. "He says he has some ideas he could draw out, so you can understand what we need."

The next interviewees were two women—a portly, middle-aged woman with rouged cheeks and a peacock feather in her hat, and her companion, thin as a rail with a sour expression.

"May we have your references?" Teresa used her formal voice.

"We ain't got any. Figured we was women. So we qualify. Names are Agnes Rich, and this here is ... Matildy Smart."

Angelina's sixth sense told her to beware. "We really need references. But we will continue the interview without them." She searched her mind for the right questions to ask. "What are you seeking to accomplish as part of the town?"

The sour-faced one, Matildy, spoke first. "Why, we want to run a business. We figured you'd set us up."

"What sort of business did you have in mind?" Teresa folded her hands in front of her.

"A business." The stout one looked at Teresa as if she were daft.

"What have you done in the past?"

"We ... we ... well, we owned a ... before the war, we ran a dance hall. Everyone likes to dance." Agnes crossed her arms, daring her to make a remark.

"I kept the books and ordered the supplies." Matildy looked at her feet. "Irene—I mean, Agnes—ran a clean, respectable business. Then the war come, and things got bad. Agnes lost the business. Now we work in a factory."

"I'm getting too old for it." Agnes—or Irene—added.

"There will be no saloons." Angelina's eyebrow rose along with her voice. "No dance halls. No form of entertainment for men."

"Miss, I know you mean well. But without men, you ain't gonna make a town. You need 'em to tote and carry and make the hard decisions." Agnes' syrupy tone tinted with disgust.

"I fear you don't understand my vision." Angelina crossed her arms and stared at the duo.

"We're hard-working women, and that makes us your best choice." With Agnes' chin high and eyes narrowed, Hiram's face replaced Agnes' for a moment in Angelina's mind.

"You are wrong in your insistence that we need men to make the hard decisions."

Teresa rose, and Angelina followed suit as her friend delivered her verdict. "Ladies, you have no references, and as Miss DuBois stated, you don't have the same vision as we do. Although you may be capable businesswomen, you are not the type we are seeking for our venture. We bid you a good day." Teresa gestured toward the door.

"I've never been so insulted. You'll be sorry you turned down Irene LaRue. I got connections." Her voice rose as her rant continued. Her companion patted her shoulder and pointed to Shamus, who'd entered the room. Irene glared but said no more.

"Thank you, Shamus." Angelina's chest relaxed as he escorted the rude women out.

Edward and Caroline stood at the front door of the DuBois estate. He had long admired the well-built, three-story brick structure with Corinthian columns and a brick walkway. Before they could enter, a large woman shoved the door open, accompanied by a thinner companion. "Imagine the nerve of that prissy tart. She wants women, but apparently, we ain't good enough." She slammed the door hard before Edward tipped his hat.

"Ladies."

"Don't waste yer time, sir. Iffen she don't want we two, who obviously fit the bill, she ain't gonna consider the likes of you." They flounced away, chattering loudly about being insulted.

Edward opened the door and let Caroline enter first. People lined the walls. The majority were women and a plethora of children. Some sat quietly near their mothers, trying not to wiggle, while others ran about chasing each other. A red-headed woman sat at a table near a door. She motioned for them to come forward. "If you'd kindly fill out these forms, Miss DuBois will interview you in turn."

They finished the simple forms, and Edward offered his sister the last chair while he stood beside her. The room filled with happy exclamations and inappropriate declarations as interviewees left. Maintaining composure during the three-hour wait jangled Edward's nerves. A clock somewhere chimed twelve times when their names were called. Straightening his tie, he nodded to his sister. Caroline gripped her references as he guided her toward the door.

Two well-dressed women sat at the table, and the older one indicated the chairs. The younger one's blue eyes offered a smile along with the one on her lips.

"I am Edward Pritchard, and this is my sister, Caroline Pritchard."

"Mr. and Miss Pritchard." The young lady nodded their way. "I am Angelina DuBois. This is Mrs. Teresa Shelling. Please present your letters of reference, résumés, and any other helpful information."

The women took the time to read the references and jotted down notes.

Edward scanned the room, noting the craftsmanship of the library. Oak bookshelves lined the walls, and an overstuffed chair and sofa were arranged in front of the brick fireplace with a hand-carved mahogany mantel. The detailed artistry of the carving impressed Edward. A bust of Homer stood in the far corner, and a large painting in a gold filigree frame of a couple with a wolfhound graced the remaining wall.

Light shone from the window and reflected off the jeweled clip in Miss DuBois' raven hair as she examined their papers. *Why is such a beautiful woman not married? Why do I care?* He crossed his legs to appear more relaxed. Caroline wiggled beside him and took a few calming breaths.

Miss DuBois straightened. "Mr. Pritchard, I am very impressed with your references. We have yet to find a builder. And your credentials are impeccable." Her smile made his heart soar. "But …" The word flattened it out quickly. "We need to ask a few questions, if you please."

Edward nodded and found his voice. "Of course."

The two women looked at each other, and the older one spoke first.

Mrs. Shilling crossed her arms. "I am an attorney. Does that bother you?"

"Bother me?" Edward paused. "In what way?"

"Does it bother you that I, a female, am an attorney?" Teresa leaned forward.

He glanced Caroline's way. Her smile of encouragement made him less nervous. "Congratulations on your achievement. I understand it is a difficult course of study." Edward composed his thoughts, not wanting to stammer or say something that would offend. "A female solicitor is not common." Again, he paused.

"Would you hire a female attorney?"

"I've never known a female attorney, so I can't say. But I am open to new ideas. Especially with my sister here constantly reminding me that women have great potential."

"And you, sir, are very wise to consider her admonitions." Miss DuBois' laughter washed over him. "Would you be uncomfortable working for a woman? I'm the architect and will be the contractor. I will be overseeing and double-checking every building. This is my opportunity to prove a woman is as capable as a man to design a town. I insist things are done my way, and if you don't have a well-thought-out and reasonable appeal, my answer to all changes will be no." Her voice rose with each statement.

"I appreciate your passion. I'd very much like to prove I can build quality structures that stand the test of time. Working on this project will give me the respect I need to get contracts for large projects in the future. I will do whatever it takes to make your dream a reality."

"And in your past jobs …" Miss DuBois fingered his résumé. "How did you get along with your supervisors?"

"Very well, overall." Edward shifted, rotating his hat on his knee. "But I won't lie. I'm honest. And I'll speak up for doing things the right way, even if the employer sees things different."

Her eyebrows arched, and her lips pursed as she considered his statement.

As Caroline stiffened beside him, Edward hastened to reassure Miss DuBois. "But I promise to leave the final decision to you, even if I disagree."

The women nodded and turned to Caroline. Miss DuBois began the interview. "You have no newspaper experience, but would you consider being my assistant until a newspaper is established? Perhaps journal our adventures? We've hired a widow, Mrs. Collins, as editor. Her son Martin will also be a reporter. The three of you should be able to produce a weekly paper. Mrs. Collins will come now with her three younger children while Martin finishes college. Do you have any experience taking care of children?"

Caroline's fingers clenched over her reticule. "Yes, while my brother served in the war, my parents passed, and I was only thirteen.

The neighbor hired me to tend their eight children."

Edward coughed back a laugh at the angelic smile Caroline pasted on. Hadn't his sister referred to those children as brats? She must be determined indeed if she sugarcoated her past dealings with young ones.

Miss DuBois flicked a glance in his direction, then back to Caroline. "Mrs. Collins has well-behaved children, and your help with them at times could help ensure the paper's success."

"Yes, of course, I aim to help any way I can." Caroline's shoulders slumped for a moment, then she straightened her spine. "I also want to make a name for myself as a reporter. My name, not a masculine pen name."

Miss DuBois' radiant smile fell on Caroline as she handed them both a packet. "Miss Pritchard, we welcome you." She extended her hand, then turned to face him. "Mr. Pritchard." Her smile faded to a straight line. "I feel you are the best candidate for the job. But if you go back on your word and insist on doing things your way, you will be fired quicker than quick, and your sister will leave with you. Is that understood?"

Edward's misgivings melted when he glanced at Caroline's hope-filled eyes. "Yes ma'am."

"Very well, we will see you at the train station on May first. Be on time and have everything on the list in the packet. Anything you forget will be—forgotten." Miss DuBois gave them both a firm handshake, her expression all business.

On the way home, Caroline practically floated beside him.

"I can't believe I'm going to become a real reporter." With her index finger, she wrote her name in the air. "By Caroline Pritchard." Her hands went to her heart. "World famous reporter extraordinaire." She swung around in a circle, then grasped his arm. "Imagine, you're working for Miss Angelina DuBois. Her father's architecture firm is known around the world. You'll be famous in no time."

Or infamous for working for a rebellious aristocrat whose experiment failed while trying to prove something to the world.

CHAPTER 4

November 1868

The fellowship hall of First Congregational Church thronged with women dressed in their finest, sitting at tables with tea services and finger sandwiches. Latecomers sat along the walls.

Stuffy air filled Angelina's lungs as she waited for Margaret Asbury, president of the Women's Progressive Thinkers Society, to finish the old business. The lectern stood in the middle of the stage. Angelina sat at a table with Teresa nearby, eyeing the exit on the farthest wall, blocked by a myriad of tables full of women.

Angelina took a breath and placed her hand on her throat. Her enthusiasm had waned with each previous fundraising talk. She leaned in and whispered to Teresa. "Are you sure they'll invest?"

"Stop worrying. I know these women. They are not like the old-money-enslaved you've been wasting your time on. Trust me, dear." Teresa patted Angelina's gloved hand. "You are a businesswoman, not an aristocrat looking to gain accolades from the masses."

Teresa's words grabbed her sensibilities, and her fear rescinded. She was not like Hiram. Seeking venture partners of the feminine persuasion to take a portion of the financial burden made sense. On paper, the business plan appeared solid.

But a paragraph from a recent women's periodical rotated in her mind. *Miss DuBois' vision of a habitat in the western prairie is reminiscent of Marie Antoinette's quaint village where the sheep wore bows, and the villagers were paid to be cheerful. The queen lost her head. Will Miss DuBois suffer the same fate?*

Angelina's corset chaffed from perspiration.

Teresa squeezed her hand again. "It will be a success. I promise." Teresa's reassuring smile fell short of its calming intent.

They were only a third of the way to the financial goal. Ladies' organizations clamored to hear Angelina's story after it appeared in the paper. They were fascinated, but their purses stayed closed. The investments so far were small.

Angelina sipped her now-tepid tea to wet her parched throat as time crawled by. She stopped her musing when the president raised her voice to be heard over the chiming of the wall clock.

"Ladies, the minutes have been read and seconded. Is there any new business?" Margaret Asbury looked about the room, then focused on Teresa. "If not, Mrs. Teresa Shilling, a member of our board, will introduce our guest speaker."

Teresa stood. "As a group, we share the same progressive thinking, goals, and convictions. Therefore, I've asked Miss Angelina DuBois to speak on an important undertaking that will create wonderful opportunities for women." She nodded to Angelina. "Let's welcome Miss DuBois."

The room gave polite applause, and Angelina rose on shaky legs.

Teresa set up an easel as Angelina organized her notes on the podium. She'd memorized her speech, but having the notes buoyed her confidence.

After Teresa perched in a chair to one side of the platform, Angelina lifted her chin and scanned the audience. "Ladies, thank you for allowing me to share my exciting vision with you. While Horace Greeley and other men are striving to create a utopia with men as the patriarchs, I have a different goal." She smiled around the room at the curiosity on many faces. "A town where women are treated equal to men. A town of female business owners." She stepped to the side of the podium. "Resolve will be an example of what a truly equal society can accomplish."

Angelina went on to share the details. Teresa removed the cloth from the architectural drawing of the town. "I am resolved to show the world that women are intelligent and capable of pursuing any career path they choose, regardless of their station in life."

Exclamations of approval filtered about the room. Teresa nodded encouragement. Angelina gulped and pressed on. Now the time to ask for investors and donations had come. At this point in her presentation, things always floundered. "What I am looking for are women who are willing to contribute to the success of this venture." Teresa placed the plaque showing the benefits of each level of investment on the easel. "As you can see, I offer a fair return rate. If investing is something you are uncertain about, for those who choose a onetime donation, a building will bear your name. If a few of you would like to make a joint donation, then you create a street name."

Murmurs circulated as she spoke, the voices nearly distracting Angelina. Nods of approval and thoughtful looks, as well as scowls, were present amongst the ladies.

Angelina completed her talk with instructions and thanks. Bright smiles and applause accompanied her from the platform. The enthusiastic response lifted some of the heaviness from her chest.

Angelina assisted Teresa in passing out envelopes to each table before returning to their seats.

The president stepped back to the podium. "Ladies, I'm inspired. This is a wonderful opportunity. Here in Chicago, we all know this is a hard-pressed battle. Just think. A fresh canvas to create a society of equality."

A stout woman harrumphed. "Margaret ... Madam President. How do you expect those of us who have no finances of our own to contribute?"

"Matilda, dear. We shall do what we always do—have a fundraiser." Margaret's words were followed by buzzes of conversation about the room.

"Our husbands would turn apoplectic over that." The remark came from a well-dressed, bejeweled matron.

"We'll call it a bazaar for the less fortunate. The men need not know who those less fortunate are."

A young woman seated next to Matilda laughed. "Mother, you know Father will do anything I ask." Giggles erupted from a few young ladies at an adjoining table.

"I am sure Miss DuBois needs funds now, and it will take us time to arrange a fundraiser." Margaret's words brought silence. "I propose those of us who can give generously now do so. Then we organize a bazaar, and later a dance, to raise further funds. A project like this is bound to have unexpected expenses."

"Hear, hear," the women exclaimed.

Angelina's heart warmed with this outpouring of support. A warm blush crept to her cheeks. A few deep breaths and her composure returned.

She leaned closer to Teresa. "You were right."

"I told you." Teresa refilled their teacups

Angelina looked around the room, catching snippets of positive conversation about her project. By meeting's end, she'd gotten pledges from investors and donations to cover seventy percent of her goal.

Margaret Asbury helped her pack away their things. "Teresa, Miss DuBois, please come to tea tomorrow afternoon. I have a proposition to discuss. Shall we say one o'clock?"

Teresa spoke for her. "I'll bring her by. Thank you, Margaret. We couldn't have raised the funds without you."

"After tomorrow, I hope to add to the amount you've collected. Bring the financials when you come."

Angelina found her voice. "Thank you, and I look forward to our time tomorrow."

Margaret escorted them to the front door. "I want to thank *you*. This project should get The Society off their pretty bustled backsides and rolling up their sleeves to work. We haven't done more than visit members when they were sick, bereaved, or have recently given birth. I want to accomplish something significant during my presidency besides having guest speakers spout high ideals. You gave us something to sink our teeth into. Good day, ladies."

The brisk air, more frigid with the wind blowing off Lake

Michigan, chilled Angelina's cheeks. Her carriage pulled up, and her driver scrambled down to open the door. He assisted them inside, then took his place above. The wheels rocked over uneven paving stones as they headed toward Teresa's home.

"I feel Mrs. Asbury is going to invest handsomely." Angelina almost squealed. "And I am so happy I hired Emily Jameson to keep the books for this project—she is a wonder. I'll have her work up all the figures tonight."

Teresa removed her hat and fanned her face. "It is stuffy in here."

"Really? I'm chilled." Angelina frowned when Teresa dabbed her brow with her handkerchief. "Are you well?"

"Just fighting advancing years." Teresa placed the lace-trimmed square of cotton back in her purse.

"I'm grateful you're coming with me tomorrow. With your legal expertise, you can negotiate the final details." Angelina stopped speaking as Teresa stuck her head out the window for a few moments. "Teresa, what will people think?"

Teresa pulled her head back inside. "No one saw me. I feel better now." She chuckled. "My body heats up like a fireplace for a time. My Aunt Minerva used to complain about the same thing, and I thought she was daft." She pointed at Angelina. "You must never disrespect your elders on things you have yet to experience."

Angelina stifled a smile. Her friend always surprised her—that was for sure. "I shall keep that in mind."

Teresa laughed as she drew out her fan. After a few moments of vigorous fanning, she shook her head. "You know, women want liberty, but we have yet to speak freely about the function of our bodies."

Angelina blushed. "And such things will probably remain private and unspoken for years to come."

"It is a shame no female doctor wanted to join our venture." Teresa closed her fan. "Women would feel more comfortable talking to one."

"Dr. Potter came highly recommended. Educated at Oxford and

had a residence at … I forget the name of the hospital in New York." But it was true, male doctors often misdiagnosed women's health concerns. "Perhaps female patients might talk to his wife. She's a nurse and could pass their complaints on to Dr. Potter."

"Perhaps." Teresa had a faraway look. "We're still uncomfortable speaking of female afflictions, so we medicate ourselves with old wives' remedies and laudanum."

"You use laudanum?"

"No, of course not. I'm referring to women in a general sense. Good gracious, I saw how laudanum changed my sister from a sweetheart to a crazed fiend as she doctored her female problems. Let's hope Dr. Potter won't prescribe laudanum and other opiates freely."

"Thank you for giving me one more thing to worry about." Angelina sighed and looked out the window.

Teresa patted Angelina's hand as the carriage rolled to a stop. "Remember, tomorrow has enough care of its own. You must give your worries to the Almighty."

She nodded politely. What would the Almighty do with them?

Angelina stared at her face in the hall mirror to be sure the morning puffiness around her eyes had melted away. She turned her head from side to side, then pinched her cheeks to give them color. *Thank you, Teresa, for putting worries in my head.* She'd finally surrendered her doubts about Dr. Potter and drifted off to sleep hours past the time she'd laid her head on the pillow.

"Emily." Angelina walked toward her office. The girl came through the door carrying a folded document.

"Here you are, ma'am. I can't believe you raised all that money last night. God is certainly answering our prayers."

Angelina took the document and placed it in her bag. Teresa, not God, had brought about this success. "Thanks to you, Emily, everything is kept in order."

"This job has helped finance my brother's supply list." Emily offered a smile. "We will be well prepared to set up the blacksmith shop."

"Is Caroline here yet?"

"She's in the office writing thank-you notes for all your supporters."

Hiring Emily Jameson as her accountant and Caroline Pritchard as her personal assistant had been wise moves. The two young women believed in her vision. And Angelina was confident the business plan would impress Mrs. Asbury. This savvy woman's financial help and support would go a long way to keep the naysayers at bay.

Teresa Shilling's carriage was already at Margaret's two-story Colonial manor when Angelina arrived. The gentle drizzle that had graced the streets of Chicago all morning had grown into a steady rain. Margaret's footman greeted her with an umbrella, ushering her into the parlor, where a roaring fire chased away the dampness.

"Angelina, I am delighted you've come." Margaret showed her to a straight-backed chair next to Teresa. "Please." She pointed to the tea service. "One lump or two?"

"Two, thank you." Angelina settled the skirt of her green poplin gown around her as she sat down.

Margaret served her guests, passing out petit fours and small cucumber sandwiches.

After some time of small talk, Margaret glanced at the clock. "Let me get to the point of your visit. May I see your financials?"

Angelina handed over the documents. "I've included our business plan."

Margaret took her time examining them. "Excellent. My late husband insisted I understand, as he called it, the money side of life. He knew if I saw the numbers, it guaranteed less frivolous spending. It taught me more than that." She handed the papers back to Angelina. "I am prepared to cover the remainder of your funds."

"That is quite a substantial amount." Her heart raced. "Are you sure?" Angelina waited in silence.

"Yes, I am. There is a string attached. And he will be here momentarily."

I hope she doesn't expect me to marry someone. A knot formed in her throat as she stared at Margaret's serene face. One of the things she abhorred about the wealthy was arranged marriages for financial gain.

Responding no doubt to her wide-eyed perusal, Margaret patted her hand. "My nephew went to seminary. He knows his Bible and is looking for a church."

"You want him to be the pastor for the town." Angelina sighed loudly, and warmth covered her neck as she gathered her composure.

"Hezekiah is a wonderful boy. However, he gets nervous in front of a congregation. His sermons are ... well ... but he is a wonderful counselor. And if you need prayer, I have found great comfort in his."

A maid entered. "Reverend Hezekiah Asbury is here."

"Send him in."

"You'll like him." Margaret gave a sheepish grin as a tall, thin man with kind green eyes and unruly blond hair gave his aunt a kiss on the cheek. "Thank you for inviting me today, Aunt Margaret."

He took the seat next to his aunt on the settee. She fixed his tea. "I would like you to meet Miss Angelina DuBois and Mrs. Teresa Shilling."

He nodded and smiled. "My aunt has told me about your plan. And I am sure she has told you about my plight." His face turned a soft pink. He reached into his pocket and produced a packet of letters. "These are my references."

Angelina and Teresa read a few. Each one lauded Pastor Asbury's ability as a minister.

"If you look a little further, there are a few who mention my less-than-stellar sermons." His eyes turned pleading. "I do much better with small groups and teaching Bible studies. I propose we have small meetings available throughout the week. May I add to my résumé that I play piano, guitar, and violin? We can have times of inspirational singing without any preaching on Sundays, perhaps."

He looked from Teresa to Angelina with a hopeful face. "At the least, there will be a need for a pastor to perform weddings and funerals."

"You've thought this out." Angelina turned to Teresa, who gave a slight nod. "Rev. Asbury, I shall treat you as any other candidate. Teresa will have the packet of information and requirements delivered to you. You have until May first to get your things together. You will work alongside the others in manual labor. And when and if a church is built, you will be responsible for its upkeep." Angelina sounded like her father, and it irritated her. But a man born to wealth willing to pastor a church in a fledgling town set off alarms. "You will live in the men's dormitory. I have not designed a parsonage, or for that matter, a church. So, until that is done, you will hold services where you find a place and the time."

His spine straightened and chin lifted. "I'll be a missionary until the church is built. A wonderful opportunity. You'll not find me a slacker."

"That is good to hear. I trust Margaret's recommendation won't be tarnished in any way." A scowl formed on Angelina's face as memories of arrogant pastors taunted her. "I did mention you would need to financially support yourself?"

"I expect nothing less." He turned and gave his aunt a firm nod.

"Of course, dear." Margaret patted his hand. "Now, if you will excuse us, we ladies have business to discuss."

Beaming, Rev. Asbury bowed over their hands. Was this a wise decision? Angelina's father had little use for spiritual things. Surely, the reverend's enthusiasm didn't indicate a belief that she embraced his doctrine.

Margaret spoke again after the door closed behind him. "Let me add, I've watched my nephew after he told the family he received the call. We were skeptical. He's not pious and haughty, which pleases me. He prefers to meet people's needs wherever they are. That way, they are more willing to hear the truths of the Scripture. I think he will fit right in." She set down her teacup. "Now ... where do I sign?"

Teresa grasped Angelina's hands as they stood before their carriages. "I can read your mind, missy. I'm sure the pastor will work out fine."

"Rev. Asbury better not have plans to put himself in a position of town leadership once he has a flock to shepherd. Father always claimed mixing business with religion created chaos. If he truly gives people a choice, then he'll fit nicely. But the minute he chooses to overstep his place and direct the community, he'll be out on his ear." Bitter acid rose in her throat.

"If you want, we can have a detective check beyond these letters of recommendation." Teresa's practical advice offered a balance to Angelina's anxiety.

"I'm sorry for my sharp tone. A member of the clergy took my father aside after my mother died and suggested Mother wasn't in heaven but that a large gift in her memory would ensure her entrance."

"What a horrid man." Teresa scowled and squeezed her hand.

"The detective is not necessary. If manual labor is not to his liking, I'm sure Mr. Pritchard will inform me, and it will seal his fate."

CHAPTER 5

Edward found Angelina's carriage outside the railroad office. He raised himself on tiptoes to speak up toward the window. "Miss DuBois, I'm here."

She peered down at him. "Good, you're on time."

He snapped the folding steps down, opened the door, and helped her to the ground.

"Really, it is quite a bother to wait for a man to accompany me." Angelina had her hair done up in ringlets that framed her face. Her bonnet matched the pale blue dress, drawing attention to her sapphire eyes. The sweet scent of her perfume—rose and jasmine—drew him in. He cleared his throat.

"A woman alone is easy prey for pickpockets." Edward took the proffered leather cylinder containing their plans, and she took his elbow.

"I carry a pocket derringer in my reticule. I shot a pickpocket once. He got a hole in his shoulder, and I had a hole in my new bag." She smiled sweetly and patted his arm.

Edward shook his head, and churning erupted in his middle. No doubt he might be her target if he disturbed her designs.

They entered the building and were escorted immediately to the president's office. A balding, middle-aged man with a handlebar mustache and mutton chops rose from his desk. "Miss DuBois, I am delighted to see you." He extended his hand and clasped the tips of her fingers.

"Mr. Worthington, may I introduce Edward Pritchard, my building contractor? Mr. Pritchard, Samuel Worthington III, president of the CB&Q Railroad. Our families have been friends for years." She gave a coquettish smile to the president. Mr. Worthington eyed her form, ignoring Edward as he took a seat beside her.

Worthington grinned and leaned against his large oak desk. "Miss DuBois, how may I assist you today?"

"I need a railroad line." She opened her fan, stirring the perfume scent. Mr. Worthington blushed and cleared his throat. "Mr. Pritchard, would you show him the map, please?"

Edward took the cylinder and extracted the map. Mr. Worthington placed a paperweight on each edge to keep it flat.

"As you can see, I need a line in Kansas." Angelina remained seated, calmly playing with her fan and lifting her eyebrow to get Edward's attention.

He pointed to the area of the map where the line was needed, feeling like a stable boy who'd been handed the reins of a horse to groom. No speaking, only action. Edward resisted the urge to grunt.

"I don't know."

Angelina's pout met Mr. Worthington's upward glance. Edward suppressed a frown. The woman expertly engaged her womanly wiles when it suited her.

"Now, Samuel." She sighed and fluttered her eyelashes. "You've done business with my father in the past. Don't forget, I'm the one who encouraged him to invest in your rail line."

Mr. Worthington pulled on his collar. "Well, I wish I could assist. But we have no tracks extending that far."

"Ah, but you have connections. I'll be investing heavily." Her smile could melt a rock. Edward waited as the president stared at Angelina.

"Of course." Mr. Worthington came out of his daze. "I do have a business associate who has invested in tracks going west. He might be persuaded to create a small spur."

"How very kind, Samuel. I knew you were the man for the job." She fanned more scent into the air, and the man's knuckles tightened on the edge of his desk.

"I assume this is the town I read about in the paper?" Worthington stared at the drawing, avoiding her gaze. "You're quite a determined woman." He removed the paperweights, letting the map roll up. "Horace Greeley may beat you to the punch, my dear."

"This is not a competition. I care not who finishes first. My project is not an experiment. I don't want to create a community of perfect, pompous piety. Rather, allow individuals to reach their full potential by the sweat of their brow and intelligence."

"Well said, Miss DuBois, well said." He smiled, and she fluttered her eyelashes, the shrewd businesswoman once again hidden behind her gender. "I believe I would like to invest in your venture."

"Why, thank you, Samuel." She fingered a curl. "Mr. Pritchard, show him the contract."

Edward pulled it from the stack of papers. "As you can see, this is fairly boilerplate. Basic agreement of intent. You will save money on your investment by offering every railroad worker an opportunity to start a business or farm in lieu of pay and as an extra incentive to finish on time." He handed over a copy of the employee contract.

Mr. Worthington studied the map and contract for several minutes before a frown began to form.

Again, Angelina employed her fan. Mr. Worthington's admiring smile confirmed the hook was set. He signed the agreement and set an appointment for the meeting with his business acquaintance. Edward's face hurt from maintaining a serious expression.

With a swish of her skirt, Angelina came to her feet. "If you have any concerns, Samuel ..."

The man touched her gloved hand, making Edward cringe.

"No, none." He removed his hand with a glint of longing in his eyes. "Members of the DuBois family have always kept their word regarding business." Mr. Worthington escorted them to the door.

Edward finally allowed his face to relax when he opened her carriage door. "I must say, considering your philosophy that women are equal to men in every way, you certainly poured on the charm."

"I may believe that, but men do not. I use whatever means legally necessary to seal the deal."

"Dressing like a debutant heading for a ball was intentional."

"I haven't been a debutante in years." Angelina laughed and squeezed his arm as he entered the carriage. A warmth spread through him. "Once I've built my town, doors will open that have been closed thanks to my loathsome cousin, Hiram, and I'll no longer have to resort to feminine wiles."

Edward nodded. "My understanding is that Hiram DuBois now runs DuBois Architectural Interests. And that your father left it to him." He waited until she nodded. "Rumors around town are, he's lost another contract." Edward had also heard he drank too much.

"Yes, Hiram will not budge on his design. Never mind it's the client's money, and they need to be appeased."

"Sounds like someone ..." He stopped himself, but his neck heated.

"I know I can be difficult." She settled herself on the bench across from him, her voice showing no irritation. "This is the first time I've had a free hand. I am the client *and* the contractor." She flashed a radiant smile, unsettling him. "Multiply my stubbornness by ten—no, twenty—add a large dose of deception, and that's Hiram."

"I've heard that too." Edward had investigated the DuBois family thoroughly after the interview. His military training taught him to gather as much intelligence as possible before the battle. "Now ... the telegraph office. Will you approach its president the same way?"

The vehicle moved through the crowded city streets. Horses whinnied, and the sound of a police whistle and vendors hawking their wares filtered through the confines of the carriage.

"No. Mr. Carson, the president of the telegraph company, respects my business sense."

Angelina leaned forward, inches from his face. He focused on her lips, then pressed back into the carriage wall. Edward doused the heat rising inside with a reminder—she was his boss.

Taking no note of his sudden move, Angelina chattered on. "I'm the one who invested in the telegraph and encouraged my father to do the same. Mr. Carson will be happy to add a telegraph station in Resolve. That's the name I've chosen because I resolve to make a difference for women."

Her optimistic attitude, though commendable, was a bit fanciful. The whole thing could go to wrack and ruin. How would she respond to that? Had this woman ever confronted disappointment or hardship?

Edward stared out the window at the masses walking to their destinations. He envisioned the streets of Resolve, crammed to overflowing with homeless laborers.

What had he gotten himself into?

Angelina concluded her business regarding the telegraph with professional ease. No flirty lashes or fanning. Mr. Carson gave her a firm handshake and showed her the same respect he'd show a male investor.

They made three more stops—the lumber yard, mercantile wholesaler, and the coppersmith. Angelina's energy appeared boundless, while weariness crept over Edward.

Finally, she paused to assess him. "Shall we stop for some refreshment? All this excitement has given me an appetite."

"As you wish." Edward refused to admit he was bone-tired and starving.

She knocked on the wall. The driver opened the window. "Yes, milady?"

"Sherman House, please."

Sherman House Resort enticed the wealthy from all over Chicago, and its extravagant décor drew envy. Edward had studied the blueprints. The thirty-foot-wide hallways seemed a waste of space to Edward's practical thinking, but this would be his first time seeing the structure and eating in the restaurant. He felt extremely underdressed in his plain brown suit.

The carriage stopped. She glanced at his apparel and smiled.

"Don't worry, I always get a table in a secluded corner. Less opportunity for gossipy people to disturb me."

He touched his nose, searching for an imaginary ring. Was he under the same spell as all the bulls in her pasture of investor cattle? She would be paying for a dinner that would have set him back at least a month's salary.

No. This was strictly business. He took a deep breath to clear his head. But the captivating scent of perfume filled his senses as he eyed the gorgeous woman who set his heart beating a strange cadence. No battlefield skirmish was as fearful as being in this woman's presence when she was dressed to manipulate men to her will. Life as he knew it, as a man in charge, shifted before him.

CHAPTER 6

February 1869

"Ma'am." Bridget peered around the library door. "I'm sorry to disturb, but ye have a visitor."

Angelina glanced up from her book to the grandfather clock in the corner. Too early for her dinner guests.

Bridget delivered a filigreed card with the name *Madeline Fry* embossed in silver script across the front, with delicate flowers etched in one corner. Madeline ... Maddy ... Maddy Fry. *Poor woman.* Angelina never attended the socialite's parties and paid little attention to gossip, but Madeline's sad story struck a chord in her suffragette heart.

"Show her to the parlor."

Angelina stood in the doorway unnoticed by the petite Mrs. Fry, who faced the display of family portraits on the wall. She still wore a hoop skirt, the style fading in the fashion world. Her sleeves were worn and her bonnet freshened up with tiny blue and green feathers around the bill.

"Mrs. Fry, what a pleasant surprise." Angelina extended her hand.

"Thank you for seeing me." After her initial start, Mrs. Fry straightened her back.

"Take a seat, and I'll ring for Bridget to bring some light refreshment."

"No, thank you. I'll be brief." Mrs. Fry continued to stand.

"Very well. But please, do sit." Angelina indicated the overstuffed floral chair near the fireplace. The scent of cherry wood wafted around them, battling the chill.

Her guest perched on the edge of her seat and removed her gloves before speaking. She cleared her throat and gave a haughty stare. "I'll skip the pleasantries, Miss DuBois. I assume you know my story?"

"I've heard rumors, but I'd like to hear it from you, if you care to tell it."

"My husband's mistress came to be with child. I couldn't give him children." Tears glistened in her eyes. "That became grounds for an annulment. Less messy financially than a divorce. My now-former husband's family has connections in the courts. I received a tiny stipend, which I've been stretching to get by. Soon I'll have nothing."

Silence fell between them while a hammer of pity beat a cadence in Angelina's heart. "How can I help you?"

"Do you have a place for me in the town you're building? I don't cook, and I'm no farmer. I have no marketable skills unless you consider needlepoint and embroidery a way to earn an income." Mrs. Fry pursed her lips and gripped her reticule.

Angelina saw the desperation and shame in the woman's eyes, despite her rigid comportment. "What kind of education do you have?"

"I completed finishing school, of course, then I attended teacher's college on a lark because I fancied myself in love with the schoolmaster." She gave a wry laugh.

"How were your grades?"

"I excelled in math and graduated tenth in my class." Her shoulders slumped. "There were only twelve students."

"Mrs. Fry, may I call you by your given name?"

"Yes."

"Madeline, no one needs to know your class rank. Never again reveal that fact to a living soul. Say, instead, *I graduated from teacher's college.*" Angelina stepped before her and lifted the woman's chin with one finger and nodded.

Madeline's eyes held a determined glint. "I graduated from

teacher's college."

Angelina moved to the other chair near the fireplace to continue the interview. "Have you ever taught school?"

"No." Madeline said, then added, "but I loved teaching children their catechism lessons. And I've taught a few of my maids to read."

"You're hired."

"Excuse me?"

"There will be children who would benefit from an education while their parents work. Depending on the number of children, I may be able to get you some help." She smiled at her guest.

Madeline smiled for the first time, filling her features with beauty.

"Come back tomorrow. I'll have a head count of possible students for you. Then you'll go to Duncan's mercantile to order school supplies."

"Ma'am, may I ..." She dropped her eyes again. "May I have an advance? Mr. Baker, the landlord, is threatening me with eviction. I'll lose my place at the boardinghouse. Just enough to catch up on my rent."

"I would rather—"

"I understand." She stood to leave, shoulders sagging.

"No, dear, I think you misunderstand. I would prefer to offer you lodging." Angelina caught her hand. "Here, at no charge."

She covered her mouth with her other hand. "You're too kind."

Angelina continued, rising. "When you come tomorrow, bring your things. I have several unoccupied rooms. You can stay here until we leave for Kansas."

"I can't impose."

"You said you are good at math. I'll have Emily teach you how she keeps the books for our enterprise. Once we are in Kansas, Emily will be dividing her time between helping her brother and me. When you're not teaching, you can continue keeping accounts as well."

"Thank you, Miss DuBois."

"Call me Angelina."

Madeline's throat worked as she swallowed. "Angelina, I won't be able to claim my belongings if I owe rent."

"I see. I'll provide the funds, and they'll come out of your salary." Angelina met her new employee's gaze.

Madeline extended her hand. "You are very generous. Thank you. I'll be here bright and early tomorrow morning."

Edward took a deep breath as he escorted his sister up the stairs to the DuBois mansion. Interviewing here was one thing ... dinner at Miss DuBois' invitation, quite another. After employing the knocker, he smiled at Caroline. Her new yellow frock complemented her womanly attributes, reminding Edward she'd crossed the threshold of childhood.

A butler answered, but as he took their wraps, Angelina hurried down a curving staircase. She swept her hand toward the hall, and her diamond bracelet caught the light. "Welcome to my home."

Edward offered a brief bow. "Thank you for having us."

"It's an honor, indeed." Caroline beamed, admiring the gold-embossed wallpaper and the crystal vase on the foyer table. Her dress appeared homespun in comparison to Angelina's silver dinner gown. Their hostess' complexion glowed as light refracted off her dress.

Edward diverted his eyes from the beautiful woman. He masked a frown as he removed his hat. They'd discussed her need for a more practical wardrobe. It appeared Angelina chose to ignore his suggestion to attire herself in a simpler manner. Dressing like a goddess dwelling on earth would certainly distract the men from doing their work or taking her seriously. Edward extended his elbow to Caroline, moving away from his hostess.

The butler took Edward's hat as Angelina led them down the hall to the formal dining room. Three place settings of china and crystal appeared dwarfed on a table that seated twenty.

Caroline chose the appropriate fork or spoon for each course—five, from soup to chocolate cake, each delicious after the simple fare they'd lived on. She then chewed slowly and dabbed her lips throughout the meal. His sister's attempt at ladylike manners pleased Edward. Then he tried not to laugh as she cleaned her plate—something a lady would never do. Angelina left a few morsels with each course. She was an enigma, equality mixed with tradition.

"Edward, have you acquired enough laborers?"

"Yes and no. Waiting until May first to start a job means some who have signed might decline if they find other employment."

"I see." Angelina took a bite of cake. "And the supplies. Is everything available?"

"Yes. But as I said, I am sure there are trees there, and we could manufacture our own building materials."

"My understanding is, the area I have chosen is prairie. Fewer trees, lots of grass, and people are making homes from dirt." She waved her empty fork in the air. "Can you imagine? That is not part of my design." She smiled sweetly at him. "I am sending enough wood to get you started building and more every month as needed."

"Surely, there are trees available for our needs in Kansas. It is going to take a few years to build the whole town."

"Two years is the projected time line. According to my research, the terrain does not seem promising to supply the wood we need."

Apparently, she'd taken off her blinders long enough to research the lumber shortage. A few years ... a long time for a spoiled rich girl to live among the masses. Edward finished his cake, and the maid collected the dishes.

Angelina came to her feet. "Shall we take our coffee in the parlor?"

Quaint seemed the word to describe the room. Not too ornate—just enough to remind guests of her wealth—but warm and inviting. The wood trim was real oak, not pine stained to look like oak. Edward appreciated the workmanship. The fresco of a pond with willow trees caught the colors of the furnishings. He turned to Miss DuBois. "A comfortable room."

"That's what I love about it. My designer was Mr. Francois."

Edward's nose wrinkled at the thought of home decorating. He knew types of woods and building materials and how to run gas lights and install water pumps.

"Do you decorate the homes you build?" Angelina indicated the chairs as she took a seat in an upholstered, straight-back chair.

"No ma'am." Edward joined Caroline in the oak chairs across from her. He wouldn't admit he'd only built two residences before the war.

"Are you acquainted with Mr. Francois?"

"We've met." And his girly touch was forever stamped on any room he designed.

The maid brought in the tray of coffee and, with a nod from Angelina, sat down.

Angelina gestured to the young woman as she explained. "You may remember Bridget O'Malley as the greeter when you did your interview. Since Bridget plans on starting a new life as an independent businesswoman, I've invited her to sit with her peers."

Bridget's face grew crimson. "Is it all right with the two of ye?"

"We have always been part of the masses, as yourself." Edward regretted his words when Angelina squirmed and touched her throat.

With a satisfied smile, Bridget poured the coffee and passed out the cups.

Angelina put three spoons of sugar in her coffee and took it up, stirring overly long without drinking. "I must ask you a great favor, Mr. Pritchard."

His brow furrowed. She'd changed the supply list and her designs on five buildings over the last several weeks. "And that would be?"

She took a sip of her brew, then placed her cup on the saucer and back on the table before speaking. "If we moved your departure date to March first, would you have enough men? That would give you two months to survey and get the area ready to build on before all the others arrive."

A strike of heat went through his spine. Why did she want to begin earlier? He pushed the question away, grateful for the extra time. "That works. The fewer people underfoot during the preparation, the better. I could use a few more hands and a surveyor, though."

"I have already secured a surveyor, and I can also offer you a doctor and a pastor as extra hands."

"The doctor would be useful. What am I supposed to do with a preacher?"

"The pastor is not opposed to hard work, and he is Margaret Asbury's nephew."

"Ah, your biggest investor."

Miss DuBois' seeking investors was a wise move that required a few concessions. A pastor willing to work with his hands would be a first in his memory. "And is the surveyor someone's kin?"

"No, but she comes highly recommended by General Sheridan himself."

Another woman. Edward schooled his face, hoping to disguise his frustration. The number of women-owned businesses proved daunting enough, but now she tossed female laborers his way. Was there no job she thought unseemly for a woman? "How does she know General Sheridan?"

"Lucinda Graves' father served under him in the Union Army. After the war, she and her father helped survey Fort Dodge and some other military facilities. They'd been surveying farm plots in Kansas until her father died a few months ago. I secured her services in exchange for land." Angelina smiled. "Isn't that fortunate?"

"Fortunate." Edward swallowed the last of his coffee before irritation formed on his lips. "When will I meet Miss Graves?"

"Lucinda is finishing a surveying job in Kansas first. She's accustomed to living off the land and has her own tent. One less inexperienced person for you to worry about." Angelina's blue eyes shone with excitement. "I'm sure you'll get along famously."

The upside to going early—he could make decisions without Angelina's interfering, fickle ways. Unless ... "Are you going early too?"

"No, I haven't begun to get prepared for the trip. I've got paperwork to finish and pledges to collect. My private train car is being refitted so I can live in it until my home is built. Which reminds me, the rail spur to Resolve isn't completed. It won't be until April twenty-ninth. I can't come until that spur is finished. Otherwise, I will have nowhere to live."

"I love the name of the town, Resolve." Caroline had remained quiet most of the evening, writing notes in her journal, but now she looked up with a smile.

Angelina nodded, clasping her dainty hands in her lap. "Yes, I have resolved to make a success of this at all costs."

The name did have a ring of hope about it. And this project needed lots of hope. Smoothing out the frown that begged to form, Edward shifted.

Fluttering a glance in his direction, Angelina tightened her fingers. "Do you think it is too forward of me to name the town? Should I ask for a vote on it?"

Caroline gave her head a brisk shake. "Naming the town makes it feel more real."

"Yes, I agree." He'd resolved to prove himself as a builder. He had to be whole-heartedly behind this endeavor, crazy as it may be. Edward smiled and held out his cup for a refill.

Bridget poured as she added, "Resolve be a fine name. Everyone who is coming with us resolves to have a better life than we got here. A better life than our parents could provide. Me ma died the year I came to America. I haven't seen me family in ten years. Shamus and I are goin' to save our money to bring 'em from Ireland."

"Have you always been a maid?" Caroline smiled and opened her notebook, slipping out the pencil marking her place.

"Nay, I was a cleaning lady in a fine hotel when Miss DuBois' personal maid eloped. Miss DuBois stepped outside her room, where she found me polishing the stair railings. Next thing I know, I had me a plushy job. Pretty good for a sixteen-year-old farm girl. I been with her ever since."

"And a wonderful job she has done, although I'd lay odds that I have the only maid who wants to open a bakery." Angelina's remark made Bridget smile and blush. "Bridget wanted to practice her cooking skills, so she prepared our dinner tonight. She's thinking of opening a restaurant too."

"You're a wonderful cook, Bridget." Caroline sat forward and touched the maid's skirt. "It was a feast fit for royalty."

Bridget's blush rose from her neck to her ears. "Thank you. Such high praise I shall cherish in me heart always. If you'll pardon me, I need to fix a plate for me brother. He's been working long hours at various jobs to add to his family's traveling money." She gave a curtsy before hurrying out the door, leaving the coffee service.

"I'd like to take Shamus along when I leave early." Edward put down his cup. "I hired the Irishmen from your list, but they seem a rowdy bunch. They might respect me more with him at my side. And I've hired men, sight unseen, to drive the supply wagons from the train station to the town site. It's a few days' journey, and they know the terrain. But I don't know their character."

Angelina nodded. "If there is any trouble, Shamus should be able to handle it. I remember reading in the paper about his fighting prowess. They called him the gentlemen fighter. I'm not sure what that means, but it made me comfortable hiring him. I'm sure he'll be valuable to you. I'll pay him in advance so Bridget can get all their supplies and his family will have ample funds until the rest of us depart on May first."

"I underestimated you." Edward shifted in his seat, resting his elbow on the armrest.

"How so?" She remained poised in her chair and smiled.

"I thought you were going to fund the whole venture and name the town DuBois."

Glancing up from her note-taking, Caroline scowled. "Edward, I'm shocked. How could you think such a thing?"

Angelina chuckled. "I assume he has met many of my class who love to build monuments to themselves." She set her cup down. "My uncle was one of them." Her pert nose wrinkled. "My father brought respect back to the DuBois name. And honestly, if not for Teresa reminding me, I might not have refined my vision to benefit all the applicants. I don't want to build a monument, mind you, but instead, prove a point."

Caroline's pencil froze, held in the air. "You want to prove women can compete in business alongside men. That we are not the weaker sex, but quite capable."

"Yes, but not at the expense of the families who are trusting me. They want a better life for their children. This is not about the DuBois name. It's about a community that respects hard work, no matter your gender or race."

"You have a very forward-thinking philosophy on life." Edward envisioned the lady in men's trousers digging alongside his crew. A laugh escaped his lips.

"You find me foolish?"

"No." His face warmed. "It's an admirable goal."

"I think the goal of treating each other with respect is in the Bible." Caroline jotted another note. "I'll have to find the reference."

Edward arched a glance at his employer. "Doesn't it bother you that my sister is writing down everything we're saying?"

"Not really. It's an excellent exercise for a future reporter. If this experiment is a success, she can write a book about it." Angelina extended her open hands wide to each side of her body and shrugged. "If not, she can write a book for future generations to learn from our mistakes."

Caroline closed her notebook. "I believe we will succeed. I'm enjoying being your personal secretary."

"You're the best I've ever had." Angelina smiled at his sister.

Caroline shook her head. "I'm your first personal secretary."

"True. That makes you the best." Angelina's tinkly laughter warmed Edward. She patted Caroline's hand. "My dear, you sparkle with personality."

Caroline's eyes gleamed with the accolades. Before they'd died in a cholera epidemic, their parents had held praise as a prize to be sought rather than freely given to encourage. When he'd returned from the war, his sister was living with neighbors who treated her little better than a slave. After he'd brought her to Chicago, she'd smiled more and now had him wrapped around her little finger. Angelina seemed good for Caroline. If this whole project fell down the well of good intentions, it was worth it to see Caroline blooming into a confident woman.

Edward rose, smoothing his frock coat. "Miss DuBois, if there is nothing more to discuss, we should be going. I've a lot to do to get my crew on the train and to Resolve in two weeks' time."

"Please call me Angelina, at least when there are no employees about."

Edward wanted to object, but she was his employer too. "Of course."

"He's Eddie to his friends." Tucking her notebook away, Caroline gave him a wink, then stood and nodded at Angelina. "You're our friend."

"Eddie it is, then." Angelina gave her a sly smile. "Eddie, keep me abreast of your progress. My personal train will carry all of you and the supplies, then return to Chicago to retrieve the rest of us and the remaining supplies. Mr. Hayes, our engineer, will be contacting you."

"You own a train?" Edward shook his head.

"My father found it very practical to own an engine for his personal car. Extravagant perhaps, but for our purposes, it saves money. We will rent freight cars and passenger cars as needed."

"Mr. Hayes will not be staying in Resolve to build a depot?" Edward laughed.

"Maybe in the future. He used to be the DuBois' exclusive engineer. My father traveled all over the country. Now Mr. Hayes works for the CB &Q Railway."

Just how wealthy was Miss DuBois? Would she still be solvent if Resolve failed? And if it didn't, would his yet to-be-established reputation disappear with it?

CHAPTER 7

Chicago, March 1869

Angelina and Teresa were escorted by the maître d' to a private room on the second floor of Bon Appétit, an exclusive new restaurant on Wabash a few blocks from Adam Street. Angelina admired the fresco of a flower garden covering the walls. The round table covered with a white linen tablecloth could seat six. A floral arrangement of purple pansies graced the center, and the music of a string quartet filtered into the room.

"Welcome to our ladies' preference room. There is no smoking or inappropriate speech permitted here. We strive to make your dining experience exceptional. A waiter will be here momentarily." The maître d' bowed and left the room.

"Really, Teresa, the whole idea of a room to protect women's sensibilities is off-putting." Angelina removed her feather-trimmed hat and placed it on the chair beside her.

Teresa rested her veiled creation in another chair. "Enjoy this pampering and fine dining while we can. We'll be leaving for the Kansas wilderness in a few weeks."

A waiter entered wearing a black tailcoat, cravat, and trousers and gave a half bow. "Ladies, today your choices are beef tips, asparagus in hollandaise sauce, oyster soup, and baked apple pudding to finish the meal. Or Cornish hen with sage and onion bread stuffing, green beans, oyster soup, and, of course, baked apple pudding."

Angelina laid her gloves beside her hat. "I'll have the beef, how about you, Teresa?"

"Yes, and a pot of tea." Teresa dismissed the waiter with her hand.

"Did I mention, my butler, Griffin, has secured someone to tend our livestock on the train? I trust Griffin's judgment. He has served the Shillings for many years."

"Is Griffin coming along?"

"Land sakes, no. He is content keeping my home in order while, quoting Griffin, 'we are on our little adventure.'" Teresa raised an eyebrow and posed her folded hands in imitation of his expression.

"If all goes well, you may never reside in Chicago again." Foreign as it sounded, Angelina warmed to the idea.

"True. But until we make a success of the town, I'll keep my home here." Teresa winked. "I'm too old to abandon everything for a worthy cause. For now, my daughters leave me to my social reform ideals. I don't care to, as Papa used to say, 'poke a resting bear.'"

"If I were braver, I'd sell all I have here and make a clean break. That's what our fellow sojourners will be doing." Angelina's stomach fluttered at the prospect. *What if Resolve is an utter failure? All those families.* "They are so brave."

Teresa patted her hand. "True. But so are you. It takes courage to lead such an expedition."

The waiter came with the tea service, followed by a scowling Hiram DuBois. "My apologies." The waiter set down the tea. "He insisted it was important."

Angelina nodded consent and the waiter left.

Hiram towered over them. "Ladies, may I have a word?"

"If you must." Angelina's courage wrestled fear as she held his gaze, his arrogant smirk all too familiar.

"May I remind you, this is the ladies' parlor? No inappropriate language may be spoken here." Teresa's words triggered a deepening of the frown on Hiram's face.

He pulled out a chair with his eyes on Angelina and sat. At a crunching sound, he leapt up. Teresa's hat lay flattened on the chair. She tried fluffing it back into shape. "Really, Mr. DuBois, have you no care for other's things?" A huff of irritation was followed by a glower that seemed to melt a bit of Hiram's arrogance. "I'll be sending you a bill for its replacement."

"My apologies, Mrs. Shilling." Hiram dismissed the faux pas with a tug of his waistcoat, then double-checked the chair before sitting again. Teresa positioned her ruined hat on the table across from him. He stared at it, then focused on Angelina, his sappy tone always a prelude to nefarious motives. "My dear cousin, I have heard some disturbing news over the past several months. Until now, I've been silent, hoping this foolish notion would pass. Is it true you are leaving for Kansas to build a town?"

Angelina added cream to her tea. "What business is it of yours?"

"I forbid it." Hiram pulled on the edge of his glove and flexed his fingers, a habit he fell into when nervous.

"Ha. You are so amusing, Hiram." She raised her left eyebrow in derision as bile rose in her stomach. "You have no say over what I do." Angelina held his gaze.

"This little experiment is madness." He fiddled with his other glove.

"So say you. I have financial backers, a sound design, and well-thought-out preparation." Angelina crossed her arms. "The town is being surveyed and laid out as we speak. Construction of buildings begins when I arrive. I have fifty families and twenty single individuals ready to work to achieve their dreams."

"I still forbid it. You will squander your fortune and bring shame to the DuBois name." Hiram pounded the table. Tea sloshed on the linen tablecloth, creating a large brown stain.

The man loved to interfere and try to control her at every turn. Even Father never saw through his deception. Angelina shook her head, inhaling a calming breath.

"Cousin … though perhaps that isn't a fair title since you were adopted. No DuBois blood runs through your veins." Hiram paled with her jab. Courage found its footing, spurring her on. "I'm an independent woman, and you are not my guardian." Angelina leaned forward. "It's always about money with you. But the DuBois fortune is mine. You inherited the company your father started. I inherited a great deal more. Even without DuBois Architectural Interests, I am able to live in as grand a style as I care to." Another reference to his resentment of her. Color rose in Hiram's cheeks. Angelina refused to tremble even as the memories of Hiram's abusive antics assaulted her, but her heart told her to tread lightly. She softened her voice. "You've no claim to what is mine. If you try to interfere, I'll take you to court and sue for DuBois Architectural Interests."

"I swear, Angelina, if you do this thing, this attempt at proving the weaker sex is superior, I'll have you declared insane and placed in an asylum. Then all you have *will* be mine." The menace in Hiram's voice cut across the table.

Angelina held tight to the chair to keep from saying something more.

Teresa chuckled. "You don't have a leg to stand on, sir."

"What do you know?" Hiram pointed with his chin. "Are you an attorney?"

"Yes, as a matter of fact, I am." Teresa straightened in her chair and pinned him with her no-nonsense look. "And I can assure you that unless they are the ones insane, no lawyer will take your case. Miss DuBois is highly respected in Chicago's social circles. She is known as a progressive thinker and is not the only one—to use your words—*experimenting*. The only difference here ... a woman is making the plans for a town run by women."

"That is what makes her insane." Hiram stood and stomped his foot.

The waiter came in with their food.

"Sir, would you mind removing this gentleman?" Teresa smiled sweetly.

"Yes, he is spewing inappropriate threats. Our sensitivities are hurt." Angelina fluttered her hand over her breast in her best damsel-in-distress impression.

"As you wish." The waiter placed the tray of food on the table and took Hiram's elbow.

"Unhand me, you lout." Hiram jerked away and straightened his jacket. "Good day, ladies. Mark my words. This isn't over."

The waiter shepherded him to the door, then returned with a fresh tablecloth. He placed the tray on the sideboard. In a few moments, the table had a fresh cloth, and he served their oyster soup. "I hope it is to your satisfaction."

Mouthwatering aromas filled the room.

Angelina tasted the soup, then smiled at the waiter. "Perfect."

"Will that be all?" He wiggled his mustache in response to her smile.

Teresa sipped her tea and wrinkled her nose. "Perhaps a fresh pot of tea?"

"Yes, this one reminds us of our uninvited guest," Angelina added.

"Very good. The rest of your meal will arrive soon."

The waiter left.

Angelina's hand went to her throat. "You don't think Hiram will follow through on his threat to get me committed, do you?"

"I wouldn't worry. There have been several positive articles in the *Chicago Times*, thanks to Caroline. Editorials have been supportive of your venture."

"There're just as many articles opposing it." The cutting words of both men and women had given her restless nights.

"True, but the DuBois name sets you apart from other crackpots."

"Crackpots." Angelina sighed. "That is not reassuring."

Teresa winked, and the two chuckled.

The waiter returned with a fresh pot of tea and poured. Angelina dismissed him, wishing Hiram could be dealt with so easily.

"He is more bark than bite, in my opinion." Teresa chortled. "I doubt he has much of a plan."

"Hiram is not to be trusted. He was my father's ward after Uncle Robert died when he was ten. When Hiram came home from boarding school, my life became insufferable. He'd tell tales to Father so that I was punished for the least infraction."

"We shall proceed despite Hiram's groundless threat. When Resolve becomes a thriving town, no one will pay much heed to your false cousin." Teresa finished her soup and cut her meat. "Don't let that pompous fool ruin our luncheon. Hiram can't even afford to eat here. I heard he lost another contract."

"And that, my friend, is why Hiram is not above sabotage." Angelina took a bite of asparagus. But the vegetable fought its way through the knots in her stomach.

Kansas, April 1868

The plat of Resolve consisted of several tents and mud puddles, and the constant, drizzling rain made everyone edgy. A small hut housed the cooking fire on the edge of a large dining tent. Edward was regretting hiring the mule team drivers in order to use their mules for the heavy work. Now he stood in the mud next to the dining hall surrounded by the lot of them.

A glob of tobacco splatted on Edward's foot. "That's what I think of your suggestion." Morton Slader, head mule skinner, held his fists at his side. "I ain't giving up my whiskey because some woman wants this to be a dry town. It's nothing but a mud hole right now." Mr. Slader stood with his feet apart and arms crossed, fire in his eyes.

"Those are the rules." Edward stared at the man, twice his size but half drunk. *That might give me the advantage.* Sweat beaded on his forehead. *Or not.* "Let's settle this like gentleman." Edward unbuttoned his collar and started to remove his coat.

Shamus O'Malley stepped forward. "Sir, I'm in charge of these ruffians. I shirked me responsibility in letting 'em drink." He had warned the mule skinners and smashed their whiskey bottles, yet they persisted with their heavy drinking. It was a mystery where they stashed the liquor. The rainy weather provided too much idle time. If their mules weren't needed for grading and removing boulders, they could be sent on their way. Hat in hand with a sheepish expression, Shamus continued. "Let me be the one to settle this."

Edward grimaced. Slader would probably pound him into the dust. *What choice do I have? I might get in a lucky punch, or more likely,*

I'll get put in bed for days … or weeks. Shamus' declaration allowed Edward to step aside without losing the men's respect.

He wrestled with his sense of honor for a few minutes before turning to his foreman. "All right, Shamus. Show Mr. Slader we mean business."

"It'll be me pleasure to teach this blowhard a lesson in respect." Shamus rolled up his sleeves and took his pugilist stance.

"I've been wanting to pound you, O'Malley. Stinking Irish needs to respect his betters." Morton's smirk widened as he squared his shoulders. He only came to Shamus' shoulder but with the build of a brick wall. Morton spit into his hands before forming fists.

Shamus let the man take the first swing. The blow to his midriff would have doubled over any other man. He stood there, unmoved. "That be yer best, is it?" Shamus grinned.

Morton roared, then swung again. Shamus ducked and feathered his opponent with punches about his face. The man's head bobbed with the action. He staggered back, dazed. Morton shook his head and let his fist fly. Shamus stepped away from the punch, faked left, then pounded Morton's face with three blows in quick succession. The man fell backward into a mud puddle, blood pouring from his nose. Two mule skinners pulled their unconscious comrade from the puddle and hauled him away.

Shamus scanned the now-silent group and stretched to his full stature. "If any of the rest of ye be inclined toward rule-breakin', you'll find yerself fired. Anyone else questionin' the rules?"

Not a man spoke as they fetched bottles from tents and wagon beds and emptied them into the puddle.

Edward let out a breath.

Shamus stepped to his side. "Thank ye. Slader needed to be put in his place, and it gave me great pleasure to do it."

They walked toward the large, ecru canvas office tent in the center of the tent city next to the site of the men's dormitory.

"It's humbling to have someone step in for me. I can hold my own in a fair fight." Edward shook his head, releasing a spray of water.

"Slader outweighed you, and he's a brawler, that one." Shamus followed him into the tent. "It be hard to keep a rowdy group toein' the line in good weather. This muck has brought out the worst in 'em." He stood in front of Edward's desk, rotating his hat in his hands. "I've broken up a few fights between the Irish and this lot."

"I appreciate you doing what needs doing to keep things moving forward." Edward looked up at the man and shook his hand. "But in the future, keep me informed. Otherwise, I'll be viewed as a spineless creature relying on others to fight my battles."

"I apologize. Just so's you know, I've been spreading the word about your heroism in the war and how you handled yourself in hand-to-hand combat."

"Who told you about that?" Edward frowned. He preferred to forget the war.

"Caroline. I thought spreading that story would keep the men in line."

"My sister tends to exaggerate." Edward sat behind his desk. "But if fear gets the job completed on time, then so be it."

Shamus didn't move.

"Is there something else?"

"Aye, someone has been stealing from the supplies. A few pieces of wood, nails, and a bit of canvas. Nothing anyone would notice right away."

"Sounds like someone is building a shelter."

"All the men are accounted for."

"Look into it for me."

Shamus nodded and left.

Now what? If the rain didn't let up, the site wouldn't be ready on time for building. And that rail spur Miss DuBois expected to be completed in a week might be delayed as well.

Two days later, Lucinda Graves marched into Edward's office, shaking water from her floppy hat. Mud-splattered, baggy trousers and boots attested to another day of drenching rain. Her red braid bobbed to a stop as she drew up, frowning, before his desk. "Mr. Pritchard."

Edward set aside his paperwork. The woman before him exemplified pioneer determination. "Miss Graves, how may I be of assistance?" He indicated the chair to the right. She shook her head and stood straighter. What now?

"Mr. Glummer is unacceptable as my assistant." Lucinda stomped her foot. "I refuse to have such a lecherous cad disgrace the surveying trade."

"Can't he do the work?" Edward had assigned the man to her when Mr. Glummer, a former factory foreman, expressed an interest in learning the trade of surveying.

"When he isn't leering at my form, his work is only passable." She crossed her arms over her chest and harrumphed.

"If you wouldn't wear trousers, perhaps he wouldn't stare." Edward cringed when Lucinda's face turned a few shades lighter than her red hair.

"You do see I am covered in mud. A dress soaks up the mire and makes it unsafe to do my job. My father, God rest his soul, encouraged me to wear trousers. Take a good look." She spread her arms wide. "There is nothing attractive or revealing about my baggy ensemble."

"But they're men's clothing." Edward's irritation at being interrupted carried in his words.

Lucinda shook her head. "No sir, they are *my* clothing." She turned in a circle. "Sewn to my specification. Special pockets for my tools. This is a uniform. And Mr. Glummer refused to wear my father's uniform, referring to it as women's clothing." She paced before him, mud dripping off in small blobs onto the plank floor forming the base of his tent. "A child would be more help. I insist you replace that man with a more suitable assistant immediately."

"I'll look into it." His jaw tightened, and his tone matched hers.

"No." She shook her finger in his face as her voice rose. "You will assign me a new assistant by tomorrow, or I quit, and Miss DuBois will know why." Lucinda stormed out.

Edward huffed. "Good grief, she's as troublesome as the mule skinners."

"Excuse me, sir." Shamus' form blocked the light as he stood in the entrance. "I've found our thief. I need ye to come with me."

Edward pulled on his rain gear and followed.

"Mr. Pritchard, I couldna help overhearin' Miss Graves' complaint." Shamus adjusted his hat and pulled up his collar against the drizzle. "Mr. Glummer is everything she says and more. I pity his poor wife."

"I've until tomorrow to fix this problem." No one else had jumped at the chance to work for a female surveyor.

Edward followed Shamus into a copse of trees. A small wooden structure, no bigger than a shed with a canvas roof, stood in a small clearing. Edward started to draw his revolver.

"Ye wonna be needin' that." Shamus pulled back the flap.

A boy and a man sat together, wrapped in a blanket. The man leapt to his feet, pushing the boy behind him.

"Shamus, you scared the devil out of me." The man's eyes grew even larger when they focused on Edward.

"Mr. Pritchard ..." The man pulled the boy forward. "Mr. Pritchard, this is my son, Teddy. He's ten. I got no family to leave him with."

"Your name?"

"Gabriel Clark, sir." His son wrapped his arms around his father's waist and stared. Edward remembered seeing that same expression of fear in the eyes of Confederate children.

"How did you manage to keep him hidden all this time?"

"I fixed him a place with the baggage, then volunteered to keep a watch when the train stopped along the way. That's when I brought Teddy food and took him to stretch his legs. Teddy rode in the feed wagon for the last leg of our journey. He ran for these trees and built a right fine lean-to. I borrowed a few things to give him better shelter from the rain."

"You'll have to return what you *borrowed*." Edward regarded the pair.

"Yes sir. I'll collect my things." Mr. Clark nodded to his son.

"Wait." Edward turned to Shamus. "What kind of worker is Mr. Clark?"

"Hard worker, no complaining. Not even when workin' in the mud." Shamus patted Gabe on the shoulder.

The man nodded. "Yes sir. I'll work double shifts to pay my son's way."

"How well does Teddy follow instructions?"

"He's obedient. Without a momma, he's had to grow up fast." Mr. Clark ruffled the boy's blond hair.

As Lucinda's words came back to him, Edward knelt at eye level to the boy. "How would you like to learn how to survey?"

"I ..." He looked at his father.

"Teddy's smart. If you need him to help that surveyor lady, he follows directions well."

"A ten-year-old canna defend the lassie from wild animals, savages, and men the likes of Mr. Glummer." Shamus' observation was true.

Edward nodded to Mr. Clark. "Wait here." He signaled for Shamus to follow him outside.

Shamus spoke first. "I think Teddy could learn the surveying trade, and Gabriel Clark could keep watch."

"Keeping watch is what got Mr. Glummer in trouble."

"Nay, he is an honorable man. I'd trust him with me life. She'll be safe, and it'll be good for Teddy."

Edward considered the man's suggestion. "Fine. You take the Clarks and introduce them to our surveyor. If she's satisfied, then go assign Glummer a different job far away from Miss Graves. Disassemble this shanty and return the materials. Teddy can bunk with the men."

"Yes sir." Shamus turned to reenter the shanty, then glanced back over his shoulder. "You be doin' a fine job, Mr. Pritchard, a fine job indeed."

Edward loved building but hated being in charge—a quandary made lighter by his foreman's kind words.

Two weeks later

Edward stood at the entrance to his office tent. The persistent rain had pounded big holes in the dirt, turning the whole town plat into a mud puddle. They were getting more behind schedule with each rainstorm.

Miss Graves headed his way, stomping in puddles in her beeline for his tent—hopefully, to remove the mud, not a declaration of her mood. Edward sighed.

"Mr. Pritchard." Once inside the tent, Miss Graves removed her floppy hat. Water drizzled on the floor. Taller than most women, she looked him in the eye. "It looks like the storm is moving south. I can get back to work despite the mud by this afternoon if I'm reading the sky right."

"Sounds encouraging." Edward sighed. When he looked at the sky, he only saw rain clouds. Lucinda had proved invaluable with her knowledge of Kansas weather and the native population. And her new assistant and protector had, thankfully, worked out. "Miss Graves, would you be willing to stay in Resolve a while after your surveying is done?"

"Whatever for? Once I get my land, I plan to fulfill my pa's dream and farm."

"I'd like to call on you to help out if we have more dealings with the redskins. I understand you speak their language."

"They don't have red skin." Her eyes narrowed. "They're Comanche and Kiowa, and please refrain from calling them redskin or heathen. My stepmother was Kiowa and a fine woman."

"You said 'was.' When did she pass?" Edward knew the pain of losing both parents, and she'd lost three.

"Some white man killed her while my father served the Union Army and I was in finishing school." Miss Graves placed her wet hat on a nearby chair. "After the war, Pa took him to court and got our home back, but no one cared about a dead squaw." She drew a handkerchief from one of the many pockets of her uniform and blew her nose, then dabbed her eyes.

"I'm sorry about your stepmother." Edward steeled his emotions in case her glistening eyes overflowed to her cheeks. Weepy women caught him off-guard and muddled his good sense.

Lucinda sniffled. "Gabriel and Teddy have been a comfort."

Edward smiled at the use of Mr. Clark's Christian name. "Good to hear."

Miss Graves stared out at the falling rain. "You know, before the war, I wanted to be a painter. When White Dove died, all the world looked ugly." She turned toward him. "Rainy weather makes me sad. Bad things always happened to my family when it rained. Pa died during a thunderstorm. Our wagon got stuck in the mud, and Pa's heart gave out trying to free it."

A reverent silence filled the tent for several moments.

"Just wanted you to know about the sky." She replaced her hat and headed back to her tent. Teddy ran toward her, Gabriel on his heels. The three changed directions and headed to the dining tent.

Lucinda never said more than a handful of words at a time. All that unexpected talk today, yet she'd never committed to staying on after finishing the surveying. His disdain for the woman melted as he considered the trials she'd endured. Maybe Angelina's idea wasn't so harebrained, after all. Here was a woman wounded by the laws made by men.

He went back to studying blueprints. Could he be the kind of man open to change? Were women equal to men intellectually? Caroline thought so. But did he? This experiment was testing more than his building skills.

CHAPTER 8

May 1, 1869

Angelina gazed about the Great Central Depot, a hub of activity as rail cars lined eight tracks, waiting their turn to disembark. She wrinkled her nose at the depot's plain, functional design. It was obvious it lacked an architect's creativity. Smoke belched from steam engines, and a murmur of voice carried across the platform.

"Mr. Hayes, everything is in order." Angelina stood with the engineer beside the tracks. Excitement beat a fast rhythm in her heart. "All passengers are accounted for."

"Mr. DuBois tried to waylay me yesterday." The conductor wiggled his eyebrows. "But I'm no fool."

"What did Hiram do now?" A headache started forming behind her eyes. "Nothing would surprise me at this point."

"He fired me." Mr. Hayes shook his head. "You can't fire someone who isn't your employee. I appreciate the copy of the notice from your lawyer telling me that you alone could change anything."

"Mrs. Shilling sent that notice to all the service and material suppliers. Then another letter directing those committed to this project to ignore instructions from anyone but me. Before those letters went out, I had to stop cancellations on materials numerous times. Firing you was his last lame attempt."

Mr. Hayes pulled his pipe from his vest and stuffed the bowl with tobacco. "I'm curious to know if the rumor is true."

"Which one?" Angelina had become the topic of conversation all over Chicago.

"That he tried to commit you to an asylum?"

"A doctor did come by my home." Angelina sighed. "We had a conversation, and I sent him on his way." *And he'll be back to chat next week ... if he can find his way to Kansas.*

"Good to hear." Mr. Hayes puffed his pipe, then stepped to the stairs of the engine. "I'm pleased to be the one escorting you to your destination. Are you aware the spur isn't complete?"

"Mr. Pritchard telegraphed me." Angelina tugged on her gloves. The decision to leave even though the track was not completed came partly from fear of Hiram's threat. "There will be wagons to meet us at the end of the line. It's a short trek by wagon to the town site."

The engineer towered over Angelina from the engine's door, his silhouette framed by the sun as she squinted from her position on the ground. "My son hopes to find a place in Resolve. He'll know how to handle any problems with the train cars you may have after I leave." Mr. Hayes smiled around his pipe.

"I appreciate your help. The freight cars won't be unloaded until a few buildings are completed."

"If you're planning a depot, my boy is your man." Mr. Hayes nodded and stepped into the engine cab.

"I'll keep him in mind." Angelina pasted on a smile. Irritation settled in the pit of her stomach. Another relative she hadn't interviewed whose family had brought them along. She raised her voice to be heard over the steam engine. "Mrs. Shilling will have a contract for your son to sign before we reach Resolve. Perhaps he can guard the freight cars until they are emptied. Be sure to direct him to me."

Mr. Hayes leaned out the window and waved. "Yes ma'am, and thank you."

As Angelina walked toward her personal car, children called her name and waved from the train windows. Their enthusiasm warmed her heart while her stomach turned. Resolve had to prosper, for these little ones more than her reputation. Twenty cars, all filled with supplies and hopeful people anxious to build a bright future. A heavy burden to bear.

Could she sacrifice herself to ensure these families had a better life? Her father never would. And Hiram served as a prime example of the DuBois mindset gone awry. *I can do this. I must.*

The early morning sun peeked out from behind fluffy white clouds framed in a deep blue sky. An omen of success.

A young conductor with dark brown hair and the same mustache as Mr. Hayes waited to assist her into her car.

"Thank you."

"I'll be here to help you at every stop."

"Your name?"

"Barnaby Hayes. My father is the engineer." He doffed his hat.

Bridget O'Malley and Teresa Shilling had stowed their luggage and found seats in Angelina's private car while she'd double-checked last-minute details. Angelina handed her wrap to Bridget, then joined Teresa on the settee positioned along the wall of windows. The car had been refitted as a home, complete with a kitchen and bedrooms. Coal rested in a bucket near the stove.

"Young Mr. Hayes instructed me on how to start a fire and use the stove while the train is moving." Bridget fidgeted with her hankie. "There are hooks to keep the pans in place." She wiped her hands on her apron. "I'm a mite anxious about it. For now, we have crackers and tortes for teatime."

"That's fine, Bridget, I understand." Angelina placed her arm across her stomach. "I'm too nervous to eat."

Teresa dabbed her forehead with her handkerchief. "Let's not make this place any hotter than it is." The women laughed.

Angelina pulled aside the lace curtain as the train jerked forward. They traveled past the ghettos, reminding her of where most of the passengers had come from. The living conditions were deplorable, and fires often broke out due to overcrowding. A sense of satisfaction enveloped her, knowing she was an instrument of deliverance for some.

"We are on our way." Turning to her friends, she asked, "Where are Caroline and Emily?"

"Emily wanted to ride with her brother." Bridget paled as the train began to pick up speed.

"Caroline wanted to get some first-hand impressions from the passengers." Teresa smiled as she fanned herself. "That girl is taking your notion of writing a book about our adventure very seriously."

"I don't mind some time without having to monitor my every word. You know, Caroline uses something she calls shorthand. It's what stenographers use now. It looks like gibberish to me. But Caroline says it's easier to get all the words down." Angelina chuckled. "Poor girl spends her evening transcribing all those squiggles into English in her journal."

"Some form or other of shorthand has been around since Socrates." Teresa laid her fan aside and took off her hat, resting it beside Angelina's on a shelf. "I've seen lawyers use it in court to make notes."

"If Caroline would teach me, I'd be able to keep me recipes a secret." Bridget gripped the seat, her face ashen. "I heard tell train travel is dangerous. Me Da heard it scrambles your brain."

"Don't be ridiculous. We'll be fine. Every new thing that comes along has its naysayers." Teresa removed her waistcoat and rolled up the sleeves on her blouse.

Angelina nodded in agreement. "This train is perfectly safe. My father kept it well-maintained, and the tracks will carry us safely to our destination." *Unless there is some unforeseen difficulty.* A cow had stalled the train once, as had some masked robbers. Fortunately, a marshal had been onboard at the time to arrest them before they made it to the DuBois private car. Angelina reached over and held Bridget's hand. "You will be far more comfortable here than in the passenger cars. Relax and enjoy traveling in luxury."

Bridget smiled as color returned to her face. "I'll do just that." She took a seat near the window. "Everything is moving so fast. I can't believe it."

Yes, everything is moving fast. Angelina leaned back on the settee and took in a deep draft of air to calm her shaking. It was too late to turn back and too early to call it quits.

Edward sat on horseback surrounded by wagons, mules, and mule skinners waiting at the end of the tracks two miles from Resolve. Tall prairie grass and scrub bushes lined the rails.

"I'm looking forward to seeing me family." Shamus shifted on his gray stallion.

"I wish they'd have postponed their trip a week." Edward rubbed his chin.

"And leave all them people out on the street? They'd already given notice to their landlords." Shamus adjusted his hat. "I'd have run back to fetch my girls meself before I'd let me family sleep on the street." The man had shaved for the first time since he'd arrived. In fact, most of the men came clean-shaven and in fresh clothes to meet the train.

"I hadn't considered they would be homeless." Edward leaned forward in the saddle, looking up the track. "I can't imagine Miss DuBois sleeping in a tent."

"Aye, it will be interesting." Shamus patted his horse and stood in the stirrups to get a better look as well. "I see the smoke."

Nervousness trickled through Edward. Would what he'd accomplished be enough? Miss DuBois expected him to stay on schedule despite the weather. It was hard to judge her mood in a telegram.

The train came around the bend and stopped two feet from the end of the track. Within minutes, the passengers scrambled from the train. Laborers gathered near the freight cars to unload building materials and supplies. Angelina, Teresa, and Bridget exited their car, dressed in simple gowns. They were fancier than most of the female passengers but appropriate for living in the tent city. Apparently, she had taken his advice. Edward rubbed a smile from his face. Even in a plain red cotton dress, Angelina exuded dignity.

Bridget ran to meet Shamus and gave him a warm hug. He

picked her up and swung her around and set her back on the ground. "Good to see ye made it safe."

"Good to be seen." Bridget picked up her carpetbag. "Me trunks are with the rest of the baggage."

Shamus hurried to meet a petite woman and two little girls. By the exchange of kisses and hugs, Edward assumed he'd found his family. The big man left them near a wagon with other families, then headed to the baggage car. He was so engrossed in watching his foreman, he almost didn't notice the three women approach him.

"Good day, Miss DuBois, Mrs. Shilling, and Miss O'Malley." He tipped his hat. "I'm afraid there is no carriage, so you'll be riding with the others in these wagons."

"I understand. Ladies, shall we?" Miss DuBois smiled and headed toward the first available wagon. People moved to give the trio a place on the bench.

Shamus hoisted his daughters in beside his sister and helped his wife get settled before mounting his horse. Five wagons filled with families and single women waited in exhausted silence. What would they think of the sparse comforts awaiting them?

"Welcome to Resolve." Edward assisted Miss DuBois and her companions from the wagon.

Mrs. Shilling raised her eyebrow. "What is that horrid structure?"

"A soddie." Edward sighed. "A few of the mule skinners said they were dryer than tents. Miss Graves agreed and paid them to build her one."

"I specifically said no dirt buildings." Angelina frowned as she glared at it. "I provided adequate tents." The tinge of irritation in her voice made his hackles rise. Of course, she'd blame him for the one thing beyond his control.

"I know what you said, but Miss Graves does things her way." *Like someone else I know. It'll be interesting to see those two butt heads.*

Angelina looked around and gave a nod. "Fine, but as soon

as possible, it will be replaced with a proper structure." She lifted her skirt and walked a few paces, then turned to take in the whole of things. Tents stood in three neat rows, and several building foundations were partly dug. Incredibly, she smiled. "It's actually happening. We are building a town of my design." She focused on him. "Thank you, Mr. Pritchard, for assisting me as I strive to reach my goal. You have done a fine job of laying out the plat."

"Why, thank you, ma'am." Holding his hat against his chest, he ducked his head.

Her grateful smile lit up her whole face. Sapphire eyes twinkled as they rested on him. "Eddie, I think we'll work well together." His nickname spilled like honey from her lips and set his heart racing.

"I appreciate your vote of confidence ... Angelina." He tested her given name on his tongue.

"Now, where is my tent? I wish to rest and unpack. Tomorrow we begin building." She touched his shoulder. "We'll meet over breakfast."

"The third tent on the right."

As the women scurried away, chattering, Edward shook his head, trying to dislodge the unwanted feelings stirring inside. He had no desire to pursue a strong-willed woman. That sort henpecked their husbands and bullied their children. His aunt of that ilk had sent his uncle to an early grave. No, thank you.

"A penny for your thoughts?" Caroline came up from behind and reached around his waist. "I missed you."

He turned around. "Let me give you a proper hug." Edward held her close and kissed her forehead. "I'm sorry I didn't greet you at the train."

"I know you had to attend to Miss DuBois. That's fine. I was busy interviewing people."

"Were you, now?"

"I'm having such fun." She hugged him again. "Thank you for doing this. If you hadn't gone on that interview with me, I doubt Miss DuBois would have given me a second thought."

"She said she needed a reporter."

"That was the second thought. She needed *you* to sign on. But I've proven my value. And I owe the chance to you."

"I'll get your trunk and take you to your tent. Once our house is built, you'll live with me. Until then, you'll live in the women's dormitory that's being built first."

"I like getting to know other people. It is what a journalist must do."

The glow of joy on her face made Edward smile. "You'll be a fine journalist. No matter the outcome here, you've got a story." Hopefully, the title wouldn't be *My Brother, the Failure*. Pushing the melancholy thoughts away, he escorted her to the women's tent.

Shamus hailed him from the bench of an overloaded wagon. "I've found all the ladies' belongings, including Caroline's and the furniture you ordered. I'll haul it to wherever you say."

Edward jumped aboard. "Life, as we are accustomed to, will be changing quickly now that the women and children are here."

"It'll keep the mule skinners and me people in line trying to impress the single lasses."

The men laughed as the wagon rolled down the muddy road of the tent city. Only a fool would try to impress Angelina. He caught a glimpse of her as she peeked out her tent door, having changed into a blue frock, his favorite color on her. He turned away. Risking his reputation by working for a female boss had branded him among his peers as being weak. A double fool he would not be.

CHAPTER 9

Angelina's hair sagged to the side. "Argh. This isn't easy."

"Allow me." Bridget removed the pins and took up the brush. "Don't be discouraged. You'll be doing up yer own hair in no time." In moments, Angelina's tresses rested in a modest bun at the nape of her neck. "It may take time, but ye'll succeed."

"I'm determined to get dressed without assistance." Angelina slumped in her chair. "I feel foolish needing help to put on my clothes. The wealthy think it's their right to be waited on when in truth, they are enslaved."

"There are a few fashions that need more than two hands." Bridget passed her a pair of boots. "These do not require a buttonhook."

Angelina slipped into the boots and stood before the full-length mirror she'd brought from her private car. "Yes, very practical, as Edward insisted. Wise man. Not afraid to speak his mind."

"And he respects you as the one in charge." Bridget handed her a shawl.

Angelina draped it over her arms and glanced in the mirror to see if it hung evenly. "I wonder how long Edward will comply before he blows his top. I'd worry if he never disagreed with me."

"Shamus says he is pretty even-tempered in dealing with the men. Mr. Pritchard is not afraid to get his hands dirty and work alongside the laborers."

"Then I shall do the same."

"Miss DuBois, I donna think that's a good idea."

"Why?" Angelina's tone brought a blush to her maid. "You don't think I can do it?"

Bridget crossed her arms and shook her head. "If ye canna dress yerself, how do you expect to do manual labor?"

Angelina sat with a huff. "Baby steps, as my mother used to say. We learn everything in baby steps."

"There you go. You've taken giant leaps in your professional life. You donna have to be perfect at everything."

Angelina secured her straw hat with the elaborate bow on the brim with a hatpin. "Now I'm ready for my first meeting as an architect-contractor."

"Should I bring ye lunch?"

"No, I'll eat with the others."

"Very good, then I'll head for the dining tent. My bread should be risen by the time I get there."

"You were up quite early."

"A baker must tend her dough in the wee hours."

Bridget put on her hat, and they headed out, zigzagging to avoid puddles. They paused at the area marked off for the fountain. Bridget went left toward the dining tent, and Angelina stood for a moment, envisioning the fountain with its cherubs holding bowls overflowing with water.

"Good morning, Miss DuBois. You look ready to work."

Edward's baritone greeting sent a delicious quiver through her. "Yes." She offered her brightest smile and stared into his chocolate eyes. She cleared her throat, refusing to be the first to break their gaze. "I'm looking forward to meeting with everyone and giving instructions for the day."

His brows furrowed, and his eyes flashed almost imperceptibly before looking away. "Shall we?" She placed her hand in the crook of his arm. "I'll make introductions. And each supervisor will give an update on their progress. Then you have the floor."

"Fine." Her voice came out sharp. She sighed and smiled his way. "You've thought this all out."

"Every contractor I ever worked for who is worth his salt does the meetings the same way."

So I'm not worth my salt. What does that mean? She schooled her irritation. "Thank you for explaining what the men expect." *Now I'll need to show them what I expect.* This was her project.

They entered Edward's office tent where four men and Shamus stood waiting. "Good morning, gentlemen. I'm Angelina DuBois. Please introduce yourselves and tell me what you do and your progress thus far."

The men glanced Edward's way before answering, the room thick with tension at her bold move. Edward nodded without showing the irritation she suspected he squelched beneath his nonplussed look.

A short older gentleman removed his bowler hat, revealing a bald pate. "Miss DuBois, I'm Cornwall Hanson, a mason by trade. Right now, I'm overseeing the laying of the foundations, then helping with the construction."

"Mr. Hanson." She shook his hand. "You'll be quite busy once the brick arrives with the next shipment. For now, I'd like you to explore and see if there are any natural stones in the area we can use for building materials."

"Yes ma'am. I'll do that in my spare time so as not to slow down the construction. Mr. Pritchard said he needs all hands."

"Very good." She nodded at Edward, then pointed to a tall, thin gentleman with muttonchops and unruly hair. "And you, sir?"

He stopped twisting his cap in a roll to shake her hand. "I'm John Thomas, the plumber. I've been marking where the plumbing lines will be in each building per your specification regarding water pumps. I've supervised the digging of one well and scouted out two other locations. Based on the topography of the area, I suspect we'll find more than one underground stream. I don't believe there is another town in Kansas with indoor plumbing."

"Have you dug many wells, Mr. Thomas?"

"I've worked on crews back in Chicago and New York."

"And will you be doing that in your spare time?"

"No ma'am, Mr. Pritchard said finding water is a top priority."

"And so it is." Angelina schooled her face lest it reveal she knew nothing about finding water. "Are you two brothers?" She offered her hand to the last two men.

"Twins, ma'am," the first tall, muscular redhead said. "I'm Sean and this is Derek. We be the Sullivan brothers." They shook her hand, wearing sheepish grins.

Derek spoke up. "We're wood craftsmen. Anything you need from wood we can create."

"And we're very good at our job." Sean grinned. "We've been making chairs and tables from the wood Mr. Pritchard brought along."

"We've also been scouting out all the trees about to see which have sturdy wood for building furniture," Derek added, then he yanked off his rumpled hat and pulled his brother's cap off. "We're also supervising work crews."

"Very good. I'm impressed." She flashed her best smile at Shamus. "Mr. O'Malley, I imagine you're keeping everyone in line." She shook his hand. He returned the smile, and a blush rose to his cheeks.

"Yes ma'am, I oversee work crews and the mule skinners."

"Mule skinners?" She crumpled her nose.

"Yes, ma'am, they's the men who work with the mules, driving the teams and whatever we need the mules for."

"Interesting." Angelina walked behind the table and rolled out the blueprints. "Now let's go over what our next step will be."

Edward fumed underneath his pleasant façade. He nodded and said all the right things as his authority waned. "You've laid out a pretty aggressive timeline, laying all the foundations for the main street in a week. Not to mention framing the dormitories."

"I believe we have enough manpower to do it now that all the townspeople are here."

"Unless they have building experience, they'll slow things down." Edward shook his head, releasing a bit of frustration with the action.

"You have an excellent point." Angelina looked around the room, catching each man's attention. "You are all such capable craftsmen."

Her smile brought their nods. "Why not teach the new arrivals how to do various tasks? Then use your skilled laborers to oversee each site."

Edward had to admit her idea had merit. "Does that include the farmers?"

"No, tomorrow, we'll get deeds sorted, and they'll be on their way to their homesteads, although a few have volunteered to continue working on the town a few days a week. They need to start planting right away. Mr. Sanders brought fruit trees, and Mr. Jones brought turkeys. His brother is bringing hundreds more turkeys overland. They should be here in two months. So he'll be busy building pens. That will leave fewer children underfoot. And it reduces the female population in town to thirty. The women who remain are willing to roll up their sleeves and work right alongside the men to get the town built."

"With our twenty laborers and the additional forty-nine who arrived with you, we can get the main street built on schedule." Edward's assessment brought a murmur of agreement.

Mr. Thomas interjected. "The womenfolk will have enough to do cooking, sewing, and tending the young'uns."

Angelina scowled at his remark.

"True, but the *womenfolk* plan to run businesses, so they will be doing much more than cooking, sewing, and looking after the young'uns." Her voice rose with each pronouncement. Angelina noted the uncomfortable looks on the men's faces. She paused, a blush rising to her cheeks, then spoke in a softer tone. "I apologize." She flashed that melt-a-man-to-a-puddle smile and added, "Shall we all get to the task at hand?"

The men nodded and left the tent. Edward waited. Angelina turned her sapphire eyes on him. "As you can see, Mr. Pritchard, I prefer to do things my way. I appreciate your support and wise suggestions." She sat in his desk chair. "Now, let's discuss the timeline for the rest of the project and what needs to be done. You've been here long enough to get a feel for the area."

Edward grabbed another chair and sat, pushing aside his masculine pride. The smell of her perfume tickled his senses. *Focus.*

Together, they put a clear timeline in place. Two years, and the work would be finished on the town. And he would be free to build his own career.

She tapped on his desk. "Tomorrow I'd like you to meet with Mr. Merriweather Paulson. He will be living on his son Fred's homestead. Meri has a gift for growing businesses and creating commerce. Although he says he's retired, I have persuaded him to help us market Resolve to continue its growth."

"Market?" Edward wasn't sure he'd heard her right.

"Yes, we want the railroad to travel farther than Resolve. That's why a railroad depot is in my design. It will put us on the mainline of civilization. He is working on getting the contract to build an observatory. Those two things are the beginning of many ideas Meri had to help keep the town solvent."

"An observatory?" Edward scratched his head, a bit dazed by her elaborate plans.

"Astronomers study the stars and chart the universe. The flat land and wide-open space here in Kansas is a good location for an observatory. Federal funds and donations pay for it. And we benefit financially from visitors."

"Your plans go far into the future." Not wanting to show how impressed he was, Edward pushed back from the desk and stretched.

She shrugged. "My father and his friends discussed economics. I learned a lot sitting in a corner and pretending to read."

She was a sharp one, no doubt. Too sharp for him?

The dinner bell clanged, and Edward escorted her to the dining tent. The aromas of fried chicken and fresh baking filled the air. The women had taken over the task of cooking. Not a man had come to eat without washing up and combing his hair. Resolve was a bachelor camp no more.

CHAPTER 10

The smell of dying campfires filled Angelina's nose as another rooster disrupted her reflections. The previous night's chill still clung to her even as the sun warmed the tent. Yesterday, she, Edward, and Teresa had greeted the wagon train of farmers and their livestock—all arrived on schedule. The wives and children who'd traveled by train joined their husbands in a ruckus of noisy voices. She had escaped to her tent, overwhelmed and fearful.

What had she gotten herself into? Never in her life had she been responsible for others' livelihoods. She'd never hired or fired anyone while working with Father. Even the household staff was handled by the butler. Angelina pulled her covers up to her shoulders as tiny hairs stood up on the back of her neck. Fear trailed her self-doubt.

The dread produced a picture of her father's scowl. All her growing-up years, he rarely smiled her way. Had she been a son, things might have been different. Angelina pushed her fear aside, threw back her blanket, and straightened her back.

By the early morning light, she dressed and managed to pull her hair into a neat bun. In the meantime, her sleepless mind reviewed every conceivable potential problem the community could face and its solution.

Bridget entered the tent with a kettle of hot water and a basket. Angelina must have slept because she never heard Bridget leave her cot.

"Good morning, ma'am. Did ye sleep well?" Bridget gathered the tea service from the side table and prepared Angelina's tea, then pulled bread from her basket and laid out Angelina's morning meal.

"Do I look like I slept well?" Angelina grumped.

"No." Bridget grinned. "I was trying not to hurt your feelin's."

Angelina slid her feet into her work boots and searched through her trunk for a handkerchief. "I may look like a banshee, but at least I'll have my lace hankie to identify me as a lady."

Bridget chuckled while placing the tea service plus some fresh bread and jam on the table. "For a banshee, you are fairer than any woman here."

"Your flattery will not get you a raise, my friend." Angelina spread the jam on her bread.

"Ye canna fault a girl for tryin'." Bridget smiled and hummed as she did up the cots and set the tent to rights.

"Why are you in such a cheerful mood?" Angelina savored another bite of Bridget's fresh baking.

"I guess all the beauty of God's creation about me." Bridget swept the wooden flooring. "Clean air and a lovely sunrise to cheer me heart. Makes me happy to be alive."

Envy perched on top of Angelina's weariness. "I suppose all the nighttime noise didn't rob your sleep?" She swallowed the last of her tea.

"I come from a big family. It reminded me of home."

A few minutes later, Bridget took Angelina's empty dishes. "What be your schedule for today?"

"Get the farmers sorted and sent to their homesteads. And check on the progress of the spur. I need my private car here, sooner rather than later. These primitive conditions are not to my liking." Until arriving here, she'd taken her feather bed, quiet moments of reading in her library, and a warm bath for granted. Embarrassing how quickly her fortitude had stumbled when the noise of tent city and a hard cot robbed her of her sleep.

Edward pinned the map to the wall of the temporary lean-to erected in the center of the tent city—a gathering place for workday assignments. Now that the residents had arrived, the workload would shift. He didn't know the new arrivals or their work ethic. These were city dwellers staking claims to land in an untamed country.

A crowd gathered. Shamus and Gabe carried a table to use for the distribution of the homesteads while Rev. Asbury followed with two chairs.

Angelina and Mrs. Shilling stepped forward with a woman he hadn't met. "Mr. Pritchard, let me introduce ..." The woman whispered in Angelina's ear. She nodded and turned to Edward. "This is Miss Harper, our schoolteacher."

"Pleased to make your acquaintance." Edward frowned. "I thought the schoolteacher was a Mrs. Fry."

"I go by my maiden name now." Miss Harper straightened her back as if daring him to question her. One more woman with a stubborn streak. What she called herself meant less to him than how well she did her job—same as he expected from the men.

Angelina patted her hand and addressed those gathered near. "Miss Harper is cutting all ties with her past and starting fresh. I think she is wise, don't you?"

"Everyone here is startin' fresh." Shamus nodded at Miss Harper. "Some Irish got new names when they come here. I couldna read when I first arrived in America, but me fight manager taught me to sign me name. Me wife told me I'm spelling it wrong. It should be S-E-A-M-U-S, but the man taught me S-H-A-M-U-S. When I was a fighter, people claimed I put me opponents to shame. So Shamus it is in me new country. Me wife taught me to read. She's a smart one, she is. Miss Harper, if ye be needing any help, she'd be happy to lend a hand. You'll find me girls are bright ones too."

Miss Harper appeared more relaxed at Shamus' warm welcome. She stood near Angelina with her chin up.

"Miss Harper, I'm sure you'll do a fine job." Edward offered his hand, and she shook it. Her pasted-on smile told him he'd have to be more careful with his remarks in the future.

Angelina stared at the crowd of chatting people. "May I have your attention?" Her words drowned in the din of voices.

Rev. Asbury executed a deafening whistle. The whole assembly came to attention, and Edward, standing right next to him, rubbed his ringing ear. The preacher swept his hand toward the table. "Miss DuBois, you have the floor."

"Hello, I'm Miss Angelina DuBois, and I'm delighted that you've all arrived safely. Before we begin, I'd like to introduce a few people. First, we have Dr. Andrew Potter and his wife, Stella, his nurse. Their tent is located at the end of this row. On my left is Mrs. Teresa Shilling. She is an attorney and will be available to handle any legal disputes. She will ensure all your deeds are properly registered. On my left is Rev. Hezekiah Asbury. You can find him ..." She turned to the minister.

"Working beside the men building this fine town. I have the blisters to prove it." He raised his hands, palms up to the gathering.

Titters of laughter followed his remark.

"For now, I'm in the men's dormitory tent," the preacher continued, "and will be available each evening right here for a time of Scripture reading and prayer for those who'd like to join me. I'm also available to perform weddings. Once you're all settled, I'll be making my rounds to each of your homesteads." He stepped back and nodded to Angelina.

"And this is Miss Madeline Harper." Angelina signaled her to step forward. "I have secured her services as a schoolteacher. Any of your children are welcome to attend the town school."

Miss Harper nodded to the crowd. Children waved at the teacher, and she smiled toward them.

Miss DuBois stared at the mass of ragged humanity. Hopeful smiles met hers. "Now if one member of each family will come forward to form two lines, Mr. Pritchard, Rev. Asbury, Attorney Shilling, and I will give you deeds to your homesteads. Understand, although I'm placing these deeds in your hands, you are expected to work hard and prove up your claim in accordance with the Homestead Act."

Murmurs of assent rippled through the crowd.

"This is Mr. Edward Pritchard, the general contractor. If you have any construction questions, he has answers." She nodded to Edward to take over.

He raised his hand. "Once you have your deed, step over to Mr. O'Malley and his sister, and they will give you vouchers for seed, a plow, and any additional staples necessary to get you started. If you traveled by train, you may collect the wagon you purchased from the Wrights, as well as a team of horses per your work agreement. All those supplies can be found at the end of the road near the corral where Emily and Michael Jameson will distribute them." Edward waited as the group began to organize into lines.

Miss Harper tilted her head toward him. "I am amazed at how fast the Wrights built all those wagons."

"All the wood, wheels, and parts came on the first train with the laborers. Carl and Henry Wright finished the last wagon yesterday, working late into the night."

"I heard the fathers are widowers with six bachelor sons between them." Mrs. Shilling smiled. "They are a handsome lot. Rev. Asbury might be performing some weddings if the way the single ladies are looking them over is any indication."

Angelina frowned at her. "You're probably right, but that is a shackle I intend to avoid."

By noon, all the deeds save one were distributed and recorded. Angelina placed her hand on her back and stretched. An angry voice drew her attention as a squabble broke out near the wagons. "What on earth?"

When she hurried over to join Edward and Shamus, an angry farmer glared at them. "What are we supposed to do with this wagon?" His growl sent a shiver through Angelina. "Pull it to the homestead?"

She grimaced. There was not a horse in sight. "I am so sorry, Mr. …"

"Morgan. Timothy Morgan. I agreed to come early. For my hard work, you promised a wagon with a team of horses."

"And you shall have them." Angelina smiled sweetly, only to receive a frown from his wife. "A Texas rancher was due to arrive yesterday with some horses and cows I purchased. In all the excitement with the wagon train arriving, I hadn't realized he was late."

"Doesn't surprise me, you being a woman and all." Mr. Morgan turned to Edward. "I need those horses now. How long we gotta wait?" He nodded toward five other families who were horseless.

Mr. Morgan's attitude galled her. How dare he assume only women made mistakes? Flames lit her cheeks.

Edward cleared his throat and spoke, his voice conciliatory and his eyes avoiding hers. "We received a telegram from Mr. Wingate explaining his delay. I expect him sometime today, tomorrow at the latest."

What telegram? Angelina screamed inwardly.

"Excuse me." A slight man in a bowler hat approached the group. "My name is George McCray. I got me six of the finest Belgians you ever laid your eyes on. I'd be happy to lend them so you can get your families to your homesteads. One of them big beauties can do the work of three regular horses. I'll hitch one up to each wagon, and when your horses arrive, me and Bessy—that's my lead horse—will bring your teams out and trade you."

"Thank you kindly." Mr. Morgan fumbled with his hat. "But we can't pay to rent them from you."

"Who said anything about renting? I noticed you all got some strapping sons among you. I got six lovely daughters. Consider it a neighborly welcome." Mr. McCray waggled his eyebrows, defusing the tense situation as everyone laughed, and the farmers shook hands with Mr. McCray on the deal.

"Thank you, Mr. McCray, for offering such a fine solution to the emergency." Angelina smiled, hiding her irritation at the men ignoring her authority. But resentment bubbled in her middle.

Edward shook Mr. McCray's hand. "When your Belgians are returned to you, I could use you and your team to help with building the town. There are a few mule skinners I'd like to give walking papers. And horses don't have the stubborn streak of mules."

"Aye, my beauties love me even better than my wife and daughters, and their loyalty has no match. My brother will be arriving with his family in a few days—along with twelve more of these fine workhorses. His wife went into labor the day we left, so they stayed back awhile. They're traveling with some other families."

"Who are these others?" Angelina snapped. Fatigue and worry fueled her irritation. More uninvited kin, perhaps.

"My brother and I made their acquaintance before we left." Mr. McCray kept his voice even. "They have homesteads already. Because you're only required to live on the land six months out of the year, they went home for the winter to fetch their families. Said the cold season is mighty fierce out here."

One more thing to prepare for. Angelina's already exhausted mind began calculating what would be needed to combat a fierce winter. What else had she forgotten or failed to prepare for?

Edward escorted Angelina away as the men left to hitch up the horses. Once out of earshot, she stopped in the middle of the street and shook her finger at him. "Why did the telegraph agent give you the telegram if it was addressed to me? And why were you reading it?" She planted her feet firmly. "I am in charge here, not you. How dare you read my private correspondence?"

"There's no telegram." Edward lowered his voice, glancing about for eavesdroppers. "I would never open a telegram addressed to you without your permission."

"So you lied to defuse the situation." Venom laced her voice while her fists rested on her hips.

Edward's gut twisted in a knot at the disappointment in her eyes.

A shadow blocked the sun as Shamus joined them.

"And it be a dandy plan." He smiled. Angelina blushed and looked away. "I'm sure the horses will be here soon." He tipped his hat. "I'm off to meet me family for lunch."

They watched Shamus until he was well up the street. Edward prepared for a further onslaught. Instead, Angelina crossed her arms and whispered.

"I'd have taken another tack." She let out a long breath and swept a stray hair behind her ear. "As Shamus said, it worked, so that's that." She glanced around before continuing. "In the future, please don't resort to lying." Their eyes met. "I'm sorry for my reaction, but that's how Hiram handled things. My cousin is a well-established liar."

Shame assailed Edward with the comparison. The creaking of wagon wheels and the joyful shouts of children chasing after one another drowned out the silence between them.

"I'm truly sorry, Angelina," Edward said. Losing her respect stung.

"In the future, do your best to be honest." Angelina fidgeted with the fringe on her bodice. "I fear the rancher took my money and left us wanting." She crossed her arms and stared at the ground. When her head came up, fire blazed in her eyes. "If he has, I'll have him arrested."

Edward needed to exercise diplomacy in his response. "If he isn't here by tomorrow, I'll send a few men out a day's ride to see if they can find them."

A softness replaced the ire in her eyes, then she frowned. "Can we afford to take men away from their work? Mr. McCray says the winters are fierce. We need sturdy shelters for everyone." She sighed as a strong breeze swirled her skirt tight to her body, emphasizing her form. He stared at his shoes until the warmth on his neck cooled. She touched his arm. "Do you think they'll come?"

He reached back in his mind to recall what they were talking about before he'd fixated on her. *Can't forget she's the boss.* The rancher, they were talking about the rancher. "Without a doubt." He offered a silent prayer that, despite the lie, God would show mercy and bring the livestock soon.

They continued walking toward the dining tent. She turned her heart-melting smile on him. A shield of resistance struggled to guard him against it. He needed his focus on his job, or he might just lose it.

"Could I impose on you for something?"

"What is it?" He looked down into her misty eyes. The frail wall of resistance came crashing down. "Whatever you need."

"I need a decent night's sleep. I need my personal train car." She stifled a yawn. "Can we check on the progress of the spur today? It feels like I'm sleeping in a circus tent with all the voices and animal sounds."

"You'll get used to it."

Angelina tried not to glare at him. "The last time someone said that to me, I was sixteen and traveling abroad. We stayed a week in a villa infested with mice. The scratching and squeaking were maddening. No one else noticed, but I did. Hiram scoffed at me, then pinched me for being petty."

Edward smiled. "I understand about mice. Noisy little vermin. But today is half over and it will be too dark by the time we get there. How about tomorrow morning?"

"All right, but I give you fair warning, I may become a she-bear by week's end if I don't get some proper sleep."

Edward extended his elbow. "Would you join me for lunch? The aromas from the dining tent are calling my name."

She placed her hand on his arm. "I think I need strong coffee more than food. Lots of strong coffee."

They entered the tent to find Bridget waving from one end of a long table, surrounded by her brother's family. Angelina smiled and tugged Edward toward her. Shamus glowed in the presence of his girls. One, a tall, slender Irish beauty listened intently to a small duplicate of herself. "Ma, when are we building our home? I miss having Da with us."

Angelina had missed her father every day as a child even though he sat across the table from her. The little girl from her past envied these sweet girls.

"Lily, it'll be a bit. Be patient, luv, like your sister Pansy." Mrs. O'Malley turned and noticed Angelina. "'Tis a pleasure, Miss DuBois, to have you join us. Shamus has been a wee too busy for proper introductions." She elbowed her husband.

He stared at her a moment as she eyed him. Understanding showed on his face, accompanied by a blush. "Excuse me, I'm an oaf. Miss DuBois, let me introduce you to the love of me life, Daisy O'Malley, and my darling daughters Pansy and Lily."

Lily ducked her head into her mother's arm.

Pansy smiled and offered her hand. "'Tis a delight to make your acquaintance, Miss DuBois. You're the most beautiful woman I ever seen."

"Please, excuse Pansy's forward ways. She gets that from her da." Daisy extended her hand across the table.

Angelina liked the woman instantly. "Delighted to meet you, Mrs. O'Malley."

"I've heard so many wonderful things about ye. Thank ye so much for getting us out of the ghetto and helping us get a new start. I'm happier than ye know that Shamus won't be earning his way with his fists any longer." Tears pooled in her eyes.

Angelina offered her lace hankie. Daisy took it, wiped her eyes, and offered it back.

"Please keep it. I've many more. I'm delighted to assist your family in this small way." Angelina patted her work-worn hand. "Shamus is a fine man."

"The best foreman I've ever had." Edward pounded Shamus' back.

"Ach, I'm dense. This here is Mr. Edward Pritchard, my very demandin' boss."

Daisy shook his hand. "Glad to hear ye be keeping him in line."

The laughter and pleasant conversation over lunch relaxed Angelina. A twinge of envy pinged in her heart. The O'Malleys were a loving family. Shamus doted on his wife, and she glowed in his presence.

Angelina glanced over at Edward. He tugged on Lily's braided pigtail and laughed. The little girl giggled and shared her cookie with him. Her insides twisted. He'd make a good father someday and a good husband … for some woman who was willing to play the obedient housewife.

CHAPTER 11

Edward leaned against the makeshift corral, inspecting the shipment of horses and cattle that had finally arrived. Over the last hours, he'd overseen the cowboys filling the corral with horses and the pasture with cattle. Angelina now stood beside him, glaring at the cowboys conversing with Shamus and some others. Her stiff back and her white-knuckle grip on the railing sent a warning alarm through Edward.

"Two weeks is a far cry from a few days." Angelina's words clipped.

The green pastel dress fit too well, and her favorite lavender scent stirred thoughts in Edward not appropriate to have toward a boss. He moved along the fence, struggling to focus on the livestock while retrieving his wits. Since Angelina's arrival two weeks ago, she hadn't worn the same dress twice. Although plain, each had complemented her womanly curves and natural beauty. It would be so much easier to keep things strictly business if she were homely.

"I've asked George McCray and Shamus to join us." Edward cleared the huskiness from his voice with a cough. "McCray knows horses, of course, and Shamus grew up on a farm. I'm a city boy."

"Very wise." Angelina nodded, relaxing her grip on the fence.

His gaze went to her scooped neckline. Would Caroline's admiration for Angelina extend to her fashion? It was challenging enough protecting his sister from the overt advances of some single men. It would definitely be more difficult if she wore a dress like that. "The tall gentleman in the tan Stetson is Mr. Wingate."

"Stetson?" Her confused look was endearing.

"His hat. The gentlemen left of the black horse is Robert Wingate."

Edward accompanied Angelina toward the cowboys and Shamus, signaling George McCray to follow.

"Welcome, Mr. Wingate." Angelina stepped ahead of Edward. "You're late."

The rancher's eyes traveled her form, and Edward's hands fisted. Wingate had no cause to look her over like a horse at an auction. Hypocrisy called his name, reminding him he'd just done the same.

Mr. Wingate doffed his hat and smiled. "Sorry, ma'am. The river had overflowed its bank at our usual fording spot, making it unsafe to cross. Our alternative route was longer but allowed us to deliver the livestock unharmed." He gave her a wide, toothy smile.

Angelina crossed her arms, a defensive stance Edward knew well. She raised an eyebrow and glared. "You couldn't send a telegram informing us of the delay?"

"No ma'am, we were in Injun territory. I had to pay them for safe passage. It cost me my best saddle horse and five head of cattle."

"You gave them my cows?" Angelina's shrill tone didn't dislodge the man's grin.

Wingate grabbed his kerchief from his pocket and began wiping the sweat off his forehead. Then he placed the material back in his pocket before answering. "No ma'am, there were three steers among 'em."

Shamus and McCray drowned out snickers with coughs. Edward grimaced.

"Are you mocking me, Mr. Wingate?" Angelina's voice, icy.

Edward stepped beside her, and with no forethought, placed his hand on the small of her back. "I think five is a fair price to get the rest here safely."

Angelina glared at him, then faced Mr. Wingate. Stepping away from Edward, she transformed. "Yes. I'm happy to reimburse you for your saddle horse." Her smile softened her tone and drew a grinning Mr. Wingate closer.

"Not necessary, miss." He leaned in. "A small price to pay to admire a fine-looking woman such as yourself."

Edward's fists formed against his will once again.

Angelina's face relaxed into her *I-must-tolerate-you* look. She turned to Mr. McCray. "Please, inspect the horses."

"With pleasure." McCray walked toward the herd.

"Mr. O'Malley, inspect our cows. I mean cattle." Angelina addressed Mr. Wingate again. "Mr. Pritchard will escort all of you to the dining tent. Please make camp outside the perimeter of the town plat until we've concluded our business."

"Much obliged."

Angelina joined McCray with the horses while Edward led Wingate and his cowboys to the dining tent.

"This here is my son, Robert junior." Wingate patted the younger replica of himself on the shoulder as they walked to the dining tent.

Edward shook his hand. Wingate introduced the others, and they nodded their greetings as they entered the tent. Edward poured them coffee while Bridget and a few other ladies prepared the men a meal.

"So ... Miss DuBois isn't spoken for?" Wingate grinned up at Edward from his place at the table.

"She's my fiancée." The words tumbled out before he could retrieve them. *What is wrong with me?* When the hackles on his protective nature went up, the results weren't often pretty.

"Mighty bossy for a fiancée." Wingate laughed.

Edward returned the coffeepot to the stove before he acted on the temptation to spill the brew in the man's lap. "Angelina's an architect and gets very intense during the construction phase. This is her project. I'm just the contractor." Edward tried to sound matter-of-fact. Stomach acid churned as shame whispered. Having a female boss was a challenge enough without feeling the need to lie.

"And you can tolerate her notions?" Wingate shook his head and reached for his coffee. "She is quite the looker." After taking a sip of his brew, he pointed the cup at Edward. "That's the kind of woman you hide away and treat special, so no other man turns her head." Wingate winked.

"You've a hard-pressed battle if you think you can turn her head. Angelina isn't interested in ... anyone else." He almost said *men*. "Don't even entertain the idea of flirting." Edward's tone brought a nod from the man.

"Understood. I respect a man who stands up for his woman."

Bridget and two others brought out chicken and dumplings, with biscuits and pie. Mr. Wingate tried charming Bridget as the other women scurried back to the kitchen.

She smiled politely. "Have you met me older brother Shamus?" She placed a crock of butter on the table.

Edward added, "The big, tall man who went to check out the cattle."

The rancher laughed as he picked up his fork. "Y'all certainly watch out for your womenfolk."

His companions all winked at Bridget and shoulder-bumped each other as she served them at the adjoining table.

Wingate took a bite of food and began shoveling it in. "This is right good vittles."

"And that surprises ye?" Bridget poured refills of coffee.

"No, miss." The rancher winked her way.

Edward gritted his teeth. Standing guard over the cooks was not on his agenda.

Young Wingate spoke up. "Pa and I figured any woman's food's probably better than Max's fare." He flashed Bridget a smile. "But ..." He pointed to his meal. "This here is vittles from heaven, prepared by an angel."

Bridget laughed. "Let me introduce you to the angel. Mary Price, if you could, please come here." A tiny woman with mousy brown hair, wearing an apron over her red-floral dress, approached the table. Bridget nodded to her and pointed at the cowhands. "These men think an angel prepared their meal."

"That's a kind compliment, thank you." Mary smiled, her face beet-red, and scurried back to the stove.

"Is she the camp cook?" Young Wingate asked.

"No, she's opening a seamstress shop. As you say, any woman can cook a fine meal." Bridget's lips pursed for a moment. "Now, if you'll excuse me. We've a lot of dishes to wash and the evening meal to prepare. Tomorrow there'll be other angels to feed ye."

Edward left them to finish their food. Bridget could hold her own with the flirtatious cowboys. Now to tell Angelina he'd lied again. He was an honorable man. Caroline trusted him. But truth went hand in hand with trust. *I'm an idiot. Angelina can take care of herself.* She'd kill him, and he'd given her the gun to do it.

Edward found Angelina in an animated discussion with Mr. McCray and Shamus.

"You're sure?" Angelina's killer scowl sat firmly in place. "I'll not be made a fool of."

"What's going on?" Edward looked between the two.

Shamus shook his head. "I fear the man traded the best to the Indians. These bovines are not the quality Miss DuBois be expectin'. Those over there"—he pointed to a group grazing nearby—"are too thin." He tossed a nod in the other direction. "And those behind you are too old."

"And the rest?" Edward ran his fingers through his hair.

"The others be in fair shape to serve in the dining tent."

"Do we have enough to provide meat through the winter?" Angelina asked.

"Aye, but not much beyond that." Shamus turned to McCray. "Tell him about the horses."

McCray adjusted his bowler hat. "Again, half the herd be fit if not a wee bit long in the tooth, but the others are mavericks. I'll need time to break 'em. There be a few strong young ones in the bunch. No thoroughbreds, mind you, but good working stock."

"I specifically asked to purchase horses already trained to the saddle and wagons." Angelina's foot tapped an irritated rhythm. "I'll not pay the deceiver." Her scowl shifted to Edward for a moment before a frustrated sigh escaped her lips.

Oh, how he wanted to pull her into a comforting hug. "Let's

go have a conversation with Mr. Wingate. Do you have the written contract?"

"No." Was that a blush on her face? "He sent me a letter, and I responded by telegram."

"How could you not have a written contract? You had every man jack of us sign contracts, as well as the railroad, telegraph, and building suppliers." Edward stared at the cattle calmly grazing. *This is what comes from trying to control every iota of this project.*

Angelina joined him at the fence. "At the time we corresponded, I was dealing with Hiram's deceit. Agnes Moorhead's brother served with Mr. Wingate during the war, and she vouched for his character." Her chin quivered slightly while her eyebrows collided. Those sapphires always sparkled when she was angry.

Shifting his gaze to her pouty lips, his neck warmed. He jerked his view toward the ground, where an ant colony carried crumbs into their anthill. The insects worked with precision. The rhythm of their movement brought calm to Edward.

"Find the correspondence. We don't want to make accusations until we see what was said between you." Edward patted her shoulder. She didn't jerk away, surprising him as warmth spread up his arm to rest under his collar.

"Join me in the office." She turned to the others. "Are you prepared to show this …" She bit her lip, then continued. "Show Mr. Wingate your findings?" The men nodded. "Meet me … us … in an hour. Once we have our facts straight, we'll speak to Mr. Wingate." After the others left, she faced Edward again. "I'll ask Teresa to join us at the office tent."

Edward pored over the two letters and telegrams. "It appears your understanding of the request is different from Mr. Wingate's."

Teresa nodded. "Mr. Pritchard is correct. Why did I not know about this transaction?"

Angelina paced the tent. "What do you mean, different ideas?"

"The price you negotiated for the herd of horses and the cattle was insulting." Edward pointed to the telegram.

Angelina scanned it. "What's wrong with my price?"

"You get what you pay for." Teresa shuffled papers into a neat stack.

Edward waved the telegram in the air, producing a snapping sound. "I'd buy a half a dozen quality horses for that price, but twenty … and cattle are selling at a premium right now. If you had been clear you wanted breeding stock …" Edward's voice trailed off for an instant. "But this telegram makes no mention of that. Besides, why would you? Are you planning on running a ranch too?" Edward pulled back his frustration, lest the conversation take a trail that might jeopardize his job. "What you requested was beef to feed the town."

"Oh." Angelina sighed and shook her head. "This is what happens when I try to do business out of my element. Length and size of lumber, I know. I can create and read blueprints. But with livestock, I'm ignorant."

Edward squelched a smile at her confession.

McCray and Shamus entered. Edward shared their findings.

"Well, if that be the case, you got what you paid for." Mr. McCray smiled. She scowled, and he pulled off his hat and turned it in his hands. "I'm sorry for offending ye."

"I'm sorry for being so foolish. It's not any of your faults." She looked at the men. "Now what?"

Shamus spoke first. "I noticed a few of the cows are pregnant, so that's good. You asked for cows, so that's all you got, not a male among 'em. They're no good for milking."

"Why is that? Can't any cow be milked?"

"Aye, but these be wild beasts. Ye'd have to gentle one enough to let ye touch her udders without getting impaled on those long horns." Shamus let out a sigh. "Some homesteaders brought Guernsey milk cows. Perhaps they'll trade for a few calves."

"What about the skinny ones?" Angelina worried her bottom lip.

"I'll be asking Mr. Klaus, as he has a gift for tending sick animals. I imagine they're just worn thin from the long walk here."

Angelina's eyes misted, and she crossed her arms. "Mr. McCray, your assessment?"

In the short time Edward had spent with George, the man tended to find the silver lining in most situations.

"Now that I know the way of things ..." McCray hooked his thumbs on his suspenders. "I'll ask the ranch crew which ones are saddle- and wagon-broke. We can provide five of those to the farmers who borrowed my Belgians. The older mares are still healthy. Nice saddle horses for ladies, children, and city boys." He grinned at Edward. "Isn't a horse alive I can't teach to pull a wagon. What mavericks are left, we'll need time to train. Then they'll be the best of the lot."

"Sounds like we have a plan." Edward glanced toward Angelina, gauging her response.

"I'll pay Mr. Wingate and send him on his way." She sat behind his desk. "Mr. McCray, can you select a horse for my personal mount?"

"I'll get right on that."

"My sidesaddle is still stored on the train."

"You be wantin' to ride sidesaddle?" McCray stopped in his trek to the tent door. "Well, now, that will take a bit longer."

"Because?" Angelina drummed the desk with her fingers.

"These horses were probably only ridden by men."

"And you're implying?" Angelina's daggered look fixed on him.

McCray stretched to his full five-feet-three inches and folded his arms, returning her stare. "I'm not implying anything, but I'm stating the truth. Horses are particular beasties. You always mount 'em on the same side. They may not care for a certain bit in their mouth, and a lady riding sidesaddle can scare 'em quicker than quick."

Edward jumped in before Angelina said something she'd regret. "A woman riding sidesaddle sits different on the horse's back. A horse must be trained to it."

McCray added, "I seen a horse take off at a gallop because the lady's skirt fluttered in the wind and scared it."

"I see." Angelina's tone subdued.

Shamus and Mr. McCray departed. Angelina pulled a key from her bodice and opened the strongbox in the bottom file drawer. She counted the gold coins. "I need a more secure place for this." She tapped the box with the tip of her finger.

"The safe in your private car would be better."

"It needs to arrive first."

"Tomorrow."

"Really?" Her voice dripped with joy. "How?"

"There's an unexplained holdup on completing the spur. But Mr. McCray and the Wright brothers have built a conveyance the Belgians can pull."

Angelina's eyes shone brighter than her smile. "Thank you, Eddie. No one has ever been so thoughtful."

She'll change her tune when I tell her I lied.

Angelina patted her elaborate hairstyle as she peeked into her speckled mirror. She'd changed for dinner into a silk gown—not as formal as her evening attire in Chicago, but far superior to work dresses. She put on her pearl drop earrings and pulled on her elbow-length gloves. The dab of French perfume gave her confidence as she grabbed her fan and prepared to slay the dragon.

I'll get that oaf to agree on a lesser price. No one takes advantage of Angelina DuBois. No one.

Every head turned when she entered the dining tent. Edward frowned as he pulled out a chair between Mr. Wingate and himself. Rev. Asbury, Teresa, Madeline Harper, and the Potters filled the remaining chairs at her table. The rancher's men sat at an adjoining table flirting with the ladies who served food. Their laughter dominated the dining tent. Each guffaw deepened Angelina's irritation.

"Your men are an uncouth lot." She deftly maneuvered her fan, covering her mouth.

"Yes, indeed." Mr. Wingate leaned closer. "They may not have citified manners, but I'd trust them with my life in any situation." He breathed in her scent, then leaned away again. Angelina took a slow intake of air. *How forward.* The rancher scooped up some mashed potatoes. "This is quite a change for my men. Usually, at the end of our annual cattle drive, they collect their pay and let off steam in the saloon." He winked.

"The women of Resolve are not to be trifled with." She tried to sharpen her glare. His eyes searched her face, then rested on her bosom for a moment. Mr. Wingate's overpowering masculinity sent a shudder up her spine. She fanned her face, collecting her poise.

"You can't blame the men for teasing the gals a bit. It's lonely on the trail and the ranch. None of us have a wife. And if you weren't spoken for, I'd be hanging around to persuade you to marry me."

Angelina choked on her coffee. Edward patted her back, then leaned forward. "Are you all right, darling?" His eyes held a warning. What had he done now?

"Mr. Wingate, I find your forwardness disturbing." She straightened her back. "A decent man would be more discreet with his words."

"I don't have time for the foolish games of courtship. If you weren't engaged, I'd not be leaving tomorrow."

Engaged. She pulled the word back off her tongue before it spewed out in angry surprise. She shot a glare at Edward, then turned her best smile on Mr. Wingate. "I assure you, there is not a single woman here who would say yes to you. They are here to start businesses."

The rancher laughed. "That's the most ridiculous thing I've heard. Most often, I don't take these trips to deliver a little livestock. But I couldn't pass up the chance to see your reckless venture for myself. Land sakes, here's a town full of eligible women. They'd be fools not to want a husband."

"Miss DuBois is correct in saying marriage is not the priority of these women." Edward placed his arm on the back of Angelina's chair.

"They all planning on being old maids?" Wingate's eyes twinkled.

Miss Harper frowned. "Mr. Wingate, it has been my experience that men will say anything to get their way with a woman. They spew promises that turn to ash, which flies in our faces and leaves us heartbroken. I, for one, am enjoying being an independent woman."

"I'm sorry to hear you're soured on men. We are not all cads." Mr. Wingate's tone gentled as he raised his cup of coffee and nodded toward Miss Harper.

Angelina signaled for Bridget.

"Yes, miss?" Bridget approached with a coffeepot.

"Mr. Wingate and I have a difference of opinion. I thought you could clear it up."

"I'll try." Bridget refilled cups.

Mr. Wingate leaned toward her. "If I ask you to marry me and come back to my ranch tomorrow, would you?"

"And give up on me dream of owning a bakery? Never." Bridget jutted out her chin.

Teresa joined in. "Mr. Wingate is under the impression any woman who would say no to him would prefer a life as an old maid."

Bridget's head snapped up. "I canna speak for every woman here, but most of us hope to marry in the future. First, we must build this town. As for me, I'm helping me brother save money to bring me family here."

Rev. Asbury interrupted. "Miss O'Malley, might I trouble you for a piece of your fine pie?" He smiled sweetly.

"Of course, Reverend." Bridget left to retrieve pie, purposely avoiding the cowhands' table.

"Mr. Wingate." Dr. Potter looked over his glasses. "Are all ranchers this frank?"

"Can't speak for others, but I speak my mind and don't mince words."

"I'll not mince them either." Angelina had everyone's attention.

"There may be a maiden or two who'd consider your proposal."

"And which ones would those be?"

Angelina pointed toward the table where McCray sat with his six daughters, the oldest being thirteen.

Wingate laughed again. "Well played."

The rest of the meal, he acted the perfect gentleman. Edward remained silent while Dr. Potter and the reverend carried the conversation.

"You'll be leaving tomorrow, Mr. Wingate?" Rev. Asbury pushed his empty pie plate away.

"That's my plan at present."

"If you decide to stay, there will be some interesting entertainment tomorrow." The reverend had his attention.

Angelina groaned inside. Her plans for the evening were foiled, thanks to her tablemates. Hezekiah had many redeeming qualities, but one irritating thing about the minister was his ability to make a big production out of a small thing.

"And that would be?" Mr. Wingate finished his pie.

"McCray's Belgians are pulling a railroad car."

"And why is that?"

"The last remaining two miles of the rail spur are not completed yet. Unforeseen delays." Rev Asbury nodded toward Angelina. "Miss DuBois needs her private car."

Angelina wished Rev. Asbury hadn't reminded her of the constant struggle to finish the line. Now she was the center of the wrong kind of attention.

Mr. Wingate shook his head and turned toward her. "Why are you in such a hurry to bring it here?"

The rancher's smoldering stare and crooked smile irked her. How dare he laugh at her?

"Angelina, you need not explain your business to this man." Edward's use of her first name in public confirmed the engagement ploy. She swallowed the truth trying to escape through her lips. It drowned in her soured stomach. Here was another irritating man.

"It's all right, *Eddie.*" Her tone was sarcastic as she tipped her head toward him, then turned her attention to the rancher. "I will rest easier knowing my valuables are not sitting unguarded in the middle of the prairie." It sounded so vain saying it out loud but seemed nobler than admitting she hated sleeping outdoors.

"That settles it." Wingate slapped the table, making the ladies nearby jump. "Watching those fine specimens of horseflesh will be worth resting a day longer." He glanced over at the table where his men were flirting with a very attentive woman. "Who knows, maybe one of my men can persuade one of these fine ladies to marry 'em by tomorrow."

Angelina strode a few feet ahead of Edward as he trailed her back to her tent. "Miss DuBois, if you please." She stopped and turned toward him. Edward ran his hand through his hair, then used both hands to smooth it back down. "Let me apologize and—"

"Explain yourself." She crossed her arms and glared, anger simmering just under her corset.

"Mr. Wingate indicated his intentions to woo you. And before I had time to think of a better response, I said you were my fiancée." Dusk did not hide the red glow on his cheeks.

The pent-up anger spewed forth. "Do you think I am some foolish girl who can be swept off her feet by a few flattering phrases?"

"Of course not. It's just ..." His face became redder, and he tugged at his collar.

"Then you consider me a weak female who needs your protection." She stepped closer and tapped his shoulder with her fan.

"No. I'm sorry." He stepped back, holding his hands up.

She poked him in the chest. "How do you think I felt when Mr. Wingate referred to my engagement? To be the laughingstock of everyone at the table? Not to mention, my plans for negotiating a lower price for the animals flitted away, thanks to your lie."

Edward's eyes almost glowed in the dusk light. "Seriously, Miss

DuBois, you would use your womanly wiles on him? Unlike the old fop of a railroad president, Mr. Wingate is not to be trifled with."

"I can handle myself." She tried to relax the muscles of her face that were stone tight in agitation. The cool night air ruffled her hair.

"Angelina, I am disappointed in you." His remark stabbed a hole in her pride. Drawing near, Edward softened his tone, slowing the rage inside her. "I respect your business savvy. I respect your intelligence. But your flirtatious tactics are going to get you in trouble out here."

Edward stared into her eyes. For a moment, she thought he'd kiss her. Instead, he stalked away without a backward glance.

She walked to her tent, hot tears trailing her cheeks. Pulling her handkerchief from her sleeve, she wiped her face. Why did she even care what he thought? He didn't understand the inequality of things. Then she groaned at the thought of Mrs. Potter spreading the news of her engagement through the whole camp before she had a chance to quell it. She might be shy around men, but she had quite a little clutch of chickens to gossip to.

Her chin rose, and her heart pounded as anger at Edward's attempt at gallantry replaced her tears. This made twice the man had lied to protect her. She lit the lamp and began preparing for bed. She flung her lovely gown across the room. While struggling to remove her corset, she weighed the pros and cons of her contractor. Once free of the garment, her hands no longer trembled with rage.

Angelina resettled her party gown on a chair, then slipped out of her camisole and into her nightgown. She spoke to her reflection in the mirror as she brushed out her hair and braided it. "Do you think maybe there is some wisdom in his words?"

CHAPTER 12

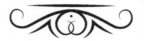

O n the east edge of town near the corral, Edward helped the Wrights and Mr. McCray hitch his team of eighteen muscular Belgians to the eight-wheel wagon. The whole town had turned out to watch, and murmurs of excitement filled the air as the first lights of morning filled the sky. The brothers' impressive ingenuity had created a vehicle with a larger axle and wheels to carry the train car from the end of the rail line to Resolve.

McCray secured the last horse and called back to him. "All set. If all goes well, we should be back in town by dinner time."

"And we should be finished with the dorms by then," Shamus said as he rode up on horseback. "I donna understand why Miss DuBois canna live there until her house be built."

Edward took off his hat and rubbed his forehead. "It's what she wants, Shamus, both for her comfort and the security of her things."

"All right, then. Safe travels." With a mock salute, Shamus turned his horse toward the clatter of hammers at the dormitories.

As they rode out of town, Mr. Wingate and crew followed on horseback, much to Edward's irritation.

"Hey, Pritchard." The rancher pulled his horse alongside Edward's. The wind whipped his neckerchief up toward his face. "Can I have a word?"

"Sure." Edward kept his eyes on the wagon ahead of him. Dust flew into his face, making him wish he'd worn a kerchief and not volunteered to take up the rear.

"I need to apologize for last night. I enjoy flirting, but I've no intention of marrying up with a stranger."

"Miss DuBois will be glad to hear it." Edward debated with his conscience. If the rancher never knew the truth, it didn't matter now. But he owed it to Angelina. Edward turned in his saddle to face the man. "But the truth is, Miss DuBois and I are not engaged, courting, or any way promised."

"I see." Wingate grinned.

"You don't." Edward couldn't let the remark lie. "Miss DuBois has no intention of ever marrying. Her focus is on making a name for herself as an architect. The woman is difficult to work with and foolish to think she can manipulate men with flirting and no harm will come to her. That is why I said she was my fiancée."

"Perhaps she wants a man without the fetters of marriage." Wingate winked.

"If you weren't on that horse, I'd punch your smug face for such an insult." Edward's voice rose as his jaw tightened.

Wingate's men gathered close, hands on their holsters. The rancher's eyes didn't leave his. "Back to your places, boys."

As they dispersed, Edward glared. "Angelina is not that kind of woman."

"Maybe you're right, or maybe she just isn't that way with you." He tipped his hat and rode back toward his men.

Edward fumed at the insinuation. Angelina was forward thinking but not ... He blew out a breath and spurred his horse toward the departing wagon.

The wagon covered the two-mile distance in no time. Its larger, wider size—with the wheelbase wider than the tracks—required careful maneuvering on George McCray's part to align it with the end of the rails. The challenge in moving the wooden train car came in leveraging it onto the wagon. The men put house jacks under the car and raised it to wagon height. They backed the wagon underneath the car. Everyone held their breath as the jacks were lowered. The car teetered, then settled. The jacks were removed, and a cheer rose. Finally, the men scurried to secure the car to the wagon with ropes.

McCray climbed on the buckboard. The Wrights double-checked the wheels and axles on the wagon before heading out.

Men were stationed around the wagon with ropes to help guide it by turns. The Belgians pulled at a steady pace. A new knot formed on top of others in Edward's stomach as their progress slowed. The weight of the train car forced the wheels well below the dry surface. Damp earth clung to the spokes, and deep ruts formed in the road.

"Stop the wagon." Carl Wright yanked at some grass holding fast to one of the wheels. "Bring me a shovel."

Every Wright grabbed a shovel and set to work freeing the wheels from the thick sod. And every half hour, the wagon paused while men cleared the mud again.

Sweat rolled down Edward's face as he assisted. "That's it, boys, put your back into it."

Even Wingate's men took a turn at removing the mud. At least they made themselves useful, Edward mused.

"I'll wager my wife's apple pie my men can clear the wheels faster." McCray challenged Wingate with a narrowed gaze.

"Throw in some bread pudding, and you're on." Wingate dismounted to take his turn with a shovel.

The friendly competition between the townsfolk and the cowhands kept the wagons moving despite the day's swelling heat. Near dinnertime, they arrived in Resolve covered in mud.

"We're almost there—I can smell the apple pie." McCray laughed. "Now, me beauties, to the finish line." He clicked to the Belgians, and they hauled the wagon to the designated spot at the end of the main street.

A cheering crowd gathered, Angelina among them. She wore a simple calico dress, and her raven hair fell in a braid down her back, her smile radiant as she watched the men secure her new home.

McCray unhitched his horses. The Wrights placed the jacks under the wagon, then removed the wheels and lowered the load to a foot above the ground.

"How are you getting the car off the wagon?" Wingate asked Carl Wright.

"We aren't. The wagon will be a bit of a porch for Miss DuBois. We'll add some stairs, and she'll have a dandy place to live."

Angelina clapped her hands. Pleasure filled her lovely face. "Thank you so much, gentlemen. I'm honored that you would go to so much trouble for me." She shook each man's hand and flashed her winning smile. "And now I must go pack."

Edward doffed his hat. "I'm on my way back to the office. I'll escort you to your tent."

Angelina nodded and strolled at his side—thankfully, not too near, sweaty as he was. "You're a man of your word, Eddie. I look forward to my first good night's sleep in weeks."

"You're very welcome." Edward grinned. "It was a fascinating adventure. I'm surprised you didn't come along." And relieved.

"I'm no engineer, and the thought of watching the move ... well, it made me nervous," Angelina whispered, although there was no danger of the men still nearby overhearing them as they tended to their horses. "Fortunately, for me and all the men on the project, I'd already promised to mind Mrs. Collins' children while she and Caroline printed our first paper. That was an adventure too."

His sister must've had a glorious day, but ... "I can't imagine you playing with children."

"I was a child once." She pretended to be offended. "I still remembered how to play tag. And Anabelle and Maribel asked me to draw new faces on their rag dolls." Angelina's sparkling eyes and sweet expression showed a motherly side he'd not imagined. "Henry and I built a castle with blocks."

"Is the paper ready?"

"It will be available tomorrow. Caroline is simply beaming. Mrs. Collins' eldest son should arrive in a few months. He'll graduate with a degree in business. Martin is excited about the newspaper venture."

A niggle of unease made Edward stifle a frown. Would this Collins boy edge Caroline out of her dream?

At Angelina's tent, she touched his arm. "Could you be a dear and pop over to the dining tent and tell Bridget I need her?" This smile was so different from the one focused on the rancher last night. There was no flirtatious lilt of her voice directed his way. But why did he care?

And the moment of camaraderie dissolved with her request. Once again, he was at her beck and call. Irritation tightened his jaw, squeezing the answer through gritted teeth. "I'll do that on my way back to the office." He modulated his voice when her sapphire eyes bore into him. "Shall I see you at dinner?"

"I think I'll eat in my new home."

Of course, the queen has her castle now. He crossed his arms as she scurried into her tent.

Moving away, Edward caught a glimpse of Robert Wingate's son talking to Caroline near the dining tent, her blush in full bloom as the young man fidgeted with the hat in his hand.

Edward stomped toward the couple. "Good afternoon, young Wingate."

"Good afternoon, sir. I was just making the acquaintance of ..."

"My sister." Edward scowled at the youth, who couldn't be more than sixteen.

"Oh." A stain of red on his cheeks made him look even younger. "We were just talkin'."

Caroline smiled at her brother. "Robert was telling me—"

"Mr. Wingate." Edward employed his firm, fatherly tone. "You don't address a man you've just met by his Christian name."

Caroline fixed her *you're-not-my-boss* look on Edward for a moment, then turned back to the cowboy. The fluttery eyelashes and beaming smile Angelina so often flashed replicated itself on his sister's face. "I was telling Mr. Wingate that our first newspaper will come out tomorrow."

"Miss Pritchard promised to bring me a copy to take home. I've never met a female reporter before." The boy smiled at Caroline, doe-eyed.

"How nice of her. Caroline, I need you for something. If you'll excuse us?"

He tried to draw her away, but Caroline clasped her elbows with both hands and moved a bit closer to the enemy. "What do you need?"

"Miss DuBois could use your help." Surely, Bridget would appreciate Caroline's help moving Angelina. And it would separate her from this *cowboy*.

Caroline relaxed and smiled once again at the little weasel. "I'll go and see what she needs. I'll bring your copy early tomorrow before you leave. Good day, Mr. Wingate." She raised her eyebrow at Edward, indicating her displeasure, and flounced away. Young Wingate's twitter-pated gaze followed her.

He tipped his hat Edward's way. "Good day, Mr. Pritchard." Then he strolled toward the campsite.

Edward's mind rehearsed various things to say to Angelina about her negative influences on his sister while he sought out Bridget in the kitchen.

The irritating voice of the senior Mr. Wingate rang out as Edward entered the dining tent. The man stood a little too close to Bridget near the entrance. "That was mighty fine pie, Miss O'Malley. I've never had better."

Edward stood stunned as Bridget duplicated Angelina's melt-you smile. "I'll carry your compliment with me forever." Then she stepped back a few paces. "But all your sweet words willna tempt me away from opening me bakery."

"A pure shame, Miss O'Malley, a right, pure shame." The rancher tipped his hat and walked out of the dining tent.

"Miss O'Malley, I never took you for a flirt." Edward's frustration came out harsh.

"And I never took ye for an eavesdropper." Bridget scowled and fisted her hands on her hips. "Ye must handle a man like Mr. Wingate carefully. Let him think he's a special gift to all womankind. Then let him down easy. Otherwise, he'll be trouble. And trouble brings Shamus down on his head." She wiped some crumbs from one of the tables into her hand. "I'm sure ye didna come to spy on me for me brother."

"I apologize for my remark. I just saw young Wingate flirting with my sister."

"And she was respondin' in kind, I'll wager." Bridget laughed and tipped the crumbs in a nearby dust bin. "Caroline is a beautiful girl, and it's natural for girls to flirt a bit."

"I don't like it. Flirting could lead to trouble." Edward's stomach soured at the idea.

"I doubt it. Those cowboys leave tomorrow. Caroline will have to find another lad to practice her charms on."

"You're as bad as Angelina. I don't understand. If you want to be treated as men's equals, why are you using womanly wiles?"

"If you donna know the answer to that, Mr. Pritchard, I'll not be tellin' ya." She chuckled. "Why are ye here?"

"Angelina needs help moving her things to her train car. I sent Caroline to help too."

"Aye, that is a good idea. The task will go faster, and young Mr. Wingate will be elsewhere engaged." Bridget winked at him and swished her skirts as she headed out.

Women were strange creatures.

As Edward passed by, a wagon pulled by two mules sat outside Angelina's tent. Her mirror and other pieces of furniture were already stacked inside. He caught a glimpse of the ladies filling trunks.

Tomorrow, he'd escort Caroline to deliver the paper to that—*boy* and make sure the lot of them were gone. What if the word got out this was a town of eligible young women seeking husbands? There were enough single men working for Edward to keep an eye on. He didn't need a boatload more to moon around after the ladies. He blew out a frustrated sigh and stalked back to his office tent.

CHAPTER 13

Angelina blinked in the morning light and stretched, disappointed she hadn't slept well. The quiet seemed odd after the noise of the tent city. But the *cock-a-doodle-doo* of four roosters still filtered through the closed train car windows. Finally, a gentle tapping on the door roused her from her bed.

Bridget stood in the doorway with a tray. "I'm on breakfast duty, so I thought I'd bring a tray rather than disturb your sleep banging pans about."

Angelina held the door wide. "Smells divine. How did I not hear you rise this morning?"

"Ye're unaccustomed to manual labor, and yesterday, ye spent quite a bit of time arranging and rearranging the furniture." Bridget pulled out two china place settings from the tiny cupboard and set the table. "Ye needed rest."

"Well, everything was tossed hither and yon by the wagon ride."

Angelina bit into a hot scone. "Heavenly." She applied a bit of butter to the end and took another bite before speaking. "I must hurry if I want to bid Mr. Wingate good riddance."

"What do you have in mind to wear?" Bridget poured tea.

"Something that says, *don't trifle with Angelina DuBois*." She flipped her braid behind her with a flourish.

"That might not be wise." Bridget finished her scone. "But I know ye will do what you please."

"Really, Bridget, am I that vain?" Angelina harrumphed before raising her teacup to her lips.

"Well, if I can be honest, I'll say me piece." Bridget smiled over her own cup.

Angelina nodded and waited.

"This be a different world than Chicago. Men out here are not as polite as ye'r accustomed to. Take those mule skinners. Rude lot. I've slapped a few faces. Others, like Mr. Clark and Mr. Pritchard, be gentlemen. Most of the men don't always speak kindly of ye."

"I know they don't like my no-alcohol policy." Angelina shrugged.

"True. But I've heard vulgar things about your … form. A few men have left yelling curses at me after I spilled scalding coffee in their laps."

"You need not defend me. "

"But I do. As long as a woman is in charge, all the women must be on their guard."

Shame warmed Angelina's neck. Eddie had told her the same thing two nights ago. She needed to lead by example, and that evening, she'd been a poor one.

"You're right. Help me select a more subdued gown for today."

Bridget pulled a dress from Angelina's trunk. "This be the one, a lovely color to show off your pretty eyes but high-collared and not form-fitting to show off the rest of ye."

Irritation built in the recesses of Angelina's mind, where ill will toward the opposite sex hid away. "This fight for equality is a hard battle, indeed."

"And the victory might not be realized for a few generations." Bridget sighed. "Let me do your hair."

"Yes, please. I need a bit of pampering today."

Mr. Wingate greeted Angelina with a wide-armed bow, hat in hand. "Miss DuBois, you look good enough to eat."

"I had no idea Texans were cannibals." Angelina kept her face neutral. She held out a small bag. "Here is your payment in full, in gold coins, as we agreed."

"Thank you, *Miss* DuBois." His smile widened. "Mr. Pritchard informed me you two are not courting."

"That does not mean I'm looking for a suitor." Angelina raised her eyebrow, hoping disdain showed on her face.

"Well, your performance at dinner the other night said otherwise."

"You are obviously not a gentleman. Your rudeness would not be tolerated in Chicago." She glared at him.

"And your behavior would be better suited to a saloon hall girl where I come from." Mr. Wingate smirked.

Angelina slapped his face hard before her mind could reverse the command. "That, sir, is exactly the attitude I deplore."

He leaned closer, his eyes glinting. "And you need to be educated in the proper place of women. Out here, some men would take a slap as an invitation. I, on the other hand, don't." He rubbed his jaw. "But it is a challenge. You're a filly that needs taming. I haven't made up my mind if I want to waste my time taming you or find a woman who's already gentled."

Angelina wrestled with a variety of responses before she settled on a simple nod. "Safe travels, Mr. Wingate."

He tipped his hat and secured the pouch in his pocket. "If you took the time to get to know me, you might find me a tolerable husband." He strode toward the other cowhands.

Angelina turned, holding her tears in check until she was safely inside the train car. How dare he compare her to a trollop? If he returned, she'd show him to the door faster than McCray's horses could pull a wagon a foot.

Edward escorted Caroline to deliver the paper to the younger Mr. Wingate. Caroline had argued, but he'd stood his ground. Her scowl disappeared when they reached the cowboy. They'd agreed to meet at a tree near his campsite. "Robert ..." She glanced Edward's way. "Mr. Wingate, I apologize for my tardiness. My brother wanted to wish you farewell too." She handed him a copy of the paper.

"No need to apologize. It took extra time to break camp. Just got here a few minutes ago." He handed her a bouquet of blue wildflowers.

She flashed another Angelina smile. "How very kind." She smelled them and caressed the bouquet.

"I'm glad you like them."

The boy's flushed face and twitter-pated grin irked Edward. Caroline fluttered her eyelashes in response, and Edward wanted to thrash his sister. Maybe Angelina wasn't the best mentor, after all.

"You'll find your name in the article I wrote about the cattle and horses arriving." Caroline's bright smile put another blush on the lad's face.

"I don't read much, but I'll read this." When the cowboy pressed the paper to his chest, Edward rolled his eyes.

"Well, Mr. Wingate." Edward extended his hand. "Have a safe trip home."

The boy's large hand tightened around Edward's. He responded in kind. Young Wingate tipped his hat to Caroline and mounted his horse. "Have a nice day, Miss Pritchard."

His horse stood on its hind legs and pranced. Stilling the mount, the youth waved his hat and galloped away.

"Caroline, you've been taking flirting lessons from Miss DuBois. That poor boy is ready to eat out of your hand." His fists rested at his side, quelling the urge to choke Angelina. "I don't approve."

"You really think I acted like Angelina?" The wonder in Caroline's eyes would have been laughable if she wasn't his sister. "Now I know how she feels."

"What?" Edward stared, even more confused.

"Don't look at me like that. I'm not in love. Good grief, he lives on a ranch in the middle of nowhere. I'm a journalist. What would I write about—cattle?" She laughed.

"You know, it's very unladylike and cruel to lead the boy on."

"I know." She looked up at him and heaved a sigh.

"Young lady, you are to cease all flirting. We have too many lonely, single men in Resolve, and flirting will tempt them more than whiskey."

"I'm sorry." She dropped the bouquet to her side. "I promise, if any man truly turns my head, I'll seek your approval." She gave him her newly acquired melt-a-man smile.

"Stop that." Edward scowled, then hugged her. "Seriously, I'll need a rifle handy to keep away all the men whose hearts you break."

"I love you, too, overprotective brother of mine." She kissed his cheek.

"How's your book coming?" This particular subject change would distract her.

"I'm enjoying doing interviews. I asked Robert about ranching." Edward scowled, but before he could say more, she raised her hand. "I promise, my motives are pure. I don't have time to waste playing the courting game."

Edward kissed her forehead. "Good to know." He lifted her chin. "Promise me, no more flirting."

"Even if I'm in love?" Caroline giggled.

"Promise." Edward found no humor in the situation.

"I promise. Even though it's a powerful feeling, it's frightening. What if he'd tried to kiss me?" Caroline's eyes widened and her face paled. "I promise."

Loud shouting erupted ahead, and Edward ran toward a worksite. A short man swore as he stuck his fist inches from a taller man's face. He couldn't recall their names, but the short man's Irish accent was cut short by the larger man's fists. Once the Irishman went down, the other man jumped on top of him. Before Edward could break up the fight, lines of battle were drawn. The mule skinners and the Irish pounded on each other.

"Stop." Edward's command got lost in the sound of the melee. He grabbed two men to separate them. Two fists knocked him down, and stars danced in his head. Crawling to his feet, he avoided a crack on the head from a two-by-four a mule skinner was wildly swinging. Edward wrestled the board from him. After disarming the man, he tripped over another man sprawled on the ground.

Rifle fire broke up the brawl.

Rev. Asbury stood, weapon raised. "Really, gentlemen. Can we not do as the Scripture encourages? Reason together."

Shamus and his work crew stood behind him. Edward rose from the dirt, wiped dust off his pants, and glared at the offenders. Angry stares directed at him, along with murmuring complaints, broke the momentary silence.

Another rifle blast.

"Enough, gentlemen." Rev. Asbury aimed the gun toward the crowd. Everyone fell silent.

Edward seized the moment. "We'll sort the particulars out later. And all damages are coming out of your pay."

Men started to argue. Edward raised his hand for silence, then signaled for Shamus to come forward. "Mr. O'Malley, I'll need the assistance of your crew to help these men clean this up. Any who need medical attention, send to Dr. Potter. And anyone who continues to argue, punch him in the mouth." Edward heaved a frustrated sigh and wiped blood from his face.

"Yes, sir! I'll tally up what's broken and have Miss Jameson deduct it from their pay."

He shouted to the men. "I donna care who threw the first punch. I donna care if you stood around and watched. Ye all will pay for the damages."

"Ain't fair, I wasn't fightin'," an Irish laborer shouted.

"That's 'cause you know I'd smash your ugly mug." A mule skinner stepped toward him.

Edward strode to the man. "That's enough." The man glowered, but Edward gave no ground. The man relaxed his fists and stepped away. "Once this mess is cleaned up, I'll see you all in my office."

Edward inspected the last of the muddy coffee in the pot in the dining hall. The ladies always kept two pots warm at the back of the stove between meals. He poured a cup and stirred in three spoons of sugar.

"Ye might add some milk to that—it's pretty nasty." Shamus scooped out a dipper of water from the water bucket and drank it down. He wiped his forehead. "What have ye decided about the fighting?"

Angelina and Teresa sat at a nearby table, poring over papers at Edward's request. Teresa pointed at the contract in her hand. "Well, gentlemen, you can't fire the men who signed on to homestead. Brawling doesn't violate the contract." She perused the paper again and frowned. "If it had been a drunken brawl, then you could fire them."

"What were you women thinking when you drew up these contracts?" As he pulled out a chair and joined them, Edward's sour comment got a sharp look from the ladies.

Teresa leaned forward. "We were assuming those committed to the project would be mature men of upright character."

"Drinking was my biggest concern. I'm almost as passionate about temperance as I am women's suffrage." Angelina shook her head. "As Teresa said, we expected men of integrity."

"Thank you for your confidence in the male gender. As you can see, not all of us are lovers of peace." Edward's head still ached from the blows he'd received.

"And some of us talk with our fists," Shamus added. "I overheard the mule skinners complain about working for a woman. They have no respect for Miss DuBois and don't think they need to work as hard. The longer the project takes, the more money they'll make."

Angelina slapped the table. "How dare they plot to take advantage?"

"Let me assure you, these types of men would do the same if a man was their boss," Edward said.

"Would they?" She pushed her chair away from the table and paced. Teresa rose and guided her back to her chair.

"Now, the good news is, you can fire every one of those ill-mannered mule-lovers. They didn't sign a contract." Teresa restacked the papers.

Angelina curled her finger beneath her chin. "How short-handed will we be?"

"We'd lose a third of our workforce." As Edward answered, Angelina's gaze swung to him, and she seemed to see him for the first time.

"Eddie, your face is all bruised." She placed her hand on his cheek. The warmth of her touch spread through him. She turned his head from side to side. "You poor man. Have you been to see Dr. Potter?"

Edward removed her hand from his face, and with it went the sense of connection. "Haven't had time. But after this meeting, I will." Perhaps Dr. Potter had a good remedy for his headache.

"We can't fire them, or the project won't stay on schedule." Angelina rested her head on the table and groaned.

"But we're already behind schedule. If we fire the lot, the rest will work faster and be more committed." Edward's voice held an edge as the headache raged on.

"We need to stay on schedule. Reducing our workforce is a bad decision." Angelina sat straight, her chin set.

"You'd rather I break up brawls every day?" Edward glared back. "I don't care to get a broken nose."

"I promise ye, Miss DuBois, the Irish and the other men with contracts won't be brawling. They gave me their word." Shamus received the same withering look from Angelina. He stared at the table.

"No one gave *me* their word. No one included me in those interviews. I have not heard one apology for their horrific behavior on my project." Angelina's voice rose with each declaration.

"Calm down." Teresa patted her shoulder. "Firing those not committed to the success of Resolve is for the best. And you know it."

Angelina slumped in her chair, sighed, then straightened again. "You're right. We can rent Mr. McCray's horses to replace the mules. Shamus, I'll trust your word that the men will work harder."

"I'll call a town meeting after dinner." Edward glanced Angelina's way. "With your permission, of course."

"Hopefully, you can rally the troops to work harder and faster. My biggest fear is that a blizzard will catch us unprepared." In an unexpected gesture, Angelina reached out and squeezed his hand.

"We have plenty of time before winter." He held her hand with both of his. Angelina's eyes dimmed to a pale blue before she stared at their hands and removed hers abruptly. Then tapped her knuckles on the table.

"If you must choose between starting my home or other families' before winter, you have my permission to delay my home until next year. I will not have anyone living in a tent when snow is on the ground."

Edward tried not to stare at this selfless side of Angelina. She did have a kind heart beating below that rough exterior, and, despite himself, he wanted to get to know that side better.

CHAPTER 14

Angelina had fired the mule skinners personally. Most took their pay and left without complaint, but a few railed at her until Shamus stepped in. They had already vacated the town site. The experience shook her and brought clarity to the decision to rid Resolve of these troublemakers. Would brawling and arguments now cease?

Trudging toward the assembly in the center of town, she silently reviewed her speech. She'd worn a conservative blue skirt with a matching waistcoat. Black filigree accented the ensemble. Her black, broad-brimmed hat with a simple, matching blue ribbon shaded her head from the afternoon sun. Would her new appearance help garner the respect she needed to keep the project moving forward?

Edward stood at the back of the crowd. Muscles bulged under rolled-up sleeves. A breeze mussed his blond hair. His broad shoulders flexed beneath his shirt. Resting her hand on his back as she drew up behind him warmed her to the core. His chocolate eyes turned her way.

Angelina clutched the notes in her hand. "I've prepared a few words to rally the workers to finish the project on time."

Edward stepped closer. His whisper dusted her cheek. "Be careful you don't disrespect the men with your words."

Irritation brushed away the calm she'd been grasping for. The temptation to stick out her tongue in response died when she scanned the crowd. Once again, responsibility laid its heavy weight on her heart. She'd asked—no, told—Edward she would prefer to rally the troops. He hadn't argued. Yet he expected her to make a blunder. Typical man. She straightened her crinkled notes.

Edward followed her to the platform in the front. This gathering spot had not been in her design but had become necessary until a proper meeting place was constructed.

"Ladies and gentlemen." She shouted to be heard over the surrounding conversations. The crowd quieted and gave her their attention. "I'm sure you're aware, we are no longer employing anyone not fully a part of this endeavor. We do not have time to police bad behavior while everyone else works. I want to thank everyone here for their hard work. Without you, we would not have come this far."

Murmurs of appreciation rippled through the crowd.

"We're a few weeks behind on the main street construction, but I am confident in your ability to finish the task." She smiled and scanned the crowd. "All of you make me proud. In the future, I will be seeking your advice on things I am … ignorant of … as in the case of cattle and horses." Chuckles filtered through the group. Angelina's face warmed, and she cleared her throat. "I apologize for any inconvenience that caused. Now let's go over our new schedule." Angelina finished her update. "Are there any questions?"

"How come the mercantile isn't on the schedule until next month?" Elmira Blake shouted from the back of the gathering.

Clyde, Elmira's husband, added, "We need all the dry goods stored in a building. If we get a heavy rain again, it'll ruin supplies."

His crossed arms and *I-dare-you-to answer-me* look set her hackles up. Folding her own arms, she glared at him. "What business do you recommend we exchange?" Angelina regretted her question the moment it passed her lips.

"Well, the telegraph and post office can manage in a tent. And we don't need a newspaper office right away." Mr. Blake's quick response made it obvious he'd been thinking on it for a while.

Mrs. Collins, the newspaper editor, came to the front. "I understand your concern, Mr. Blake, but an additional month isn't terrible. I have four children, and I'll be sharing the living space above the newspaper with Mrs. Swenson, who also has four children, thus reducing my original living space by half. The children's needs should come before yours."

"Hester, you're not the only one with children." Sarah McCray stepped beside Mrs. Collins. "I have six girls. The livery isn't slated for construction until next month either. I think if you're speaking of children, then the McCrays' building should be this week as well."

"Then there's them slant eyes." Mr. Blake sneered. "Why are they on the main street instead of white people?"

Angelina fumed. Locating the laundry on the corner near the men's dormitory made perfect sense. How dare he say such wicked things about the Ho family?

A din of voices rose around her. What was wrong with these people? This was her project, her town. But who was she to talk? She'd wasted a day of construction moving her rail car for her own comfort.

The correct response escaped her.

"I suggest we take a vote." Edward's voice carried above the murmurs of discontent.

Angelina stared at Edward. How dare he usurp her authority again?

"That's a blame fool idea," one of the Irish laborers shouted. "Boss, you have a sound schedule for the building of the town. Why change it now?"

"Mr. Hennessey, you hired on in exchange for land. You don't live in town. You got no say," Mrs. Hardy shouted.

"Begging your pardon, I been dividing me time between my homestead and building your fine town. I even helped with the cattle. My time is precious, and I don't kin to you telling me I have no say."

Voices rose again, and verbal battle lines were drawn.

Edward tried shouting above the din. Then, catching Rev. Asbury's attention, he nodded. The minister executed his shrill whistle, bringing silence.

The crowd refocused on Edward. "Before summer's end, barring unforeseen interruptions, this first phase of the project, the main street, will be completed—although some single women will share shop space until their storefronts located on the cross street are completed next year. In my opinion, if we build by family needs, the patchwork of building sites will make us further behind schedule. We need to make sure everyone is housed before bad weather hits. It's much more efficient to move to the next lot than move around helter-skelter. However, I can promise that if we take a vote and it calls for us to build based on family size, we will work hard to get those buildings up before winter."

To Angelina's amazement, faces calmed, and many nodded in agreement. Would she ever receive this kind of respect?

George McCray joined his wife and pulled her close. "I believe we all are a bit weary of living in tents. But this is what we signed on for. According to our contract, we promised to work together to build this town. This is the first time I've had a real chance to follow me dream without someone sayin' I'm worthless because I'm Irish. Let's not let our own personal needs muck everything up." Turning to Mr. Ho, he nodded. "I do not hold your race against you. I know what it's like to be looked down on. As for me and mine, we bear you no ill will."

The two men shook hands.

"I think a vote is a grand idea, and my brother agrees," Emily Jameson called out. She and her blacksmith-brother had set up shop under a large tree and shared a tent while they waited for his building to be completed. "Let me add from an accountant's standpoint that it will cost more to change the plan. We've already lost money because of the time wasted by the mule skinners."

A few more women voiced their objections on both sides of the issue, mainly having to do with the needs of their children.

Finally, Angelina quelled her frustration and gave the group a warm smile. "I am as concerned for the children as you are. Even though this is my design and my timeline, I will yield to your wishes. Tomorrow ... your vote will be honored."

"Hear, hear," a woman shouted from the back. Applause broke out, then everyone dispersed to go back to work.

Edward touched her arm. "You've gained their respect." The

kindness in his expression melted the ire she still harbored over his taking over the meeting.

Angelina shrugged, then tugged her waistcoat back in place. "I hope you're right. And I hope they vote to leave well enough alone." She shook her head. "After all I've done to raise the funds, give them the wonderful opportunity for a better life, and get them here safely …" Her words sounded petty when spoken aloud. So much like her father. "I'm sorry. That was mean-spirited of me."

"Let's pray God turns their hearts in our favor." Edward's reverent tone stopped a sarcastic remark regarding God's intervention from tripping off her tongue.

Angelina's heart warmed as history was made. The women stood in line with the men to cast their ballots in front of the doctor's office. At noon in the dining hall, the results were announced by Rev. Asbury.

"First, I'll say the vote was close. But the final tally fell in favor of continuing with Miss DuBois' timeline. Thank you to Miss DuBois for her very democratic way of dealing with this issue." Applause followed. "Let us commit one hundred percent to work diligently on each building without complaint. The Scripture reminds us, the hands of the diligent are made rich."

Would their diligent efforts complete the project on time now that the labor force was reduced?

Murmurs from the back of the room drifted forward. "We know who plans on getting rich."

Her neck warmed. *How dare they assume I'm the only beneficiary?* She crossed her arms to hold in her desire to argue.

Rev. Asbury smiled, then his voice took on a mock growl. "And I'll not mention what happens to the lazy and the dissenter."

The crowd quieted.

Angelina glanced at Edward across the table. "I'm so relieved."

"As am I." Edward's smile thawed her anxiety.

Caroline and Madeline joined them. Madeline spread jam on her bread. "I'll admit there were lots of persuasive talks in the women's dormitory."

Caroline chimed in. "We actually had a debate on the subject. You won hands down, Angelina."

"Do tell." The idea that the women had decided in her favor after a logical discussion pleased her. Men accused women all too often of being too emotional and weak-minded to make important decisions.

"Beth, Elmira, and Sarah took the opposing side while Lucinda, Madeline, and I took your side. We presented the facts again." The shine in the young woman's eyes matched the excitement in her voice.

"Yes," Madeline added. "One thing I learned from my former husband is the art of persuasion. So I encouraged the ladies to prove to the men that they could make a sound decision without consulting their husbands. I painted a picture of half-completed structures and crying children in the dead of winter."

"So the emotional appeal won the vote." Angelina's disappointed sigh wasn't lost on her friends.

"The vote went your way, Angelina." Madeline patted her hand. "I've learned to take my victories any way I can."

"Be grateful we don't have a saloon." Edward snorted. "Men have come to blows during an election after a few drinks and a difference of opinion."

Angelina paused from slicing her steak and shook her head. "I've never understood men's need to settle things with their fists."

"I agree, it is much easier to ruin your opponent with unfounded gossip." Madeline delivered the statement in a deadpan tone.

No one laughed at her remark. Angelina recalled how Chicago's social circles had branded her friend.

"Let's hope neither fists nor tongues add fuel to the dissent that is still among us." Edward's grim expression took away Angelina's appetite.

The human part of her equation didn't balance well with the structural part in bringing Resolve from paper to reality.

CHAPTER 15

The gray clouds hung low to the ground, mirroring the frustration that lay like a rock in Angelina's heart. Construction moved along too slow. After four months, the foundations were finally set for the cross street. They were still a week behind schedule finishing the main thoroughfare, and underlying ill will from those who resented the result of the voting had raised its ugly head. Now she had to deal with Mrs. Hardy, who'd spit in Mr. Hennessey's food during lunch and stomped Mrs. Ho's fresh laundry in the mud.

Teresa joined Angelina in the train car. "I'm shocked Mrs. Hardy would do such things."

Angelina sighed. "It's apparent I'm not a very good judge of character."

A knock at the door, and Edward walked in, removing his hat. "Angelina, if you don't mind …"

She signaled to a chair across from her. The morning light streaked his blond hair and accented his strong jaw. Staring at Edward's handsome face was not on the agenda for the day. She cleared her throat. "I assume you're here to give Mr. Hardy moral support."

"No, I'm here to stand in solidarity with you. Mrs. Hardy's behavior is reprehensible."

Angelina tapped her foot, letting some of the irritation flow away with the action. "I hate it. But I intend to send them packing, so others know I'm serious." A rooster crowed as if in agreement, and they all laughed. Edward's chuckle made his eyes twinkle and her heart calm.

Teresa shifted in her chair. "I think I have a better solution."

Angelina respected the wisdom of her friend. "I'm listening."

She patted Angelina's hand, then shared the details of her plan.

A gentle knock announced the arrival of the Hardys. Edward opened the door, and the couple came in. Mr. Hardy stood with cap in hand, while Mrs. Hardy scowled and crossed her arms.

"Please don't send us away." The poor man came close to kneeling at Angelina's feet as he pled. "My wife is a bit high-strung. But we got nowhere to go if you do." He swayed on his feet, crushing his cap in his hand.

Angelina nodded to Teresa, grateful for the alternate plan.

"According to your contract, Mrs. Hardy, Miss DuBois is within her legal rights to ask you to leave. You promised to behave in a civilized manner, and yet your treatment of Mr. Hennessey and the Ho family are in clear violation." Teresa's commanding presence and authoritative words wiped the scowl off the woman's face. She stared at her worn shoes. "What do you have to say for yourself?"

"I'm sorry I behaved like a child." She looked them each in the eyes, holding Angelina's the longest. "Please, for the sake of my children ..." Swallowing, she turned her head away.

The angst on the fool-hearted woman's face touched Angelina. "I suppose everyone is entitled to a second chance." She offered the olive branch and gauged the response.

Mrs. Hardy's head jerked up, and relief flooded her face. "Thank you."

"You do understand ..." Teresa pinned her with a stare. "There are consequences for breaking the agreed-upon rules. You are banned from kitchen duty because everyone will wonder if you'll spit in their food. Instead, you will be the sole provider of cow chips to fuel the cookstove for a month."

The horror on Mrs. Hardy's face showed the wisdom in Teresa's plan.

"And you will spend one day a week helping in the Ho's laundry for the next month."

Mr. Hardy patted his wife's arm. "I'll help you, dear."

"No, you will not." Teresa's stern tone brought a blush to his face. "If I find out you or anyone in your family or a friend helps Mrs. Hardy, I will make collecting cow chips her permanent job for an entire year. Is that understood?"

The couple paled and nodded.

"Good, then you may go." Angelina dismissed them with a gesture toward the door.

They turned liked whipped pups and departed the train car.

"Teresa, your wisdom is invaluable." Angelina smiled at her friend. "Do you think she'll complete her punishment?"

"If she wants to stay, she will." Edward rose to leave. "I know Bill—he won't allow himself to be embarrassed again." He turned. "Tell me, Teresa, why picking up cow chips?"

"Madeline and Bridget were complaining about her refusal to touch the cow chips. If the stove needed fueling, they had to do it."

"Such a clever woman, indeed." Edward's approving smile brought a blush to Teresa's face, the sincere compliment from a man regarding her mind a long overdue prize. "Ladies, if you'll excuse me." He smiled at Angelina as he doffed his hat and left the train car.

Her hands touched her warming cheeks. His kindness to her friends went further to recommend him than kindness to herself.

A few hours later, Edward was meeting with Lucinda Graves when Angelina called to him from the entrance of the office tent. "What on earth? Edward, come here." Panic laced her voice.

He stepped outside with Lucinda, who took one look at the low, dirty cloud racing toward them in the gloomy afternoon sky and shouted, "Grab your rifles."

"What?" Terror echoed in Angelina's question as she stared at the surveyor.

"Buffalo." Lucinda cocked her rifle. "If we don't turn them, they'll wreak havoc on the town."

"Angelina." Edward grabbed her arm and gave it a little shake. "Get the women and children in the dormitory." She stared at him, face pale. "Now."

She nodded, lifted her skirt, and ran, shouting toward the dormitories.

Lucinda raced toward the corral. Rifle in hand, Edward followed, sounding the alarm. "Stampede! Buffalo!"

Already the earth shook as the sound of thundering hooves rumbled their way.

Lucinda grabbed the mane of the closest horse in the corral and heaved herself on its back. "We got to turn them, now." Her shrieked command got the nearby men moving.

As several of them mounted up and followed her toward the stampede, Gabe Clark shouted, "Don't shoot into the herd."

Fear pounded a rhythm through Edward. Lucinda's experience and knowledge of the massive beasts brought no argument from the men as to who was in charge. Per her instructions, the men started shouting and shooting into the air. Gabe led a group to flank the animals. The bison began to turn until a few fools shot into the herd.

Now, buffalo stood their ground, prepared to charge.

"Get behind them and keep shouting." Lucinda shot in the air again.

Some bison began to move, but others resisted with bellows. The few men experienced with lassos whipped them toward the furry monsters to distract them. The herd shifted direction.

Bill Hardy fell off his horse only feet from the disgruntled herd. His scream caught Edward's attention. Terror pushed him forward. Shamus also galloped toward the fallen man. Edward extended his hand, and Mr. Hardy grabbed it while Shamus snagged the back of his pants and heaved him upward. Bill scrambled behind Edward, and they raced away from the herd. Mr. Hardy's empty mount darted toward the corral.

Lucinda continued to shout instructions. Gabe's group rounded the strays away from town. After what felt like hours, the bison turned, leaving a rutted path north toward the river.

A train whistle blew in the distance.

"Do ye think it be stupid fools shooting at the beasties from the train that caused the stampede?" Shamus scowled as he wiped sweat from his brow with his shirt sleeve.

Edward kept his eyes on the departing buffalo as Bill Harding dismounted and walked with wobbly legs back to town. "The railroad encourages it, to keep the herds off the tracks. But I've seen a few men open their windows and shoot at herds nowhere near the tracks."

Once the danger passed, Lucinda rounded on a few men. "We could have turned them far quicker if you fools hadn't shot into the herd. Did you not hear Gabe tell you not to?" The men hung their heads as she glared at them. "If my father had acted as you men have, I wouldn't be here to tell the tale. If not for Mr. Pritchard's and Mr. O'Malley's quick action, Mrs. Hardy would be a widow." She turned her mount toward town.

Silence followed her rant, and the men scanned the scene. The grass was mashed, and holes pitted the ground where hooves had broken through earth.

Edward left off further lectures. "Well, I see we have three dead buffalo. Any of you know how to butcher them?" For now, action needed to be taken. The buffalo meat would go a long way to feed the town, saving the cattle to slaughter as winter approached.

"Mr. Pritchard, I can handle that." Gabe pulled his horse next to him. "My father was a buffalo hunter. Give me a half a dozen men, and I'll show them what's needed. Leave the skinning to me. Buffalo fat works as well as whale oil, and you'll never find a warmer blanket than a buffalo hide."

"Excellent, Gabe." Stifling a groan, Edward shifted on his horse's bare back. Good might come of this yet.

"Maybe a few men can scout near the railroad track and see if there's any other dead bison."

"I'll get a few of me men, and we'll ride out to see." Shamus

123

slid from his mount and rubbed his backside. "After we saddle our horses."

Edward left Gabe and five volunteers to the task and headed back to the corral as additional men fetched wagons to haul the meat and hides back to town. The day was well spent when they returned. Some of the women prepared the bison meat for smoking and salting, while the others prepared a fine meal. The children begged to hear about their adventure. By the time the meat was secured and everyone had eaten, dusk set in.

"We rise with the sun tomorrow, men. We have to make up for lost time." Edward's words were met with weary but firm nods of ascent.

Angelina found Lucinda watching the sunset near her unfinished women's dorm. "That was a brave thing you did today. I couldn't have done it."

"It's survival. They would have destroyed the town and killed or injured people." Lucinda adjusted her hat. "Men shooting buffalo out the windows of the trains is cowardly. We are wasting a perfectly good food source."

"Well, I'd not eaten it before."

"We may not eat it too much longer." Lucinda's eyes glistened. "My father said the government would eliminate the buffalo so they could control the Indians."

"But I've read articles in the *Chicago Times* saying the savages need to be controlled. They massacre innocent settlers." Angelina wrapped her arms around her middle, quelling a shiver.

"The newspaper hardly depicts the whole story." Lucinda stared over the prairie as the sun began its descent. "The white settlers take their land, destroy their hunting grounds. The Indian agents cheat them and allow them to starve." She faced Angelina. "If someone decided that all the land your ancestors had given you should be theirs, wouldn't you fight for it?"

Hiram's face appeared in Angelina's mind. As a child, she'd felt helpless when he took her things and destroyed them. Her mother had encouraged her to be kind to the wayward lad. But Hiram's whole goal in life … take all that was hers. "Yes, I would fight to keep my inheritance."

Lucinda walked away, leaving Angelina to ponder her words. The wind still held the smell of the stampede as the sun's final rays disappeared over the horizon, ending a day full of unexpected things. Angelina headed toward her train car, passing a few worksites. Building this town and living a simpler life stretched her preconceived notions about many things to their limits.

Edward wiped sweat from his brow with his handkerchief while the sound of hammers and saws drummed a fierce cadence. The men had been working since the crack of dawn. Voices of foremen shouting orders filled the humid air. Edward paused and dipped his handkerchief in a nearby bucket of water and wrapped it around his neck. He'd grown familiar with the oppressive summer heat while fighting the war in the blasted Southern states. He'd seen too many soldiers sicken from lack of water marching in the summer heat, so now, he made sure buckets of water were placed around the work areas. His kerchief dried quickly, and a heavy layer of sweat coated him once again.

Soon they would need to cease work and continue later, working until dark. Edward looked forward to the few hours out of the sun. Some men napped while the wood craftsmen worked on trim or furniture in shady spots.

Lucinda shouted down from a roof trestle she straddled. "Agnes, bring me more nails."

The woman nodded and headed up a ladder with a bucket. She wore a split skirt rather than trousers. Agnes and the others Lucinda had brought along to help kept pace with the men. Edward had tried to refuse their help, but the women surprised him daily with their diligence and fine work.

"Mr. Pritchard, may I speak with ye?" Shamus called as he approached. The two stepped away from the workers. "I spotted a group of redskins heading this way."

"Fetch Miss Graves. We'll need a translator." He scowled at Shamus. "Don't let her hear you call them redskins."

Shamus nodded, and a blush covered his cheeks. "I'm grateful Miss Graves is still here with us."

Edward left in search of Angelina. He'd rather leave Angelina here in town, safe. But there was no way she'd stay behind. Keeping her safe by his side was his only alternative. Why couldn't she leave these sorts of encounters to the men? Then again, without Lucinda, this would be even harder. *Lord, protect us.*

Edward and Lucinda brought four saddled horses from the corral as Angelina and Shamus joined them. Lucinda gave them instructions. "Edward, you go forward while Angelina follows behind. They will expect a male leader." She raised her hand, not allowing Angelina to object. "We don't want them confused."

Angelina remained silent, twirling a loose tendril of hair, and sighed. "I don't wish to endanger anyone." She placed her derringer in her skirt pocket, then glared at Lucinda. "Don't you dare tell me to go out there unarmed."

"Fine. Follow my lead. Could be friend or foe." Lucinda turned to Shamus. "Hang back just behind us and keep watch."

They mounted their horses and rode out. Anxiety rolled through Edward. He shook it off and straightened in the saddle, heading toward the group of mounted Indians moving toward the outskirts of Resolve. Angelina was as pale as the spots on her horse. Shamus wore the expression that put fear in the laborers, his rifle clenched in one hand. As Edward drew closer, he stifled his surprise. Three women, a few children, and four youths made up the contingent of Indians. One youth swayed, then righted himself.

Lucinda dismounted. There was a lot of chatter once she approached, and then a tall woman with a ruby necklace and a beaded buckskin gave Lucinda a hug. The surveyor spoke over her shoulder. "These are White Dove's sisters, Red Bird and Standing Doe." She touched the necklace with reverence. "Red Bird still wears the necklace my father gave her."

"White Dove was her stepmother," Edward explained to the others.

Angelina's fear-filled face relaxed as she dismounted.

Edward dismounted and stood next to Lucinda. Red Bird held his gaze. "Welcome to Resolve." He hesitated to extend his hand in greeting in case it would offend.

Lucinda's translation continued far longer than his greeting. "I told them you were the chief and wish them no harm." She nodded, and Red Bird shook Edward's hand. He noted the same youth swaying on his horse. How long had they been out hunting?

Angelina stepped forward and shook their hands, and Lucinda translated her greeting.

"Red Bird wants to know if you are Edward's squaw." Lucinda's playful glint wasn't lost on them.

"Of course not." Angelina's beet-red face needed no translation.

Edward held back a chuckle. It was a shame, really. The natives would not accept her leadership any better than most men did in the white culture.

Red Bird was animated as she rattled on in her native language, her tone more agitated now that the formalities were done.

Lucinda continued to translate. "They were out hunting. The boys were tracking game when some white settlers began shooting at them."

The same youth he'd noticed before fell from his pony, blood flowing from his side. Battle scenes flooded Edward's mind. For a moment, he was frozen in time, hearing the screams of the dying, the smell of death embedded in his brain forever.

Angelina's scream jarred Edward out of his stupor.

He removed his shirt as he ran to the boy, calling behind him to Shamus. "Tell Dr. Potter we're bringing him a patient." Shamus kicked his horse and galloped away. "Lucinda, help me."

Edward tore his shirt into strips and bandaged the wound. Then he helped the lad back on his horse. The Indians rode slowly along with them toward Resolve. People stopped to stare at the group as they headed toward the infirmary.

Shamus met them at the doctor's office and carried the injured brave inside. Red Bird trailed behind him, matching his steps as if Shamus might harm the boy at any moment. Was she that afraid of whites, or was this her son? Lucinda, Angelina, and Edward escorted the others to the waiting room.

Noting the Indians' gaunt appearances, Edward whispered to Lucinda. "Can you take them to the dining hall?"

"They'll not leave the boy's side until they know he is well. Besides, they don't trust us."

Angelina's eyes glistened. "I am so sorry this happened."

Edward rubbed his chin. "What if we bring food here?"

"They won't eat. Not until they know he is well. Hunger is a way of life for them." Lucinda smiled at the children, then lowered her voice. "My stepmother told me that, as a child, she learned to go without and not complain."

Edward gave her a tight smile. "I'm grateful you are still with us, Miss Graves."

"I can't imagine how we would have managed things without you." Angelina touched Lucinda's shoulder. "The boy might have died."

Edward drew near Angelina. "Let's leave Dr. and Mrs. Potter to tend the boy."

Angelina nodded and placed her hand on his arm. "Let's head to the dining tent and collect some food for them. Perhaps they won't eat now, but they can take it with them. It's the least we can do."

Lucinda followed them out. "I promised Gabe I'd tell him what happened. Then I'm heading back to Red Bird. She understands English but doesn't speak it well. I don't want her to be afraid."

Timothy Morgan and McCray's brother Arnold came riding

fast into town. Edward and the ladies stopped in the middle of the street near the livery. Arnold slid from his horse and started shouting, "Indians attacked us."

"What are you bellowin' about?" George McCray ran out of the livery and approached his brother, who repeated his declaration.

Arnold's panicked expression turned into anger. "I said we'd been attacked by Indians."

"How many were there?" Edward frowned.

Morgan answered. "At least a dozen. I shot one, and they ran off like the vermin they are."

"So you're to blame for this," Angelina snapped as she stepped within inches of the man's face. "You would shoot a boy trying to feed his family?"

Lucinda nudged Angelina to the side, and her anger released itself with a hard slap to Morgan's face.

Morgan grabbed her hand. "Have you lost your mind, woman? No one slaps me and gets away with it. Settle yourself before I take my belt to you."

Edward stepped between them. "If I ever hear of you taking a belt to any woman, including your wife, you'll answer to me."

Morgan scowled but dropped Lucinda's hand.

"The Kiowa you claimed attacked you are here. Come with me, and I'll show you the women and children you shot at." Lucinda pointed toward the doctor's office, then marched in that direction.

Arnold blustered. "It's a trap. There are more hiding nearby."

"Settle down, Arnold. Shamus said they be alone." George crossed his arms. "You always act like the world is ending when there be a bit of trouble."

Whispering in Lucinda's ear, Angelina drew the surveyor away. "We'll fetch food," she murmured to Edward. He nodded. He and George took Arnold and Timothy to the clinic, where Arnold viewed the group in the waiting room through the front window.

Angelina, Lucinda, and Gabe arrived with baskets of food. Brushing past the men, they entered and offered the contents to the

Kiowa. The children glanced at their mother before taking biscuits from the basket.

When Angelina came back out alone, Morgan scowled at her. "Since when do we feed the likes of them?"

"Since you shot the boy who does the hunting." She glared back at him.

"We got mares ready to foal any time. What were ye doing at the Morgans' in the middle of the day?" George leaned closer to his brother and took a whiff. "You smell like a brewery. Leave it to you to find alcohol in a dry town. Should be interesting to see you explain it to your wife."

Arnold stared at the floor. Edward appreciated George dealing with his brother.

Angelina planted her hands on her hips and glowered at Tim Morgan. "You signed a contract not to drink."

"When I've been asked to work in town, I don't." His voice rose. "What I do on my own land is none of your business." He glared, fisting his hands as if looking for a chance to bring her down a peg or two.

Gabe Clark edged in front of the man, his jaw taut and eyes fierce. "Lucinda told me you threatened to beat her." He rolled up his sleeves. "You can take that up with me."

Morgan appeared to debate with himself, his fists flexing. Edward touched his arm and shook his head.

As Morgan retreated to the side of the porch. George followed Arnold, employing a calming tone with his brother. "If you'd been sober, you'd be seeing this whole situation differently." He turned back to Morgan. "Perhaps you can hold your liquor, but my brother can't."

Edward joined the McCrays and spoke quietly to Morgan. "Miss DuBois gave you this opportunity. If you don't appreciate it, then it can be taken away. If you can take an occasional drink and meet the requirements of proving up your land, then fine. But when it impairs your judgment so that you fire on women and children, then that, sir, is a problem that affects everyone."

Morgan nodded, his face flaming as he pushed his hat down on his head. He stared at Edward, his eyes throwing accusations, but without another word, he strode off the porch in the direction of the livery.

"Oh, what a mess." Angelina groaned, running her hand over her face. She nodded to Edward and George. "Thank you, gentlemen, for defusing a tense situation."

The sound of hooves heading out of town could be heard a few moments later.

Lucinda stepped out onto the porch and closed the door behind her. "The doctor wants to keep Walking Deer overnight, but Red Bird said they will take him and care for him themselves."

Angelina blew out a breath. "Little wonder, with the welcome they've received?"

Lucinda gave a grim nod. "They'll make a travois and haul him to camp."

Edward frowned. "Where is their camp?"

"I persuaded her to camp near the river so Dr. Potter can check on Walking Deer a few more times." Lucinda turned to Gabe. "I told her you would bring her buffalo meat in payment for her son being shot. In a few days, they will return to their people."

Unease stirred in Edward's gut. They didn't need trouble with the natives. Perhaps sharing the meat would help forge an alliance with the Kiowa.

The dining hall hummed with argumentative conversation regarding the Kiowas' presence. Edward's dinner soured in his stomach as he defended the Indians against those who wished them harm.

"My father was scalped by a raiding party." A woman at an adjoining table went on to tell every disgusting detail.

Another man pointed his finger at his tablemate. "An Injun saved me from drowning, then nursed me back to health. They ain't all bad."

*Amen*s and accusations continued to volley about the dining hall.

"That's enough." Edward's voice carried, and the room quieted. "We obviously have different views of the Indians. For the remainder of the evening, can we find something less distasteful to discuss?"

"Hear, hear." Rev. Asbury rose. "While you all finish your meal, I'll read a few passages of Scripture." He pulled a small Bible from his pocket and began. "'Trust in the Lord with all your heart ...'"

He chose several passages that directed the diners to the Heavenly Father and His peace. The sound of utensils on plates formed the backdrop to his reading. Much better.

Edward left his half-eaten food and went for a walk, his mind dissecting the day's events. Heading toward the riverbank north of town, he found Angelina sitting under a tree. "It's not safe for a woman to be out alone."

Angelina gasped. "Must you sneak up on me? Announce yourself as you approach. I might have shot you."

His eyes widened, for indeed, she gripped her derringer. "I hope you can hit your target."

"There are two bullets, so I have a second chance." She resettled on the blanket she'd placed under the tree.

"May I sit?"

She smiled her consent.

"Trying day." Edward lowered himself onto the end of the blanket. Crickets chattered and mosquitoes buzzed. He swatted them away.

"A trying few weeks." Angelina sighed and tore a piece of grass into shreds. "I never anticipated buffalo stampedes and Indians."

"How did you not consider the Indians and the buffalo?" Edward slapped his arm as another insect droned nearby. "You appear to have figured every other contingency into your grand plan."

"You mock me." Angelina stared at the sunset, expression firming.

"Not at all." The sky pinked as he searched for the right response. "Just an observation."

Angelina leaned back against the tree, looking small and

vulnerable. "My focus seems short-sighted now." A mosquito buzzed near her face and met its demise on her cheek. She wiped it off, not missing a beat as she added, "Lack of resources was more on my mind than Indians."

"That's understandable." Edward wanted to lift some of the sadness from her. As much as she irritated him with her bossy ways, this mood was far harder to handle.

"I suppose I was naïve enough to assume the Indians would be dealt with by the army. And I had no idea buffalo would be a danger. I did read about the atrocities befalling the settlers. Because there were peace treaties made, I assumed—now that Kansas was a state—it was more civilized." She glanced toward the river. A gentle wind blew hair in her face, and she wiped it away. "Foolish, indeed."

"The papers report only one side of things." The damp night air nestled around them as another mosquito met its demise on Edward's shirt. "The Indians have lived here for thousands of years. I can understand why they're not too happy with us claiming their land." Edward scooted closer to Angelina.

She tucked her skirt around her as if creating a barrier. "After all this, I worry that my project will fail because everyone leaves out of fear."

"They're a hardy lot. And like the Bible says, don't borrow worry from tomorrow." He got to his feet and reached out his hand. She took it, rose, and then folded the blanket.

"The Bible really says such a thing? Being free of worry would be wonderful." She headed toward town, and he followed.

Her lack of faith created a chasm between them. Until the gap was closed, how could he hope for more than friendship?

CHAPTER 16

August 1869

A tap on the door woke Angelina. Bridget entered with a covered basket. "I stopped by earlier, but ye looked so peaceful I couldna disturb ye."

She grabbed her robe and pushed her hair from her face. "I was tireder than I thought. Good thing it's Sunday. I can justify my laziness. But you must never let me sleep in again. There is too much to do."

Bridget set the basket of pastries before her. She smiled as she poured from the hot water kettle on the stove into the china teapot and added her tea ball to steep. "This will be the last time I serve ye breakfast."

Angelina stared at her friend, then sighed.

"Yes, indeed, you will be too busy with your bakery and restaurant to continue to serve as my maid." A pang of regret ached in her heart. "I'll miss the best personal maid I've ever had."

"I'm not leaving the country." She chuckled. "Ye can come and eat at me establishment any time. But I will miss our private conversations."

Angelina touched Bridget's arm as she poured. "My door is always open for a chat."

Bridget rested the teapot back on the table and hugged Angelina. "Thank ye for all you've done to make my life better. Thank ye for helping me follow my dream."

Angelina smiled as tears flowed. By the time Bridget poured herself a cup and sat beside her, Angelina had found her voice. "You've taught me so many things. I'm no longer a slave to society's expectations of the wealthy. I can dress myself, do my hair, and even wash it with no assistance. I know to some it might sound petty. But for me, it's freeing. I'm in charge of the town. I ought to oversee my personal needs too. Now if I could only make a cup of tea as fine as yours."

"I want to be sure you invite me to tea often, so I'll hold back that instruction." Bridget winked and took a pastry. "I've been smelling me own creations all morning and saved the tasting to share with you. Tomorrow I open me doors for the first time."

"I'll pop by later today and see all the work Shamus and Mr. Clark have done. I heard from Edward that the interior matches the finest restaurants in New York."

"Ach, 'tis a bit of blarney. But it is grander than I ever imagined. I sewed me own linens, and Mr. Clark is a true craftsman. His filigree trim makes things look wondrous indeed. Shamus has learned so much and wants to make furniture as nice for his girls."

"Wonderful. I am so amazed at Mr. Clark's talent. He's a wood craftsman and knows how to butcher buffalo too."

"Shamus said Gabe's a man of many talents. He learned furniture-making from his uncle before the war." Bridget dabbed her mouth with her napkin. "After the war, he'd lost both his wife and mother, God rest their souls." She shook her head. "Poor Teddy."

Angelina pushed away the sad thought. So many had suffered similar losses. "Well, I'm glad he chose to join us. I suspect we'll be attending a wedding soon."

"Aye, Lucinda Graves is smitten. She's been wearing dresses more often."

"I'm glad—otherwise, she would have left us to farm her land much earlier, and we'd have sorely misjudged that nice Kiowa family."

Lucinda's kin had left after a few days without incident. Some of the townsfolk had gone out to the camp out of curiosity, bearing small gifts. She'd not taken the time to get to know them. Building a house was easier than building friendships.

Bridget rose and started cleaning up the meal. "I need to get back to the bakery. I've got to get pies in the oven, and the bread should be ready to shape into loaves. I'll leave the rest of these pastries for your breakfast tomorrow."

"Perfect." Angelina drew a reticent breath. "Eva Blake will start as my personal maid tomorrow."

"I'm sure Elmira will be glad to have her daughter associated with you."

"Mary Price has worked with her in the dining tent kitchen and recommended her."

Bridget paused to press a reassuring touch to her shoulder. "Eva is a bonnie lass. A little direction from you, and she could become a fine lady."

"Thank you for your vote of confidence. Honestly, my final decision rested in appeasing Elmira and her husband when they lost the vote for changing the construction timeline."

"Well, it worked. They be singing your praises and bragging about Eva's opportunity." Bridget gave her a hug. "I'm off."

Angelina closed the door behind her friend. After dressing, she took up her embroidery and watched the town through her window for most of the morning. Dark clouds formed in the distance, spreading high and wide as they moved toward the river. Women called their children in from play. Angelina set her needlework aside and closed her windows. Storms on the prairie seemed more ominous than those in a large city. "A rainy day is a good excuse for a nap." Sunday was the only day Angelina allowed herself the luxury.

"Mr. Pritchard, a tornado!" Gabe rushed into Edward's office, Lucinda on his heels.

"What?" Edward rose from his desk as the tent undulated with the increasing wind. His mind raced to find calm.

Lucinda pulled back the tent flap. "Look to the west."

A tiny funnel stretched from the earth to the blackening clouds.

The strong wind tore at signage and tents.

"What do we do?" As he threw ledgers into his haversack, Edward's heart pounded. He'd not experienced a tornado, and the stories of survivors raised the hair on his neck. Hail began to pelt the canvas of the tent.

Lucinda gestured for him to follow. "I'll keep the children secure in the school. A soddie should be sturdy enough. Everyone else needs to find a place low to the ground. The dormitories have root cellars out back."

"The mercantile also has a cellar," Gabe yelled over the howling wind. "But we need to hurry."

Women shrieked and small children wailed in their mothers' arms as they scurried past Edward toward safety. Mr. Blake jerked open the cellar door behind the mercantile, and a few men threw out boxes to make room for people. The cellar doors behind the dormitories were already closed. A few men dove under porches.

Edward scanned the area as the hail stung his skin. Where were Angelina and Caroline? Surely, they'd been among the first to seek shelter in the cellar of the women's dorm. There was no time to check.

Neighing and lowing carried on the rising wind. Edward dashed toward George McCray, who was struggling to open the corral gates.

"It be best to let them run. They can sense these things," McCray explained. Edward helped him shoo the livestock from the pen, then they raced toward the mercantile's cellar door.

They stumbled down the stairs, and Bill Hardy and Clyde Blake struggled to close the doors. Edward grabbed a broom from the corner and slid it through the inside door handles. Candlelight cast an eerie glow from the corner as people huddled close together.

Loud pings overhead awakened Angelina, her head still foggy from her nap. She peered out the window as the hail beat harder. When she opened the door to get a better look, the train car rocked and pitched her out onto the ground. She tried to rise, but the wind slammed her down, and the rain soaked her to the skin. Damp hair wrapped around her face. Groping about, she grabbed onto the footing of the porch. Fear gripped her spine, producing strength to hang on tighter. Roaring winds drowned out her screams. A weight slammed into her head. Blackness prevailed.

Edward covered his ears as a loud roar went overhead. The screams of women and children didn't muffle it. The ringing in his ears died with the sudden silence. The gentle whimpers of the children echoed the cry of fear he held in check. Waiting. Listening.

"Is it over?" a small girl asked.

Edward removed the broom, and the men shoved the cellar door open. They helped the women and children step over the debris of twisted wood and the shattered contents of the crates left outside. He struggled for a full breath as he climbed out and took in the devastation.

The roof of the men's dormitory lay in pieces on the ground, snapped like kindling over a knee. The women's dormitory had lost the back wall. Bridget's bakery had half a sign and the front window was shattered, and the tree the blacksmith forge sat under had been uprooted.

Clyde shouted from the front door of the mercantile. "The blacksmith's anvil smashed clean through the roof, the ceiling, and the counter."

"Anyone hurt?" Edward asked.

"No, thank God." Clyde hugged his wife as his children joined him on the porch.

Edward peeked inside the few remaining tents, now shredded, for any injured. Empty, thank God. He continued through the debris-covered street toward the women's dorm, keeping an eye out for any wounded. Flashes of battle-weary men clinging to one another shadowed the sight of men and women coming out of hiding, calling family names. Lucinda and Madeline brought the children to their parents. The soddie had indeed stayed intact.

Gabe's son Teddy ran to his father as Edward approached. "Miss Lucinda nailed the door shut and pushed desks in front of it. We all huddled near the far wall. Then a roaring noise like twenty mountain lions made me cover my ears. All the girls cried and screamed. Some of the boys too. But not me, Pa. I stayed calm like you taught me. But I was awful scared."

Gabe hugged his son and then kissed Lucinda on the lips. "You're Teddy's hero. Guess I need to marry you to keep us both safe. Would you do me the honor, Lucinda?"

Tears streamed down the couple's faces, as they hugged the boy between them.

Edward didn't catch her answer, but the additional kisses told him she'd accepted. A close call with death could make people more grateful for what they had. Heart thudding a heavy rhythm, he searched an approaching group of women. "Caroline?"

His sister broke free, ran into his open arms, and sobbed.

"I'm so glad you're safe." As he smoothed her hair, she hiccupped and hugged him again.

Bridget called from her shop. "Would you believe the coffeepot stayed on the stove? Come on over if you need a cup to fortify ye." Mr. Hennessey and Michael and Emily Jameson headed her way.

Caroline shook her head. "A full coffeepot and a lit stove were spared, while the front window is shattered and her tables are lying out here."

Edward wrapped his arm around her and scanned the area. "By the looks of the street, the same random destruction took place with every business. For the most part, the buildings are still standing."

Shamus carried his daughters in his arms as his wife leaned on him. Others shouted for joy as family members crawled out of their hidey holes under porches. The roof would have to be replaced on the laundry, but the happy chatter of Chinese told Edward the Hos had all come through unscathed.

Everyone began sorting through debris. Dr. and Mrs. Potter

walked among the gathering crowd to check for injuries. A few horses wandered back into town, and several chickens squawked from roofs and porches.

Looking toward the end of Smithton Avenue, Edward could see clear to the river. "No." A lump caught in his throat. Angelina's train car was gone, the platform it rested on a shattered heap of broken and bent wood. He took off running. "Help! I need help."

Gabe, Shamus, and George McCray joined him. Without a word, the men searched the rubble. Caroline, Bridget, Teresa, and Lucinda lent a hand, calling Angelina's name.

Edward jumped when Gabe shouted, "Here." He pulled a broken section of the platform away. Soon the men were pitching debris. Angelina lay unconscious on the ground, a bloody gash on her head. Her ashen face sent fear through him. Edward squatted down and pushed loose strands of hair from her face. Blood covered his fingers. *Please God, don't let her die.*

Dr. Potter nudged people out of the way and knelt beside Angelina. "She's got a pulse, but her breathing is shallow." He nodded to his wife.

Mrs. Potter wrapped Angelina in a blanket, and Edward tenderly deposited her on the stretcher the couple had brought. His heart in his throat, he followed as Gabe and McCray carried her toward the clinic.

Angelina's head pounded as she struggled to open her eyes. A bit of white cloth blocked the vision in her left eye. Turning her head slowly, she saw a bedraggled Eddie, his shirt dirty and rumpled and whiskers covering his chin. A relieved smile broke out on his face.

He stepped to the door and shouted. "Doc, she's awake." Then he came back to her side.

Her parched voice squeaked. "Water."

Bustling in, Dr. Potter tucked his hand under her head and placed a glass to her lips.

She took a sip. "Thank you. What happened?"

"A tornado." Edward's worried expression pricked her heart.

"Was anyone killed?" She'd heard of the 1855 tornado that touched down in Chicago and only damaged one home, but lives had been lost.

"Mr. Paulson."

"Oh my. Such a sweet gentleman." Her mind wrestled with the information. His poor son, Fred, must be heartbroken. And who else could now help market Resolve the way he would've? Tears choked her voice. "Dear man. Was he in town?"

"No, the tornado's path hit a few homesteads too." Edward's tired eyes glistened with the sad news. "We had his funeral yesterday."

Dr. Potter checked her pulse. "Thank God there were no other casualties, just a few bumps and bruises."

"Wait. Yesterday?" Angelina frowned.

"Miss DuBois, you've been in and out of consciousness for three days. You'd been knocked out by storm debris."

She placed her hand on her pounding head. "What about the town?"

"The town will recover." Edward stroked her cheek. "We're all worried about you."

Dr. Potter laid a cold hand on her forehead. She shivered. "Sorry." He pulled the blanket over her shoulders. "I've been monitoring you closely and believe you're on the mend."

"I need to get up. There is so much to do." Angelina struggled with the bedclothes, but dizziness seized her, and she lay back down.

"Whether you agree or not, I can handle everything until you're well. I'll come by every day with a report." The touch of Edward's hand with his reassuring tone went a long way to calm her.

"You promise?" Her eyes drooped, and her head hurt trying to process his answer.

Three weeks later

"Boss, we found Miss DuBois' train car about five miles east of here." Shamus held out a piece of lace curtain.

Edward took the lace, his chest tightening. How close Angelina had come to flying along with the train car. He gripped it, thanking the Lord that hers wasn't the first grave in the cemetery.

He'd kept his promise to report daily on repairs to Angelina as she recovered from her injuries. Edward looked up the street toward the clinic. After three weeks of bed rest, she sat in a chair on the clinic porch and visited with the townsfolk.

"When I told her the train car was gone, she took it in stride." They both had been advised by Dr. Potter to share things with her a bit at a time. Yesterday when Angelina had talked about returning to her home, he had had no choice but to tell her the truth. She'd turned away, wiped her face, then flashed him a faint smile.

"Took ye long enough to get up the nerve." Shamus chuckled. "Ye might be a wee bit scared of her."

"Enough of that." Edward took the good-natured teasing.

"If she hadna been thrown free of the car, she'd have not survived." Shamus' observation knotted Edward's stomach.

"Anything salvageable? Bringing her some of her belongings should lift her spirits."

"The car is twisted down the middle. What things of hers we could free from the rubble, we hauled back to town in the wagons." Shamus walked him out to a wagon to have a look.

The stove appeared in surprisingly good shape. He wasn't so sure about her clothing. There was an assortment of soggy books and chipped china. The knot in his stomach tightened more at the thought of almost losing her.

"Gabe hauled the other wagon with her furniture behind the men's dormitory. He wanted to see if any of it could be repaired. Ach, it looks fit for the rubbish heap to me. Gabe sees it different."

"Well, I guess I'll have to tell her." Edward sighed. "I've kept the worst of the town's damage from her."

"I'm glad ye volunteered to reveal the whole truth." Shamus smiled. "But ye did the right thing holding back the worst of it until now. She'd have tried to jump out of bed to fix the mess herself."

Edward wasn't looking forward to her scowl, but it couldn't be helped. When she knew the full extent of the damage, she'd understand his motive. Or maybe not. But that might not be all bad, for her to get her fighting spirit up. He rather missed going toe to toe with her.

"Where do you want me to take her things?" Shamus handed him a necklace. "Found this."

"Ask Bridget." Edward rubbed his thumb over the locket, cleaning the dirt away, then pocketed it.

Shamus climbed aboard the wagon and headed to Bridget's bakery. The vehicle passed the clinic as Edward approached the porch.

"Is that my stove?" Angelina leaned forward to get a better look as the wagon rumbled by.

"Sure is, but there's not much else to speak of." Edward climbed the porch steps. She appeared smaller, more fragile in her recovery.

"Well, it's a small price to pay for my life, I suppose." A deep sigh escaped her lips. Edward hurt with her as she processed another disappointment.

"God surely had His hand on you." He took the chair next to her.

"And the Almighty will not keep me from finishing this project." Angelina's mouth formed a stubborn, straight line.

Edward kept his smile in check. Angelina was returning to her old self. "What makes you think God is against it? He spared your life."

"The Bible is opposed to forward-thinking women. It demands women be under the thumb of men."

"I've never seen those passages." Edward leaned toward her. "Can you point them out to me?"

"I've never bothered to read the Bible."

"My, for a woman who gathers the facts before making a

decision, you certainly surprise me." Edward crossed one leg over the other and shook his head.

"Fine. Send Rev. Asbury here with a Bible, and I'll read it. Then I'll have the ammunition I need to make my case." Angelina fanned herself as perspiration dotted her face.

"Making a case is my job." Teresa stepped on the porch with some wildflowers.

"Where on earth did you get those?" Angelina took them from her, pressed her nose in the bouquet, and breathed deeply. A smile replaced her sour mood.

"Red Bird stopped by to help Lucinda with her wedding. She thought you might enjoy these." Teresa took the remaining chair.

"That's right. Lucinda's wedding is soon." Angelina sighed.

"In two days, in front of the women's dormitory." Teresa pulled a fan from her sleeve.

Edward picked up a flower that had fallen to the floor and tucked it back in the bouquet. Angelina stroked the flowers at the same moment. Their hands touched, and a wave of want washed over him. He sat back in his chair, schooling his feelings. "You'll ride in a wagon to the ceremony. And if you're not too tired, you can stay for the festivities afterward."

"At last, a foray beyond the clinic." Angelina clapped her hands, and her eyes sparkled like a child's at a birthday party. She smiled at Teresa. "Would you mind seeing if any of my dresses are presentable? Shamus just drove by with my things from the train car on a wagon." Then she turned her gaze on Edward. "I assume I'll need to find a new home?"

Edward wasn't ready to see the joy wash from her face. He handed her the locket.

"Oh! It belonged to my mother." Angelina pressed the heart-shaped pendant to her lips. "I'm glad it survived."

"May I?" Edward rose. She held out the locket, and he fastened it around her neck. Tendrils of loose hair feathered across his hand as it rested on her shoulders for a moment after the locket was secured.

Then he took his seat again. "Do you want to order a new train car?"

"No." A tinge of fear widened her pupils, and her voice softened. "I think I'll move into the women's dormitory. There are fewer residents now that the shops are built."

"You can have the Hardys' home." Teresa pointed across the street to the large, two-story structure. "They decided to move to Indiana to live with her sister. A millinery shop didn't hold much appeal after the tornado."

Angelina assessed the abandoned building with its few sagging shutters and front steps that listed to the left. "Can we fix the porch?"

"How about we put my law office in the shop, and we share the living quarters? It has three bedrooms. The Hardys had a large family."

Angelina brightened at Teresa's suggestion. "Eva can have the third bedroom if she still wants to be my maid. I prefer a live-in."

Teresa patted her hand. "It will be great fun having my dearest friend as a housemate."

Angelina nodded. "This will work nicely. My home isn't scheduled to be built until after the town is finished." A faraway look came over her. "By then, I hope for thriving commerce and perhaps a train depot."

Edward cleared his throat. "Angelina, the depot may have to wait. There is still damage that hasn't been repaired." He waited for the scowl that didn't come.

"I thought you weren't telling me the whole truth. You have a propensity for lying if you think it's in my best interest." Angelina shook her head.

Edward's neck warmed under his collar. He leaned back in his chair and frowned. "In my defense, I was following the doctor's orders to dole out information only as you gained your strength."

"Apparently, he didn't tell his wife the same. Mrs. Potter and Elmira Blake kept me abreast of the devastation." Angelina laughed. "Don't look so surprised. It's what they do best."

"Gossip." Edward wanted to strangle the hens.

"And you do know, Caroline has been bringing me the latest *Resolve Chronicle*. I've read the last few this past week. Mrs. Collins always prints the truth." Another barb aimed at him. It was obvious her mind had recovered before her body. Edward could almost see her brain whirring into action. The excitement brought color to her otherwise pale complexion. Now that she felt well enough, she'd redirect the project, and he would take second chair once again. If not for her near-death experience, he might be irked at the reversal. Instead, he thanked God she was her old self. "If we have a crew on repairs and the others on new construction, we can get back on schedule. I need that train depot. A few more feet of track and ... what has taken so long to finish the tracks?"

"We've had our hands full with completing phase one. Then we had all the repairs since the tornado. Finding out what's delaying the completion of the track to Resolve was not a high priority."

"I'll telegraph Griffin right away to make inquiry." Teresa rose. "I suspect Hiram is at it again."

"Ask Griffin to contact Mr. Hayes. I want to be sure Hiram hasn't tried to sell the tracks and easement out from under me." Angelina pursed her lips.

Edward shook his head. "Our latest calamities have not been of his making. Perhaps he's given up." He wouldn't put anything past her cousin, but Angelina was already anxious to get the town back in order without another worry.

"Hiram is a sneak. He waited a whole year to get even with a friend for winning his month's allowance at cards. When Lawrence least expected it, Hiram tripped him on the stairs and put him in the hospital."

Teresa paused with her hand on the porch post. "Surely, that was an accident."

"Oh no, he confessed the whole thing—or rather, gloated about it to me. Then he threatened bodily harm if I told anyone." Angelina's voice trembled as if she were reliving the event.

Edward refrained from reaching out to comfort her. "Well, it's a bit of a challenge to knock you down the stairs hundreds of miles from here."

"Even so, I think I'll have Teresa telegraph her friend Allen Pinkerton to investigate." As if reading his mind, Angelina reached for his hand and squeezed it. "I'd rather be vigilant than be caught by surprise."

CHAPTER 17

Edward helped Hennessey carry the bunting-decorated archway in front of the women's dormitory. Wildflower arrangements dotted a makeshift platform. Wagonloads of people had been arriving for the last hour to attend the wedding. The laughter of children filled the air as they played tag, waiting for the festivities to begin.

"Does it seem like a small turnout?"

Hennessey positioned the archway. "You betcha. Fear of being caught in town by another tornado kept my neighbors home. I offered to bring their daughters with me, but their pa wasn't keen on it."

"I'll wager they were less keen on you than fear of another tornado."

Edward's tease was met with a playful shoulder bump.

"Leaves me more options of young ladies to dance with later." Hennessey grinned.

Together, they shoved the archway into the ground. Hennessey wiped sweat from his brow before taking up his hammer to nail support posts on the back. "Did you hear three homestead families packed up and went back east? The tornado scared 'em, for sure."

"It's to be expected." Truth be told, Edward had feared many more than three would pull up stakes and leave.

"Their plats of land are being offered up after the wedding to any interested party." Hennessey nodded toward the bank. "Once we're done here, I'm gettin' me a loan. The O'Toole property backs up to mine. Sign my John Hancock, and I'll double my property." He gathered his tools. "I'll see ya at the wedding."

The festooned area had begun to fill with guests. The mixture of accents as people greeted one another reminded Edward that Resolve was populated by many from Europe. Surely, crossing the Atlantic and living in tenements made these people more determined despite the prospect of another tornado.

Edward walked through town on his way to his room to change clothes.

The mercantile, the seamstress, and the laundry were doing a crisp business. The single men needed clean clothes for the reception dance. A few of the men had already expressed an interest in finding a wife amongst the single women of Resolve. His mind went to Angelina, and he dismissed it out of hand. She'd made her preference clear—spinsterhood.

"How do I look?" Angelina stared at the ugly scar on the left side of her forehead near the hairline. Teresa and Eva joined her at the mirror.

"It's healed nicely," Eva offered. "I'll ask my mother for her salve. It lightens scars."

"Thank you. I'll try anything. This is horrible." Angelina felt foolish grieving over the mark on her forehead after almost dying. The stark reminder shadowed her resolve to move forward.

"Consider it a badge of courage." Teresa patted her shoulder. "This is a great undertaking. It proclaims to the world you've given Resolve your all."

Angelina smiled. "What would I do without your silver-lining speeches?"

"Mope about and whine, I suppose." Teresa gave her a silly grin.

"You know me so well," Angelina said. "Everyone in town has surely seen my bandaged forehead by now."

"Miss DuBois, a careful application of cosmetics may cover it." Eva held a jar in her hand.

"I've never been one to use cosmetics in excess. They can be more torture than a corset. A friend of mine endured hair being sewn on her eyelids to give her thicker lashes. And I don't want to look like I am wearing flour on my face. It can get pasty and gloppy when one perspires." Angelina examined her scar more closely in the mirror. "What do you think, Teresa?"

"Let's get you dressed. An attractive dress can draw attention from your scar." Teresa spread the gown over her bed.

Angelina scowled. "I've worked so hard to be independent, and now I'm back to having others dress me."

"This gown requires assistance. There are too many buttons down the back, and the flounce may get tangled." Teresa smoothed the skirt. "Even independent women need a bit of help now and then. We can't do everything ourselves."

A knock at the front door sent Eva downstairs. Angelina stroked the green silk. Mary Price had worked a miracle with her needles since yesterday to restore the gown. The new creation had additional lace at the collar and cuffs after Mary had removed any torn fabric.

"What a lovely dress," Bridget purred as she swept in. "I'm here to fix yer hair. And Eva told me about the scar. I think I can cover most of it."

"That's encouraging." Angelina sat in a chair, and Bridget went to work.

Eva pressed Angelina's gown and searched through what jewelry hadn't flown away with the tornado. "You have these pearls." The necklace hung from her right hand. "Or these emeralds?" The more ornate jewels dangled from her left hand.

"Do I have the earrings to match either?" She'd had a bad habit of throwing her earrings helter-skelter into one of three jewelry boxes. Only one survived the tornado. Who would find the lost jewels? Or were they embedded in a rock somewhere, as Clyde's fancy watch fob had been?

Eva sorted through the jewelry box. "One of each, I'm afraid."

"Lassie, check for the silver dangle ones." Bridget added hairpins to Angelina's coiffure.

"I found the pair." Eva smiled.

"Let's get this dress on, Miss DuBois, then we'll see what's needed." Bridget and Teresa slipped it over her shoulders. The gown fell nicely over her loosely tied corset and her modest bustle.

"Before you peek, put on the earrings." Bridget waited for Angelina to put the bobbles on her ears. "Now turn toward the mirror."

Angelina stared. Only the tiniest bit of the scar showed. Bridget had curled several strands of her hair and arranged them around her face. A curly mass rested on top of her head, surrounded by multiple braids that drew attention away from her forehead. The silver earrings provided the perfect complement.

"Elegant simplicity." Teresa nodded her approval.

A few minutes later, Angelina filled her lungs with fresh air as she took a seat behind the bride's family. She admired Red Bird and her sister's beautifully beaded buckskin dresses. Their children wore buckskin and cotton shirts. How much more practical their clothing seemed than the layers of undergarments and the uncomfortable bustle Angelina endured in the heat of the day.

Gabe stood near the front with Shamus as best man and Rev. Asbury in his clerical collar front and center. He gave a nod, and Arnold McCray played the wedding march on his hand organ. Caroline came down the aisle dressed in a yellow frock. Lucinda wore a beaded buckskin. Her hair flowed to her waist with two small braids lifting from her temple and joining at the back. The joyful looks between the couple brought tears to Angelina's eyes.

"That's her stepmother's wedding dress," Teresa offered in a whisper. "So lovely."

Angelina caught sight of Edward seated on the groom's side. He was clean shaven, with his hair freshly trimmed. His black suit sported a burgundy vest and a black silk cravat under his stiff collar. His attire could hold a candle to any fine gentleman's in her former social circles in Chicago. She gave him a subdued smile, and he returned it.

Edward shook Gabe's hand and gave Lucinda a kiss on the cheek as he walked through the receiving line. "Gabe is a lucky man."

"Thank you, Mr. Pritchard. I am the lucky one. No ... blessed. Gabriel and Teddy are truly a gift from God." The glow on her face brought wishful thoughts. Would God bless him with such a gift? He moved from the receiving line and spied Angelina sitting in a chair with a view of the festivities. As he approached, his heart beat a cadence of admiration. "Your gown is as lovely as you are."

"Thank you." Her radiant smile broke forth. "You look like the lord of the manor."

Edward's face warmed. "Miss O'Malley, Miss Shilling, you two are stunning as well."

"Thank you, sir. 'Tis one of Angelina's gowns." Bridget smoothed the front of the skirt.

"It appears you salvaged a few from your wrecked trunk." He sat beside Angelina.

"Mary says she can repair most of my gowns. She brought me many new serviceable dresses while I convalesced. Her new creations were a delightful daily distraction."

Strange, to listen to Angelina talk about fashion after months of discussing blueprints and deadlines. Her eyes sparkled with pleasure, making her seem more like a woman and less like his prickly boss.

"How kind of Miss Price." Edward faced forward, avoiding the depths of her eyes.

"After staring at those clinic walls for days, I suggested Mrs. Potter find artwork to decorate the room. I'll telegraph an artist I know in Chicago and ask her to send a few landscapes."

"Are you homesick for Chicago?" His stomach tightened. Did she regret giving up so much?

"No. Why would you think that?" Angelina's eyebrows collided in that cute way they did when she questioned something.

"I suppose landscapes of Chicago would make you less homesick."

"Oh, no." Her nose wrinkled. "Meadows and green pastures, perhaps a seascape. Patients need lots of details to stimulate the mind. My friend wanted to come, but she is confined to a wheelchair. She will be thrilled to have her work a part of Resolve."

"I imagine it would be a distraction for someone confined to bed." Edward recalled his two weeks in a ward recovering from pneumonia during the war. The daily monotony had been more tiring than the illness.

Lucinda and Gabe made their way to the food table. Rev. Asbury said a blessing, and people formed a line behind the newlyweds.

"May I escort you to the line?" He offered his arm to Angelina.

She nodded and tipped her head to the side, offering a sweet smile before taking his arm. A man could get used to this kind of attention.

"Good to see you out and about." Mrs. McCray waited behind a table filled with delectable food to serve them. "Which would you prefer, turkey or roast beef?"

"I haven't had turkey in ages. I'm anxious to see if it's as tender as Mr. Jones brags about it to be." Angelina accepted her plate, but her progress through the rest of the line was slow, as everyone stopped to inquire about her health.

Finally, Angelina found a seat at one of the makeshift tables between the McCray girls. Edward stifled a frown. The only other spot open was near George, far down the table.

Clyde launched into his plans for the mercantile. "I lost precious stock during the tornado when we had to throw crates in the yard to make room for people in my cellar. Figure if we build a large root cellar out back, we'll have more room if a tornado comes our way again. They say it's common around here."

"There should be root cellars near every building in town." Edward hated the thought of more people losing their lives.

Angelina's face lit up as she engaged with the McCray girls. Edward smiled as they burst into giggles. His first impression of her had been misdirected. She'd welcomed people outside her class into her heart. The women respected her, and it inspired them to keep going. Even the men admitted, out of her earshot, how much they appreciated the opportunity she'd given them.

Rev. Asbury whistled for attention. "Now that we've eaten our fill, Lucinda has asked me to invite you to join her and Gabriel in a wedding dance. It is in honor of her late father and stepmother, who began their life together in the same way."

Red Bird's son beat a drum and chanted while Lucinda, Gabe, and an animated Rev. Asbury joined the Kiowa in a circle.

"How delightful." Angelina left her seat, dragging Bridget along with her while the men sat with crossed arms. As they melded into the ring of dancers, Angelina nodded his way.

Edward rose and adjusted his waistcoat. "Well, gents, we *are* celebrating a wedding." With a smile, he stepped between Angelina and Bridget.

Angelina's small hand against his callused palm felt more natural than he'd care to admit. Soon Shamus took Bridget's hand, widening the circle with his wife and daughters. Several of the single men inserted themselves between the young ladies, grinning like schoolboys. George and his brother smiled at Red Bird's son and matched the drum's rhythm on the tabletop. The steps were simple and the rhythm easy to follow.

Angelina smiled up at Edward and tripped over her own feet. She giggled. He laughed, and they continued in the circle. The carefree spirit of the moment took away some heaviness of daily responsibilities. After a few more minutes, the dance ended, and the crowd broke out in applause. Edward escorted Angelina back to her seat.

"Thank you all for helping me remember my parents." Lucinda turned to the musicians. "Arnold, Rev. Asbury, shall we have a waltz?"

The men took up their violins. Lucinda joined Gabe as the music began, while other couples filled the makeshift dance floor. Angelina fanned her face, and Bridget handed her a glass of lemonade as she took a seat beside her. Edward hesitated. Should he ask Angelina to dance? The women had their heads together, speaking in low tones. He took it as his cue to mingle with the other guests.

After dancing with half a dozen single women in a variety of quadrilles and reels, Edward approached Teresa for another couples' dance, a schottische. "May I have this dance?"

"I'd be delighted." Teresa placed her hand on his shoulder. "But do tell me the real reason you asked me to dance."

"Is it not inappropriate for a man to dance too often with the same woman?"

"True. But no one would think less of you if you fancied one of them." Moving with the grace of a woman well-trained to dancing, Teresa glanced toward Angelina. Edward refused to follow her gaze. "Anyone come to mind?"

"No ma'am. A few of the ladies ... well ... they lack certain social graces." Edward's ear still tickled from his last dance partner's whisper as she pressed too close.

"So now you chose the older widowed and married women." Teresa teased.

"Exactly." Edward laughed as they moved around the floor.

"How about invalids?" Teresa signaled toward Angelina with her head. "She is a lovely dancer."

Angelina sat chatting with people while her foot tapped to the music.

"Your suggestion is duly noted." Edward's reluctance to ask Angelina defied his feelings.

The dance ended. Edward bowed to Teresa. He tugged his frockcoat to straighten it. Dancing to honor Lucinda's request with his hand in Angelina's was quite different from partnering in a couples' dance. Aha, the reverend was announcing another reel. But was she well enough for something so vigorous? He sighed, smoothed the front of his vest, and went to her.

"Angelina." Edward extended his hand. "Would you do me the honor of a dance?"

She rose. "Dr. Potter admonished me not to overdo, but I've been sitting here enjoying the music for ever so long." She tipped her head and grinned. "I'm thoroughly rested, mind you. So, yes, please."

They found their place in line. As they went through the series of stars, do-si-dos, and casting off, Angelina glowed. And Edward's heart sped every time their hands touched. When the music ended, he assessed her lovely face for signs of fatigue and asked, "Shall I take you to your chair?"

"Oh no." She took his hand as they join three other couples to dance a square. She held her own, and when the music slowed to a waltz, she waited for him to lead.

Edward didn't inquire about her health as they rotated in three-quarter time. Instead, he enjoyed the closeness of Angelina in his arms. Not needing to pass her off to other partners throughout the dance gave him more time to gaze into her eyes uninterrupted. Her lavender scent beckoned him to draw her close. He resisted, maintaining a proper distance. She missed a step and stumbled as the music ended. He held her close to steady her. "Are you tired?" They stayed that way a bit too long for polite society. She pulled away and fanned her face.

"As much as I'd like to dance until dawn, I must be an obedient patient and follow doctor's orders." Angelina took his offered elbow.

The distance from the dance floor to her chair was much too short. Edward smiled down at Angelina, tempted to kiss the hand he still held. "Would you like some refreshment?"

"I see Teddy is bringing me lemonade." Angelina removed her fingers from his. She smiled at the boy and kissed his cheek as she took the glass, bringing a red glow to his face. He ran back to his playmates, who elbowed him and laughed.

Edward chuckled.

"Would you fetch the reverend for me? I've been waiting to have a word with him. I know he loves playing his violin, but the poor man needs a break by now. George and Clyde are waiting to relieve him, anyway."

"My pleasure."

Angelina had graciously dismissed him with her request. Gracious or not, it still stung. *Let's not forget she is my boss.*

Angelina pulled her shawl over her shoulders as the temperature dropped with the evening breeze. The minister walked toward her through the crowd. He'd visited her often while she recovered, offering to pray without being pushy.

"Good evening, Hezekiah." He'd become her friend over the weeks of her recuperation. It seemed less awkward now to call him by his first name.

"Good evening, dear lady. It is so good to see you out and about. God has truly blessed you with a strong recovery."

He took her hand and bowed. "Edward said you wished to speak with me." He took the chair beside her. All her tablemates were on the dance floor.

"Yes, I've discovered I'm not as well informed concerning the Bible as I thought." She cleared her throat. "My father's pastor said God has no hand in the affairs of men, and we must work hard to prove ourselves worthy of the Almighty."

"I disagree. God cares very much about every aspect of our life. He even knows our thoughts." Hezekiah smiled.

His sincere expression contrasted the condescending, brow-lifting scowls of pastors her father had entertained for the obligatory clergy-to-Sunday-dinner quota. Once, she'd dared to ask a question, and the harsh response indicated the pastor's opinion was the only correct one.

Angelina tugged her shawl crisscross over her chest. "I see. I am also curious about the verses that command women to stay under the thumb of men."

"Angelina, my dear friend." Hezekiah sighed like a mother comforting her confused child. "Someone has been leading you down a false path." He patted her hand, then turned in his chair to face her. "God has given men the role of protector and provider. He's given women the role of overseeing everything else."

"Really? What about …"

"The thumb part?" Rev. Asbury chuckled. "God created woman so man would not be alone. He took man's rib, not his foot bone, so she walks beside him, not under his boot."

She loosened her grip on the shawl at the revelation.

"Men who demand obedience but haven't learned to love their wives as Christ loved the church are out of God's will."

"Interesting." Angelina had been too afraid to seek out the truth before.

Hezekiah leaned back in his chair. "As for single women, God will bring protectors and providers through their family or the church. And those men are not to put the women under their thumb but nurture their gifts and talents so they can serve the Lord."

"Hezekiah, this is new to me." Confusion over her experience and what the minister claimed as truth battled in her heart. "Do you have a Bible I may read? I'd like to study this for myself."

"I brought a crate full of Bibles and hymnals when I arrived. And if you'd allow me, I can give you a reading guide." His smile lit his whole face.

"That would be most appreciated." Angelina sensed his aunt was right—Hezekiah had the right heart for his profession. His ability to make people comfortable and appreciated would serve Resolve well.

He lowered his voice. "Since your confinement, you seem less skeptical of spiritual things."

"Almost dying has a part in it." She sighed. "When Edward remarked that God had spared me, my first reaction was not to let God beat me down. In truth, it took Edward asking me where I'd gotten such a faulty idea for me to admit I've never read the Bible." Angelina's face warmed.

"And now you want to gather the facts."

"Yes. But don't tell anyone. Please."

"Of course." Hezekiah nodded. "If you have questions, I'm at your disposal." He rose from his seat. "Shall we dance?"

"Ministers dance?" Angelina put her hand over her mouth and looked about to see if anyone heard her outburst.

"I enjoy a waltz now and again." He took her hand, and they joined the others.

As they swirled to the love ballad, Angelina caught a glimpse of Edward, watching them through the crowd. When the music ended, the minister escorted her back to her chair and joined some men near the refreshment table. She was content to sit and sip her lemonade. Angelina sensed a small crack in the armor around her independent spirit as she pondered the minister's words.

A week later

Edward waited in line to purchase a few staples at the mercantile. Many unfamiliar individuals gathered near the counter, exchanging cash for goods. A half hour later, Mrs. Blake greeted him. "I am sorry for the wait."

"Who are all these people?" Edward asked.

"They came from Flat Ridge, a good ten miles from here. They say I have a better selection than their grocer. And we have a doctor." She gave a nervous smile.

"Interesting." Edward took out his list. "Can you fill it? Seems like all these newcomers could cause you to run out of supplies. The needs of the town come first."

She nodded and scanned his list without looking up. "No problem." Another nervous smile from the proprietress set Edward on edge.

The mercantile worked on a credit system. The families' contracts promised credit in the mercantile with the hopes the credit lasted until their businesses were established. Angelina wanted to ensure no one was in want while they worked to make Resolve a success.

Clyde stepped beside his wife. "Don't forget the train tracks are repaired, and the depot is supposed to be finished soon." Then he leaned toward Edward and whispered. "Besides, with Miss DuBois' and Mrs. Shilling's connections, they can get whatever we need."

Clyde's assumption the ladies had unlimited reserves at his disposal irked him. "I assume you've spoken to them about this?" Until the Blakes owned the store outright, all additional purchases beyond the town's needs had to be approved by Angelina.

"Not yet." Clyde looked at his wife, then gave him his best customer-greeting smile. "I'm sure Miss DuBois will appreciate a little extra coin in her pocket."

Edward took his purchases and said nothing further. Heading back to his office, he debated about mentioning his conversation with Clyde to Angelina. He'd give him a chance to speak up first. No man needed to feel tattled on.

Edward now shared space with Teresa's law office. She received clients in the back room, which meant people traipsed through his office to hers, reminding him of the lack of privacy in the tent when he first arrived. He had just poured a fresh cup of coffee when a couple came in.

"We is lookin' for da ..." He spoke to his wife in German.

"Attorney," she added.

"I'll see if she's in her office." The woman needed her own secretary. And not him. At least, if Angelina were here, she could serve in that role. The doctor hadn't pronounced her well enough to work yet.

He knocked on the door, then opened it. Teresa stared out the window. "Mrs. Shilling, you have a couple here to see you."

"Thank you. Please send them in."

Edward opened the door wider, and the couple entered. Returning to his desk, he continued his task of drawing extra copies of the blueprints. One copy secured in his safe had not been blown away. Angelina had redrawn the original plans with some modifications since the tornado. A second copy would make it easier to carry one with him—unless Angelina woke up tomorrow with an epiphany and changed things again.

Another couple entered.

"I heard there's a lawyer abouts." The stocky man held a cigar between his teeth, his shirt stained and his boots dusty. His wife's clothes were clean but worn. She kept her head down, her bonnet covering her face.

"Take a seat. She's with someone."

They took chairs along the wall. The German couple emerged, and the man leapt to his feet. "Mueller, what are you doing here?"

The taller German man remained expressionless. "Like you." He tipped his hat and escorted his wife out of the building.

"I'll be switched. That dumb German got the jump on me." He stared at Teresa standing in the open door. "Tell that lawyer I want to see him. I'll pay double what Mueller did."

"The lawyer isn't taking any more clients." Teresa pursed her lips and crossed her arms. "I suggest you go to Abilene. There are several lawyers there."

"Surely, he ain't taking on that German." He puffed on his cigar. Smoke wafted toward Teresa. "I cain't understand him most times."

"The attorney is fluent in German." Teresa fanned the smoke away.

The man stomped out red-faced, his wife hurrying behind him.

"What was that all about?" Edward asked.

"According to Mr. Mueller, he has a rightful claim to his homestead. The Browns are squatting on their property, claiming they were there first. Mueller has all the legal paperwork. His deed is valid. Now, if the angry gentleman produces another deed, then we'll have to go before a judge to determine whose land it is."

"You're enjoying yourself."

"Yes, I am." Teresa's smile lit her eyes.

"When did you learn German? I thought French was the preferred language for females of means." Edward teased.

"I love language. I'm fluent in several. My late husband and I often traveled around Europe. But I learned German at my mother's knee. We spoke it at home. It is delightful to speak it again. The

Muellers are lovely people. I encouraged them to study English so no one would try to cheat them in the future."

"You may have more new clients. I saw lots of strangers in town. Clyde says they're from Flat Ridge. Apparently, we have better shopping and a doctor. Now it appears a lawyer is an advantage too."

"If you have a moment, I need to show you something." Teresa's joyous expression sobered. Edward followed her into her office. She retrieved some papers from her desk and handed them to him.

"What's this?"

"I've had a private investigator following Hiram DuBois since we came here. This is his report." Teresa crossed her arms. "Angelina didn't want to bother with it. She's happy to be far away from him. I, on the other hand, am less confident he won't try something."

Edward read through the report. "Hiram is trying to declare Angelina insane. How is that possible?"

"Did you not catch this paragraph?" Teresa tapped the paper.

"He's paying witnesses to testify regarding her mental state and has attempted to take over her bank accounts based on those statements." He skimmed the pages again. "It appears he's not been too successful in his goal."

"I've known Hiram for years. Robert DuBois adopted him when he was twelve, after his mother died. She was Robert's wife's sister. Hiram has never demonstrated the high moral character of the DuBoises. Over the years, his sneaky ways have become more refined. I received a letter from my butler, Griffin, informing me he attempted to contact my daughters."

"What?"

"He left a packet addressed to their eyes only at my home in Chicago. Hiram has no idea where they moved to after they married. I can't believe he thought Griffin would send it on without question." Teresa shook her head. "Griffin opened and read it. Hiram claims I've been seeing a doctor for ladies' nerves, and they need to intervene."

"I'm surprised Griffin opened it." He knew the man to be honest and trustworthy. But perhaps Teresa had directed him to monitor her correspondence.

Teresa rubbed her hand over her face. "Griffin caught Hiram, when he was fifteen, attempting to molest my eldest daughter when she was thirteen. Hiram's father, Robert DuBois, paid my husband handsomely to avoid a scandal. That's the only time I heard Griffin express his displeasure."

Righteous anger rolled through Edward. "I would say so. The scoundrel."

She fidgeted with the hem of her waistcoat and began to pace the room. "My husband took the money and banned Hiram and his parents from ever attending any social gathering our family attended. No one ever heard of it, including Angelina's family. Elizabeth, Hiram's mother, doted on him. Believed every lie that came out of his mouth—Robert too. After Hiram's father passed, Angelina's father took him in. He was seventeen. John did a lot for Hiram. Too much, in my opinion. And Hiram had John fooled as well." Teresa took the papers from Edward and placed the stack on her desk.

"If not for John's deathbed promise to Robert, Angelina would have inherited DuBois Architectural Interests." Teresa slid behind her desk and took a seat. "Now that Angelina's father is dead, Hiram is trying very hard to prove he deserves the respect of a DuBois and their fortune."

A chill crept down Edward's neck. "You think he won't be stopped."

She turned her chair and stared out the window. "I know he'll not give up. I hope I find out what his next move is before he executes his plan."

"Does Angelina know what is in this report?"

"Yes. When we received it in this morning's mail, she wanted to keep it between us. But I insisted on telling you. I was waiting for a discreet time. No one else in town needs to know. I trust you to use good judgment in keeping watch."

"I'll do my best." Edward wasn't sure what he could do to prevent action on Hiram's part, but he was certainly willing to try. "Thank you for trusting me with your concerns."

He went back to his desk, his coffee as cold as any ideas he might have to protect Angelina. He watched out the front window, worry nettling him. What if Hiram sent an imposter among the Flat Ridge residents? What would the motive be?

He took his cup and stepped out on the front porch. He stared up and down the street as he emptied the cold coffee on the dirt road. The dark liquid absorbed into the dry ground, leaving little evidence in moments. How would he identify a threat among all the strangers in town?

CHAPTER 18

Fingers curled through the handle of her flowered cloth valise, Angelina entered the newly finished newspaper office—the first stop on her to-do list now that she was back to work. The smell of ink and new construction tickled her nose. If not for her injury, she would have visited weeks ago.

Hester Collins looked up from her typesetting table and smiled. "Angelina, what a pleasure to see you looking so healthy." She came to the front counter, wiping the ink off her fingers on a rag she pulled from her apron pocket. "How can I help you today?"

"I want to discuss something with you and place an ad." Angelina noticed the clean appearance of the room, everything in place. Drying pages hung from a line in the back. "Is that tomorrow's paper?"

"I'm finishing typesetting the last page. We only have two pages this week. The papers from California and back east haven't arrived yet. Not even a telegram, so it's been a slow news week." Hester opened a portion of the countertop, making an entrance. "Please, come, let's have tea, and I'll grab paper and pencil."

Angelina sat at a small table in the corner while Hester prepared the teapot.

"I've been wanting to invite you to tea—although I envisioned it in my home upstairs."

"Perhaps another time." Angelina placed the valise on the floor at her feet and her bonnet on the chair next to her. "Your office space is wonderful. Someday I'd like you to explain to me about typesetting. Do you have everything you need now that you're moved from the tent office?"

"A few additional shelves would be nice. But Martin can build those after he comes next week."

"Martin is a good carpenter?"

Hester stood at a counter near a tiny stove in the opposite corner, arranging a tea service on a tray. "My late husband taught Martin how to build shelves and tables for typesetting. They won't be as fancy as Mr. Clark's work, but serviceable for my needs."

"Very good." Angelina sighed. "It's delightful to have some time off my feet. I've been checking in at each business to see if they need anything. I'm placing an order soon. If you need more ink or paper, now is the time. I'll telegraph my list to my suppliers tomorrow."

"I believe I'm fine, but I'll double-check." She crossed to the table. "Here we are." She placed a tray with the tea service and sweet bread on the table. "It's not much, Angelina."

"This looks delicious."

"My mother made sweet bread often. This loaf has raisins."

"Hester, where did you manage to find raisins?"

"I brought a large supply with me. I love them. Don't reveal my secret, or I'll feel obligated to share." A blush covered Hester's face.

"Your secret is safe with me." Angelina added cream and sugar to her tea. "I'd like your opinion on a women's society."

"Women's societies in general or having one here in Resolve?"

"I think Resolve could benefit from a women's club. Our goal is women running businesses. A club might put some backbone to it."

"You see a few spineless business owners, do you?" Hester took a bite of sweet bread.

"Yes. Some married women own their businesses in name only. I hate to see the opportunity I'm providing mistreated." Angelina ducked her head. She also hated being the strict schoolmarm scolding her charges.

Hester sipped her tea, then nodded. "Being a widow gives me a different perspective than you have as a single woman of means. I need to make this work. My family's livelihood rests on my shoulders. Because my husband relied on me to help in the shop, I can better run this business now." Hester set her cup down and stared at her ink-stained fingers. "Those who are married have relied on their husbands to provide, and now that they have the chance to fulfill their own dream, it's frightening. It's easier to let their husbands take charge. It hurts a man's ego to have his wife do the providing."

"I understand. I truly do." Angelina pushed a stray hair from her face. "I'm just as frightened. This is a chance to fulfill my dream too. A chance to prove women have brains and can accomplish great things." She stirred her cup mindlessly for a moment, gathering her thoughts. "The Jamesons have made it work. Granted, they are siblings. But society expects Michael to provide for Emily. Instead, they share the responsibilities of the blacksmith shop."

"I think Michael would have allowed Emily to run the business end even if he hadn't lost his voice." Hester added fresh tea to their cups. "He admits keeping the accounts is not his forte."

"That's what I mean. They make it a partnership." Angelina tapped the table with her fingers. "Mr. McCray's eldest daughter works side by side with him to learn the livery business. She wants to take it over one day. Another example of what I hoped would happen." Angelina tasted the sweet bread. "Oh my, Bridget will want your recipe."

"Well, she can't have it. Family secret." Hester chuckled. "Do you really expect the husbands to change?"

"It's disconcerting that I've worked so hard to bring my vision to reality, and husbands want to take over. I have no intention of losing investors' money because of poor management practices." Angelina placed her shaking hands in her lap. "That is the best reason I have for never marrying. Men think they must oversee everything, even if they aren't suited." Her collar warmed as memories of her own blunders convicted her of the pot calling the kettle black.

"Without getting into specifics, what are you concerned about?" Hester sliced more bread.

"I insisted the married women sign the contracts. This is a village of women. They are ultimately responsible for the success of their businesses or homesteads. This is the crucial part of my vision for Resolve. Women are smart and capable. Husbands need to partner with their wives. Work side by side like God intended." As she was learning, the Bible did have some helpful knowledge. "This way, the women should fulfill their contracts and own their businesses and farms outright, barring any natural disaster, of course."

"We have five years to pay back your investment into our businesses. Are you concerned some people will fail?"

Angelina nibbled on her slice of bread, giving her time to consider her words. She didn't want to sound bitter. "Yes. If the husbands don't work with their wives and respect their opinions and glean from their knowledge, they may fail. And I won't be bailing them out." Unlike what some people seemed to think, she didn't have endless resources at their disposal. "Some orders I received today are ill planned. A few of the merchants purchased things hoping Flat Ridge citizens will swoop in and buy them."

"Why aren't you refusing to approve their foolish orders?" Hester dabbed her mouth with her napkin.

"I don't want to be an ogre, but I plan to speak to a few people." Angelina took the last bite of bread, then stared out the window. "I wouldn't be concerned if the men would consult Edward before ordering. He has a good head for business on his shoulders." A handsome head too. She focused on Hester again. "Back to the subject of a women's club. I'd like to have a meeting once a week to educate women on good business practices."

"Will women's suffrage be part of the agenda?"

"That goes without saying." Angelina smiled and reached for her valise.

"How are you going to persuade the women that the club has value? We are all busy. Why would we want to make time to come?"

"Good questions. Here." Angelina pulled a sheet of paper from her valise. "I'm hoping my editorial encouraging them to take responsibility for their own futures will be a start."

Hester read through the page. "I see there's a veiled hint you may revoke some contracts for unwise business practices." She picked up her pencil. "May I reword this a little? This is my area of expertise." She winked at Angelina.

"By all means. And here is my ad announcing the meetings. I'd like to call it something besides a women's club, but all the ideas I had didn't capture my vision. My brain is still tired from my injury, so any suggestions you have are welcome."

"Give me a few days, and I'll get back to you with some ideas. There is no room for the ad in tomorrow's paper. You have the meeting set for two weeks from now. I can make a flyer to place on the announcement wall, then run the ad in the newspaper next week. I'll ask Caroline for ideas too. She's due back from her latest interview soon."

"How has Caroline been working out?"

"My girls adore her, and Henry has settled down now that an extra set of eyes is watching him, but I feel guilty having Caroline sit with the children when she is such an excellent reporter. I've asked Mrs. McCray if the children can go over and play with her daughters when Caroline is on assignment." She sighed. "It was so much easier when school was in session."

"Caroline is indeed a wonder." Angelina smiled. *That girl has her brother's fine work ethic and his stubborn determination.*

A summer wind whipped strands of Angelina's hair loose from under her hat. She tucked the stray strands behind her ear and tied the ribbon of her bonnet more securely as she headed down the street.

"Excuse me, madam." A portly stranger in an expensive suit greeted her. "I'm looking for a Mr. Edward Pritchard."

"Follow me, for I'm headed that way."

"Would you be Mrs. Pritchard?"

"No. I'm Miss Angelina DuBois. Mr. Pritchard works for me."

He gave her an odd look and remained silent until they entered the office. Edward sat at his desk, engrossed in the accounts.

"Mr. Pritchard, you have a visitor." Angelina stumbled as the man pushed ahead of her. *How rude.* She scowled at his back.

"Let me introduce myself." The man extended his hand. "I'm Oswald Quinn, and I'd like to rent one of your new buildings."

"Mr. Quinn." Edward shook his hand, then redirected his attention to Angelina. "Let me introduce Miss Angelina DuBois. She is the one you need to speak to."

"She really is your boss?" Mr. Quinn squirmed. "My apologies, Miss DuBois."

"A very competent one." Edward's praise warmed her cheeks. She looked away with the pretense of hanging up her bonnet. The boss should never be caught blushing like a schoolgirl.

"Take a seat." Edward pointed to the chair in front of his desk.

Mr. Quinn sat. Edward surrendered his chair behind his desk to Angelina, took her desk chair, and placed it next to their visitor.

Angelina crossed her arms and leaned forward. "Tell me why you would think we have any rental space."

"A few people in Flat Ridge told me about the fine town of Resolve. I thought I'd like to set up shop here."

"What kind of business do you run?" Angelina shook her head as Mr. Quinn pulled a cigar out of his pocket. "Not in my office, please."

He nodded and put the cigar away. "I run a saloon in Flat Ridge and want to open a second here."

Edward laughed. "You can't be serious."

Mr. Quinn stared at him. "I am." He cocked his head and smiled. "Every town needs a place where men can relax."

"This is a dry town." Edward glanced at Angelina. "Miss DuBois had it put in the town's charter. And Resolve is a town with businesses run by women."

Angelina's heart raced a bit as Edward defended her dream.

"Well, I could find a woman to run the saloon."

The man's off-handed remark galled Angelina. She laced her fingers on the desk in front of her. "Did you not understand Mr.

Pritchard? This is a dry town, and that means no spirits of any kind are allowed." She glared at the vile man and fought a tremor that whispered in her core when he leered.

Mr. Quinn addressed his next remark to Edward. "For the right price, I believe I can persuade you to make an exception." He pulled out a fat wallet.

Edward rose from his chair. "Again, whoever suggested you come here has left out some facts. Money would not persuade Miss DuBois. And neither can I be bought." He glowered at the man. "And don't even think of selling alcohol to the mercantile."

Angelina stood up as well. "We are all temperance-minded here. A saloon will never be a part of Resolve."

"I see. Sorry that I wasted your time." Mr. Quinn rose and stalked out, pulling the door closed a bit too hard.

Edward stepped outside and stared down the street. "He got on a horse and left. Good."

"It's hard to believe he didn't know our founding principles when articles about Resolve have spread across the country." Angelina pulled her desk chair back in place and sat sorting papers.

"Very peculiar, indeed." Edward tapped his pencil on his ledger. "I'll spread the word to keep a watch for that man. Something tells me we'll see him again."

Edward leaned back in his chair an hour or so later and assessed Angelina. He had enjoyed having her back in the office these past two weeks. Since Mr. Quinn had stomped out, they'd reworked the next leg of the project and had a heated discussion over her new designs. He appreciated her ability to stand her ground on her ideas, then set the discussion aside during breaks. "Shall we adjourn for luncheon?"

"Yes. I'm famished." She tied on her bonnet. Edward had been too distracted by the uninvited guest to notice it matched her dress. White feathers trimmed the bill. No matter how much she longed to be equal to men, she would always keep up with the latest fashions. Edward was grateful for that. He'd read recent accounts of a woman who insisted on wearing men's suits, including a top hat. "Mary ordered the feathers from a New York shop. Red is one of my favorite colors."

"It looks very nice on you." As they walked toward the restaurant, Edward glanced to his left. "Speaking of color ... who is that?"

A woman in a garish green and purple dress pranced around handing out flyers. She approached them and offered Edward one with a wink. He took one glance at the paper and frowned. "Miss, miss?" He left Angelina and strode after the woman.

"You cain't stop me passing out flyers." The woman's red hair had black roots, and her heavy cosmetics gave her a sensual look. As she leaned toward him, too much above the bodice came into view. He diverted his gaze.

"He can, and I can too." Angelina stepped beside Edward. He handed her the flyer. "There is no soliciting of this nature in Resolve. Liquor is not allowed within the city limits."

"Our establishment ain't in your city limits." She turned her attention back to Edward with a slow, sultry wink. "A man needs a drink now and again. We have a nightly show featuring dancing girls."

Edward wrenched the flyers from her hand. "This is a dry town. If I catch you or anyone from your saloon in this town again, I'll have you arrested." The idea of needing a sheriff crossed his mind for the first time. Shamus, perhaps? "Now leave and do not return."

She stalked away and mounted the same horse Mr. Quinn had ridden. Edward had noticed the three stockings and the white patch on the mare's chest. "Go on to lunch. I'll see if she left any flyers about."

"I'll help you." Angelina squeezed his arm.

Michael Jameson, the blacksmith, headed their way, a pile of handbills in his fist. He handed them over with a note. Edward read it out loud. "I think I found them all. She came to my shop and left

172

a pile. I followed behind her and collected what I could.'"

Angelina sighed. "Thank you, Mr. Jameson."

Edward appreciated the man's commitment to staying sober. "I'll hold a meeting and inform the men of the consequences of violating our covenant." Drunk laborers were the last thing he needed.

Michael scribbled something on a slip of paper, passed it to Angelina, then nodded a farewell and headed back to his shop.

Edward craned his neck. "What does it say?"

"Nice hat." Angelina laughed, and he joined in.

CHAPTER 19

One week later

The light breeze contrasted with the heavy rock in Edward's stomach. He found Shamus hammering the new bank sign over the door. "Shamus, I have something for you." He pulled a brass star from a box. "I ordered this for you. There's a few more if we ever need deputies."

"Mighty fine." Cromwell Hanson stopped mortaring the river stone trim to the bank wall to admire the star. "I know a few good men you could deputize."

"Let's hope it never comes to that." Shamus laid aside the hammer and took the star. "You know I'd rather be building alongside ye. We have so much yet to do, and Daisy isn't happy about this. I promised I'd not be fightin' again. She understands, but this must be temporary. It's the only way me wife will agree."

Edward gave a grim nod. "I understand." Hopefully, once the unsavory Flat Rock elements saw that they meant to uphold their laws in Resolve, things would settle down.

"She's been getting up early to help Bridget bake, so I'm escorting her to work. I can patrol a bit each morning afore I go home to see to the girls' breakfast, then maybe take a pass at lunch and after dinner."

"My wife would shoot me herself if I ever thought of being a law man." Cornwell's remark elicited a scowl from Shamus.

Edward pointed toward the unfinished wall, and the mason went back to work. He and Shamus stepped a few paces away.

Edward placed the box in his pocket. "You can keep working for me unless things get out of hand. Then patrolling could become your full-time occupation for a time."

"I'll do me best."

"I suppose we should have a swearing in, but there's no city council. Besides, everyone looks to you to keep the peace, anyway. We'll leave it with your promise to do your best." Edward shook his hand and pinned the badge on Shamus' shirt. "I promise this is temporary. We'll hire a sheriff if we must. Hopefully not until next year. That's when Angelina has scheduled town elections."

"She has every bitty detail planned, then?" Shamus wiped the star with the cuff of his sleeve.

"Yep, and every bitty detail keeps getting changed. Once she lets go of her need to control it all, things will go more smoothly." Edward looked out over the new construction.

"And when do ye think that'll be?"

"When it snows in July."

The men laughed.

"There you are." Angelina approached, the wind rustling her yellow floral dress.

Edward and Shamus looked up at the bank sign, expressions innocent. Edward attempted to direct her attention away from their conversation. "Hasn't Shamus done a fine job?"

"His work is always superior. Mr. Clark made the sign, I see. It's like a little bit of Chicago in the middle of Kansas." Angelina pointed to Shamus' shirt. "I see the star arrived. It looks very impressive. You'll make a fine sheriff."

"It be only temporary."

"I hope so." Her nose wrinkled. "Crime was not on my schedule."

Edward gave Shamus a knowing look.

Angelina sighed and crossed her arms. "Is something wrong?"

"No, n-not at all," Shamus stuttered.

"We were just wondering if it might snow in July." Edward glanced down at the ground to hide his smile.

"I don't believe you for a minute." Angelina laughed. "I'm off to double-check the work on the plumbing. Mr. Thomas has been doing a fine job. I've learned a lot about wells and pumps from him."

As she walked away, Shamus looked at Edward, and the two guffawed. Laughing relaxed the knot that had formed in Edward's chest at the prospect of a liquor-guzzling criminal element slinking into Resolve.

One week later
Edward enjoyed his second piece of Bridget's fine apple pie. When she'd mentioned she'd used the last of the apples, he'd bought the entire last pie.

"More coffee?" Jenny Blake, Eva's younger sister, poured his refill.

"Why aren't you working in your mother's store?"

"I do. But she doesn't pay me. I come and help on Fridays when Bridget has more customers. I'm saving for some books. There's no library in town, and I've read most every book anyone brought with them. I have several picked out and want to order them all at once. Momma refuses to buy them for me."

"You have a wise mother." Edward pointed his cup toward her before he took a sip.

She moved away from the table as the Sullivan twins approached with a small boy in tow.

"Take a seat, boys." Edward pointed to the three empty chairs at his table. "Lunch is on me."

The Sullivans flanked Edward, while the thin child sat across from him. The men had a week's growth of beard, and the boy could use a bath. Jenny brought them the lunch special and coffee. The three ate like starving men. Especially the boy.

Edward had sent the twins to Flat Ridge as spies. The men had been working their homestead the last two months without coming to town, so none of the people from the neighboring town would recognize them. He hadn't expected them to bring home a child.

"By the look of you two, you haven't been home. I went out there with a few men and finished your soddie and plowed your garden just as I promised. I'm impressed with how much you've gotten done in a short time." Edward's words were answered with smiles between bites.

"Dessert?" Jenny poured more coffee.

Sean spoke for them. "Bring whatever you got."

"Peach cobbler."

"Sounds fine." Derek wiped his mouth with his napkin. He watched her leave before giving his full attention to Edward. "I'm glad to be back in Resolve. Flat Ridge ain't a place for respectable people."

"Our father would have loved it there. They got two saloons, a dance hall, and a brothel," Sean added. "The mercantile is poorly stocked and dirty."

"Kids go begging in the street. Broke my heart." Derek shook his head. "We brought Ian home after we checked around. His ma died. She worked …" His pause told Edward it had been the brothel, and he didn't want to speak in front of the boy. "We could use the extra hands at the farm."

"The boy should be in school." Edward's remark received a scowl from the child.

"I don't need no school." Ian sat up. "I promised to work for the Sullivans."

"You can do that, boyo, and go to school when Miss Harper starts the new term in the fall. All the homestead children are home helping with the crops for now." Sean took off the lad's hat and set it aside. "A little education will give ya a great advantage."

The boy nodded and devoured the cobbler in a few bites.

"Miss Blake?" Derek got Jenny's attention. "Can you take Ian to your mother? Ask her to choose clothes the boy needs. Two sets for every day and one for Sunday. We'll be by later to collect it. Whatever he needs, have her deduct it from our credit. And if you could add a washtub to the bill, I'd appreciate it."

"I'll tell Bridget where I'm going." She nodded to Ian to follow.

"Add soap and towels too." Sean raised his voice and winked at Ian, who shuffled slowly behind Jenny. She spoke to Bridget, then grabbed the boy's hand to hurry him along.

Once the two were out the door, Derek got down to business, leaning toward Edward and lowering his voice. "Mr. Quinn set up a tent saloon about five miles out of town. He's got a few dance hall girls and the other kind available. We stopped by there and ordered drinks. Nasty rotgut." He wrinkled his nose. "I think he mixed turpentine in it."

Sean frowned. "We didn't want to look out of place by not drinking. They weren't offering food. We waited a while before asking the bartender why the tent saloon when there are saloons in Flat Ridge."

"He said Mr. Quinn hoped to grab some homesteaders and men from Resolve who didn't have time to go to Flat Ridge." Derek finished the tale and took his last bite of cobbler.

"I appreciate this, and you'll keep it to yourself." Edward rubbed his jaw.

They nodded, then looked at each other. Sean sighed. "A few men from Resolve were there. Hennessey, Curtis Sinclair, and a couple of farmers."

"They usually go to the Morgan place for his homemade brew. But there aren't any pretty ladies to entertain them there," Derek added. "Morgan is going to be angry once he finds out. He was making extra money selling to his guests."

"Did you buy it?"

"No sir. Our pa was a drunk." Sean balled his meaty fist on the table. "You won't find liquor on our place."

"We did go to Morgan's to play cards." Derek blushed with the admission. "He offered us liquor, and we drank only a little. And I'll say, it tasted like heaven compared to the rotgut the tent saloon sells."

"Morgan signed the temperance pact." Edward's jaw clenched as he held back angry words.

"No sir—his wife did. The homestead is hers. But Morgan was

a brewer by trade, and he works the land with a vengeance. He's plowed more sod than anyone else. At the end of the day, he likes a pint." Sean laid down his fork and nodded to Derek.

"You can't make a man change his ways. He's got to be willing." Derek placed his napkin on his empty dessert plate. "Miss DuBois said no liquor in Resolve, not on the homesteads."

"And not outside the town." Sean rose, and his brother followed. "We need to head home. Tomorrow we meet with Gabe. He has a big furniture order he needs our help with."

"Sean and I got a chance to make something of ourselves thanks to Miss DuBois, and we're happy to help any way we can." Derek pulled his cap from the table.

"If she wants a dry town, then that's what she'll have." Sean shook Edward's hand. "If you need us for anything else, let us know."

"We told Shamus as much before we left." Derek pulled on his cap, and Sean adjusted his new Stetson. "We need to collect our purchases at the mercantile and take that boy home for a bath and a comfortable bed."

Edward watched the twins leave. He'd never pegged them as the fatherly types. It was good to know these fine young men were loyal to Angelina. Loyalty would go a long way to preserving her dream, especially during hard times. His gut told him hard times were doomed to plague Resolve.

Angelina admired Edward as he stood at the front of the crowd in the men's dorm. His sleeves on his dingy white shirt were rolled up past his elbows, his hair rumpled from running his fingers through it. His determined looked mirrored her own. She gauged the crowd's response to Edward's announcement as she pressed her shaking hands together. Mrs. Collins had printed up the rules, and the Sullivan brothers passed them out. Murmurs floated around the gathering.

She hated the compromise. Edward had argued with her. How

she wished she could make all the men abstain from liquor. But diplomacy was needed, and she respected his gifting.

"You all signed a contract with Miss DuBois. No liquor in town was part of that. The rules restate what you signed. If you come to work with alcohol on your breath, you'll be fired on the spot. If you wander around town inebriated, you'll be fined fifty dollars. If your drinking leads to violence, you will be arrested and fired. Shamus is our acting sheriff, and I'm sure none of you care to pick a fight with him." Edward scanned the crowd. "I've seen the shoddy workmanship that results from workers with hangovers. I will not tolerate it. I've been giving you the weekend to rest. But if work keeps you out of trouble, then I'll go back to a seven-day workweek."

"Are you saying we can't drink in our own homes?" Hennessey bellowed from the back of the room.

"I'm saying don't come to work drunk. If you can drink and be stone-cold sober on Monday, then that is your business. But if you come to work with even a whiff of liquor on you, you're fired."

So much for diplomacy. Eddie appeared more irritated over the liquor issue than he expressed to her. *Why? Does he know something I don't?* She sighed. *He'll tell me soon enough.*

Angelina had relented her no-alcohol stance with the compromise partly because she'd been the victim of intolerance as a woman in a man's world. *I suppose if there are no saloons in Resolve, I'll not argue.*

The sound of men swearing under their breath as the meeting broke up soured her stomach. Now would be a good time to learn how to pray. Because it would take an act of God to change the rise of discontent.

CHAPTER 20

A week later

Edward hurried to meet Angelina at the well site. A smile pulled at his lips. When she'd called it a bit of Chicago amid the wilderness, she had not exaggerated.

The area around the well had been cleared away and paved with river rock. Mr. Thomas' crew had taken a few days lining the well and running the pipe. Then Cromwell's brick-laying skills had provided an elegant look. Even the pump house was brick. Cromwell's daughter, Ada, apprenticed under her father, had created an elaborate floral design inlaid in the mortar. Soon all the homes on Smithton Street would have indoor plumbing. *All this modern innovation seems a bit premature for a fledgling town.*

Curious as to how secure the well's covering was, Edward lifted the lid and peeked inside. "What?" He leaned over farther and squinted. The sunlight barely touched the dark recesses of the interior, and the smell reflected his suspicions.

"Mr. Pritchard, I see you arrived early." Angelina's greeting startled him.

Straightening, he acknowledged the group accompanying her with a nod—Mr. Thomas, Teresa, Cromwell, and Ada.

"What do you think of the well?" Mr. Thomas beamed with pride. "It's my best work to date. A bath can be had by our townsfolk without hauling water from outside. Eventually, outhouses will be replaced with water closets. That would be at the expense of the business owners, of course."

"I think there's something in the well." Edward peered inside again.

"The reflection of the water can give the illusion of something being there." Mr. Thomas leaned over to look. He stared for several minutes, then went to the pump house.

"Did you see something?" Angelina asked as she and Teresa peered over the edge. They wrinkled their noses.

"What is that awful smell?" Teresa's hand went to her chest. "Oh, my."

Cromwell clicked his tongue. "Some vermin. That's not good."

Ada reached for her hankie.

The plumber returned with a bucket and rope. He lowered it into the well. After a few attempts, he pulled up the bucket containing a dead skunk.

Teresa covered her nose with a handkerchief, while the others pinched their noses.

"I don't understand." Mr. Thomas frowned. I secured the cover on the well myself."

"It was secure when I arrived." Edward stared at the bloated creature. "Cromwell, was the well covered while you did all the masonry?"

"I removed it for a few hours while Ada finished the trim." He patted Ada's shoulder and she nodded. "We never left the area. And we secured it in place again by noon."

Angelina's eyes shone fire. "Obviously, the poor creature didn't fall in by accident."

Edward examined the corpse without touching it. "There's no bullet hole, so whoever did this shouldn't be hard to find."

"Who hasn't been at work the last few days?" Teresa adjusted the handkerchief.

"Everyone. We gave them the weekend off." Angelina sighed. "How long does the odor of skunk linger?"

"Don't worry, we'll get to the bottom of it." Edward's jaw hurt with the rage building inside. Why would anyone in town do this?

It didn't make sense.

"It's a good thing you got curious, Mr. Pritchard. I'd not have been able to live with myself if contaminated water took lives." The plumber wiped his face with his neckerchief.

"It's a good thing we haven't started the pumps." Edward stared at the dead creature. "Everyone will have to continue to take buckets to the stream a little longer."

"I'll track down my crew." Mr. Thomas frowned. "But first, I'll bury the skunk."

Edward touched his shoulder. "Keep this under your hat." He turned to the others. "All of you, until we get answers."

Mr. Thomas retrieved a shovel, grabbed the bucket, and headed toward a copse of trees behind the pump house.

"My daughter and I are the only masons. We've been together all weekend." Cromwell furrowed his brow. "I've got a few apprentices among the older school children. I'll go visit them. I'll say I saw a skunk in town. Just not one dead in the well. If the guilty parties among 'em, I'll know it."

"Who would want to sabotage the waterworks?" Edward ran his fingers through his hair as anger battled to influence his logical thoughts.

"Hiram is the only one who comes to mind." Angelina splayed her arms wide on the edge of the well, then dropped them to her side. "He's still in Chicago, and I can't imagine him going anywhere near a skunk."

"You know, Hiram wouldn't do his own mischief." Teresa scowled and crossed her arms. "Someone in this town might be his lackey."

"But why?" Angelina leaned against the well.

Edward lifted her chin. Unshed tears rested in her eyes. The urge to wrap her in his arms wrestled with his duty to his boss. "Angelina, you said yourself, Hiram is vengeful."

"The thought he'd stoop so low as to endanger the whole town seems too cruel, even for him." Angelina stepped away and turned to Teresa. "Are you up to holding court?"

"I look forward to serving justice to the miscreant who poisoned the water. Let's walk over to the telegraph office. I know a few people I can have inquire discreetly."

"Edward, how do ..." Angelina sighed and reached for his hand. "How do we tell everyone without creating a panic?"

"We don't." He squeezed her hand and held it for a few moments. Lost in the sea-blue of her eyes, he almost forgot his place. *Control yourself, Pritchard.* Dropping her hand, he headed to the pump house, Angelina close on his heels. Mr. Thomas joined them at the door. "You need to order a part."

"Why, yes, I do." The plumber went into the pump house and returned with a handle. Without a word, he tucked it in his pocket. "I must have misplaced it."

"They need to know." Disappointment weighed down Angelina's words.

"Not yet. We don't want a panic." Teresa came to Edward's defense. "Mr. Thomas, how long before the water is safe to drink?"

"I'd say a week, but let's give it two."

"It's for the best." Teresa nodded toward Angelina, and she sighed. "We have to keep this quiet until we find the culprit. If Hiram is somehow connected and it isn't just a childish prank, we don't want to show our hand."

Edward escorted the women to the telegraph office. No one spoke. Angelina held tight to his arm. The feel of her nearness stirred confusing feelings. When she released his arm, the separation was palpable.

"I'll find Shamus, and we'll find who did this." Edward tipped his hat.

"Thank you, Edward."

Encouraged by Angelina's willingness to let him handle this without her oversight brought a lightness to his chest.

Angelina missed the assurance of Edward's strong presence. As he'd walked with her to the telegraph office, the ribbon of dread circling her heart had loosened. She waited while Teresa wrote out three telegrams.

"What do you think?" Teresa handed them to her. "The first one is to the Pinkertons, the others to my butler, Griffin, and the bank. Read them and tell me if I made myself clear."

Angelina perused the missives. "Telling them to keep an eye on Hiram's activities seems a bit vague. Add that a letter is forthcoming." She flipped to the second message. "I never thought to check my bank account. Sign my name to this one. Mr. Kirkwood set up the Resolve account. He was given strict instructions not to speak with Hiram. Ask him to inquire if any of his other employees may have been persuaded to reveal my business to my cousin. There is still a substantial amount of money in that account to complete our project." Angelina sighed. Bile rose in her throat. What if Hiram got his hands on those funds? "After tornados, rainstorms, and a buffalo stampede created delays, now there could be sabotage."

"My dear, it will all come out right in the end. God is on our side." Teresa patted her hand.

"Say you and Hezekiah. It doesn't feel like it." Angelina reviewed the telegraph messages one more time, then handed them to Miss Sloan, the telegraph operator. "A cup of tea would be nice before we send off detailed letters."

"I have half a mind to board the train to Chicago and slap some sense into Hiram." Teresa cocked her head and smiled. "But the other half of my mind wants to see him in jail."

Angelina chuckled, but even laughter couldn't remove the anxiety encircling her heart and mind at the prospect of Hiram ruining everything.

"Hopefully, our ladies' tea goes better than our morning." Angelina pinned her straw hat in place and checked her reflection in the hall mirror before descending the stairs. Visions of the bloated skunk lingered in her mind. She glanced up to see Teresa adjusting her hat in the same mirror before joining her at the front door. "Do you think all the women will attend?"

Teresa patted her shoulder. "Tea and Bridget's pastries will bring them out, I'm sure."

Angelina straightened her lace collar. "We're making history. Women discussing the welfare of a town has never happened before. It's been difficult for the ladies to find their places as we've laid the foundation of the town. The men have done a splendid job building. Now it's ..."

"Now it is time for the women to step forward." Teresa finished her thought.

Angelina paused halfway to the women's dormitory. "What will I tell the ladies about the progress of the indoor plumbing? It's on the agenda."

"You can skip that bit of business or say a part is missing." Teresa reached over and pulled Angelina's hand into the crook of her arm. "It is the truth. A part is missing. We don't have to tell them we saw where it's gotten off to."

They arrived to find the room full, including the homesteaders. The beds had been pushed aside to make room for more chairs. The buzz of conversation halted when Angelina entered. She placed her hat on a nearby hook and made her way to the table at the front.

"Welcome, ladies." She smiled and removed her gloves, placing them on the table near her notes. "I'm so delighted at such a wonderful turnout." She licked her lips before continuing. "This is far more than a tea."

A mixture of smiles and nervousness covered the women's faces. Caroline sat posed with her pencil and notebook to Angelina's right.

"Teresa will open our meeting by reading the bylaws she created for our Progressive Women's Society. Bylaws, by definition, are the rules we promise to adhere to. Anyone can make suggestions for change. We will vote to accept or reject these bylaws after they're read and discussed."

Elmira Blake raised her hand. "Shouldn't we ask our husbands' opinions before we vote?"

Madeline Harper elevated her voice from the back of the room. "Elmira, this is a unique opportunity. A town run by women." She eyed the whole assembly. "Don't let any man tell you you're not intelligent enough to make these decisions."

Applause followed her comment. The women took their task seriously, listening carefully as Teresa read the bylaws. A few suggestions were made before they were unanimously passed. Then they discussed the progress on the town and the homesteads.

"Has anyone got new recipes for salt pork?" Mrs. Owen, a homesteader, asked.

Sarah McCray gently shook her head. "That's not official business. We can talk about recipes over tea. Let's get on with it, then we'll have tea and Bridget's delicious pastries. The smell is making me hungry."

The ladies laughed.

"For this to be a proper business meeting, everyone should rise to speak after they have been recognized," Teresa added, then took her seat.

Angelina looked at her notes and cleared her throat. "The waterworks aren't quite ready, I'm afraid. A part is missing. We should have running water to every home in town in no more than three weeks."

Bridget rose. "We didn't have no running water in the tenements in Chicago and not at the farm back in Ireland. Resolve, by comparison, is a bit of heaven on earth, even without the waterworks. I, for one, can wait." More murmurs of agreement, and the meeting continued.

"Ma'am." A young lady rose. "I'm Ida White. I'm engaged to be married. But I'm waiting for the church to be built. There is going to be a church, right?"

Angelina's face warmed. "Rev. Asbury agreed to raise his own funds to build the church. I'll donate the lot between the schoolhouse plot and the cemetery. In exchange, I will be permitted to design the exterior to complement the rest of Resolve's architecture. Miss White, why don't you form a committee and help the reverend raise the funds?"

"I don't see why you just don't up and build it," someone in the back of the room shouted.

Sarah McCray came to Angelina's rescue. "I attended a church where powerful men with lots of money financed it. They demanded to be on the church board and gave everyone grief who didn't agree with them. Raising the money ourselves makes it our church. No one will be excluded or treated differently."

Mrs. Ho raised her hand, then stood. "Excuse, please. I am Christian. Missionaries came to our village. I want church too." She smiled at Angelina. "Rev. Asbury teach me read English. My husband too. We want to be true Americans. We move Resolve to be equal. We help build church." She resumed her seat in the back of the room.

"Thank you, Mrs. Ho, for being the first to offer to help build the church." Angelina tugged on her bodice. "I agree with Sarah's observation. When someone finances the building of a church, they feel they have the right to control everything that goes on within its walls." She shook her head. "I don't think you'd appreciate that."

Teresa gave her a knowing smile. "I'm sure you've heard from your husbands how Miss DuBois oversees every detail of the construction—and not in the kindest terms." The ladies laughed as Teresa fanned herself. "A church should be built by its congregation. Anyone interested can meet here next Tuesday evening. You can bring your husbands." Giggles interrupted her. "We'll start the planning and fund raising. And thank you, Angelina, for your generous donation of land and a design."

"Sounds wonderful." Miss White took her seat. Everyone applauded.

Mrs. Jones rose to speak. Angelina couldn't recall her Christian name. The woman wrung her hands, but her voice was strong and steady. "The homestead gardens are small this year. It might not get our families through the winter."

"You all should have enough credit at the mercantile to buy what you need. Miss DuBois made sure no one would starve this winter." Teresa glanced Caroline's way.

"Ain't so." Another homesteader stood. "Mr. Blake refused us any more credit."

"He told me the same." Sarah jumped to her feet. "I keep careful records. It is not possible that I would have run through the line of credit Miss DuBois provided before winter. I came right from the mercantile to this meeting. I haven't had time to tell my husband. When I do ..."

Women whispered and eyed Elmira suspiciously.

Teresa posed the question for them all. "Elmira, is this true?"

Her face paled. "I ... I ... I don't manage the books. Clyde does."

Voices raised, and chairs scraped the floor as several women tried to be recognized at the same time. They spoke over each other, creating a cacophony of angry words.

Angelina raised her voice. "Silence! Silence, please, ladies. Please take your seats. We can't proceed until you do." At last, there was silence. She stared around the room. "Let's not act like brawling men."

The women laughed, and the tension eased for the moment.

"Elmira, I'll be by on Friday to check your books." She turned to the rest of the women. "And there will be no more discussions until I get to the bottom of this."

Murmurs and nods offered agreement.

Angelina continued in a gentle yet firm tone, addressing Elmira, who shrank beneath the accusations. "You're accustomed to your husband managing things. But you agreed to handle the books and the running of the store when you signed the contract." She took time to scan the room. "This is a new concept for men. All married business owners, remember you violate the terms of your contract if you are owner in name only. We will not judge Elmira for the miscalculations of her husband. If any of you need something before next week, charge it to my account. I'll straighten this all out very soon, and your accounts will be adjusted accordingly."

Teresa led the applause. "Hear, hear. I move we adjourn for refreshments. Do I have a second?"

"Me—I mean, I second," said Caroline, waving her hand.

"All in favor?" Angelina smiled as they all shouted, *aye*. Her heart swelled at the women following the rules. *Not as addle-brained as men think we are.*

Elmira slipped out the door before anyone stopped her.

Angelina moved among the ladies seated at tables, thanking each one for coming and listening to any concerns or comments they didn't care to broach in the group. She approached a table where Mrs. Morgan and her eldest daughter sat with Bridget and Sarah. "Nice to see you, ladies."

"I have never been so thankful for a skunk in my entire life." Mrs. Morgan laughed.

Her daughter added, "If Pa and Jefferson hadn't been sprayed, we'd have never been allowed to come to this meeting."

"While he's banished to the barn, he has no idea what I do in town." Mrs. Morgan grinned as she took a sip of her tea.

Angelina kept her tone matter-of-fact. "How did this happen?"

"Jefferson and my husband went hunting. They took Sadie, Jefferson's dog. She came upon that skunk. They tried to get the dog to leave it. The skunk spray got all of them."

"When was this?" Angelina smiled but couldn't bring herself to laugh with the others.

"Yesterday. It's been quiet in the house without Tim bellowing about something."

"I've got some pine tar soap that might help," Bridget offered. "I could bring it by tomorrow."

"I'll come along, Bridget." Angelina disliked people inviting themselves, but she had to get to the bottom of this. "I've wanted to visit a few homesteads. I hear your husband has done a fine job getting you all settled."

"My Tim's a hard worker, that's for sure." Pride filled her face. "He'll be a bit embarrassed he can't show you around proper."

The woman seemed to have no clue of any skunk mischief. Angelina tilted her head. "When will we taste some of that cheese you told me about?"

"I have a little, but once my nanny goats deliver their newest kids, I should have plenty of milk to make cheese. Our cow is fixing to have a calf soon, too, so it's probably good that Tim's stuck in the barn. He'll be there to help the goats and Millie. That's the cow."

Soon all those who didn't live in the women's dorm left, and the room was set to right.

Angelina and Teresa walked out with Caroline, who clutched her notes to her chest. "I have just seen history being made. I need to head over to the newspaper office and write my article."

"How kind of Mrs. Collins to let you cover an event she attended," Teresa said.

"I hope when Martin arrives, she'll still trust me to write the news." The girl hurried down the street, her bonnet bouncing by its ribbons.

Caroline's remark bothered Angelina. Surely, Hester Collins wouldn't let Martin take over because of his gender. *What would happen if I left Resolve?* Would the men take over from the women even though they were doing a good job? Would male pride destroy all her hard work? And if Mr. Morgan was the culprit who threw the skunk in the well, his whole family would lose their place.

Her own excitement over the first all-women town meeting soured in her stomach.

CHAPTER 21

Edward sat at his desk, scrutinizing blueprints. Angelina had modified the plans once again. There was no building she hadn't redrawn since the project began. Her desire for perfection became more irritating with each revision. The tornado's destruction had finally been repaired and cellars dug behind every building not constructed over a cellar. All new construction had cellars included— even the train depot. Fear added to the expense of building.

Soft footsteps on the stairs alerted Edward to Angelina's presence. An uneven rhythm told him Teresa was carefully maneuvering the steps behind her.

"Are you sure?" Teresa's voice carried from the bottom of the stairs.

"I'm sure ..." Angelina stopped speaking in his presence. "Edward, you're here early." She fidgeted with her waistcoat.

"I wanted to take a careful look at your revisions before we went to inspect the foundation at the depot." He rolled up the blueprints and placed them in a leather tube.

"That's today?" Angelina's forgetfulness was out of character. She glanced toward Teresa. "Yesterday, we promised Mrs. Morgan we would pay her a visit today."

"Your schedule has us at the depot site in ten minutes. Mr. Barnaby Hayes arrived a few days ago. Angelina, we discussed this. He's the new depot manager, and we are giving him a tour of the site and going over the blueprints."

"Of course." Angelina threw on her cloak and pinned her hat in place. "Teresa, please tell Bridget to bring some pastries for the

192

Morgans. Tell Lucinda we'll be leaving in an hour."

"Planning a party?"

"What?" Angelina's eyes shifted left, then she smiled too brightly. "No, Bridget, Teresa, and I need a driver. Lucinda has been teaching us how to drive a wagon. I love the independence, but I'm not that confident yet."

"Perhaps I should come along for protection." The Morgan homestead was a half-hour drive, and with the tent saloon so near, Edward worried for their welfare.

"Don't be silly. Lucinda and I are dead shots." Her laugh seemed forced, and her face flushed.

There was more to this trip to the Morgans. Now who was the liar? Why? Hypocrisy apparently didn't bother her. He squelched the irritation. They needed to get on with the construction.

Angelina's maid, Eva, clattered down the stairs, interrupting any further discussion. "Miss DuBois, I'll see you tomorrow." She stopped long enough to curtsy.

"Eva, where are you off to in such a hurry?" Edward smiled at the girl.

"Mama asked if I could help with canning. If I have time, I'll probably dust and reorganize the store shelves. My brother Everett is a lazy soul. He'll dillydally over a few shelves all day long." She curtsied again and dashed out the door. Teresa followed.

Angelina watched them go, then turned toward him. Yep, she was up to something when her smile didn't light up her eyes. She seemed to reach for conversation. "Our small apartment isn't hard to keep in order. Once my house is built, Eva will be quite busy. I may need to hire additional help."

Edward held the door for her as he put on his hat. A chilly breeze, a harbinger of the impending autumn, joined them on their walk to the depot. "The sooner we get the inspection over with, the more work the men can do before the day heats up. Caroline keeps pestering me about completing our home before winter."

"I'm sorry, I put it off again for the depot. Now that everyone has shelter, I felt the depot was the next priority. Why don't you take the building across the street?" She swept her hand out. "Its former occupants didn't care for the isolation or the weather. They left on the train this morning."

The space was smaller than Teresa's office, but he'd have privacy. And having his sister share the apartment would allow them to regain some of the closeness they'd lost while she stayed in the women's dorm.

"Caroline will be delighted. I'll move my office as well, and then Teresa can have a waiting room."

"You don't like being her receptionist?"

They laughed and continued to the worksite.

"I'm glad you're taking that space. Postponing your office and my house are the only things we can fudge on with the vote to stay on my original schedule. I may need to postpone my home again because the women want a church."

"Isn't that Hezekiah's responsibility?"

"I said 'may' because the ladies are forming a committee to raise the funds." Angelina sighed. "I need to allow the women to make decisions. This is their town too." She leaned closer to avoid a puddle. The warmth of her nearness, if only for a moment, pleased him.

"The men aren't happy about being excluded from the decision-making." Edward understood their angst.

"Teresa and I are encouraging the women to take responsibility for their futures. We have more widows than married women who want the best for their families." Angelina stopped and faced him. The wind blew tendrils of brown hair in her face. She pushed them aside and seemed to examine him. Was she waiting to see if he would argue with her? He had no problem with women running businesses, especially widows. But swallowing his pride and giving Angelina's vision a chance was a daily challenge. "The unmarried, young ladies need to feel they can take care of themselves. Marriage should be an option based on love, not necessity." Her sapphire eyes pleaded with him to understand.

"So you're not opposed to marriage?" Edward's lips quirked into a teasing smile.

"Only as an institution that enslaves women. But one built on love would certainly be preferred." Angelina turned away, her cheeks reddening.

They began walking again. Was her blush a tell? Did she think of him as more than an employee?

"City elections are on the agenda for next year. Teresa wants to run for mayor." Angelina again searched his face.

"Be prepared for some resistance from the male population— especially Clyde Blake." Edward took Angelina's elbow and steered her around a pothole. "Might make for an interesting election."

"Get some men to fill that hole. Next year, we lay brick streets."

"You're changing the subject." Edward could almost hear her brain spinning.

Angelina wrapped her cloak tighter around her middle, then stopped walking yards from the worksite. "At the meeting, a few women said Clyde claimed they'd used up the credit line already— which seemed ridiculous when I made sure there was enough for each family to draw down until next year. Most of these families are frugal. They've heard about the harsh winters. Elmira admitted her husband keeps the books. I intend to go by Friday to review the accounts. I reminded all the women this is not an in-name-only venture."

"Is it possible ..."—Edward knew to tread lightly—"that Emily miscalculated the monies needed per family?"

Her eyebrow raised and her jaw clenched. "I'm shocked you would even suggest such a thing. But that's why I'm waiting until Friday—so Emily and Elmira have time to be sure their calculations are correct." She glared at Edward. "It sounds like you're assuming because she's a woman, her calculations are off. Do you know most married women keep the household accounts?"

"I meant no disrespect to Emily or any other woman in this town." Edward pulled the collar up on his jacket against the cool breezes and her icy stare. "Mistakes are made."

"Emily researched the cost to feed a large family for a year, then adjusted the budget according to family size. We'll know on Friday if Emily's math isn't true."

"The rumor is, you'll be sending the Blakes packing." Edward wanted to pull her close when her shoulders sagged.

"That's all it is—a rumor." Angelina's eyes sparked. "Gossip is the bane of my existence. I suspect Mr. Blake, who, by the way, has no experience running a store. His wife ran her father's mercantile. Elmira is the owner on the contract. Mr. Blake won't let her use her talents."

"They do have three children." Edward's face warmed despite the cool morning air. Surely, she didn't think it was a father's place to care solely for children.

"Old enough to help in the store. Jenny works for Bridget and Eva for me. Their son is fourteen." Her sharp look told him she wasn't finished. "Have you noticed extra crates addressed to Clyde with the last shipment of building supplies?"

"You didn't order them?"

"I have supplies for the mercantile sent in quarterly. He can order additional things at his own expense."

"You think he's charging you on behalf of the mercantile in anticipation of more profit from outsiders shopping here?" Edward knew that was exactly what Clyde was doing.

"Clever man, Eddie." She turned toward the worksite. "And if he is unable to pay it back, then Mr. Blake may have sealed his family's fate."

She began walking toward the depot again. He matched her pace, their unpleasant conversation ended.

"Mr. Hayes, you're here." Angelina shook the young man's hand. "What do you think of Resolve?"

His black handlebar mustache framed his smile. "I've been exploring your town. Impressive."

"Resolve is not *my* town." Her eyebrows furrowed. "Have you seen the blueprints for the depot?"

"Yes ma'am." Mr. Hayes tapped his leg with his bowler hat.

"Not the revised version," Edward said. "We'll go over those changes."

"Yes sir."

"Are you comfortable in the dormitory?" Angelina always asked after people's comfort, a quality Edward appreciated.

"Yes ma'am." Mr. Hayes looked at the ground.

She gave him a welcoming smile. "If you are anything like your father, you will be a wonderful depot manager."

"I hope so, ma'am. I'm a bit nervous."

"I never properly thanked you for guarding the freight cars while we awaited the spur's completion. And let me apologize for sending you back to Chicago with the empty cars. I should have found a place for you sooner." Angelina's voice took on an edge. "My cousin Hiram managed to delay the completion of my rail spur. Then Mr. Paulson died, and some negotiation with the railroad had to be assigned to his former colleague."

"No need to explain, but thank you for doing so." His face pinked.

"Shall we begin?" She swept her hand toward the worksite. The men followed her.

Angelina hurried through the inspection, grasping her watch pendent and checking the time frequently. Finally, she shook Mr. Hayes' hand. "Thank you for joining my venture, Mr. Hayes. Now I need to be somewhere else." She nodded to Edward to follow her. They stepped toward the street. "I trust you to report back to me anything Mr. Hayes suggests regarding the revised blueprints."

Edward nodded and crossed his arms. "Shall I accompany you Friday?"

"Whatever for?" She wrinkled her nose.

"Clyde—"

"I can handle Clyde." She dragged out the name and raised her eyebrow.

Edward tamped down his irritation as Angelina sashayed toward the livery a few buildings over. He glanced back at Mr. Hayes, who kept his eyes locked on her backside.

"That is one fine-looking woman. It's a shame she's stuck up."

"Mind your tongue. Show some respect." Edward pinned Barnaby with a scowl.

"Sorry, sir." Mr. Hayes returned his stare. "But it's clear she doesn't know her place."

Anger flared in Edward. "And what place would that be?"

He took a step back and shook his head. "Forgive me, sir. But a woman's place has always been in the home. Are you and Miss DuBois courting?"

"No. Why would you think that?" If Angelina had moved him beyond the friend stage, she hid it well.

"You seem a might defensive."

"No, we are not courting." Edward crossed his arms and maintained eye contact. "Miss DuBois is our boss. You will keep such remarks to yourself if you value your job."

Barnaby nodded and adjusted his bowler hat. "Yes sir."

He gave himself a count of ten. "Shall we look at those blueprints? I'll pass along your suggestions to Miss DuBois."

It was so out of character for Angelina to leave a meeting before it was complete. He rolled out the prints on a makeshift table. Barnaby perused the design.

"Looks fine to me." Barnaby nodded. "I don't understand blueprints, so I'll have to wait and see what it looks like."

Suppressing a frown, Edward shook Barnaby's hand, and the two parted company.

His gut ached, a sure sign something was amiss. Not just with the new stationmaster, but with Angelina. His bet was on her sudden need to visit homesteaders. The silent walk to the office gave Edward time to formulate a plan.

Angelina found Lucinda checking the traces on the wagon in the livery. Fiona McCray stood nearby. "I told you my pa taught me how to hitch a wagon. I don't know why you doubt me." The thirteen-year-old's childish pout belied her more mature hairstyle.

"I always double-check, even my own work. You've done a fine job." Lucinda patted the horses and split a carrot between the two.

Teresa and Bridget approached, carrying covered baskets.

"Climb aboard, ladies." Lucinda jumped up on the seat and took the reins. She wore trousers and a floppy hat.

"Thank you for agreeing to drive us. I know you're busy helping your new husband." Angelina took her seat next to Lucinda, and the others took the second bench. Their skirts billowed with the autumn breeze. Angelina tied her bonnet more firmly and clutched her shawl.

"I'm finding the process of making furniture interesting, although the Sullivan brothers work circles around me. The three of them are building a fine reputation for quality work." She pushed the brake free. "Hey, get up there."

The horses moved forward.

"How are you managing the homestead too?" Teresa spoke from behind.

"Like any good partnership, we take turns helping each other. Gabe planted trees on most of the property. Together with Teddy's help, we've spent the last few weeks canning and drying vegetables. Now we're catching up on furniture orders. The Sullivans spread the word in Flat Ridge, and we got several from there."

Angelina almost asked what the twins were doing in that godless place but decided she didn't want to know.

Lucinda's smile broadened as she continued. "I never told you I went to art school."

Teresa laughed. "You are full of surprises. Such a strong pioneer woman is an artist."

"Can't a pioneer woman be one?" Lucinda winked.

Angelina blushed. Would she ever get past her own hypocrisy? She'd assumed Lucinda had no genteel inclinations since she'd been raised in the West.

"I've been painting scenes on bedposts and chair backs. I love it."

Lucinda's face glowed.

A prick of envy ached in Angelina's heart. This woman had managed to find the perfect combination of love and marital equality. "I'm happy for you. Will you continue to survey?"

"I'll fulfill my commitment to you. After that, I'll pass the tools on to Teddy. He's doing a fine job. He'll need to apprentice to someone else when he's thirteen."

"He's apprenticed to you." Angelina felt her ire rise.

"No, he's my assistant. By the time he's thirteen, I hope to be raising my own family and creating more art. Gabe wants to create custom pieces with my signature design on them. Can you imagine— *my* signature design?" Lucinda squealed her delight.

"Good for ye." Bridget cheered. "And for Gabe—a man who encourages a woman to spread her wings. That's what I'm hoping to find someday."

Would Bridget find another man like Gabe among the single men in Resolve? Would she? Was Edward that man? Angelina's face warmed, and she turned to face the prairie. Why did even the thought of him make her blush?

Angelina glanced over her shoulder. "Before we reach the Morgans', I want to reveal my true motives for this visit to you two, Lucinda and Bridget. Teresa already knows." She shared the details of the dead skunk and Mrs. Morgan's confession. "Ask questions whenever you get a chance about the skunk encounter, especially of the children. They are not as guarded in their speech."

The wagon jerked, jostling them. Teresa gripped her side of the rear bench. "My, my, these ruts barely qualify as road. I miss the cobbled streets of Chicago at times like this. My bones feel like they're jarring loose." She rearranged herself. "Let's find evidence, ladies. It's important we either confirm Angelina's suspicions or rule them out. Maybe we won't have to make this bumpy ride again anytime soon."

The Morgans' homestead consisted of a neatly whitewashed house with a soddie barn. Crops Angelina couldn't identify grew in the north field, while haystacks and cornstalks rested in the others. Mr. Morgan perched on the top of a partially framed structure. Seeing them, he waved and descended a homemade ladder. "Ladies, my wife said you were coming. I'll be keeping my distance."

"What are you building?" Teresa called as Lucinda set the brake and they all climbed down.

"A silo to store the corn. Once those stalks are dry, I'll put the ears in here."

"I grew up on a farm." Teresa put her hands on her hips. "Would you show me around?"

"Under any other circumstances, but I was skunked a few days ago." He hung his head.

"I'll show her, Pa." A small, pudgy boy appeared from behind the silo. "I'm Timmy. I'm named after my pa." Turning to his father, he offered, "I can show the lady."

Mrs. Morgan and the other children filtered out of the house as Teresa shook the boy's hand.

"That would be lovely."

Timmy smiled and took her hand.

Teresa looked back at the father. "Mr. Morgan, might you narrate my excursion? From a distance, of course."

"You've been warned." He nodded and led the way.

Mrs. Morgan greeted her guests with handshakes, then glanced toward her husband. "Tim is so proud of this place. Even though he had to rebuild after the tornado."

"You lost your home?" Angelina shook her head. Why had they never mentioned it?

"No, my husband just had to fix the roof. But the barn frame blew away. That's when he built the soddie barn. I'm lucky he's smart. He built a root cellar first thing when Mr. McCray told him what he'd heard about the tornados and the bad winters. We hid in there when he spotted the strange cloud. Tim's determined to keep us all safe and warm."

Bridget handed her a basket.

"Oh, we are blessed, Miss O'Malley. I'm not much for baking fancy things." Mrs. Morgan showed her children the treats. They minded their manners and waited in wiggly anticipation. She opened her door, and the smell of lavender greeted them. "I've been making candles. My ma taught me how to create different fragrances. Mr. Blake agreed to trade them for supplies."

More evidence of who was in charge of the mercantile. Angelina's mouth tightened.

Bridget nodded at Angelina and changed the subject. "I fancy your fine goat cheese would be lovely on my pumpernickel bread."

Mrs. Morgan set out coffee and pastries. A stocky lad stood nearby, eying the basket. "Johnny, take this plate out to your father and Jefferson and let Mrs. Shilling know tea is ready. Clara, honey, help serve our guests."

"Yes ma'am." Clara, a mirror image of her mother, laid the cheese and a butter ball on the table.

"Jefferson is one unhappy child. He hates sleeping in the barn. The hay makes his eyes run."

"My stepmother cured me." Lucinda offered. "If you have some paper, I'll write down the recipe." She placed cheese on the bread. Angelina did the same. "My, this is very tasty."

"Whenever you are ready to sell this, I'll be your first customer." Angelina's praise brought a smile to Mrs. Morgan.

She found a scrap of brown paper and a pencil and placed them before Lucinda. "Much obliged for sharing your receipt."

Angelina and the women chatted about lighthearted things for several minutes. As Teresa entered and served herself, Lucinda managed to bring the conversation around to the goal at hand. "Tell me about the skunk." She had been seated across the room at the ladies' tea when Mrs. Morgan shared her tale. Now, Clara and her four siblings added their own details.

"Jefferson heaved a rock at it. Broke the varmint's neck." Clara laughed. "Pa said he'd never seen such a thing. Jefferson was aiming for his head. The rock hit its neck and slammed the skunk into a boulder nearby."

"Pa said that made him even stinkier," Johnny added between bites of oatmeal cookie.

"I almost forgot." Bridget reached in her reticule. "Here is the pine tar soap."

"Thank you kindly." Mrs. Morgan smiled and nodded to Clara. The girl gave Bridget a lump of cheese wrapped in cloth. "I'm happy to trade if it helps Tim and Jefferson get clean enough to join us in the house. I just finished another set of clothes for them. We had to burn the others, and what they are wearing now may meet the same fate."

"We need to be heading back." Angelina rose. "Thank you for your hospitality."

The ladies said their farewells as Tim hollered from the barn. "Grace, you've had your womenfolk visit. It's time you all got back to your chores." His scowl turned to a polite nod toward their guests. "You'll wanna get back before dusk, being unprotected as you are." He tipped his hat and then raised his voice again to be heard over the children saying their goodbyes. "You planning on fixing vittles any time soon, Grace?"

His grumbling brought a nervous smile to his wife's face. "My apologies. He likes his meals on time." She walked toward the barn as Angelina and the ladies took their seats on the wagon.

"Lands sakes. Two hours …" His words were lost to their hearing as the wagon rumbled from the yard.

Once out of earshot of the homestead, Angelina looked at the others. "I worry about her."

"As do I." Teresa frowned. "But I don't think any of them threw a skunk in the town well."

"Did Mr. Morgan tell you the same story?"

Teresa gripped the seat as the wagon traveled the same rutted trail. "Jefferson was in the barn, and he told his sad tale exactly as the children said. Mr. Morgan went to bury the skunk the next day, but it was gone."

"Perhaps someone else found it." Bridget spoke what Angelina had been thinking. "Surely, we'd smell the troublemaker."

Teresa tipped her head to one side. "I don't recall whether the bloated creature in the well had a broken neck. But none of us were curious enough to examine how it died."

The women were almost to town when Lucinda pulled the wagon to a stop and drew out her rifle. "Someone's following us."

Two horses came over the horizon. As Edward and Shamus drew near, Angelina's anger erupted. "Why are you following us?"

"I almost shot first and asked questions later." Glaring, Lucinda lowered her weapon to her lap.

"We got a wee bit worried when you hadn't come back." Straightening in his saddle, Shamus showed no remorse. "I'm the sheriff, and it's me responsibility to watch over the people of Resolve."

"What's your excuse, Mr. Pritchard?" Teresa beat Angelina to the question.

Edward's cheeks reddened as he cleared his throat. "I'd be remiss in my duty to Miss DuBois if I didn't make sure she was safe."

Lucinda rose from her place, aimed her rifle, and fired. The women shrieked, and the men struggled to calm their mounts. "There's one less snake to worry about."

A headless reptilian corpse lay several feet from Edward's horse.

"I'm a deadly shot with the two-legged kind too." She calmly took her place once again and clicked to the horses.

The other women exchanged silly grins. Angelina took a calming breath and exhaled slowly, then smiled at Lucinda. She'd never admit her own fears of traveling with only women.

As nice as it felt that Eddie cared enough to worry over her, he'd already taken over more of the project than she'd intended. Compromise was necessary to keep the male population happy and get the work done. But protecting her was not her contractor's job. Often a protector became a ruler. Her father had ruled over every project she designed, taking full credit. This was her project, her credit. Edward Pritchard would be wise to remember that.

CHAPTER 22

Friday morning, Angelina went to collect Emily Jameson at her brother's blacksmith shop. The heat from the forge warmed her chilled hands. Michael smiled and nodded a greeting before plunging a horseshoe into a basin of water. Steam rose toward him.

"Good day, I'm looking for your sister." Angelina kept her voice natural, avoiding talking louder because the man was mute.

He pointed to a door behind him.

"Thank you." She skirted a table of broken items needing repair and assorted horseshoes. Opening the door, she peered into the tiny office. Emily's full attention rested on a ledger in front of her.

"Emily, have you forgotten we have to meet with the Blakes shortly?"

"Miss DuBois, you startled me." Emily's face, full of worry lines, did not relax as she rose. "I've been going over my figures. Yesterday after Madeline dismissed the students, we went over the ledgers again. I thought I might have dropped a page of entries when I brought them here from your office, but Madeline confirmed all is in order."

"Emily, I'm confident once you compare our figures to the mercantile's, we'll find the error." Angelina patted her shoulder. "Come along. We can't be late. Teresa is meeting us there."

Michael signed to his sister. Emily translated. "He asked if I'd like him to go with us."

"Don't tell me—he wants to protect us." Angelina shook her head and faced Michael. "We will be fine." She took one of the ledgers from Emily and tucked it under her arm. "I'm sure Mr. Blake is a reasonable man."

Michael nodded and signed.

Emily translated. "He would feel remiss if he didn't offer." She waved goodbye and turned to Angelina, and they headed up the street. "The gossip is, Mr. Blake keeps a rifle at the ready." Her face paled as she held the ledgers close.

Angelina tugged Emily into a shoulder hug. "Don't concern yourself with the town gossip." She took her elbow and guided her toward the mercantile. "I should imagine any shopkeeper would keep a rifle handy. We both know he's not going to shoot us."

Nervousness wrapped its tendrils around Angelina's spine. These sorts of confrontations weren't supposed to happen. At least it had seemed that way when she wrote out her business plan and created the contracts. Assuming everyone would be honest had been quite naïve on her part.

One of these days, when her hands were less full, she'd unmask the teller of tales and give them a piece of her mind. For now, she would ignore the gossip.

The two women entered the mercantile. Teresa waited with Mrs. Blake while Edward and Shamus came through the door. She scowled at them. Did no one see how ridiculous this was? Angelina didn't want the Blakes thinking they would be arrested. She approached Elmira. "Is there a more private place we can do our investigation?"

"There's a table in the back room." She looked at her husband. Angelina followed her gaze. "Clyde, once we've examined the books, I'll want to see you as well. For now, go about your business."

His jaw twitched as he nodded.

Once they were seated, Elmira teared up. "I'm so sorry I haven't been doing my share. I know the contract I signed. But you see ..."

Angelina raised her hand, and Elmira stopped. Teresa handed her a lace handkerchief. She dabbed her eyes. Fear paled her otherwise olive completion.

"Elmira, we aren't here to condemn you. Let Emily and I go over the books. If there is an error, we'll address it. Emily may have underestimated what was needed to support these families until next year. Some families may truly have run out of the funds I allotted them. Or ..."

"My record keeping could be off." Elmira finished the sentence.

"Do you keep the accounts?" Angelina made eye contact.

Elmira's face reddened as she shook her head.

Angelina smiled. "Don't worry, I'm a firm believer in second chances." She reached to pat the woman's hand.

Elmira grabbed her fingers and squeezed hard. "I'm so relieved."

The shopkeeper sat quietly as they perused the accounts.

After about fifteen minutes, a grim expression passed over Emily's face. "Elmira, why were the families charged for food items the first month they arrived? Everyone was eating in the dining room. There wasn't even a mercantile."

Elmira glanced at Emily, then at Angelina. "I'm sure there's an explanation. Let me—"

"Then there are these individual discrepancies. I know for a fact I didn't order a hundred pounds of flour last month. Even Michael doesn't eat that much." She flipped another page in the ledger. "The Gordons have pigs, so they would have no reason to order salt pork." She turned to another entry. "The Joneses raise turkeys. Why would they order eggs?" Her finger ran down another page. "Mary Price places orders with Angelina for her yard goods, yet she has several entries for material. I could believe a few buttons or a few yards of something if she came up short. I wonder, are the McCray girls wearing trousers now? The ledger has recorded six pairs of men's trousers. The McCrays are too frugal to order that many pairs for George. Every ledger has identical items. Miss Price wouldn't order tobacco. I know my brother doesn't use it."

Elmira burst into tears. "I told him he best let me handle the books. I told him he should ask Miss DuBois before he ordered anything extra. I told ..." Her hysterics turned her words to gibberish.

Clyde came through the door. "What are you doing to my wife?" His fists at his side, anger flashed across his face.

Angelina rose and returned his gaze. "The better question is, what have you done to her?" She stared until he averted his eyes. "Where is my money, Mr. Blake?"

"I have no idea—"

"Don't lie to me. You are not skilled at hiding your embezzlement."

"How dare you accuse me?" His voice rose. "Get out of my shop."

Teresa stepped up. "No. This is not your shop. It's legally your wife's, and she will not gain ownership until the completion of her contract."

"No court of law would support a woman owning a business."

"You are mistaken, Mr. Blake." Teresa held up her hand to keep him from answering. "And don't even suggest a woman attorney is incapable of defending the law."

"Elmira, it's time you fixed lunch."

"Yes." Elmira rose to leave, but Angelina motioned her to sit, then faced her husband.

"You are in serious trouble, and because your wife's name is on the contract, she is in more trouble. By shirking her duty, she has violated the terms of the contract. I could have her arrested."

"No, please." Clyde put his hand on his wife's shoulder. "I'm responsible. A man has to take care of his family."

"Violating the terms of the contract is not taking care of your family." Teresa glared.

Clyde's shoulders slumped. "So you're saying Elmira gets to make the decisions while I tend the home?"

"Is that why you've stolen my money?" Angelina crossed her arms. "You feel emasculated?"

"I don't know that word, ma'am. But I don't feel it's a woman's place to support the family when she has a well-bodied husband to do it."

"So, you can't share the responsibility?" Angelina pointed to the empty chair. Clyde sat with his head down. "Elmira successfully ran a mercantile for years before she married you. Did you help with the home while you farmed?"

"I helped with what needed doing, like Saturday baths and such. You work together on a farm. It's different when you work in a factory. I guess I'd forgotten."

Angelina paced the small space. "The two of you, correct the entries in this ledger, restoring everyone's credit. And give an accounting of what you borrowed from me. Then you will go to the bank and secure a loan to pay me back."

"I don't believe in loans." Clyde's steely voice unnerved Angelina.

Teresa placed a reassuring hand on her shoulder. "But you believe in stealing?"

"No ma'am." Clyde's pride deflated. Elmira took his hand.

"We will do whatever we need to. I'll fix the books and get the loan." She squeezed Clyde's hand. "Together, we will make this store a success."

"All right. How you going to help me and keep house?" Clyde jerked his hand away from his wife.

"Your children can help in the store." Emily smiled at Elmira. "That's how Michael learned to be a blacksmith. And my grandfather taught me how to keep accounts when I wasn't much older than your son. And I learned to cook and keep house from both my parents."

Clyde sighed and shook his head. "My mother was a terrible cook. Pa fed us and taught me all he knew about cooking. He always told us children how disappointed he was that Ma shirked her duties. Not Elmira." He smiled at her. "She's a gem at keeping house and smart as a whip. I suppose we can try to share responsibilities."

"That's a good start." Angelina extended her hand and Clyde shook it. "I expect to review the books again next Friday. Shall we say, after the store closes?"

"Yes ma'am." Clyde turned to his wife.

She nodded. "Everything will be in order."

When the women opened the door to leave, Edward and Shamus moved away. "Listening at the keyhole, gentlemen?" Angelina frowned.

"Am I arresting them?" Shamus asked.

"No. We've sorted it all out. They've a second chance to make things right." Angelina breathed a sigh of relief.

Shamus smiled. "I'm grateful my sheriffing duties weren't needed."

"Things might have turned out differently." Edward's worried brow—somewhat endearing, Angelina had to admit—lifted. "May I walk you back to the office?"

"No, thank you." Angelina moved away with a swish of her skirt; the others followed her. She turned to wave goodbye to the Blakes, reveling in the positive results. Edward winked at her, warming her face as she left with her friends.

CHAPTER 23

The little stove fought to warm the cold air permeating Edward's office. Caroline squatted near its opening and flung more buffalo chips into the fire. Then she wiped her hands on a rag with a disgusted shiver. "If someone would have told me a year ago I'd be burning animal droppings to keep warm, I would've thought them looney."

"Our new supply of coal isn't due for two weeks. It's cooler than we anticipated for September." Was this a prelude to winter blizzards? "I could bring over some scrap wood from the worksites." Edward rubbed his eyes from the strain of staring at rows of numbers. "I'll be glad when it's too cold to build."

"Then you can help me nail some pictures to the walls in my room. Oh, wait. First, you need to paint them." Caroline rose and stretched her back. A frown creased her brow.

"It'll be too cold to paint." Edward grinned and laced his hands behind his head, the chair creaking as the front legs left the floor.

"Drat."

"If you look in the bottom drawer of my desk, you might find a solution."

Caroline's breath caught as she pulled out rolls of delicate rose wallpaper. "Oh, Eddie." She planted a quick kiss on his forehead. The front legs of his chair clacked as they landed back on the floor. Her eyes sparkled. "You promise to get this done right away?"

"I promise." Edward never tired of bringing her joy. "I ordered it last month."

Caroline squealed. "When can you start?"

"Tomorrow. My crews can manage without me for one day." He squeezed her hand.

The bell over the office door bonged.

"My, my, a bell." Angelina ducked and squeaked as she entered before pushing back the hood from her green cloak. Her cheeks were pink from the chilly wind. She examined the bell over the door as she patted her hair with trembling fingers. "The sound startled me."

Edward took her cloak and hung it on the coat rack. "Sometimes, I'm not here and Caroline is upstairs. We've had a few people who've wandered around in search of me. One man, who shall remain nameless, found me in the outhouse."

Angelina's raised eyebrows made him chuckle.

Caroline replaced the wallpaper in the drawer. "He didn't want anyone searching for me in there." She smiled at Angelina. "Tea?"

"Yes, please. Perhaps a bell is a good idea for Teresa." Angelina covered a yawn.

"Maybe she should come over and take a look." Caroline went to the stove.

"Her clients from Flat Ridge have entered our private quarters when we're gone. She posted a sign on the door stating she was out to lunch, but apparently, those men can't read. The door locks we ordered still have not arrived. It was foolish to assume our town would not need locks." She crossed her arm and sighed, staring at the floor for a moment. "We put a chair under the doorknob at night."

"Teresa should hire a male secretary to ensure no one enters uninvited."

Edward had happily renounced that responsibility when he moved his office across the street, but Caroline's suggestion sent heat through Edward's spine. Angelina's presumption that everyone would be forthright caused him to watch their building from his office window when he should have been working.

"A male secretary? Is that another way to prove female equality?" He frowned, then bit his tongue a second too late. Truth be told, the idea of any other man spending that much time in Angelina's presence waylaid his normal caution to watch his words.

"What about Barnaby Hayes?" Caroline leaned against his desk. "He has nothing to do until the depot is finished. We only have one train arriving every few weeks."

"That's a splendid idea. He's not handy with tools, and right now, there is no other work." Angelina warmed her hands at the stove. "The train tracks from Resolve to Abilene and other destinations throughout Kansas won't be completed for quite some time. Right now, I don't need a full-time depot manager, so it feels as though I'm paying him to be idle." She sipped her tea, then added, "Teresa can pay his secretary salary until he is working full-time at the depot."

Edward studied her. She wore a generous amount of powder, and a touch of rouge colored her lips. She had rarely worn cosmetics since coming to Resolve. It did little to cover the dark circles under her eyes. "Have you been sleeping well?"

"I'm fine." Angelina gave him a weak smile.

"Caroline, why don't you run across the street and tell Teresa your idea?" With a pointed look, Edward stepped to the coat rack and helped his sister into her cloak.

"I'll be back to report." Caroline winked at her brother and gave him her *I-know-something* look. Edward ran a finger between his neck and his collar, trying to suppress a rising heat.

After she left, Edward placed a chair in front of his desk. "Sit. How about coffee instead of tea?"

"Yes. Please."

"Caroline just made a fresh pot." He poured two cups of coffee, then set the pot on the back of the stove to stay warm and stood beside the desk, sipping his brew. "I don't have any cream."

"That's fine. I need it strong."

The clinks of her spoon circling the cup filled the silence. Angelina's faraway look worried him.

"Tell me the truth. How much sleep are you getting?"

"Less and less." Moisture glistened in her eyes. "Since the tornado, I haven't slept well. I dream that I'm trapped in my private car and the tornado is carrying me back to Chicago. Sometimes Hiram is there, reminding me I'm worthless. And last night, skunks joined me in my nightmare."

As ridiculous as that last might sound, Edward experienced not the least temptation to laugh. "I understand." He set down his cup, leaned on the desk, and held her trembling hands until they stilled. "I have nightmares too."

"About the tornado?" She didn't remove her hands from his.

"No, the war." His voice became husky. "I spent the war in an engineering regiment building bridges and dirt works for defense. But … I killed a man." The confession startled him. Even Caroline didn't know. "I was on guard duty when some Rebels snuck into camp. One of them grabbed me from behind and attempted to choke me with my rifle. I managed to break his hold and shot him. I'll never forget seeing life leave the man's eyes as blood gushed from his mouth."

"Oh, Edward." Her fingers tightened on his.

"Whenever things weigh heavy on me, I have a nightmare that I'm the one dying."

Angelina's face blanched paler than the light powder on her face. "I'm sorry."

His shoulders slumped before he straightened his back. "I'm sorry for mentioning it." Sharing his pain hadn't lightened her load. But her compassion touched the wounds in his heart.

"How do you overcome those nightmares and rest?"

"A small amount of sleeping powder. I awake a bit groggy. But after a few days of good rest, the nightmares are gone, and I don't need the medicine."

"I'll ask Dr. Potter." Angelina held his gaze. Need rested in her eyes.

"You never have to bear these things alone. I'm always here to listen and help in any way I can." Edward knelt in front of her. Her finger trailed his jaw. The impression of her touch tingled on his face even after she dropped her hand.

"Thank you, Eddie." Moisture dampened her cheeks. He wiped her tears with his thumb. "It's nice to be understood."

He touched her inviting, red lips with his own. She didn't pull back but matched his ardor. Edward wrapped his arms around her, balancing himself on his knees as he leaned into the kiss. He feathered kisses along her cheeks and returned to capture her lips once more. She moaned and locked her arms around his neck.

The doorbell bonged. Edward leapt up and once again leaned against the desk as Caroline entered with a humorous smirk. He crossed his arms, trying to look casual.

"Did I miss something?" Caroline's playful smile brought guilty heat to his ears.

"What did Teresa say?" Angelina sounded breathless.

"She wasn't sure she liked the idea at first. Then a Flat Ridge client came by without an appointment. She wants Barnaby to report to work on Monday." Caroline pursed her lips as she winked at him.

"Excellent, I'll head over to the men's dormitory and tell him." Angelina went for her cloak, but Edward reached the hook first and assisted her. Lavender fragrance drew him to stand a bit closer for a moment. She put her hood back over her head. "And I'll see if Dr. Potter has any sleeping powder." She fumbled to button her cloak, never looking at him.

The bell bonged as the door closed.

"It's about time." Caroline laughed.

"What are you talking about?" Edward crossed his arms and stared at the floor.

"It's about time you kissed Angelina." She patted his shoulder.

"You were spying on us?" Edward's irritation didn't erase her smile.

"Anyone walking by could have seen your amorous embrace through the large front window."

"It was a mistake." Edward jerked away from his sister, still feeling the heat of their kiss.

Caroline frowned. "Don't you dare tell her that. Don't you lessen that sweet moment with such hateful words."

"But it was. We talked about our nightmares." He shoved his hands in his pockets. "She looked so ..." *desirable, vulnerable, kissable.* He groaned, then turned to his sister. "She's my boss."

"It looked as though you both were enjoying that kiss. It wasn't a mistake." Caroline took off her wrap and warmed her hands at the stove while silence reigned. "She is more your equal than your boss. Angelina knows full well that without you, this town would still be a drawing on paper."

Angelina stopped a block away from Edward's office to pull her cloak more firmly around her. *What was I thinking?* Propriety would have demanded she slap his face. But ... her own response would've made such a gesture not only ridiculous but insulting. Her gloved hand touched her lips as she began walking again. Even though cloth separated her fingers from her lips, she still could feel the warmth and passion. She'd never been kissed like that. Hiram had cornered her once in the stable and slobbered over her face. She'd screamed, stomped his foot, and slapped him before running. Until Edward had kissed her, she had no idea it could be sweet, delicious, and oh, so desirable.

CHAPTER 24

Angelina shivered under the covers. The early gray sky seeped in through the window and filled the room with gloom. Wind howled against the walls. This cool October morning appeared to have no chance of ushering in a warm afternoon. Lucinda had been right when she'd warned the town to prepare for an early winter.

Wrapping her robe around her, Angelina padded to the window. Small, dry snowflakes floated across her view, dusting the town in white. The temptation to go back to bed almost won out as the sun lost its battle with bleakness. Her mind's fogginess from the sleeping powder hadn't worn off yet. She scurried to her wardrobe and changed into a heavy cotton dress. Her shawl did little to warm her. The wool dresses she'd ordered from Mary Price would not be finished until next week.

She sat at her vanity and combed out her hair. When it was coiled in a neat braid atop her head, she went downstairs.

Opening the stove door in Teresa's office, she added a few sticks of wood and struck a match. She wanted the office toasty before Teresa started her day. Lighting the stove was Eva's job, but she had taken another day off to help her family with the last of their canning. The Blakes were struggling to repay what they owed. Elmira had pled to pay Angelina directly and not get a loan. Angelina had agreed when Eva requested her salary go toward their debt. She admired the girl's loyalty. At fourteen, she was far more responsible than Angelina had been.

A pounding on the door caused her to drop the lighted match. She stomped on the tiny flame before it could do any damage to the wood floor. Angelina took a deep breath before answering the door.

Edward held a wheelbarrow full of scrap wood. How handsome he looked with chilled red cheeks and windblown hair across his forehead. She resisted the urge to smooth it back into place. He wore his business face.

"The coal shipment is late. Perhaps these scraps will get you through until it arrives. Shamus is taking some scraps to a few needy families as well." He scooped up an armful of wood and laid the stack near Angelina's stove, then started a fire. "If the cold lingers for a while, you might consider using only one stove to preserve your wood supply."

"An excellent idea." Teresa's voice startled Angelina.

Why was she so skittish? There was no danger lurking about in the weather or otherwise.

"Good morning." Edward shut the stove door.

"What I wouldn't give for a lovely fireplace." Teresa grabbed her coat from the rack, shrugged into it, and began buttoning it up. "I'll collect what's left of our wood from out back. How thoughtful of you to bring us more."

Angelina watched her leave, then turned to Edward. "We gathered all the wood that was unsalvageable for rebuilding after the tornado. Teresa's had Barnaby chopping it into smaller pieces for our stoves."

"I was concerned a wheelbarrow full would be too little." Brushing off his pants, he stood.

"As you can see, we will not be caught in a moment of weakness." Angelina studied Edward. He got her meaning, for his ears reddened. She tried not to smile at the cuteness of his blush. It'd been three weeks since the kiss. When he pulled his business mask back on, she couldn't decide if she was relieved or sad.

"Caroline is pleased to have an alternative to chips." He finally faced her, a smile playing on his lips. "I'm impressed with your resourcefulness."

His compliment thrilled her almost as much as the kiss.

"Thank you." She flashed him her best smile, hoping to coax the amorous Edward out of hiding. His cheeks flushed, but he kept his distance. "You're always so thoughtful. Thank you for the wood."

Oh, how she wanted to speak of the kiss. Come to an understanding. But if he said it was a mistake, she'd slap his face and ... regret it later. He stood there, saying nothing while her pulse raced.

"The sleeping powder Dr. Potter gave me three weeks ago has helped. Thank you again for recommending it."

Edward started to reach out to her, then dropped his hand to his side. Angelina turned away to hide the disappointment surely visible on her face.

"Don't take it too often, or you'll come to depend on it."

"Thank you for the good advice." The stilted conversation was maddening. "Can we—"

The front door flew open, bringing in snow and Barnaby Hayes.

"Why is there a wheelbarrow out front, filled with wood?" Barnaby hung his wet coat and scarf on the coat rack as Teresa came through the back door with an armful of wood.

"Mr. Hayes, take those wet things and hang them on a chair near the stove." She barked the order, and the young man complied with a frown. "Stop. Take off your shoes. You're tracking bits of snow all about." Teresa grabbed a rag and handed it to Barnaby. He glared at her. "Please, sir, clean up after yourself."

Barnaby removed his boots and tugged on the toe of his sock. "I'll need to buy some house shoes to wear when I remove my boots in the future. Otherwise, everyone can see my holey socks while my boots dry." His big toe wiggled free from his dark sock. "Such is the state of a bachelor. The lovely Miss Eva is making me a few new pairs." He grinned and attempted to fold the holey portion under his foot.

Eva had taken quite a shine to Barnaby, and Teresa had reminded her of work upstairs on more than one occasion. The more time Angelina spent around Mr. Hayes, the less she thought of him. Besides his uncomfortable stares, he often left his desk and wandered outside. At times, Teresa had to ask him to redo handwritten receipts because they were illegible. The train depot manager's position required a neat hand. Surely, his father had explained this to him. Didn't he want the position? Or was it his father's idea?

Angelina focused on Edward, less than eager for him to leave. "With the bad weather bearing down, have you heard an update on the church?"

"Rev. Asbury said he's raised enough money to build the basic frame for the church and the pews. The rest of it will have to wait until the funds are available. If winter truly has begun, the church will barely get completed in time."

"Indeed." Angelina drew a quick breath when he turned toward the door. "Edward, would you be willing to join me for dinner tomorrow night?"

He faced her again. His brown eyes sparkled, and a smile slowly curved his lips.

She felt the stares of the others in the room. "We should prioritize the construction we can accomplish before winter shuts us down."

"Of course. Shall we say six at the restaurant?"

"Let's say six here. I'll order dinner." Before Edward could object, she added, "Madeline is teaching Teresa how to quilt. They'll be down here all evening."

"Yes, and a few others will be joining us." Teresa gave an odd smile. "Bridget, Lucinda, and perhaps Daisy O'Malley and her girls. There is much more room to set up a quilting frame down here than upstairs." She made no mention of the impropriety of them being upstairs unchaperoned.

"All right, I'll see you tomorrow at six. Perhaps we can also go over your plans for the spring." Edward wrapped his scarf more securely around his neck and left.

Angelina went to the window and watched him maneuver the wheelbarrow across the street. As much as she wanted her independence, her heart wanted more. This man was everything she needed. After tomorrow night, would he still want to be here next spring?

CHAPTER 25

The sun dipped below the horizon as Edward walked toward the river. Angelina's invitation that morning repeated in his head. Evening strolls helped him sort his feelings. He hadn't stopped thinking about Angelina's delicious lips and how she felt pressed against him. The ardor between them had come as a surprise. Avoiding her had made things awkward. Tomorrow his fate would be sealed—but how did he claim a kiss that felt so right was a mistake without using that word? Without hurting her? Hurting himself. Angelina had stolen his heart. If she didn't feel the same, things would be more awkward—no, painful. His men might view any courting as Angelina surrendering her leadership. No. He couldn't do that to her.

He'd worked hard at keeping their relationship professional. But when the tornado nearly took her, he realized the attraction went far deeper than infatuation. *Now what do I do?* If only God would cool his heart. Then he could keep on task without distraction or risking his reputation and hers.

Water splashed him as he neared the riverbank.

"Turn away." The voice coming from behind a clump of prairie grass belonged to Teresa. Edward looked away from the stream toward the trees. After a few moments, footsteps followed him. "Edward, were you spying on me?"

"Goodness, no, Mrs. Shilling." Warmth rose from his collar. "I walked this way to clear my head." Edward peeked her way. She'd paused to tie her shoe. "Forgive the intrusion."

Teresa laughed, rose, and fished a pair of gloves from her

waistband. "I wasn't bathing, just wading. The cold water of autumn is invigorating. During the hottest days of summer when I went swimming here, I swear, there was a peeping Tom. Never caught him, though."

"If you would refrain from swimming in the river, perhaps there would be no peepers." Edward's initial embarrassment unfurled into irritation, and his jaw twitched. "There are Indians and many single men about."

Teresa snorted. "Cheeky fellow, aren't you?" She pulled on her gloves. "Come, let us walk back to town." When he didn't move, she gave a conciliatory smile. "Mr. Pritchard, I shan't go swimming in the river in the foreseeable future."

The older woman placed her hand in the crook of his arm. Edward's hand covered hers as they set out. They walked toward the woods. Crickets began their serenade as the light faded amidst the trees.

With a pitying glance at him, Teresa spoke, interrupting his private musings. "Edward, no matter how hard you try, you'll never get Angelina out of your head—because she's captured your heart."

"Did Caroline say something to you?" His sister generally kept her own counsel.

"Aha, my suspicions are confirmed." Teresa chuckled. "No. It's painfully obvious you care for her."

Hopefully, the evening shadows hid the blush warming his cheeks—a further confirmation of her suspicions. The last time he'd blushed this much, he'd been a child.

"I know she feels the same way about you."

In mid-step, he paused and stared at her. "Did she tell you that?" Fear and excitement battled in his heart.

"Of course not." Teresa patted his arm. "Don't worry, that doesn't discount what I say. In all the years I've known her, she has only shown disdain for men. Hiram's cruelty and her father's self-centered interest presented her a dismal picture of the male gender." Teresa frowned. "Are we going to stand out in this frigid weather?"

Edward continued their trek back to town as she leaned closer.

"You make her smile. She respects your opinion, and you're not afraid to disagree." Teresa lowered her voice. "Trust is hard-earned from Angelina. She seems to not only trust you, but it appears her heart is drawn to you. Tell her your true feelings tomorrow night."

"What if you're wrong?" A fool with a broken heart was the worst kind of fool.

"I'm not. She may deny it, or she may kiss you passionately. Either way, she'll know your true feelings, and that will help her deal with hers."

Smoke filtered into Edward's nostrils as they neared the edge of town. "Something's burning." They increased their pace. Smoke billowed near the end of the block. Edward's chest twisted in a knot. The law office roof was aflame. "Fire!"

Edward raced toward the law office with Teresa right on his heels. "Angelina!" Teresa's scream drew the attention of the already forming crowd.

"Angie." Edward's heart clogged his throat as he pounded on the locked door.

"When I left, she was napping." Teresa reached his side. "I don't have a key."

Barnaby rang the bell in front of the men's dorm. Men poured out into the street, some pulling up their suspenders, others stumbling to shove their feet in boots.

The cry spread. "Fire!"

Moments felt like hours as the town went into action. The Blake family carried several buckets. Women and children joined the men in a line and began hauling water from the well toward the law office. Men stationed on ladders handed up buckets while McCray and Shamus poured water on the roof. Noisy voices and children crying echoed in the night air.

Smoke billowed out the one open window. Angelina could be trapped upstairs. Edward looked around. "Barnaby, help me."

Together, they crashed through the door and were quickly

enveloped in smoke.

A rock formed in his gut. Edward stepped outside and dipped his handkerchief in a bucket as it passed up the line from hand to hand. He tied the wet cloth over his face. Entering the building, he paused, the thick smoke irritating his eyes. "Angelina."

Racing up the stairs, he found smoke billowing from the stove in the parlor. He felt his way along the wall toward Angelina's bedroom. He pulled open the window and stuck his head out, gasping for air to soothe the burning in his lungs.

Arnold stood at the top of a ladder next to the window, handing a bucket to George, who stood on the roof. "Edward! What are you doing?"

"I think Angelina's in here." Although it was too smoky to see everything. Edward pulled off his face covering and handed it to Arnold.

"Be careful." Arnold dipped the face covering in the bucket and handed the dripping cloth back to Edward.

Edward took another breath, retied the cloth, and turned into the room. He groped along the wall until he bumped into the bed. Indeed, a soft form lay under the covers. "Angelina." He shook her. "Angelina." Fear gripped him. *Please, God, no.*

He folded her unconscious form in his arms. Stumbling, he made his way back to the open window. Arnold reached for her. His lungs burned. The smoke followed him as he stretched his head for clean air. Angelina seemed to float down on the arms of strong men. Dr. Potter appeared with a few women and a stretcher.

Edward relaxed only a moment. "Arnold, hand me a bucket."

"Don't go back in there."

"It's the stove." Edward took Arnold's full bucket.

Gulping the air tainted with smoke, he held his breath as he turned back inside. Stepping to the stove, he grabbed the red-hot oven handle. Screamed. He ignored the pain long enough to pour water on the coals, then knock the stove pipe away from the ceiling. Darkness overtook him.

Edward struggled toward consciousness. Smoky dreams and Angelina's unconscious form haunted his sleep. His eyes flitted open, and a cough overtook him. He gasped for breath.

"Drink." Dr. Potter offered him water. "Sip it slowly. It will help with the cough."

"Ange—" Another cough stole his voice.

"She's coming around. You saved her life. I fear she has relied on the sleeping powder too much. If you hadn't gotten to her when you did, she would have died from the smoke she inhaled." Dr. Potter brought more water to his lips.

Edward drank deeply and coughed. His lungs felt less tight as he looked around the client room. Where was Angie?

"You'll recover." Dr. Potter set the glass on the night table.

An aching pain in Edward's right hand made him wince.

"Your hand was badly blistered," Dr. Potter said. "In a few days, I'll remove the bandages."

Edward drifted off to sleep and woke again when the morning sun shone over his covers. Shamus sat beside his bed. "I'm grateful to the Almighty for sparing ye and Miss DuBois. When ye be a wee bit better, we need to talk."

"Talk now." Edward's voice was harsh from the smoke. He rose and sat on the side of the bed.

"The fire weren't an accident. Teresa told me they was burning wood because the coal shipment hadn't arrived yet. Yet there be coal in the stove."

No accident. The revelation bounced around in Edward's foggy mind. "Are you sure?" He coughed out the last few words, then took a breath. Shamus held out a glass of water. He drank it down, then nodded for Shamus to continue.

"I found a sock stuffed in the stove chimney." Shamus showed him the blackened sock.

Edward jerked up straighter, which brought more coughing.

Shamus patted his back. "We also found a piece of coal near the back door. It smelled of kerosene. I'll be deputizing a few men to help me patrol."

"How is—" Another cough interrupted Edward's question.

"The roof will need replacing and the whole building cleaned and repainted."

Edward started to rise, but Shamus held him down.

"Sleep now. I'm the sheriff, and I'll be getting to the bottom of it."

He left before Edward could ask more questions. Dr. Potter entered and gave him laudanum-laced water that brought more sleep.

The next day, Edward was up and dressed before anyone could tell him to lie down. Mrs. Potter opened the door as he pulled on his jacket. "Where is Angelina?" His voice was less husky.

"Well, I suppose you've had enough bed rest." Mrs. Potter guided him to an adjoining room—the same room Angelina had recovered in after the tornado. Twice, he'd nearly lost her.

Angelina, wrapped in a robe, turned his way. Her dark brown hair hung past her shoulders as she sat in a straight-back chair near the window. She greeted him as he approached with a happy smile. Looking him over, she took his bandaged hand in hers and kissed it. "You suffered this for me." Tears glistened in her eyes.

Pulling her from the chair, Edward drew her close. She came willingly. "I was so afraid. Afraid I was too late. Afraid I'd lose you."

He kissed her, and she returned his kisses, then stared into his face. "If not for you, I would have died."

He kissed her nose, her cheek, and possessed her lips again. He pulled away, then leaned his head against hers. "Angelina, if you had died … if you had died before I told you I'm in love with you, I'd have hated myself."

"I'm glad." Her cheeks flushed crimson. "What I mean is, I'm glad you don't hate yourself." She gazed into his eyes, and her slender fingers stroked his unshaven face. A sigh brushed his cheek. She stepped out of his arms. "Thank you for not saying that first kiss was a mistake and for sharing your true feelings."

Teresa is a wise woman. Edward smiled to himself as he waited for Angelina to say more. This smart, feisty woman had just admitted their kisses meant something. An unreadable expression crossed her face. Was she confused or happy?

Angelina bowed her head for a moment, then focused on him, unshed tears in her eyes. "I don't know what I'm feeling, but it is closer to love than anything I've ever experienced. I need to know I feel the same way when my life is not in danger."

Edward hugged her close, and she clung to him. Their bodies molded to one another. This woman was who he wanted. Rushing her to confess she loved him, too, would prove he was no better than her perspective of the male gender. He kissed her hair, then held her at arm's length. "Fair enough."

"Thank you, dear heart." She pulled him close again, wrapping her arms around his neck, and initiated a long, passionate kiss. In it, Edward felt all the love she couldn't express. She ended the kiss, then they lingered in a hug. He fingered her silky hair, envisioning it resting on a pillow beside him.

Angelina stepped away, breaking the spell. She gazed at the window. The silence went on longer than Edward could bear. He took her hand with his unharmed left hand.

"Shamus is looking for whoever did this."

She squeezed his hand, her composure intact. "I wouldn't doubt it all leads back to Hiram." She crossed her arms, her brow furrowed as she lowered her head. "We need answers."

"Until Shamus finds out who's behind this, I'm staying by your side." Edward ran the exposed fingers of his bandaged hand over her cheek.

"Eddie, I would enjoy all the extra time with you." She gently removed his injured hand from her face, planting a kiss on his cheek, which stirred desire. "But there's the construction schedule." This time, she didn't argue that she could take care of it herself.

"All that is left before the weather gets too bad is the church. I think my crew and the church members can handle it without me." Edward kissed her nose. He thumbed her fingers that rested in his hand. Oh how he wanted to draw her to him again, but the temptation to do more than kiss was too great. "I know I just promised not to leave your side, but I do need to get a better look at the evidence and learn what Shamus has discovered. I'll be back." He kissed her forehead. "I promise. Truly, I do."

The smile she offered was different. Full of hope and trust.

On the way out, he found Mrs. Potter. "Be watchful." Edward glanced back at Angelina's door.

"I understand. It's all over town that someone tried to kill her."

Dread touched his heart. Who would want to kill Angelina? Surely, no one in town. It had to be an outsider. Would Hiram extend his reach to Resolve to get the DuBois fortune?

"I'll have Shamus send a deputy." For once, Edward was glad for the gossip telegraph. Anything untoward would be noticed.

Angelina snuggled under the covers. Warmth filled her. Was it love? She played his romantic declaration over and over in her head. Did she love him? Or was it more that she loved being protected? Her independent spirit and fierce determination intimidated most men. Eddie was different. The list of his fine qualities grew daily.

But what would others think if she pursued a romance with Edward? Would it appear she was less independent? Would the men in this town assume Eddie made all the decisions? Would the women think she was weak?

Angelina sighed and closed her eyes. What was wrong with her? She'd never cared what others thought of her. Why now?

She flipped to a more comfortable position, remaining still until sleep brought dreams. The man she thought she loved transformed into Hiram, and shackles held her behind a prison door. Perspiration covered her as she struggled to escape her nightmare. Her eyes flew open.

"Let me help you." Mrs. Potter's sweet face leaned over her as she straightened the tangled covers, then offered her some water. "There, now. Want to talk about your dream? Sometimes it helps."

Angelina shook her head, and Mrs. Potter patted her hand and left the room

The closed door was not as ominous as the one in her nightmare. Hiram represented all the men who'd come calling but couldn't see past her form and funds. Even Father had seen her as a commodity to be used to better the DuBois fortune. His promise to leave her the architecture firm was another way to manipulate her. She tugged her bedding toward her neck. Lies and deception from men who claimed they loved her had plagued her life.

A sunbeam spread across the middle of the closed door. Maybe if she allowed herself to love Eddie ...

A tingle went through her. Perhaps she'd allow her heart a bit more authority over her head.

CHAPTER 26

Edward grasped the edges of his office desk to keep from punching the man sitting in Caroline's desk chair.

Barnaby Hayes squirmed under Shamus' glare. "Why would I do it?"

Edward grabbed the evidence from atop the desk, anger growing in his chest. He flattened the filthy sock. "Notice the hole in the toe?"

"Wait, I'm not the only man around who doesn't know how to darn a sock." Barnaby jumped up, fire in his eyes, and slammed his hand on Caroline's desk. "I wasn't even in town two nights ago." He glowered at them.

"Where were ye?" Shamus leaned a little closer.

Sweat beaded on Barnaby's brow. "I was …" A blush covered his face. "I was at the tent saloon."

"Did anyone see ye?" Shamus' expression darkened.

"Yes sir. Mr. Hennessey and a girl named Lucy."

"I'll ask him." Edward frowned. Hennessey spent time there, but that didn't mean Barnaby had covered himself. A few dollars toward spirits could provide an alibi.

"Wait—Arnold McCray was there too." Barnaby wiped his brow with his sleeve, then crossed his arms

"I'll be asking." Shamus stepped away from the young man. "Don't leave town, boyo."

Barnaby put on his hat, glared at his accusers, then stormed from Edward's office.

"I'll go speak to Arnold. He's at the livery today." Shamus grabbed his hat and exited with a bong of the bell. Then it bonged again as he poked his head back in. "You be going to me sister's birthday dinner? It be a week from today."

"Of course." Edward shook his head as the bell bonged once more. He was beginning to regret its purchase.

Caroline rushed in. "Mrs. Collins wants the latest news about the fire. Do you have any updates?"

"Shamus is checking information. You know I won't tell you anything else until all the stones have been turned. And even then, an arrest needs to be made first."

"Can't you give me a small tidbit?" Caroline sighed. "Lately, the only news worth reporting has been the birth of the Anderson baby."

"Aren't you still working on your book?"

"I've finished all the current chapters. Until we start building in the spring, I don't have anything to add." She removed her coat and scarf and hung them on a peg, then pulled a paper from her valise. "Besides, we have to go to press on a regular schedule whether I'm spending time on my book or not. Please read over what I've written about your first-hand account of the fire."

He read through the well-written article and smiled. "Excellent work."

"Thank you." But Caroline perched on the edge of his desk, frowning.

Edward raised his eyebrow. "How about the first Christmas in Resolve? Or the new church?"

"I suppose Christmas and the church are newsworthy. But they aren't as dramatic as the tornado or as mysterious as the fire."

Edward laughed. "Caroline, if Momma were alive ..."

"She'd say it was stuff and nonsense." Caroline scowled.

"No." He reached for her hand. "She'd be so proud of you. I overheard her tell Papa more than once she wanted more for you than keeping house."

"I never knew that." She studied his face.

"When Papa was away from the house, Ma confided in me." Edward gave her a side hug. "You were too busy getting into mischief to listen."

"Sounds like Henry Collins." Caroline chuckled. "Trouble's his middle name. It takes an extra set of eyes to watch the scamp. His older brother, Martin, is like you."

"He's arrived?" Edward noted the slight lift in her voice. Was she interested in the lad?

"Martin wanted to take over the lead reporting." Caroline crossed her arms and harrumphed. "But Mrs. Collins insisted he prove his worth." She rocked from one foot to the other. A competition between them, then, and it appeared she planned to win it.

"Are you writing the article about Miss O'Malley's birthday party?"

"Yes." Caroline sighed. "It'll probably be a small notice in the paper." She glanced at the wall clock. "Look at the time. I need to get the fire article to Mrs. Collins." She took her paper from him and tucked it into her valise. At the door, she turned his way. "Eddie, you might consider shaving again."

He ran his hand over his chin. His whiskers usually looked unkempt by five o'clock. Maybe he'd grow a beard again. It had been so much easier to manage during the war. His unit had made a covenant that together they'd survive the war. The beards represented their promise. But canon fire had ripped through the bridge and his men. He stroked his bristled cheek.

And went upstairs to shave. He'd promised to protect Angelina. Would that vow end the same way?

One week later

The sun sat lower in the sky as Angelina finished hanging bright yellow bunting over the small cake table pushed against the wall of Shamus' sitting room. She had insisted Dr. Potter release her after two days since she'd stopped coughing.

She had placed an octagonal table in the corner for the gifts. All the regular furniture had been removed to the bedrooms to make room for two long dining tables to seat guests for Bridget's birthday celebration. She'd wanted the whole town to celebrate her friend but knew that would make Bridget uncomfortable.

Her arms ached from reaching above her head. How tired her servants must have been keeping things in order when her youthful parties lasted until dawn. What a selfish girl she was back then.

Wearing her Sunday best, Jenny Blake set her cake in the center of the small table. It was lopsided, but Bridget would be pleased. Daisy O'Malley had made a variety of cookies and potato soup and her sister-in-law's favorite Irish dishes for the special occasion. Her plaid skirt matched Shamus' vest.

Angelina hugged Lily and Pansy, who wore matching pink dresses and smelled like their mother's rosewater.

In a green velvet gown that complimented her complexion, Teresa stood near Edward. Something she said made him laugh. He wore a new suit with a red vest, looking every bit the gentlemen. Angelina's heart fluttered when he graced her with his dimpled smile. Emily and Michael Jameson were the last to arrive.

"Bridget will be so surprised." Angelina had forgotten how much she enjoyed the labor of putting a party together, even though this was far simpler than the parties Father had hosted.

Bridget came from her bedroom, wearing a simple green frock that matched her eyes. Her hair sat in a riot of curls on the top of her head. She scanned the room and beamed. "Thank ye, everyone, 'tis lovely." Her eyes glistened with happiness.

Everyone found their places at the dining tables. The O'Malley girls set the food in the center of the tables, then took their seats. Laughter filled the spaces between courses of food. Angelina enjoyed the Irish dishes and friendly banter.

"I'd like to make a toast." Edward stood, water glass in hand. "Miss O'Malley, may this year bring you every happiness."

Everyone applauded and dessert was served.

"Jenny, 'tis fine cake." Bridget patted the girl's arm as she passed out more dessert. "I'm proud of ye."

"I wish it had risen evenly." She sighed.

"Don't ye worry, lass, it's the taste that counts." Bridget proceeded to finish every bite.

Daisy rose after dessert. "Now, 'tis time for more birthday cheer." She took Bridget's hand and led her to the gift table.

Bridget's face streamed with tears. She wiped them with her sleeve. "'Tis too much. Such a lovely thing, but much too much."

"Don't ye dare insult us by saying we should take it back. Ma always did that." Shamus' reminder brought a nod from Bridget.

She opened and examined each gift slowly. There was a set of new knives from Emily Jameson that Michael had made, a book from Jenny, and some perfume from Shamus. Angelina's gift was the last one.

"It's too much ... I mean, it's wonderful." She pulled out the new dress. And then glanced Angelina's way. "You've very good taste." She laughed, and Angelina glanced down at her own dress.

No wonder she loved the pattern when she'd commissioned Mary to make it. Her mind must have been somewhere else when she ordered it. Where had it been today when she dressed? The gowns were the exact same poplin print with a striped bodice. Hers was blue and Bridget's was green. Angelina joined the laughter.

"Try it on. I'm honored to see you in the same style." Back in Chicago, it was the height of humiliation to wear a dress identical to someone else's to a function. Today it seemed perfect to dress alike— twins. Why not? She was like a sister.

Bridget slipped into a bedroom and reappeared in the new frock. Everyone applauded. She twirled around and smiled. "I look every bit a fine lady."

Angelina gave her a hug.

The party broke up not long after, and Edward escorted Angelina home. The walk to the women's dorm was much too short. Oh, how she wished her home wasn't still being repaired so they would have a bit more time alone.

"Eddie, you look quite handsome in your fine new suit," she

whispered.

"When Miss Price told me it was high time I got a new one, who was I to argue?" Edward leaned down and stole a kiss. She glanced around to check for spectators peeking out the windows, then giggled. "And you were very kind to Bridget to buy her such a fine dress."

"It's purely selfish. It brings me joy, and her gratitude blesses me."

At the door, he removed his hat and gave her a chaste kiss when Teresa headed their way. Angelina grinned and reached up to pull him to her, allowing her ardor to flow through her lips. When the kiss ended, Angelina offered a dazed-looking Eddie a mischievous smile.

"Teresa dared me to kiss you in public." She grinned up at him.

"A dark night with no one about is not public. But I'll take your kisses gladly, anywhere, anytime." Edward pulled her close as Teresa joined them at the door.

"Now, now. Enough of that." Teresa clucked her tongue and hooked arms with Angelina. "Well, young man, it's time I take this brazen woman inside."

They laughed, and Edward replaced his hat and headed home.

Angelina waited. Halfway there, Edward turned and waved. She returned the gesture before entering the dormitory. Expectations of sweet dreams brought a smile.

Pounding on the door woke Edward from his romantic dreams of Angelina. He looked about the room, expecting to find her nearby. The pounding on the door persisted. He pulled on his pants and padded down the stairs to the front door. One look at Shamus' face, and Edward knew the bell tolled bad news.

"Me sister took the trash out last night as I was heading to bed. She's not at work, and her bed was not slept in."

Edward couldn't imagine Bridget leaving without a word. "Did you say something to upset her?"

"Nay. She was in a bonnie mood after the party."

Shamus had buttoned the first button on his coat into the second buttonhole, bunching up the coat front. A nightshirt hung over his pants. "We need to form a search party." The man's moist eyes were wild with fear.

Edward touched his shoulder. "First, go home, dress, and get your rifle. I'll knock on doors on this side of the street once I'm dressed. You take the other."

Shamus swayed and grasped the doorframe with white knuckles.

Edward reached for a cup from his desk and filled it with water from a pitcher. "Drink it."

Shamus released one hand and grabbed the cup, gulping the water. He wiped his mouth and inhaled a deep breath.

Edward took the empty mug. "Pull yourself together, man. You're no use to us like this."

Shamus nodded and straightened his back. "I teased her about being a lady of leisure, too good to take the rubbish out. We laughed, and she made a big show of taking it out. I went on to bed because I had to patrol in a couple hours. I did me rounds and went back to bed." His face blanched. "I ne'er even noticed she didna come back inside. It's been hours now."

"What's happening?" Caroline tied her robe as she hurried down the stairs. "Did I hear you say Bridget is missing?"

"Aye." Shamus repeated his story to Caroline.

"Don't blame yourself, Shamus. We would have done the same. You had no reason to doubt she wasn't snug in bed." Her words seemed to calm the big man. His little sister was becoming a wise woman.

Edward's mind flew to various solutions before he spoke. "Send someone for Mr. Morgan's dogs." He patted Shamus' shoulder. "We'll find her. Meet me at the mercantile once you've dressed and gathered a search party."

Shamus hurried away.

How would Angelina react when she heard her friend was missing?

Minutes later, on the street outside the mercantile, most of the men and Lucinda gathered for the search party. Angelina ran to Edward's side. "I'm going too."

"No." Edward and Shamus spoke in unison.

"I'm in charge." Angelina glared at them. A mother bear growl came from trembling lips. "Bridget is my dearest friend."

Edward melted at the sight of her unshed tears. "You need to stay in case she returns."

"There are plenty of others staying behind." Angelina placed her hand on his shoulder. "Please, I can't bear to do nothing."

There was no way she would obey his request to stay behind.

Shamus stared at her, then pointed his chin. "Miss DuBois, you'd best serve me sister by keeping the women calm and leading by example."

Edward nodded in agreement. Surprisingly, rather than arguing, she went to stand by Mrs. Collins.

Shamus turned to Edward. "Miss DuBois just needed to be reminded that she is in charge."

"You're brilliant." Edward smiled, then checked his rifle load. Angelina's presence by his side would've been too much of a distraction as he helped with the search party.

Shamus took the lead. "Divide into groups. Some of ye, head to the woods. A few of you, search around the tent saloon. "

"How about heading toward Flat Ridge?" Arnold McCray suggested.

"I'll go with him." George McCray grabbed his brother's shoulder.

Tim and Jefferson Morgan arrived with their three dogs. Mrs. Morgan stepped down from her wagon with her children. "I'll get the women organized to serve food."

"We'll search once again around town," Teresa offered. "You gentlemen, bring our Bridget home." Her voice cracked as she dabbed her eyes with a hankie.

Shamus set a slow pace on his horse as Edward and a few others followed him out of town. The Morgans' dogs sniffed the ground. Tension rested on Edward's shoulders as prayers went up for divine help. Visions of Bridget dead beside the path sprang to mind. He shook off the thought. That would be too big a blow, not just for Angelina, but for everyone.

A couple hours later, Edward and Shamus ran toward the sound of the dogs howling over the small rise ahead. The other searchers followed. A piece of material from Bridget's dress hung from a bush. Edward watched Shamus, but his face remained unreadable.

The dogs sniffed around and started south. They better be as good at finding people as Tim claimed. Time wasted on wild goose chases would surely seal Bridget's fate. He took a long draft of the cold air to clear his mind.

"There's an abandoned homestead about two miles from here." Jefferson helped his dad release the dogs from their leashes. "Me and Timmy found it when we first got here. It's a dugout, so you can't see it right off unless you're looking for it."

The men had been walking beside their horses, but now everyone mounted and followed the sound of the canines as the sun rose overhead. They lost sight of them in the tall prairie grass. The dogs howled louder as they approached a wooded area. Edward's heart sat in his stomach. *Please, God, keep Bridget safe.*

A scream echoed through the copse of trees. "Get him off!"

Shamus and Edward reached the commotion first. Tim called off his dogs as Shamus grabbed the culprit by the collar. "Where is she? If ye did her harm, you'll not live to regret it."

"Barnaby Hayes, I might have known." Edward made no move to encourage Shamus to let him go.

"Please, sir, I didn't do anything." Barney gasped under Shamus' grip.

"So you were just walking in the woods?" Frowning, Tim tied the leash back on Sadie.

Shamus threw Hayes to the ground.

"I was trailing some kidnappers." Barnaby rubbed his shoulder. "I saw them grab Miss DuBois from behind Shamus' house last night. I was returning from the outhouse when they pushed her onto a horse."

"Why would you think it was Miss DuBois?" Edward watched the man's face.

"Her dress. No other woman in town has fine silk dresses." Barnaby rose slowly. "I may not like her uppity attitude, and whether you believe me or not, I'd never do her harm. I've been trying to figure out who stole my socks and set me up."

"You expect us to believe ye?" Shamus grabbed the front of his shirt and shook him.

"Please stop." Hayes clawed at Shamus' hands as he gasped for breath.

Shamus stilled the shaking but kept a firm grip on the man.

Barnaby took in a breath, his color returning. "Honestly, I was headed back to find you."

Edward signaled for the sheriff to let him go. Shamus tossed him to the ground again. Barnaby whimpered and crawled a few feet before standing.

Edward approached Shamus as the man calmed. "May I have a word?" He and the sheriff walked out of earshot of the others. "He doesn't know it's Bridget. He couldn't have been with the abductors."

"I was thinking the same thing. Sorry. Me frustration needed release." Shamus stomped back toward the young man. He offered a hand to Barnaby. "I apologize for roughing ye up. 'Twas me sister, not Miss DuBois, who was taken."

"Really?" Barnaby dusted off his trousers.

"Did ya see where they took her?" Shamus asked.

"They were holed up in a shack dug in the ground. Not far from here. Not sure if they're still there."

Barnaby's description spurred everyone on. The Morgans released the dogs again. A few minutes later, yelps and whines of joy echoed just ahead. Rounding a bend in the dirt road, they saw Bridget surrounded by happy hounds. She patted each in turn, her dress torn and her face scraped. "I knew ye'd find me."

Her brother hugged her close, then stretched her out at arm's length to check her over. "Where are the scoundrels?"

"Probably squatted behind a tree in agony." Bridget grinned. "Once their boss come by to tell him I was a cook and not Miss DuBois, they had me make their last meal afore they shot me. I asked if I might make a pie." She pointed to a tree full of small, red berries. Edward had only ever seen birds eat them.

"Those are poison, ain't they?" asked Jefferson. "Leastaways, Ma won't let me pick 'em."

"Not exactly poison, but you get the trots and wish you was dead." Tim Morgan ruffled his son's hair, and they all laughed.

"Who's their boss?"

Bridget shuddered and leaned into Shamus. "I didna see the rogue, but I'd recognize that oily voice anywhere."

Angelina's heart soared at the sight of her friend. She had to wait her turn to hug her while the rest of the town greeted Bridget. Angelina stared at the strange men tied together, walking behind Shamus' horse. Their trousers were soiled, and their ragged shirts needed mending. The large man's greasy black hair hung about his face, and he towered over the younger man by several inches.

"You varmints fall into the outhouse hole?" Lucinda pinched her nostrils shut as the men passed the group of women surrounding Bridget.

Angelina placed a hankie over her nose, then pulled Bridget into a protective hug.

"They ate red berry pie,"—Bridget chuckled—"and it didna agree with 'em."

"Oh my." Angelina identified the smell and felt a sense of satisfaction that the men were, even now, paying for their crime.

Dr. Potter approached Shamus. "They look like dysentery has them in its grip."

Shamus shook his head. "Not exactly."

"Take them to the clinic." Dr. Potter walked beside them. "You fellas can tell me what happened on the way." Turning to Shamus, he smiled. "Whichever deputy you send may be guarding the outhouse. Once they've recovered, perhaps you can find a better place to confine them."

Shamus poked one prisoner with the butt of his gun. "I'll telegraph the US Marshals."

Teresa joined Angelina beside Bridget and placed her hand on the woman's shoulder. "Let's have a trial right here and save time. Shamus, wire for the county judge, as well. Then the marshal can escort them to prison."

A shudder went through Angelina. Crime had come to Resolve.

Once the search party was fed and Bridget properly welcomed back, the families packed up the leftovers and went home.

Edward and Angelina sat in the O'Malley parlor across from Bridget and Teresa. Shamus helped Daisy prepare tea. Their girls were spending the afternoon with friends.

Shamus brought his sister some tea. "Now ye can tell the ladies what happened and about the voice."

Angelina leaned forward, ready to offer her hand in comfort if needed. *I'd have been frightened out of my wits.*

"I was pretty sure those two halfwits couldna done it on their own. Dumb as posts, they was." She placed her arms across her waist as if holding in her peace. "I told 'em over and over I wasn't Miss DuBois. They kept saying I was crazy, and they was being paid to deliver me to the looney doctor." Bridget shook her head. "The tall one had a dastardly laugh, he did." She shivered and pressed her arms more firmly about herself before continuing. "They threatened to slap me and a few other unsavory things."

A knot formed in Angelina's stomach, imagining what could have happened to her friend. Bridget was a brave woman. *Would I be as brave if circumstances called for it?*

Bridget balled up her hands. "I just glared and told 'em me brother, who was a giant of a man with fists of iron, would be fetching me soon." She punched the air. "Fools just kept laughing."

She sipped her tea, set it down, then leaned forward. "Just as the sun rose, a wagon pulled up outside. I couldna see from where they had me tied. The man peeked in the window after they told him I was a red-headed spitfire. The sun's reflection on the dirty window made it hard to make out his face. But when he spoke—I'd know that whiny, pinched voice anywhere. Hiram DuBois is here."

Hiram is here. Angelina's worst nightmare. As she sat back in her chair, Edward reached for her hand. She clung to it, swallowing hard.

Bridget pushed a loose strand of hair behind her ear. "He told the others to kill me and dispose of my body. But an O'Malley can outwit the best of 'em." Pride coated her statement.

"Sounds as though they weren't much of a challenge." Shamus patted her hand. "How did Mr. DuBois get out this way without taking the train? The next one isn't due for a week."

Angelina wanted to know the answer to that as well. He would have to use the regular train routes. Only by special arrangement did any stop at Resolve.

Edward leaned forward. "There's a stage line to Flat Ridge from Abilene, but he must be determined indeed to have stayed in such a place. Angelina? You're pale. Are you all right?" He squeezed her hand.

"I wonder if the doctor who visited me in Chicago before I left is with him." Would her greedy cousin succeed in committing her to an asylum even after all this time? "Why else would the men use the word *looney*?"

"I imagine someone will be making another attempt to kidnap Angelina. If those two said they were paid, perhaps Hiram paid others." Teresa shook her head. "The man is like a starving dog. Even though there's no meat on the bone, he'll bite you if you touch it."

"It doesn't sound like Hiram." Angelina raised her hand to the group before they could disagree. "Hear me out. I've known the man all my life. He's not above inflicting pain ... but murder? I don't think so. Putting me in my place is far more beneficial to him."

"But I know I heard his voice." Bridget wrapped her arms around her middle.

"Killing me doesn't guarantee he'd inherit the DuBois fortune. I have blood relatives who would probably win in court if it came to that."

"You told me how vengeful he can be," Edward interjected.

Angelina squeezed his hand again and looked around at the group. "He's a fool, a bully, and a fraud, but not a murderer."

"I still think we need to be vigilant." Edward wrapped his arm around her shoulder and pulled her close.

Angelina's fear lessened, knowing he would protect her. Most of the community would come to her aid if trouble came her way. That knowledge renewed confidence. Resolve was becoming more than a project—the people were family.

"I suspect his next trick will be to make an appearance." Angelina smiled. "And we are going to be ready for him."

CHAPTER 27

Edward nailed a piece of trim to the doorframe, completing the simple, framed jailhouse. Cold blasts of air ruffled his hair. Finishing the door gave him something to do while he guarded the prisoners secured in the cells inside. While he worked, snow fell in heavy flakes, covering the village in white. Pulling his coat collar up, he shoved his hands under his arms. Angelina would be relieved the building was finished. He smiled, remembering their conversation last week.

"I'm disappointed we must add a jail to my plans." She'd stared at the blueprint of the town. "If you must, put it here, at the end of the cross street." She'd pointed at the edge of the page.

"But the sheriff's office is usually next to the jail and near the depot."

Her nose had wrinkled, and her lovely lips had pressed into a line as they always did when she was deep in thought. "I refuse to give the criminal element center stage." Then she'd lifted her chin.

"Why are there no windows in the cells?"

"Villains might benefit from time in the dark." Angelina had flashed her teasing smile but added windows to the drawing. "For now, it's wood, but in the spring, it will be overlaid in brick. If criminal activity continues in Resolve, they'll have no means of escape from such a sturdy structure."

Recalling her determined stance made Edward laugh out loud now. He opened the door and glanced toward the tiny cells. The Davis brothers were secured inside, awaiting the US marshal and county judge.

Shamus approached with a covered tray. "Brung their noon meal." He set the tray on the desk in the main room. "Thank ye for giving me a bit of a break to have the morning with me girls."

"Glad to help." Edward warmed his hands near the stove. "I sent some volunteers from my laborers to the church site. Everyone wants it finished for a Christmas Eve service."

"I think they'll meet that deadline with all the extra help today." Shamus passed the plates through a slit in the cell doors, then cups of coffee. The prisoners glared at Shamus as they took their food. Cots were the only furnishing in the cells. Mary Price had brought the two a change of clothes once their stomachs calmed. Shamus leaned against the desk. "In the spring, we'll add proper metal bars, but for now, the wood cages will have to do."

Edward walked over and shook the slats. "I see you've chained the prisoners' legs for good measure." He scanned the jailhouse. A small desk almost filled the front room, and each of the three cells was only a bit bigger than an outhouse. "This is tiny compared to the one in Abilene."

"How would you be knowing that? Were you a resident there?" Shamus raised an eyebrow.

"No, Caroline brought me a copy of their newspaper. There was an article describing the new jail. It's at least three times the size of this, but they have quite a bit more crime there."

"I'm grateful we only need a wee jail." Shamus rose from his place. "Thankfully, Worth will be here soon to stand guard. Having deputies means I don't need to live in the jail with the criminals. Once the trial is over, I won't need deputies anymore."

"Let's hope you're right."

"You thinkin' Mr. DuBois be stirring more trouble?"

"That and the crime in Flat Ridge might come our way." Edward straightened the front of his coat. "I'll be sure to ask the marshal about a replacement for you."

"Wait on that." The big man offered a sheepish grin. "I'd like to keep the job a bit longer."

"I thought Daisy didn't like it."

"After we rescued Bridget, she saw things differently. She thinks I can keep the crime at bay because I've earned the respect of the town."

"Wise woman. You did a fine job organizing the search for your sister. You've kept the men sober, and the women feel a sheriff makes the town more civilized."

"I may have found me calling." Shamus fell silent as Dominick Worth stepped through the door.

"It's getting worse out there." The man set a basket on the table and removed his coat, then stepped to the stove and added a few more coal chunks. "I brought provisions. Figured I'd stay until the storm passed. No sense Arnold risking life and limb to take his turn." Worth nodded their way.

"Suit yerself." Shamus pulled his collar up. "I don't imagine they'll be attempting an escape in this weather."

Snow clung to Edward and Shamus, and the wind pushed them forward as they headed home. They struggled to maintain their balance. Edward's ears hurt from the cold.

"Stay warm." Shamus nodded as he stepped through the threshold leading up to his residence above the restaurant.

Edward trudged on toward the newspaper office. As he opened the door, a warm blast of air greeted his frozen face. "Caroline." He placed his toolbox on the floor and pulled off his gloves.

His sister lifted the portion of the counter that opened and smiled. "I assume you've come to collect me. I'll get my coat." Caroline nodded to someone. "Come and meet my brother."

A young man with blond hair stepped from behind the printing press. He took her coat from a peg on the back wall and assisted Caroline, gently securing the wrap around her shoulders. A twinge of brotherly concern caused Edward's fists to clench involuntarily.

"I'm Martin Collins." A hint of a mustache nearly disappeared in the young man's broad smile. He extended his hand. "I've been here a while now, but whenever you've come by, I've been helping my mother with my siblings. It's good to meet you at last."

His strong, confident grip impressed Edward. Martin was at least a head taller than he was, and his frame resembled the late President Lincoln's. "Caroline mentioned Henry was a handful."

Martin laughed. "Indeed he is. My father was the disciplinarian. Mom is too soft. Now that I'm back, Henry is more obedient. He was three when Papa died, so I'm the only father he's ever known."

Caroline nodded to Martin. "I'll be back whenever the storm subsides."

"If you have some thoughts on the storm, write an editorial." Martin nodded toward Caroline. "And if you hear from others about their experiences …"

"If you'd leave the office for half a minute, you might make a few friends." Caroline's Angelina-smile caused Martin's ears to redden, and the color spread to his cheeks. Edward tried not to laugh. "Then you'd have your own sources to use for comments."

"Shall we go?" Edward escorted his sister home, the snow falling thicker as the temperature dropped. Bustling into their house, he removed his coat and winked at his sister. "So you fancy Martin?"

"What?" She frowned. "No. Why would you think that?"

"You're just practicing Angelina's *make-a-man-weak-in-the-knees* smile, then?"

"Am I?" Caroline's coy expression revealed everything. "I'll go prepare lunch."

Edward had insisted on escorting her home after Bridget's abduction. Although the kidnapping was a case of mistaken identity, he didn't want to be remiss in the care of his sister. Miss Harper had demanded a lock be installed in the women's dormitory.

Edward shook his head, remembering his sister's complaint about the lack of interesting news. *Lord, I'd appreciate an uneventful winter. I've had enough excitement.*

Angelina joined Teresa at the window of the women's dormitory.

"That is quite a snowstorm."

Her friend nodded. Women sat quilting and knitting on the first floor. Noises of pots clinking from lunch preparation echoed from the kitchen.

"Lucinda said it will get worse before it subsides." Teresa pulled her shawl tighter. "I must say, I'd hoped our home would have been habitable before winter. Edward said the roof needs to be replaced, and it could collapse under heavy snow."

Angelina stared at the white flakes moving sideways across her vision. Goosebumps formed on her arms. Even with wool undergarments, she was chilled. "I never imagined I'd revisit my finishing school days by sharing a living space with several women. And Mrs. Montague's school was far warmer. I should have insisted bricks be added to the outside of this structure."

"Your intent was to convert this to a library once the other homes were constructed. That's part of phase three."

"I sometimes hate being so organized." Angelina stepped toward the stove, where a coffeepot and kettle warmed, and poured two cups of coffee. Teresa took them to an empty table away from the others.

"I don't see Madeline." Teresa stirred sugar into her brew. "Which means someone else probably made the coffee."

"Madeline is helping Mrs. Potter wrap bandages and restock the medical cabinet. She's determined to learn new things."

"Good for her." Teresa made a sour face as she took a sip. "If any of these women ever hope to find a husband someday, they need to learn to make good coffee."

"Then I'm doomed." Angelina chuckled.

"Edward can make his own coffee." Teresa patted her hand. "There're surely a few cookies left over from yesterday." She headed to the kitchen, leaving Angelina with her thoughts.

Wind rattled the walls. Would her town withstand a blizzard? Perhaps she should have built more for practicality. She'd used fine materials, to be sure, but the finish work on each building resembled styles from around the world. The copper domes on the clinic reminded her of a trip to Moscow. The Ho laundry resembled one she'd seen in Hong Kong. Edward's office and Teresa's resembled Swiss chalets. The rest of the storefronts reminded her of the market areas of Chicago and New York. Would it all be standing when spring came? In her quest to impress the architectural world with her creativity, had she foolishly doomed the residents to danger from frostbite?

"Here we go. Two cookies each. Gwen chased me out of the kitchen before I could secure more." Teresa pushed the plate toward Angelina. "Why the glum face?"

"What if a blizzard flattens Resolve?"

"That is ridiculous."

"Is it?" Angelina sniffled.

"Indeed it is. A blizzard is not a tornado. Edward has ensured every building is strong and well-built. Your designs are stunning and practical."

"But not fireproof."

"Oh, my dear." Teresa pulled her close. "That fire was sabotage. Don't worry about something that may never happen again. Listen to me." She turned Angelina to face her. "The fire did not consume the building. It did not take all our possessions. In the spring, I'll have my apartment back, and they'll start on your house. Most of these women will be sharing homes by summer. Focus on your successes."

Angelina wiped her nose. "How do you manage to be so positive?"

"It comes from years of wasted time worrying." Teresa removed her shawl, fanning her flushed face as Angelina pushed back a chuckle. "Life is full of misfortune. I find comfort in the words of Scripture during hard times and joy in its promises. I pray about everything as the Bible instructs."

"Does it help?"

"Yes."

"I've been meeting with the reverend to answer my questions about my Bible readings. Lately, after the fire and Bridget's abduction, I've set it aside."

"Do you feel better not reading?" Teresa added more sugar to her coffee.

"No, not really. But I'm still not sure God cares." Angelina bit her lip. "Trying to understand a life with God is daunting. Has He ever actually given you direction?"

"I wouldn't be here otherwise." Teresa's warm smile touched the place in her heart once reserved for her late mother.

"That encourages me." Angelina chewed on the sugar cookie as she went over the possibility of trusting God. "Will He protect me from Hiram? Or does He want me to fail because I am striving for women's equality?"

"I know He can protect you from Hiram." Teresa finished her coffee. "Equality isn't your entire focus anymore. Although your original plan was to prove to the world you're a competent—no, spectacular—architect, your heart has shifted. Concern for this community has changed you for the better."

"You think that had everything to do with God?" Angelina's voice came out as a whisper. "My mother told me God allows hard things to make us better people. Her death was the hardest of all. And when the pastor questioned my saintly mother's eternal resting place, I never gave God much thought after that."

"I'm glad you're giving our Heavenly Father some now. Angelina, walk with Him, and God will help you." Teresa patted her hand.

"Even if I want equality for women?"

Teresa sat back and laughed. "Especially with that. God is a big advocate of women. After all, He created us."

CHAPTER 28

Several weeks later, Angelina again gazed at the snow from the front window of the women's dormitory. Worry had transformed into a giddy joy when the snow stopped and the sun came out. While snowstorms had come and gone, all her fretting over a possible blizzard had come to naught. The men had kept the wooden sidewalk shoveled, and sled runners had replaced wagon wheels on the streets. Even the train arrived on schedule.

She put on her coat, bonnet, scarf, and gloves, then checked her reticule for the list of supplies for the kitchen. Walking toward the mercantile, she tugged her coat closer against the frigid air, her cheeks freezing in the morning breeze. Edward came toward her as she neared his office.

"Good morning, Eddie."

His face was covered in a scarf so that only his gorgeous eyes showed. He pulled down the scarf, revealing a heart-stopping smile. "Angie, I've missed you." He reached for her hand.

"Angie?" She wrinkled her nose, then giggled.

"You don't like it?" The concern on his face was, oh, so appealing.

"Lucinda calls me *Ang*. I like *Angie* much better." She smiled up at him. "It sounds lovely when you say it."

Edward looked about before taking her in his arms and kissing her soundly. "Then Angie will be my pet name for you." He tucked a stray hair back into her bonnet and ran his finger down her cheek. "You're freezing. Come in and warm up a bit."

"I'm heading over to the mercantile. I'll stop by on my way home." Angelina squeezed his hand. "Where were you coming from?"

"The jail. It was my turn to deliver food to our prisoners." Edward pulled her close again.

She snuggled near, enjoying the bay rum scent lingering on his scarf. "I'll be glad when the trial's over and they are on their way." A shiver not related to the cold overtook her.

"You may be getting your wish." Edward drew away and pointed up the street. Two strangers on horseback approached, then dismounted and hitched their mounts outside of Edward's office.

As Edward drew her toward them, the men doffed their hats. The burlier of the two, a few inches taller than his friend in the bowler hat, spoke for them. "I'm Marshal Adams. This is Judge Rathbone. We're here for the trial in response to Attorney Shilling's telegraph."

"This is Miss Angelina DuBois, and I'm Edward Pritchard." He pulled her hand into the crook of his arm in a protective fashion. Now recognizing Edward's action as endearing, not overbearing, she resisted her normal inclination to pull away and be independent. "Won't you come into my office?" He gestured toward the door.

"We need to tend our horses first." The marshal patted his mount. "Always take care of your horse, and he'll never let you down. We'll head to the livery, then come back."

Edward nodded. "You can leave your belongings here. You'll be staying with me." The men handed over their saddlebags, remounted, and headed to the livery. Edward set the saddlebags inside the door before rejoining her on the sidewalk.

"Where are they sleeping?" Angelina knew he only had two bedrooms, his and Caroline's.

"It will be a little tight, but I'll set up two cots in the office to give the men privacy at night. I'd better buy a few more blankets."

"And they'll have distance from Caroline." Angelina patted his arm as they walked to the store.

"Exactly."

"I wished I'd had a brother to protect me." She would have been safe from Hiram. But architecture school might never have happened. The brother would have been given the opportunity.

The train whistle caught their attention. "It's heading back to Chicago." Angelina sighed.

"Do you miss Chicago?" Edward squeezed her hand as they walked.

"At times." She glanced his way. "I'm more content here than I ever was in Chicago, though." She leaned against his shoulder for a moment, touched his cheek, and smiled before resuming a proper distance. "I love this town and these people." *And you most of all.* The thrill of the revelation filled her, but she schooled her expression for a more appropriate time.

The mercantile always overflowed with customers after the train delivered supplies. People waited in line to have their orders filled. Edward headed toward some back shelves while Angelina stood at the back of the line, waiting her turn.

After about five minutes, a hand rested on her shoulder, and she patted it. "There you are, Eddie." But when she turned, it was Hiram who stood behind her, wearing a smug expression. Horror and disgust washed over her. She stumbled back a few steps into the McCrays, who stood in front of her in line. They both reached out to keep her from falling. Sarah McCray placed her arm protectively around Angelina's waist while her husband glared at Hiram.

"Are you all right?" McCray asked. His gentle tone softened her fear. Their presence gave her confidence.

She found her composure. "Hiram, why are you here?"

Edward approached and stepped between them, his face a thundercloud. "Mr. DuBois, what brings you here?"

"Mr. Pritchard, I wish to speak to my cousin alone."

"I'm not leaving my place in line until I've finished my business." Angelina crossed her arms. "You'll have to wait."

"Why not step to the front of the line?" Hiram raised his eyebrow. "After all, this is your town."

Bile rose in her throat, and her hands quivered. Edward placed his hand on the small of her back.

"Say what you have to say and be on your way." Edward's growl caused Hiram to flinch.

"She has you under her spell, I see." Hiram removed his hat and smirked at Edward, then winked at her. "Well done." He reached for her hand, but she hid it behind her back. While his tone was cordial, it foreshadowed more lies, and a latent fury rested in his eyes.

Angelina reached for Edward's hand. "I have built a town founded on equality." She maintained eye contact. "I'll wait my turn in line like everyone else."

Hiram stared for a few fast-paced heartbeats before offering his phony smile. "Shall we meet for lunch at the restaurant?" Now he'd added syrup to his voice. "I have someone I want you to meet." He replaced his hat. "I see it's the only restaurant in town. I had breakfast there. Your maid makes delicious pastries." He turned to leave as Shamus appeared at the door along with the marshal and Judge Rathbone.

"Mr. DuBois, ye are under arrest." Shamus took his arm.

Every head turned their way. Angelina gauged the tension in the store and resisted the urge to clap for joy.

"I think not." Hiram remained cool. He jerked his arm loose and produced a paper from his jacket pocket. "I am here to collect my cousin and take her home."

Angelina squeezed Edward's hand and waited, though the urge to rip the paper from his hands quivered through her.

The marshal perused the legal document. "I'll have the lawyer look at it. You're still under arrest for attempted murder."

"Murder? Don't be ridiculous. I just arrived in town this morning. I have witnesses." Sweat beaded on Hiram's brow. Shamus took his arm in a firmer grip.

"Sheriff O'Malley will escort you to jail." The marshal nodded toward Shamus.

"Wait, I want to telegraph my lawyer. This is all a terrible mistake." Hiram's polished demeanor crumbled as his voice rose. "I demand my lawyer."

"I'll follow you to the jail and take down your lawyer's information and send the telegram myself." The judge pulled a piece of paper and a pencil from his pocket. "I'll fill him in on the particulars."

"Who are you?"

"Judge Rathbone. It appears I'll be presiding over your trial too."

Hiram's eyes grew large, and his chin jutted toward the man. "I want my lawyer present."

"If he can get here by Friday—otherwise, you'll have to find other representation. I have other trials elsewhere." Judge Rathbone followed Shamus and Hiram out of the mercantile.

The silence that followed their departure was filled with murmurs from the other customers.

The marshal stayed behind. "We met the sheriff heading this way and came along. Say, does the train to Omaha come by here?"

Edward cleared his throat. "We can send a telegram asking for a train to stop here, although we are not on their regular route yet. Miss DuBois has a contract with the railroad to make special stops."

"Good to know. Neither of us wants to get caught in a snowstorm, especially if I have prisoners along. I hadn't expected to see a train depot in this tiny town. I'll send the telegram after we sort out when the trials will be." The marshal tipped his hat and tugged on his gloves as he headed out the door.

A strange sadness filled Angelina at the prospect of Hiram going to prison. What was wrong with her? Maybe it was all the Bible reading she'd been doing now that there was no more building until spring.

"What was on that paper he gave the marshal?" Edward asked as they neared the front of the line.

"One last falsehood to try to put me in my place, I assume." Angelina straightened the list, as it had gotten crinkled during her conversation with Hiram. She smoothed out the paper, determined not to let Hiram rattle her.

"Resolve is the right place for you." Edward nodded.

Angelina felt his words to her core. But Hiram's arrival stole her peace and a chunk of her confidence. "I hope nothing happens to change that."

"It won't." Edward put his blankets on the counter so Clyde could record the sale in the ledger.

Angelina handed her list to Elmira, her mind filled with the ways her cousin could change things. *God, I'm hoping You have Your hand on me so I can continue to live among these lovely people.* What an odd prayer. But a deep sense of rightness settled over her.

CHAPTER 29

Angelina paced Edward's office as Teresa sat at his desk and carefully read Hiram's document. Edward and the marshal sipped coffee, their eyes fixed on the lawyer. After several long minutes, Teresa placed the sheet on the table. "My word, it's hard to concentrate with you three staring at me."

"What do you think?" Angelina placed her hands behind her back to keep from wringing them. "It's fake, of course."

"The document is legal." Teresa sighed. "A Dr. Schmidt signed the request for your committal."

"How is that possible? He came for tea. We chatted. He talked about his daughter's upcoming wedding. He asked about my project. Nothing unusual. Then he made an appointment for me to see him in his office the next week. There was no visit because I was here."

"According to this document, you have been diagnosed as having behavior unnatural for a female." Teresa huffed and snorted.

"What does that mean?" Edward rose and put his arm around Angelina's shoulder.

"Normally, these sorts of documents refer to married women. Our dear schoolteacher, Magdalene Harper, agreed to an annulment rather than be declared insane. Any woman who is not obedient to her husband or doesn't otherwise behave in the way society expects her to in all things can be subject to committal."

"How can Hiram suggest such a thing? I'm beyond the age of majority, and I managed my father's finances while he was alive, just as I've been managing my own affairs. It is unusual for a woman to be as independent as I am, I'll admit." A fire burned in her stomach, and her voice rose. "But never once have I behaved in an unseemly fashion."

"Not all women keep house and mind children." Marshal Adams poured himself another cup of coffee. "My sister went to medical school and works among the poor in New York."

Did that mean he would rally to her cause? Angelina drew away from Edward. Ire toward her cousin poured over her affection for the man standing beside her. Beads of perspiration dotted her forehead, and her heart fluttered. Amid Hiram's accusations, any male touch felt controlling. "Again, I'm not married to Hiram. How can he do this?"

Teresa guided Angelina to an empty chair. "Best you sit, because you're not going to like what I tell you."

Angelina hugged herself and stared at the floor while her composure wrestled with her fear.

"Enough money can land any woman in an asylum, should someone else covet that money." Teresa's words caused Angelina's breath to catch.

"So there's a real danger here." Edward stared at Teresa. "You're serious."

"Very. Unfortunately, women have no rights. Men dictate how we should behave. And foolish women ban together to be sure every female follows those rules."

Edward's jaw twitched. He stepped closer to Angelina and patted her shoulder. She sensed his frustration. He stalked about the room, his face contemplative. "What can be done?"

"I'm sending a telegram to Allen Pinkerton." Teresa tapped the paper on the table. "I hired his agency to keep a watch on Hiram. They should have quite a dossier on him by now."

"I told you not to spy on him." Angelina's hands relaxed, and she folded them in her lap. "I'm glad you didn't listen."

"Next, while the judge is here, we will bring this before him. A sanity hearing. We will need to gather written statements confirming Angelina is not insane. Those will be presented to the judge, along with testimonies from townspeople."Teresa began to write a list.

"That shouldn't be hard." Edward smiled at her. "Even the men who find her irritating don't believe her insane."

Teresa chuckled, then turned to Angelina. "As much as I love a good legal challenge, there is an easier way to solve this. If Edward married you before the trial, Hiram would have no hold."

"I refuse to use Edward in such a way. Marriage should be based on love, not my need to get out of Hiram's grip." Angelina stood and walked to the window. The bracing wind blew bits of paper up the dirt street. If only Hiram's document would disappear as easily.

"I'd marry you to keep you safe." Edward's husky answer drew her eyes to his. Love and compassion rested there. It would be so easy to marry him. But easy was never her way.

"Thank you. But no. I'm confident we can prove me sane." Her voice quavered, defying her conviction.

"What happens to this document if Hiram is convicted of attempted murder?" Edward's question gave Angelina hope.

Teresa placed her hand on her chin, squinting as she pondered the question. "I'm not sure. I know of no precedent where someone who files commitment papers has gone to prison."

"We'll be the first, then." Edward placed his hand in Angelina's. Their fingers intertwined as comfort passed between them, relaying his determination to support her. "Angelina will win this case, with your competent help."

"Absolutely. To set a precedent would be a feather in my cap." Teresa smiled and grabbed her coat. "I'm off to the telegraph office, then I'll study my law books. I intend to be very prepared if Hiram's lawyer shows up."

"You think he'll travel all the way here in this kind of weather?" Angelina remembered Hiram's lawyer from the reading of the will. He was overweight and getting up in years.

"There are lawyers who'd be willing to go to hell to defend a client for enough money." Marshal Adams rose from his chair. "I'm meeting the judge for lunch. We haven't eaten since we arrived."

"Don't discuss—" Teresa began, but the marshal raised his hand.

"Save your breath. I've been traveling with the judge quite a bit. We keep the legal stuff out of our meal conversations." He escorted Teresa out as the bell thudded against the door.

"What happened to your bell?" Angelina laughed. The merriment helped release a few of the knots peppering her body.

Edward's embarrassed look gave him a boyish charm. "I wrapped some material around the clapper."

"I think maybe buying a smaller bell would be best."

"Such a wise woman. One is on order." Edward chuckled and winked. "Would you care to join me for lunch?"

Angelina placed her free hand on her stomach, trying to still the churning. "Hiram's arrival has stolen my appetite."

Edward caressed her cheek as he leaned in for a kiss. She turned away. How could she think of kisses when Hiram was trying to have her committed? He released her hand. "You know this is another attempt on his part to get your money, except this time he went too far, and now he'll pay for his cruelty to you."

"I hope so." She allowed Edward to pull her into a hug. The warmth of his closeness, the strength of his muscular frame, threatened to melt her resolve.

"Marry me, Angie?" His husky voice tickled her ear. A desire to say *yes* overwhelmed her for a moment.

She pulled away, breaking the intimate bond. The man was a temptation she couldn't afford. Their eyes met, and he held her gaze. "Don't you see, Eddie? Things must change for women. Winning this court case is another step toward that goal." Angelina moved another pace away, pleading. "Please, don't ask again." She turned, threw on her coat, and, with her bonnet in hand, strode out of the door, slamming it behind her.

Edward stared out the window toward the women's dormitory. Stubborn, stubborn woman. Why must women's suffrage always take first place in her affections? He slammed his hand on the desk. Marriage didn't have to be a prison for a woman. Shamus and Gabe were examples of husbands who cherished their wives. Angelina's rejection trounced his heart. If he left, would she even care? Were her kisses all flirtation and charm with no true feeling? Come to think of it, Angelina had never said she loved him.

Edward ran his fingers through his hair as his heart wrestled with his mind. She'd said from the first day she preferred spinsterhood. But since the fire, her kisses had been more than sweet. Now she dismissed him like dirt beneath her feet.

"What happened to you? You always mess your hair up when you're worried." Caroline touched his shoulder.

He startled, turning to take in her furrowed brow. He'd been so trapped in the throes of his pity party, he hadn't even heard her enter the office. He smoothed down his hair. Could he leave town without Caroline? Who would watch over her? Edward's logical nature pressed against his emotions. *I'll not do something foolish because my pride is hurt.* No, his heart was wounded and bleeding out.

"Eddie, I'm waiting." Caroline tapped her foot. "Don't shut me out."

Edward hated those words. Wasn't Angelina shutting him out? This stubborn woman had his emotions in a vice-grip and his mind in a tizzy.

He stormed upstairs to their living quarters, Caroline following. "Eddie, talk to me."

He ran to his bedroom. "We're leaving Resolve today." He wrestled a trunk from the corner. The struggle released some of his angst.

"I'm not going anywhere." Caroline crossed her arms.

"Of course not. You're a free and independent woman." Edward opened the lid and flung his dress shoes into the trunk. The thud echoed his mood.

"Edward Hastings Pritchard, stop this childish behavior this instant and talk to me." Caroline's crossed arms and a determined glint mirrored another stubborn woman.

He glared for a moment, then slammed the lid shut and sat on the trunk. "You can't print what I'm going to tell you." He shook his finger at her.

Edward started with Hiram at the mercantile and laid out the whole thing, ending with Angelina fleeing from the office earlier.

"I understand how Angelina feels." Caroline sat in an overstuffed chair across from the trunk.

"You would take her side." Edward pushed down his anger. "Men were created to protect women. Angie needs my protection."

"Eddie, you're a wonderful protector." Caroline knelt beside the trunk and touched his arm. "But this time, Angelina needs to protect herself."

"Argh." Edward jerked his arm away. "Confound it. I can fathom the need for equality. But marrying me would eliminate the threat."

Caroline matched his tone. "Another man controlling her life, putting her in a subservient position."

"I would never treat a woman like property." Edward slumped lower, placing his hands on the trunk.

"We know that. Angelina knows it too. But no one else would believe it." Caroline sighed. "This is a man's world."

"Is that such a terrible thing?" Edward was weary of this whole experiment.

Caroline remained silent. Wind rattled the windows. This discussion could escalate into an argument, making his sister an unwitting substitute for his real target.

"Most women are happy with men in charge. Most women rely on men and appreciate their protection." Edward bit his tongue before his next thought popped out. *Most women would jump at the opportunity to marry me.*

"Protecting and controlling have a ribbon line of division. Your protection doesn't squelch my individuality, my dreams and opinions. But Ma mimicked our father's words. If she ever ventured a dissenting opinion, he scowled at her something fierce. Once, Pa threatened to send her to an asylum during an argument."

"Really?" Edward's anger deflated at the revelation. No wonder Ma had become more and more withdrawn over the years. "Maybe Angelina doesn't need protecting. But Resolve does. I haven't put all my sweat and muscle into building this town to abandon it."

"That's the brother I love. Protect the town, then." Caroline hugged him.

"But if Miss DuBois loses her case, Resolve will lose credibility." Edward kissed her forehead and rose.

Caroline tapped her chin, then her eyes brightened. "Why not ask Dr. Potter to examine her and testify that she is sane?"

"When did you become so wise?"

"When we moved to Kansas, of course." She giggled. A world of new possibilities had opened to his sister. He'd not snatch away her joy, even for a broken heart.

Edward hugged her close again. When Resolve was finished and Angie no longer needed him, he'd go back east and find a new opportunity—although as much as it would pain him, Caroline would probably choose to stay. "I'll take you to lunch."

"Perfect." Caroline reached for her coat. "I'll spread the word for people to write letters to the judge on Angelina's behalf."

Edward sighed as they walked downstairs. "And the gossip train will carry the news faster than the paper."

"Everyone is still upset over Bridget's abduction. Knowing Hiram is connected should help our cause." Caroline took his arm.

Hiram's remark about the lack of restaurant choices galled him afresh. Someday, this little town would have more than one restaurant. It would become a booming metropolis of commerce. Together, he and Angie had been building this town, conquering obstacles, and solving problems. Edward wasn't ready to call it quits because of Angelina's foolishness. Despite her resistance, he would not leave her to handle Hiram alone.

CHAPTER 30

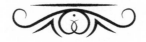

An hour later, Edward stood outside under the restaurant portico as icy snow bit his face. The cold chilled his heated thoughts.

Caroline had gotten Bridget's attention at the restaurant during lunch, and the two had spewed their views of the upcoming trial. Other female patrons had spouted more gibberish. Edward's appetite had trotted toward non-existence as his anger simmered below the surface. He'd excused himself before saying something he'd regret. Now he stood in the freezing dampness rather than listening to one more rant on equality for women. *Those women have no idea what may happen. The judge may decide Angie is crazy. Then what? They assume it will all turn out roses.*

"Dash it all." Edward shoved his hands into his coat pockets and stepped toward the sidewalk. Teresa might not win the trial, and Angelina's conviction could prove her undoing.

A wagon rolled through town, plowing through the slush, making deep ruts in the road before falling snow settled into the space once again. *My life is one big rut, filling constantly with unexpected changes.*

Snow covered the road with clean whiteness, but the muddy mess was still there below the pure surface, like the emotions swirling inside his heart. He'd put on a good front in the presence of the women, but his wounded heart had measured the conversation and found it wanting. *If she wasn't so bullheaded, her future wouldn't be at risk.* Their future—a future both had resisted. Even though she returned his affection, she refused him on principle.

Edward shuddered as the wind whipped across his face again. *God, how do I make her see marrying me is the best solution?* Did he want a wife who married him to avoid an asylum? Drat, drat, drat.

A man dressed in a wrinkled suit stepped out of the restaurant. "Excuse me."

Edward had been too sullen to notice a stranger at another table.

"Can you direct me to Mrs. Shilling?" The man's black mustache sagged around his mouth, but his eyes shone with determination.

"May I ask your business?" Edward looked him over.

"None of yours," the man snapped and returned his stare.

"I'm a close friend of Mrs. Shilling, and you're a newcomer in town. We've had some problems with strangers, so I'll ask again, what's your business?" Edward stood eye level with the man.

"I'm James Woods, a business associate of Mrs. Shilling." He extended his hand.

Since when did Teresa have a business associate? "Edward Pritchard, the general contractor for Resolve." They shook hands.

"Can you direct me to her?"

Edward studied the man for several more seconds. "Come this way." He had no intention of leaving Teresa unprotected, business associate or not. Surely, Teresa would appreciate his presence.

Edward's crew had repaired Teresa's roof and stabilized the building before the last snow. The upstairs living quarters wouldn't be finished until spring, but Edward had deemed the office space suitable to conduct business. He'd made sure the stove was properly vented and instructed Barnaby to watch it carefully. Teresa had refused to condemn Barnaby Hayes on the circumstantial evidence related to the fire and kept him on as her secretary. Angelina trusted Teresa's judgment. Women thought with their hearts, not their heads. Barnaby was bad enough—there was no way Edward was leaving Teresa alone with Mr. Woods.

Barnaby sat with his feet propped on his desk. He jumped up when the two entered. "Mr. Pritchard?" He gave the stranger an odd look.

"Is Mrs. Shilling in?"

"Yes sir, right this way." Barnaby opened her office door.

Teresa looked up from her desk. "Edward. Mr. Woods." She rose with a smile and shook Woods' hand. "Your arrival is timely." She turned to Edward. "This is the Pinkerton man I employed before I left Chicago."

"You mentioned you hired a Pinkerton to spy on Hiram DuBois." Edward nodded and directed his next question to Mr. Woods. "Did you follow him here?"

"Not intentionally." He removed his coat and draped it over his arm as Teresa indicated the chairs in front of her desk. Edward took the man's coat and his own and hung them on nearby hooks.

Agent Woods sat ramrod straight and placed his bowler hat in his lap. "I'm here to give my report and check with the other agent who has been here for several months."

"There's another agent here in Resolve?" Teresa's eyebrows raised. "Why?"

Edward wondered the same thing. Why was a Pinkerton here when Teresa had hired one to watch Hiram in Chicago?

Agent Wood interrupted his thoughts. "With your permission, Mrs. Shilling, before we begin, I'd like to introduce the other agent."

"Of course." Teresa nodded, and he stepped to the door.

"Mr. Hayes, if you please." Agent Woods signaled for Teresa's secretary to enter her office. "Barnaby, your reports have been helpful."

"Thank you, sir." The young man shook his hand, then appeared to be waiting for instructions.

Edward's jaw went slack. Teresa's expression was as blank as he'd imagine his own was.

Agent Woods turned to them. "After Miss DuBois sent him back to Chicago until she needed his railroad expertise, I recruited Mr. Hayes to watch out for Mrs. Shilling when he returned to Resolve."

Edward faced Hayes. "Your comments about women knowing their place ..."

"Were part of the persona I needed to display to draw out dissenters and troublemakers. I've been gathering intelligence."

Teresa harrumphed and crossed her arms. "Who asked the

Pinkertons to send me protection, young man?" A menacing scowl covered her face. "My daughters?"

Woods held up his hand. "Mr. Hayden Griffin asked me to send a detective to watch over you. To quote Mr. Griffin, 'I am concerned my employer will meet an untimely demise.' Mr. Hayes' mission was also to discover who was causing problems. He was never supposed to be a suspect in a kidnapping."

"I'm still trying to figure out who stole my sock off the clothesline," Barnaby added.

"It was one of those ne'er-do-wells in the jail," Teresa said.

"I think there is someone else involved." Barnaby stood a bit taller. "Maybe more than one. Shamus and the marshal have been questioning the prisoners for hours. Shamus learned the men's intent was to scare Miss DuBois, not kill anyone. They haven't admitted there is a third party."

"Once we know for certain, then we can act." Detective Woods turned to Teresa. "I apologize if Mr. Hayes' true identity troubles you."

Teresa laughed. "Griffin is a cautious man. He often acted in my best interest in Chicago, then told me after the fact. We'll see if Mr. Hayes proves to be for my good." She scowled at Barnaby. "I still expect you to continue as my secretary."

"Yes ma'am." Barnaby chuckled.

Agent Woods opened his valise. "I've been shadowing Hiram DuBois for months. He's involved in lots of questionable business deals, and he needs funds."

"Interesting." Teresa tapped her chin. "Grab your notepad, Mr. Hayes. Edward, I think Angelina is at the dress shop. Can you bring her here?"

Angelina stood before the full-length mirror at the dress shop.

Mary Price's smile reflected in the mirror. "It fits perfectly." She had another frock draped over her arm. "Try this finished one on. I have three more I need to hem. If you have time, you can try those on, too, and I can pin the hems."

"You do wonderful work." Angelina stepped behind the screen to change garments. She hung up the hemmed dress and reached for a lavender floral print.

Mary's plain face lit up in the most satisfying manner when Angelina appeared. She assisted with the buttons down the back of the dress, then bent to straighten the skirt. "Lovely. No alteration needed."

Angelina went to the mirror and turned to the side to get a better look at the bustle. "Perfect. I love the lavender, and the bustle is not too big." Trying on a new frock cheered her.

Miss Price's doorbell chimed.

"Angelina?" Edward's familiar voice sent butterflies soaring in her middle as he made his way past the front counter toward them. "Teresa has called a meeting. A Pinkerton has arrived."

"Teresa just sent the telegram a few hours ago to Allen Pinkerton." Angelina shook her head. "I'm confused."

"You're not the only one." Rather than meet her eyes, he ducked his head, his hat in his hands.

"Very well." She smoothed the front of her new dress. "Mary, I'll be back tomorrow for another fitting. I'll pick up my other dress then."

Angelina allowed Edward to help her with her coat, the awkward silence palpable.

Edward walked beside her toward Teresa's office. "You look nice in purple." His tone was flat. His arms rested at his sides. The barrier between them was firmly in place again.

"It's lavender and thank you. I feel cleaner if I have fresh clothes daily." She sighed, hating the distance between them. Angelina's heart didn't feel clean after her hasty words to Edward rejecting his proposal. Why was she still blabbering on about dresses? "I know you think I'm vain."

"Did I use that word?" Edward paused in their walk.

"No, Edward, and I'm terribly sorry." Angelina opened the closet they'd hidden their hearts in. "Your proposal was sincere, and I shouldn't have brushed it off so rudely."

"It's fine." Edward started to walk again.

"No, it's not." Angelina refused to move and touched his arm. "I appreciate all you've done—and do. You're an honorable man." She fought to control the tremble in her voice. "Right now, I …"

"Need to do this on your own." Edward took her hands and gazed into her eyes, love discernible behind his sad expression. "Let's see what the Pinkerton detective has to say before you throw me in the toolshed."

Did Edward think she viewed him as something to be used and set aside? The thought hurt. How often had she said or done something to make him feel that way? Eddie deserved better. "I'm sorry." She stepped closer. "Please, I can't do this without your support."

"I'm here, Angelina." Expression softening, Edward stroked her cheek.

One kiss and she'd capitulate, and then the foundation of all her hard work would shift. She pulled away and continued walking. When this trial was over … but for now, she'd focus on the task at hand.

When they reached Teresa's building, Edward opened the door and helped her put away her coat. Angelina patted her hair in place, then headed toward her private office and those assembled.

Teresa looked up from her desk. "Good, you're here. Detective Woods, this is Miss Angelina DuBois, the architect and founder of Resolve, Kansas."

The man who'd risen from his chair when she entered shook her hand. Mr. Hayes stood near Teresa's desk.

"This is Detective Woods, from the Pinkerton Agency." Teresa finished the introductions.

Angelina nodded affirmation and took the chair offered. Edward pulled another from the front office and sat beside her. "And Mr.

Hayes is also a Pinkerton agent." Teresa nodded his way. He gave Angelina a sheepish grin.

"Oh my." Angelina had many questions for Barnaby, but now was not the time to ask.

Mr. Woods opened a notebook. "Mr. DuBois is involved in a scheme to defraud his former architect clients, and his gambling habits have him partnering with a criminal element to sell bogus railroad stock." He continued, reading details surrounding her cousin's crimes.

Angelina felt sick. "I believe he was involved with those same unsavory people while my father was alive. They had arguments regarding adding new blood—Hiram called it—to the firm." Angelina seethed at the memory. "Father refused to expand his business by investing in the companies my cousin sought out. But Hiram, as the sole owner of DuBois Architectural Interests, can do whatever he likes. I'm not sure any of that information would help during my sanity hearing."

"There's something else." Detective Woods closed his notebook. "Hiram DuBois was on the train two rows in front of me the whole trip here. He could not have kidnapped Miss O'Malley."

"But she heard his voice clearly." Angelina's throat tightened, and she clenched her fists in her lap.

"The marshal is questioning the miscreants now. He told me they are Matthew and Thaddeus Davis, two brothers who will do almost anything for a price." Teresa's arms rested on the desk. "Even if Hiram can't be connected to the kidnapping, his motives for trying to commit you are clear. We can prove you're not insane and that he is seeking to take over your finances for his own interests."

"I was trailing those men when Sheriff O'Malley accosted me." Barnaby rubbed his jaw. "I'd have done the same if it was my sister. There was a third man, but I lost his trail about the time the posse caught up with me."

"Did you tell Shamus and the marshal you're a Pinkerton?" Edward asked.

"No. I was waiting for Detective Woods to arrive before I said anything further. Hiram could still be behind all this."

"Agent Hayes, you and I will meet with the marshal and the sheriff. We don't want any prisoners released until we've finished our investigation." Detective Woods turned to Teresa. "You've got the dossier I've prepared for you." He replaced his hat and rose. "If you have no further questions, we'll get back to the business of nailing Hiram DuBois for a number of crimes."

The detectives left, and Teresa went to her stove. "More coffee?" She filled their cups and returned to her desk.

"I had no idea Barnaby was a Pinkerton." Angelina shook her head and stirred her coffee.

"That's a long story, and I'll tell you later, after I've fully digested the revelation," Teresa said. "Angelina, can you bring me dinner later? I'll be studying my law books for a while. When I get inspired, I forget to eat."

"Of course. Thank you for doing this." Angelina hugged her friend.

"Doing what I fought to get into law school for? Pursuing a career twenty years later?" Teresa leaned toward her. "My dear, this has been the most fulfilling time in my life. I've settled land disputes, written wills and deeds, and now I have the privilege of using my God-given gifts before a judge and jury. I'll prosecute the Davis brothers. Then banish the accusations you're insane. And I believe after I show the judge this dossier on Hiram, he'll be facing more charges." She sat back and fanned herself. "No. Thank *you* for asking me to share this adventure."

CHAPTER 31

From the door where Edward had volunteered to stand to bar latecomers, he surveyed the men's dormitory, now transformed into a courtroom for the trials—the Davis brothers', then Angelina's. A table had been set at the front for Judge Rathbone, and two more were placed facing the judge's table for the lawyers. Twelve chairs were placed to the left of the judge.

Jury selection had taken some time because so many townspeople had been involved in searching for Bridget. Three of the men were homesteaders. Cromwell Hanson, who wasn't in the search party, was selected along with Mr. Ho and Rev. Asbury. Judge Rathbone had agreed to add three women homesteaders who lived a distance from town to provide an unbiased jury. Teresa's argument that women ran most of the businesses in town made the request reasonable.

"Edward." Gabe caught his attention as he entered with Lucinda and Teddy. He indicated for his family to sit in some empty chairs near the back and stepped toward Edward. "I heard a rumor even though the attempted murder and kidnapping charges were dropped against Mr. DuBois, he may still have to stand trial."

"A regular three-ring circus." Edward glanced around the almost-filled room. "The file Teresa gave the judge regarding Hiram's criminal activity in Chicago may require a hearing of its own. I don't have all the details."

"No one told him." Gabe chuckled. "When I brought the prisoners their breakfast, the man kept insisting he knew important people in Chicago who would hear about—to quote Mr. DuBois—'the horrid treatment' he'd received. Can't figure how three square meals a day and place to sleep is so bad." Gabe turned to leave. "I got appointed to stand guard by the defendant's table. Should be interesting."

"Indeed." Edward took his sentry position once again.

Gabe strolled to the front as the Davis brothers were brought in by Shamus and the marshal. The marshal took a seat in the front row behind the prisoners, while Shamus moved toward the judge's table, then walked the perimeter of the room.

Angelina sat behind Teresa's table. Bridget sat with Teresa, and the two accused kidnappers sat alone at the defendant table, Gabe standing guard to their left. Murmurs of greetings and muted conversation hummed about the room while people found seats.

Edward stepped over toward Shamus, who was now standing along the front wall. "It looks like a full house."

"Aye, sending riders to homesteads to spread the word about Angelina's trial brought them out even in the cold weather."

"These people will support Angelina." Edward cleared his throat. "At least, I hope so."

Shamus patted his back. "Ye need not worry but put yer trust in the one who knows the outcome."

Edward nodded and went back to his post.

A man reeking of liquor brushed past Edward and joined the accused at their table. The three whispered together.

As the judge entered, Shamus proclaimed in a loud voice, "All rise. The court be now in session, the honorable Judge Rathbone presiding."

The defendants' lawyer continued to talk to his clients as Judge Rathbone took his place.

"Excuse me." The judge slammed his gavel down on his table. The sound echoed through the room. The three men sat straight, finally focusing on the official. "I run my court with the same efficiency and decorum of any courtroom back east. There will be no talking during the proceeding. Anyone in the gallery who creates a disturbance will be removed at once. Every witness will be treated with respect. Both lawyers ..." He turned to the stranger at the defendant's table. "Am I to assume you're their lawyer?"

The man stood, stretched his suspenders, and puffed out his chest, then turned to smile at the crowd. "I'm Byron Tripper, justice of the peace in Flat Ridge. I'll be acting as their lawyer."

The judge scowled. "Despite your initial disrespect of this court, I will assume you're aware of how a trial proceeds. And I trust you will conduct yourself accordingly, Mr. Tripper."

"Yes, your honor." Mr. Tripper plopped in his chair.

"Each lawyer will take their turn at questioning. When all the evidence is presented, the twelve jurors will be escorted to Mr. Pritchard's office, where they will decide these men's fate. While they are deliberating, I'll preside over the commitment request. Once that is resolved, there will be another hearing involving Mr. Hiram DuBois as the last item on the docket. I don't believe in wasting time. If we run past noon, we will recess for lunch—otherwise, there will be no breaks."

Other than a few rustles as people found comfortable positions, the room remained quiet.

"Mrs. Shilling, you may make your opening statement." Judge Rathbone nodded her way. She approached the bench with a confident stride and presented a compelling argument. Seeing her in action relaxed the tightness in Edward's neck. Once she was seated, the judge nodded to Mr. Tripper. "Your opening statement."

Mr. Tripper rose. He nodded to the judge, stumbled around his chair, and straightened. "I intend to prove my clients are not guilty." He turned toward the gallery and made a dramatic appeal painting the Davis brothers as the salt of the earth.

Teresa then stepped forward to summon her first witness. "I call Miss Bridget O'Malley to the stand."

Shamus swore her in.

"Miss O'Malley, would you tell the jury what happened to you on the day in question?" With a gentle smile, Teresa coaxed the story from Bridget.

If Edward didn't know otherwise, he would have sworn she was a seasoned lawyer. Those present remained silent and attentive to every detail.

"Thank you, Miss O'Malley. I'm sure that was difficult for you to talk about."

Next, Mr. Tripper took his turn cross-examining. He smiled at Bridget, and her eyes widened when he leaned in a bit too close. "Miss O'Malley, are you sure the defendants are the men who abducted you?"

"Of course. They didn't even try to cover their faces."

Mr. Tripper paced toward the jury and turned toward Bridget. "Would you say they treated you kindly?"

"If you call shoving a bag over me head and tying me to a horse kind, then yes." Bridget glared at the man.

He stretched his suspenders. "I understand they made sure you were fed, and no harm came to you while in their care." Mr. Tripper smiled at the gallery.

"I was the one doing the cooking, and that one over there ..." Bridget pointed to Thaddeus Davis. "He made some inappropriate remarks to me."

A woman in the gallery shouted. "They kidnapped her, for heaven sakes."

Judge Rathbone banged his gavel. "This is my first warning. The gallery will keep their thoughts to themselves, or Mr. Pritchard will escort you out."

Once the room quieted, Mr. Tripper continued. "Now, Miss O'Malley, Matthew and Thaddeus Davis have expressed to me their regret for the incident."

"Incident." Bridget spat the word out. "I was kidnapped, Mr. Tripper."

Judge Rathborne brought down the gavel. "Miss O'Malley, please contain yourself. Mr. Tripper, either ask a question or be seated."

Thaddeus Davis turned with crossed arms and scowled as Mr. Tripper took a seat.

Barnaby Hayes gave testimony as an eyewitness to the kidnapping. "I saw those two grab Miss O'Malley behind her residence."

"What were you doing behind the building at that time of night?" Teresa nodded toward Barnaby.

"I was patrolling the town, as I had every night since the fire. The sheriff didn't ask for my help, but if the arsonist decided to strike again, an extra set of eyes patrolling couldn't hurt."

Edward was impressed. Barnaby managed to conceal the fact that he'd been a suspect—and also his identity as a Pinkerton agent.

Teresa glanced at her notes. "What did you do next?"

"I followed them to a cabin where a third man joined them. He seemed to be in charge."

"Did you get a good look at the third man?

"No ma'am. From my hiding spot, the sun was in my eyes."

"Then what did you do?"

"I headed back to town to tell Shamus."

Once she completed her questions, she looked toward Mr. Tripper.

He shrugged and remained seated. "I got no questions for this witness."

"In that case, I call Mr. Matthew Davis to the stand."

The young man took the chair with slumped shoulders, keeping his eyes on the floor.

"Mr. Davis—that is your name, correct?" Teresa's motherly tone brought his head up. Her smile seemed to put him at ease.

"Yes ma'am, Matthew Davis, and that's my brother, Thad." He pointed toward his brother sitting at the defendants' table and smiled at Teresa.

"Can you tell me why a nice young man like you would be involved with a kidnapping?"

Teresa spoke in a tone she might use to address a child. Edward even felt sorry for the man. When he'd brought Matthew his meals, he'd seemed a bit touched in the head. Even so, he'd refused to offer up the name of the man who hired him. The rougher the marshal had spoken to him, the quieter he'd become. Teresa's gentle prompting proved more effective.

"I was paid to."

"You were paid to kidnap Miss O'Malley?"

"No. Miss DuBois."

"Then you made a mistake?"

"Yes ma'am, a terrible mistake. When he told us we had to kill her, I near died myself." The defendant wrung his hands.

Teresa put on a sympathetic face. "I'm sure you felt terrible when … what was his name?"

"Mr. Gerard Standish."

"Shut up, Matt," his brother shouted from his seat.

The judge's gavel pounded the table. "Order in the court. Mr. Thaddeus Davis, you will stay quiet, or you will be removed."

Thad scowled at his brother. Matthew seemed to shrink in the chair.

Teresa patted his shoulder, and Matthew appeared to relax and gave her his full attention. "When Mr. Standish told you to kill Miss O'Malley, what did you do?"

"I told Thad I wasn't going to do it. I'm a Christian man, and killing is a sin."

"Are you aware that kidnapping is a sin as well?" Teresa asked, turning to the gallery and crossing her arms.

"We kidnapped the wrong person, so it's just a mistake." Matthew's knee shook. "Besides, we was told Miss DuBois escaped a looney bin, and we was retrieving her."

"Mr. Standish told you this?" Teresa continued to nod encouragement.

"Yes ma'am."

"When and where did he contact you to do this retrieving?"

"We was at the Red Rose. That's a saloon in Flat Ridge. The bartender told us Mr. Standish wanted to see us. We do jobs for him, time to time."

"What kind of jobs?" Teresa kept her voice soft.

"Deliveries, watching people, and relaying messages."

"Are you a violent man, Matthew?" Her voice rose a bit.

"Not to women. We didn't hurt Miss O'Malley, I swear. I was tempted to kiss her, but decided I'd be a gentleman instead." Matthew smiled Bridget's way, and she glowered in return.

"Thank you for your honesty, Matthew. No further questions."

Marshal Adams nodded at Edward as he left the building. With this new information, the lawman would waste no time finding the third man. And Detective Woods was taking copious notes.

The trial was over in an hour. The Davis' lawyer was useless. At one point, Thaddeus nudged him when he began snoring. Edward escorted the jury to his office, where a deputy guarded the door, then headed back for the next trial.

Shamus met him in the street after returning the men to their cell. "Appears Mr. Standish is not a man to be trifled with. The more Thaddeus yelled at his brother, the more the wee man cried."

Hiram DuBois now sat where the Davis men had been. Shamus had let him stew in jail overnight, for only this morning had he learned the attempted murder charge had been dropped. Clean shaven, with a smug expression on his face, he nodded to Angelina, now seated next to Teresa. Edward regretted his decision to guard the door, longing to be by Angelina's side.

An older gentleman wearing a black suit approached the judge. Teresa joined them for a brief parlay. Word around town, thanks to Mrs. Potter, was that she and her husband had provided hospitality for this witness, the doctor from the asylum. Hiram's arrest had left Dr. Cosgrove without introductions, and most of the town had ignored him.

Over the next few minutes, Teresa presented the judge with letters from all the Resolve residents along with some from the homesteaders testifying to Angelina's sanity. She had carefully chosen five witnesses—Tim Morgan, Clyde Blake, Caroline Pritchard, Michael Jameson, and Madeline Harper.

Standing behind her table, Teresa addressed the first witness with the authoritative tone of an attorney. "Please state your full name."

"Timothy Angus Morgan."

"Mr. Morgan, what was your first impression of Miss DuBois?"

Tim Morgan squirmed and spun the hat resting in his lap between his fingers. He glanced at his wife, seated in the back of the gallery.

Edward stretched his fingers out at his side to release the nervous fists that had formed with Teresa's question. He prayed the man wouldn't say something foolish.

Tim blushed and cleared his throat. "I thought she was too high and mighty and needed to be put in her place." Murmuring of disapproval filtered from the back of the room.

The gavel fell. "Enough. There will be silence." Judge Rathbone glared toward the disturbance. He waited until the crowd stilled, then nodded to Teresa.

"And now, how do you feel?"

"She may be rich and smart, but she don't lord it over anyone. I've come to respect her." Tim stopped fidgeting with his hat.

She retrieved a book from her desk and opened it, then stepped toward the witness. "I have here a *Noah Webster's Dictionary of the English Language,* the most commonly used dictionary to date. Let me read Mr. Webster's definition of *insane.* 'Unsound in mind, mad, deranged in mind, delirious.'" She closed the book and placed it back on her table before continuing. "Mr. Morgan, would you say Miss DuBois is insane?"

"'Course not. She's been nothing but fair to me and mine, so I got no complaints." Tim nodded and glanced at his wife again. "If not for her wanting to build this community, my family would still be living in those tenements."

"Thank you, Mr. Morgan." Teresa smiled. "No further questions."

Michael Jameson was the next witness. He wrote his answers to Teresa's questions, and she read them aloud, offering a glowing report of Angelina as a friend and businesswoman. Caroline followed and also sang Angelina's praises.

Anxiety filled Edward when Clyde took the stand. He admitted she treated him fairly when he'd overstepped his bounds regarding his contract.

Edward released a long sigh.

After dismissing Clyde, Teresa adjusted her papers. "I have one more witness, your honor, but I'd like to wait until after Dr. Cosgrove testifies."

"Very well. Take the stand, please, Dr. Cosgrove." Judge Rathbone indicated the witness chair. Shamus swore him in. Hiram rose and stood near the witness.

"Dr. Cosgrove, please identify yourself to the court."

"I am the administrator of the Chicago Asylum for the Mentally Infirm." The man sat a bit straighter.

Edward recalled the institution. What had he heard about it? He leaned forward, giving the man his full attention.

"When did you make Miss DuBois' acquaintance?" Hiram gestured toward Angelina.

"I visited her in her home back in the spring. And let me say, I am very good at reading the signs." Dr. Cosgrove crossed his arms.

"And those would be?" Hiram strolled away from him, gazing up at the gallery.

"Women do not have the mental capacity to embrace complex ideas. When Miss DuBois expounded on her idea of creating a town run by women, she proved her lack of mental clarity. Obviously, the woman was suffering from delusions."

The gallery erupted, then settled when the gavel sounded. The judge thundered from his bench. "One more outburst, and I'll clear the room."

Edward shook his head. Hadn't Angelina done just what Dr. Cosgrove claimed wasn't possible?

"Do you have any other observations?" Hiram tugged on his waistcoat.

"Yes, her eyes darted about the room as we spoke. A clear symptom of paranoia." Dr. Cosgrove crossed his legs, then tipped his chin up.

"To the untrained, she would appear normal."

"Very interesting." Hiram smirked and paced the room. "Then no matter what these fine citizens have said, they would be wrong."

"Unfortunately, yes." Dr. Cosgrove's sappy tone brought more murmurs.

"Are you quite finished, Mr. DuBois?" The judge glanced at his pocket watch. It must be nearing noon.

"Yes, your honor." Hiram took his seat, crossed his legs, and pasted on a smile.

"Your witness, Attorney Shilling."

"How long was that visit?" Teresa asked the question like a hostess offering refreshments.

"Perhaps an hour." Dr. Cosgrove relaxed in the chair.

"You could determine Miss DuBois' entire mental state in a mere hour's visit?" Teresa held eye contact, then walked toward the gallery. "That's quite impressive."

Dr. Cosgrove smirked and nodded, stroking his beard. "I do have twenty years of experience."

Teresa reached for a sheaf of papers from the table. "I have documents I would like to present in evidence."

Edward recognized the pages as part of the packet Agent Woods had given her. She held them overhead. "These are affidavits from various medical professionals in Chicago stating you have no medical training whatsoever. With your honor's permission, I shall read a quote from a Dr. Reinhardt, a leading psychologist at the Chicago Hospital."

Judge Rathbone nodded.

"'This charlatan is known to commit anyone for the right price.'" She handed the papers over to the judge. "*Mister* Cosgrove, how much did Hiram DuBois pay you to commit his cousin?"

The man's face paled. "I'd rather not say." Judge Rathbone stared at him until he pulled on his collar. "One thousand dollars."

Hiram squirmed in his seat as Teresa turned her focus on him.

"Thank you for your honesty, Mr. Cosgrove. You may step down."

Teresa had indeed prepared a solid defense. Edward relaxed as the trial continued. Once Mr. Cosgrove was dismissed, he glared at Hiram, then took his seat.

The last character witness, Magdalena Harper, took the stand.

Teresa began her questioning. "Miss Harper, can you speak to the character of Hiram DuBois?"

"I must protest. My character is not on trial here." Hiram glowered at the judge and the witness.

"It speaks to Mr. DuBois' motive." Teresa's calm demeanor reflected confidence.

"Overruled. Please continue, Mrs. Shilling." Judge Rathbone nodded. "Miss Harper, please answer the question."

"Mr. DuBois is the sort of man you don't invite to parties. He offends women with lewd comments. If not for his late uncle, he would not have a membership in the gentlemen's club because he isn't one. Even my former husband, cad that he was, refused to associate with him."

"How can you take the word of this—this *fallen* woman?" Hiram's accusation caused another murmur in the courtroom.

Again the gavel hammered, and the room quieted.

"Mr. DuBois, your remark confirms her testimony. Miss Harper, you may take your seat." Judge Rathbone smiled at the witness.

"Do I not get to cross-examine her?" Hiram stood from his place.

"No. You obviously don't understand how serious I am about treating witnesses with respect." Judge Rathbone glared until Hiram took his seat. "Mrs. Shilling, I believe I've heard enough. Dr. Potter presented his diagnosis to me this morning. I'm ready to rule." The judge nodded to Teresa and motioned to Angelina. "Miss DuBois, will you stand?"

Angelina rose, her hands folded in front of her. Edward again wished he were holding her hand rather than guarding the door.

"I find that you only suffer from the foolish notion that women are equal to men. And having an opinion does not make you insane. It is apparent as I walked through this town today that you are indeed very sane. I rule the document ordering Miss DuBois should be committed null and void."

The room exploded in applause. Hiram shrank in his chair, his arms across his chest like those of a schoolboy caught cheating.

The judge inclined his head toward Edward. "Would you check on the jury? If they are still deliberating, we will recess."

⬥

Edward opened the door to find the jury standing outside.

"They didn't want to wait in your office." The deputy shrugged.

Edward ushered them in.

"Mabel, what's the verdict?" Mrs. Potter called to a homesteader. The woman kept her face forward and took her seat with the jury.

Shamus went to collect the Davis brothers. While everyone waited for the judge to call things to order again, Edward grabbed Gabe. "Watch the door?"

Gabe nodded and took his place while Shamus signaled for a deputy to stand guard over Hiram.

Edward sought out Angelina. She was surrounded by her friends. Noticing him, she excused herself.

As she stood before him, he ducked his head. "Angie, you hurt my pride, but I understand why it was so important for you to stand up for yourself."

Her eyes glistened as she reached for his hand. "Forgive me for being so stubborn." Her gaze lingered on his face. "I wasn't angry about the proposal."

"I'm sorry I didn't trust your decision." Maintaining a respectable distance, Edward grasped and kissed her hand.

Her lips curved in a sly smile. "Thank you for admitting it." She cocked her head to the side and grinned. "It was nice to be worried over, to be honest." She squeezed his hand.

"Caroline spoke with me, and I hope we can start fresh now that the trial is over."

At that, the love Edward had thought she'd denied shone on her

283

face. The temptation to kiss her full on the lips was interrupted by the judge's gavel.

Cheers and clapping answered the unanimous verdict of guilty. Shamus took the Davis brothers back to jail. Edward sat beside Angelina behind Teresa's table and held her hand.

Celebrating and visiting ended abruptly when the judge called everyone back to order. All eyes on him, he spoke in a grave tone. "Now for the final hearing of the day. Hiram DuBois, if you will stand."

Hiram's hands trembled as he straightened his jacket. "What is the meaning of this?"

"It has been brought to my attention that there are several warrants for your arrest in Chicago."

"All lies. Who told you this?" Hiram's voice wavered.

"Detective James Woods of the Pinkertons brought the warrants with him."

"What?" Hiram's face paled. "My lawyer is not here. I object."

"You are welcome to use Mr. Tripper's services."

"Please, I'd rather defend myself." Hiram straightened his back and sniffed, raising his long nose in the air.

Edward coughed to cover his laugh, while others around him weren't so gracious. The gavel came down, and the tittering ceased.

"This is not a trial. Merely an arraignment. Detective Woods will escort you back to Chicago to stand trial. And it brings me no pain to add the charge of attempted kidnapping."

"See here. See here." Hiram blustered to no avail as Shamus wrapped his meaty hand around Hiram's thin arm.

"Your honor, I had nothing to do with the kidnapping." Hiram's whine brought Angelina's brows down. "If I tell you where Gerard Standish is, he will tell you the kidnapping was all his idea."

"How do you know Mr. Standish?" Teresa asked before Hiram could be removed.

The judge nodded, and Gabe and Shamus paused with Hiram between them.

"He's my uncle." Hiram's face flamed. "I encouraged him to invest in my architectural firm, and he lost a considerable amount of money. It was his idea to get you committed." He pointed his chin in Angelina's direction, his expression actually remorseful. For the first time, she saw her cousin as broken and desperate to prove his own worth, however misguided. "Gerard is my blood uncle, and he offered to help me get the estate for a portion. I said no."

Angelina stood. "Not because you cared about me."

"No, because I don't like to share." His eyes darkened. "Resorting to kidnapping is beneath me. And certainly murder. What purpose would that serve?"

"I believe you." She held his gaze. "I forgive you." Peace covered her, and a passage of Scripture about forgiveness floated through her subconscious.

Hiram dipped his head, then straightened. "You'd say anything to appear righteous. We both know your forgiveness is false. Those in the DuBois family do not forgive." He nodded to Shamus and Gabe, and they escorted him out of the building.

Angelina fought back tears. How sad that her uncle had such a negative influence on Hiram. Even sadder, her father had held the same attitude about forgiveness. *This DuBois does forgive, does love, and won't be painted with the same brush of selfishness—even if Hiram doesn't believe it.* This project, these people, were helping her change. Even God seemed to be on her side. Maybe all this trouble would soften Hiram too. She could only pray. The thought surprised her. Yes, she would pray, despite his action toward her.

CHAPTER 32

E dward and Angelina waited for the room to clear of townspeople eager to congratulate Angelina and Teresa. "Let me help with your coat."

Her smile sent heat across his chest. "Thank you, Eddie."

Outside, the wind had picked up, and small flakes of snow clung to their coats. He tucked his chin against the chill. "I wonder if we will get a blizzard."

"Lucinda and Gabe think this will be light, although we might have heavy snow again in January." Angelina put her hand on the crook of his arm. "Christmas is a few days away." She squeezed his arm and snuggled closer. "I wish spring followed Christmas."

Edward leaned over and kissed her cold cheek. "You are ready to build again."

"Yes." A sigh escaped her lips. "You and the men are making furniture, and most of the women are making quilts and doilies and other such things. But I'm bored."

A brisk wind grabbed snow from piles near the road and blew moisture into their faces. Angelina gasped, and Edward drew her close under his arm.

They reached the women's dorm. "Come in, Eddie. I have something for you." She didn't remove her coat but disappeared upstairs as he stood just inside the door. The few women in the parlor made themselves scarce. Returning with a small box, Angelina handed it to him. "It's not much, but I made it myself."

"I don't—"

"Open it."

His initials, E.P., were monogrammed in the corner of a large handkerchief. Delicate vines were sewn along the edge. "I had no idea you knew how to embroider."

"It's not a practical skill like knitting or making clothes, but I enjoy it."

He stroked the stitches. "Very nice. Thank you." He pulled her close, kissing her soundly. Angelina returned his ardor. Before she set him on fire, he stepped away. "I have nothing for you."

"After that kiss? Please." She winked at him. "Darling, you have given me so much. This is my way of showing you I can adapt to a simpler life."

"Oh?" She was making a commitment with her veiled words, but he needed to hear her say it.

"You've taught me what love is. You make me feel cherished. Even when you argue with me, respect is always there. Until you, I thought all men were selfish brutes." Stroking his cheek, she whispered, "I love you."

"Then marry me."

"When the last nail on the last building is hammered, I'll marry you."

Edward wanted to marry her this minute. But Angelina knew her own mind, and she hadn't said no. He smiled down at her. "You don't want to wait for the fountain to be built?"

"No, I wish for our wedding to be its own celebration."

"What if there are delays?"

"Then you'll need to work harder." Angelina laughed, then hugged him close. "You know me. I can't begin something new with unfinished business hanging over my head. I expect to be courted, and then our wedding will be the highlight of the summer."

"My, my, such old-fashioned traditions from such a modern woman." Edward kissed her nose.

They turned as a group of women came from the kitchen, placing food on the table and a cake with white icing in the middle. Bridget and Teresa pulled them toward it.

"Let us celebrate our victory, Angelina." Teresa gestured toward the beautiful spread.

Bridget chuckled when Edward wrapped his arm around Angelina's waist, unwilling to release her just yet. "It's good to see ye've found each other. I hope ye have the fortitude to wait for that last nail." She winked.

"Listening at the keyhole, Bridget?" Edward grinned.

Caroline whisked in from the kitchen and slid a plate of sliced turkey on the table. "You know, brother, it's a wonder Angelina did not do the proposing, modern woman that she is."

Edward's face heated as he laughed along with the women.

"Only if I had to." Angelina smiled up at him. "Now I know God gave me the idea to build so he could bring me the one thing I've always missed—family. And you, my love, are God's surprise addition to my blueprint."

AUTHOR'S NOTES

*A*ngelina's Resolve is pure fiction from the setting to the characters. The idea came to me in a what-if moment. While researching another story, I ran across an article about Horace Greeley, a wealthy entrepreneur, publisher, and outspoken abolitionist who embraced the teaching of his contemporaries Karl Marx and Frederick Engels. He and fellow stockholders invested in property in the Pocono Mountains with the intent of creating a communal utopia. Due to the harsh long winters, Sylvana did not survive beyond two years before it was abandoned. Greeley used his journalism skills to influence the nation. Many considered his free-thinking ideas as too extreme. Two decades later, Nathan Meeker founded Greeley, Colorado, based on the commune pattern Greeley had discussed. Many years later, the commune reverted to a more traditional government.

There is also a small town in Kansas named for Greeley as a tribute to his ideals of equality for all.

My what-if moment developed into a village of women where women ran the businesses and all residents—regardless of gender—were respected as equals.

Women's struggles for equality during the mid-nineteenth century could lead to incarceration or committal to asylums. The belief that women's brains could not comprehend complex thoughts and that certain jobs were not suitable for women formed big hurdles.

I created Angelina DuBois, a single woman of extreme wealth who, in her desperation to be recognized for her intelligence, decided to explore Greeley's idea but with a twist. Women would run the businesses and the town. Adding a contractor who struggled to find work after the Civil War was an easy reach. I love having veterans in my stories, and Edward Pritchard's experiences as a civil engineer for the Union Army offers him a unique perspective.

289

All of the obstacles (both natural and legal) the citizens of Resolve met as they built the town mirrored actual historical events. And a few additional catastrophes were delegated to the deleted scenes file.

If you have enjoyed *Angelina's Resolve*, I would appreciate it if you would post a review, even if it's only a line on your favorite book retailer's site. I love connecting with readers on social media.

Website: www.cindyervinhuff.com
Facebook: https://www.facebook.com/author.huff11
Twitter: @CindyHuff11/Huff
Instagram: @CindyErvinHuff

Made in the USA
Las Vegas, NV
27 March 2022

46400737R00173